# The Sebastian Trilogy

## Janey Rosen

*Dear Nikki*
*With love & thanks*
*Janey Rosen*
*x*

ISBN-13: 978-1512330441

ISBN-10: 1512330442

For my husband, my family and friends who have never grumbled when I'd rather write than be sociable. For my loyal readers who are walking this path with me and who have faith in my writing and put a smile on my face every single day. Thank you.

–Janey

# Secrets

## Janey Rosen

# Chapter 1

Closing the bedroom door, I pad over to the dressing table and select my most seductive perfume, spritzing myself from the waist down with the musky scent. Next, my new pink silk robe is removed from its hiding place in the lingerie drawer and slipped over my head. Switching off the lamp I sashay toward our marital bed knowing that I am irresistible; a lioness prowling toward her prey.

Pulling back the heavy feather duvet, I slide into bed and wait for him to devour me; one lives in hope. Patiently awaiting a response, a soft cough fails to wake him as he lies motionless, sprawled across the expanse of our bed. Sighing heavily, I decide he needs a little encouragement to stir. Turning onto my side, I spoon him. My hard and needy nipples rub against his back, but the heavy brushed cotton of his striped, old-man pyjama top shields him from my touch. Forgoing subtlety now, I decide upon the direct approach; impatiently reaching over his hip, I trace a demanding path along his flaccid manhood through his trousers, but apparently it's as benumbed as the body it belongs to. He stirs and groans, a good sign. When I lean in to nip his earlobe, his eyelids flutter open to my seductive smirk crafted from glossy lips. For a moment he focuses on his wife, my panted breaths breezing over his cheek. The signs are promising until he swats my hand away with an irritated huff.

Humiliated and rejected once more, I wriggle away from him to the sanctuary of my own side of the bed and lie there in the darkness as I do every night, reflecting upon seventeen long years of frigidity. Tears fall unbidden, moistening my cheeks as I seek solace from my own expert fingers. The orgasm brings a release but not fulfilment and the hatred I feel for my unresponsive husband deepens, frustration burning anew within.

An incessant buzzing heralds the start of another day. Hitting the mute button on the alarm clock, I reach across to prod Alan awake, swinging my legs out of bed. It is time to prepare the children's breakfast or we will surely be late again.

Motherhood is a gift that I thank God for every day. Conception was nothing short of miraculous as Alan's libido has always been in his boots. My ticking hormonal clock had led me to become a devious trickster, and turning my cap inside out after rare sex eventually rewarded me with a positive pregnancy test and, nine months later, my daughter. Joe's arrival coincided with the end of my frugal and sporadic sex life. He began his embryonic life thanks to two bottles of Chablis one New Year's' Eve when Alan was too inebriated to remember birth control.

Sighing at my slumbering lump of a spouse, I can't help but wonder why we married. My libido has always been high but having notched up an indecent number of boyfriends by the age of twenty-two, I was ready to settle down when I met Alan at a friend's wedding. Now I find myself, seventeen years later, living in a respectable three bedroom semi-detached house in a respectable village in Dorset, with a respectable job running my own business, but with a far from respectable secret. The secret brings a wicked smile to my lips this morning.

Retrieving the newly purchased tight, black pencil skirt and red silk blouse, both hidden at the back of the wardrobe nestled between winter coats, I quickly dress. Pulling up my sheer black hold-ups I savour the sensuality of the seven-denier hose, then slip my feet into new high-heeled black patent shoes. *Professional, with a hint of slutty—perfect.*

A cursory glance toward the bed reassures me that Alan is still dozing but just in case, I pull on a long cardigan and button it over my exposed décolletage.

"Looking a bit dolled up for Monday morning at the office aren't you?" Alan sneers as I smooth down my skirt and check my appearance in the full- length mirror in our bedroom. *Damn, he's noticed. The one time he takes any notice of my attire is the one morning I'm dressed like this.*

"Yes, some of us like to make an effort with our appearance." My reply is venomous but in my opinion, deserved. Alan grunts something inaudible in response before heaving his overweight form out of bed and shrugging on his comfortable grey suit with boring white shirt and navy tie, as he does every weekday morning. No shower. No wash. He disgusts me and I despise myself for feeling this way.

The kids are still eating their toast as I hurry them to the car, yelling a perfunctory, "goodbye, have a good day" to Alan. We are late again, which means Joe will once more lose his morning break as punishment for a lateness for which he was not responsible. I make a mental note to call his year head and apologise. As we sit, nose to bumper in the morning rush hour traffic, I reflect solemnly on the juggling act that is my life. I am mother, wife, and employer—all things to many but nothing to myself. That's why my secret is so special. It is the first thing I have done for me and me alone. Today I welcome my alter-ego Elizabeth Dove, harlot and vamp. A shiver of anticipation pushes aside the guilt that pricks my conscience. *He's pushed you to this, Beth. It's not your fault.*

After dropping Joe at his junior school and Bella at secondary school, I drive to work on autopilot. My thoughts are consumed with a recurring fantasy of a strong virile man dressed in uniform, pinning me hard against a wall and fucking me until I beg him to stop, screaming as a strong, powerful orgasm rips through my soul. I run a red light and narrowly miss a real life encounter with a man in uniform but thankfully the traffic officer is busy issuing a ticket to a youth in a black Mazda. *Crap. Concentrate.*

The morning passes quickly as I endeavour to clear a

small mountain of paperwork before lunchtime. By eleven-thirty my work is done. Closing my office door, I pick up my coffee and take it to the old saggy couch where I curl my legs under me and get comfortable. I wake up my laptop and sip my coffee, drawn in once again to the forbidden world of uniform dating.

A secret fantasy about strong men overpowering me is one that has long been harboured. I've kept it to myself shamefully. It's not the sort of thing one speaks about in today's world of women's liberation and equality, even with girlfriends. When I watch movies in which a woman is arrested, I find myself imagining it's me and in my mind I always resist arrest, wanting to feel the bite of handcuffs and powerful arms restraining me. I can't even blame these feelings on my childhood, because my father was lenient with me—overly so.

My first recollection of this perversity occurred when I was nine. I recall a game I forced my best friends to play in which Abigail Forrester had to be the teacher, David Seaford the headmaster, and I the errant and badly behaved pupil. Abigail, Miss Forrester, always had to send me sulkily to Mr. Seaford where he would have to cane my bare bottom using my pink horse-riding crop. Sometimes I left it at the stables after my weekly riding lesson, in which case Sir would use my plimsole. My punishment invariably stung but I liked it, and I liked the tingle I felt *down there.*

Abigail and David were always rewarded for playing the game, usually with bubble-gum or hard candy I'd bought with my pocket money. One day Abigail said she didn't want to play the game anymore, so our friendship crumbled. David, however, said he liked to play the game but he wanted me to punish him for a change. I tried, but hated it. Soon after, I was no longer friends with David either.

Now, in adulthood, and with a failing and unsatisfying marriage, and plethora of women's literary offerings on the subject, I'm insatiably curious to explore this hidden side of my persona.

When I enter my password and log in, I'm thrilled that my profile has been viewed by no less than twenty uniformed gods since I last logged in. When I check their profiles in return, most are either ugly or doppelgangers of Hannibal Lecter. One candidate catches my attention, and I send him a wink. Simon, aged thirty-eight, six-foot-two inches of testosterone packaged in fire fighter gift-wrapping. *Delicious.* I save his profile and hope to receive a wink in return. I check my messages and feel a warm glow between my legs as I read a new message from Prison Guard John.

*Babe, I'm so hard just thinking about meeting you today. Don't be late or I will take you over my knee, and spank your ass hard, young lady. I won't care that we'll be in the middle of the bookstore. See you by the coffee shop. Remember, no panties. I want you wet and ready for me. John xxx*

I grind myself down on my heels as I read. The excitement is indescribable. I've only been a member of the uniform dating site for three days and already I have a date with John, who works as a prison guard—if his profile is true. I suggested we meet today at one o'clock in the bookstore. It's not too far from where we live, but a respectable and unlikely place to be spotted. It's a safe meeting point in case John turns out to be a psychopath.

I know this liaison would shock my best friend Ruth Evershaw who, as a die-hard feminist, is unlikely to approve of my scheduled illicit encounter with a dominant stranger.

Reading John's message again, I can barely endure the anticipation.

Poised to reply to the message, a knock on my office door tears me away from my laptop and back to reality. Ruth steps in, her head a mess of auburn curls. She is not only my best friend but also my business partner. Together we run Evershaw Dove Recruitment, a personnel recruitment agency in the south of England. I love our business although it is a constant source of stress and has been since we founded it six years ago. Ruth and I have invested a considerable amount of time and money, and are now at a crossroad, whereby the business must expand or risk being succeeded by the larger players.

"Hey gorgeous." I smile up at her.

"You've got your nose in that computer again," Ruth observes, eyebrow raised. "You are up to no good, Mrs. Dove, I know that look."

My smile is one of pure innocence as she begins to pace while watching me.

"Wow, what are you wearing?" she asks. "You look amazing."

"Oh, this old thing? I threw it on in a rush this morning," I lie, thankful for the discretion afforded by the cardigan.

She eyes me approvingly and then raises her eyebrow almost to her hairline. "If I didn't know you better, I would say you have a date."

I blush at her intuition, which serves to reinforce her suspicion. Her eyes narrow accusingly.

"Oh my God!" she exclaims. "You do have a date."

"Not a date, Ruth, I'm a married woman. I'm having lunch with a friend. Sorry to disappoint. I know how you love to gossip," I tease. *If only you knew the truth.*

A deep crimson now, I put away my laptop. It's too late to email John anyway. He will be on his way to our rendezvous. I rise casually from the couch and remove my coat from the hook by the door. Powering down my desktop computer, I inform Ruth that her abhorrent suggestion is offensive and wrong. Clearly she knows otherwise but leaves my office with a withering look, which serves only to heighten the guilt settling in my core.

I have time to drive carefully to the rendezvous and try to catch a glimpse of Prison Guard John before he sees me. That way, I can bail if he looks remotely homicidal. *I'm so nervous. What if someone sees me? How will I explain this to Alan?*

Five minutes past one. My hands and knees are trembling with fear and expectancy as I lean against the wall adjacent to the entrance of the in-store coffee shop. I am without panties and, as instructed, wet with anticipation.

The bookstore is surprisingly busy and I'm frantically scanning faces. My line of sight is set above six foot. Prison Guard John's profile stated he stands six-foot-one. The photograph on the site personified impeccable affair material with a tousled mop of dark hair and chiselled features.

Feeling a vice-like grip on my arm, I look up. Then look down. There, standing at least ten inches below my line of sight is a receding mop of sandy coloured hair exaggerating an already too high forehead. My guilty pleasure has become my secret nightmare.

"Babe. You look even better than your pic. Come here and give Johnny a kiss." He rocks up onto tiptoes and plants a wet, firm kiss on my lips before I am able to turn my cheek to him. At five- foot-ten, I tower above the man and my ardour fizzles away instantaneously. *How the hell do I get myself out of this situation? Think quickly, Beth.*

"I'm...err, sorry, you must have the wrong person." I stutter, blushing hotly. "I'm waiting for my husband." It's lame and transparent, but self- preservation and humiliation extinguish any care I have about the man's feelings.

"It's Rosie, isn't it?" The pseudonym I created for my

illicit profile. The one sensible thing I did was use a false name, and I am thankful for that now.

"No, I'm...Tracy. I have one of those faces that looks like everyone else's, easily done, don't worry," I say less than convincingly.

"Oh, bugger. Okay, sorry about that. You sure do look like the bird I'm meant to be meeting. Nice kiss by the way! *See ya.*"

The dejected little man ambles in to Starbucks in the futile search of Rosie.

"Yeah right. See ya in your dreams. Little twerp," I mumble while making a hasty exit through the store, utterly devastated.

Back at the office, Ruth is in a meeting enabling me to slip dejectedly back, in to my safe space undisturbed. I close the door and fire up my laptop, calling up the uniform dating web page and logging in to my profile, hastily deleting John. I'm about to delete my profile when I notice a message from Firefighter69. Reluctantly I open the message.

*Rosie, you winked at me. I know what you want and I can give it to you. You need a strong, dominant man who takes the lead in bed. I am your man. You're my woman. Message me back. Si x*

My alter-ego perks up but my inner conscience screams, *delete*. Unfortunately my inner conscience is no match for my alter-ego and so begins the next chapter in my illicit journey.

By five o'clock I have revelled in a sordid dialogue with fire fighter Simon, spanning instant messages and mobile phone—all notions of my security disregarded. Having seen a photograph of Simon in his fire fighter uniform, at least I know he is genuinely attractive. Not necessarily my type, with boyish good looks, but definitely shaggable. I now look forward with eager anticipation to a sexual encounter with him on Thursday at one o'clock at the Value Inn near Bristol. The eroticism of meeting for sex is unbearable, the ache in my groin is longing for remedy, never having felt so desperate for sexual gratification in my entire life.

I'm restless. The children are home, thanks to my mother who often collects Joe from school for me, and Bella takes the bus. Alan will be arriving home with fast food for himself and the children, as is our custom on a Monday night, so I am not in a rush.

Ruth insists I go with her for an after work drink at our favourite pub, The Crooked Man. I know my dear friend will subject me to an interrogation about my mysterious lunch appointment but nothing can dampen my spirits. *I'm wanted and desired by a real man for the first time in years and it feels incredible.*

Retrieving my coat from the back of my chair, I wrap a warm grey scarf around my neck and together we leave the office and walk across the road to the pub. Our favourite corner table is available, and Ruth sits down while I go to the bar to order our drinks. I join Ruth at our table, carefully placing the glasses on the mats provided, unwrap my scarf and, removing my coat, we enjoy the warmth of the smouldering log fire next to us.

"Okay, I want to know exactly what you've been up to, lady," Ruth insists. "Blow by blow—no pun intended." She cocks her eyebrow in a way that implies only the full truth will suffice.

"Not much to tell. I went to meet a friend, but they stood me up."

Ruth rolls her eyes in disbelief, a cynical smirk playing across her lips.

"Jesus, Ruth. What kind of woman do you think I am?" I say with a mischievous glint in my eye. She is not buying my story so I divert the conversation to sex, hoping to shock her into distraction. "Here's one for you. Have you ever heard of vanilla sex?"

"Christ, Beth!" splutters Ruth, choking on her Bacardi and coke. "I'm not that naive. It's where the man smears ice cream on the woman. The things you come out with."

I love Ruth, she always thinks she knows it all and is disgruntled when proven otherwise. Shaking my head at her ignorance, she rolls her eyes once more. "Vanilla sex," I inform her, "is straight-up boring sex. But did you know, some men like to dominate women and tie them up." I just want to gauge her reaction, not give her too much information.

Ruth's eyes widen, as I knew they would. I so love to be controversial. Ruth can't resist giving me a lecture about how I'm setting women back one hundred years by even paying lip service to such matters. I declare what happens between consenting adults is perfectly acceptable, and a lively debate ensues for the next ten minutes.

"What's this all about, Beth? Is everything all right with you and Alan?" Ruth sits forward in her chair, her hand resting on my knee, a look of anxiety apparent on her face.

"I want *more*, Ruth. I'm just so tired of my life. I know I've lots to be grateful for. Alan, the house, healthy kids, good job. I just want more."

"We all feel like that sometimes, Beth. It's your age. You're nearly forty, the hormones are rampant and it makes us feel dissatisfied. Honestly, there are many worse off than you."

My friend is well intentioned but her words do not temper the emptiness I feel. Ruth has been divorced from Ed for four years and is contentedly alone. She lives for her work and never seems to complain, nor does she seem lonely. I envy her peace of mind.

"I want to feel needed. *Wanted*. To meet someone who will command me and protect me. Make decisions for me, and not put up with my crap. I want hot torrid sex, Ruth. I am sick of sharing a bed with a man who abhors touching me. I've been thinking about leaving Alan."

Ruth is shocked. "I had no idea things were that bad," she says anxiously.

"Have been for years." I keep my voice low so no one overhears. "I just don't talk about it. I just presumed it was *me*. But, the more I look into it I see that other couples don't live like us. It's not normal. He's not normal. I want what other people have."

"It's a fallacy," Ruth retorts. "All marriages are the same eventually. It's all sex and candles until children come along, and then couples settle down. Just buy yourself a raunchy book, a new vibrator, and fantasise, girl."

"That's just it, Ruth. I'm not prepared to settle for that anymore. I'm nearly forty, and if I don't change my life now, no man will want me. My clock is ticking. Wrinkles are appearing every day and before long I'll be too arthritic or senile to recognize a cock, let alone be able to do anything with it." We both break into a laughing fit, and it is cathartic.

It's been a long, tiring day. As I pull into the drive of our neat suburban house, I'm looking forward to an early night with my book and a glass of red wine. Alan, as usual, is sitting in his favourite chair in front of the television watching a sci-fi documentary he has recorded on the TV hard drive. Our evening together looks set to continue its usual routine. I'll put Joe to bed, Bella will grudgingly do her homework and then disappear to her room for the evening to chat online with her friends. Alan and I will barely talk. He will retire to bed at ten o'clock and leave me working on my iPad or watching television. He will be comatose when I turn in and I will lie awake until the early hours of the morning, feeling frustrated and bitter. No sex. I do wonder, night after night, if I'm so unattractive and undesirable that even Alan, who's no Adonis, doesn't want me. *Simon wants me and soon he'll have me*, I remind myself.

My regular source of orgasmic satisfaction is provided by the contents of my hidden toy box. My favoured toy of the moment is my neon pink Rampant Rabbit. With seven functions it is apparently, *perfect for the rampant connoisseur!* I guess that describes me. It does make me feel seedy using my toys in private, but a girl has needs. Usually my rabbit accompanies me to the bathroom, the only room in which I have privacy. Recently I treated myself to a tiny vibrator the size and shape of a lipstick and this has perked up many a boring day at the office.

Alan and I have had many arguments about sex. I would never divulge to anyone, even Ruth, that we've only made love three times in five years. I think it must be me. I must be detestable. *Simon doesn't think so.*

My self-esteem is at its lowest ebb despite constant reassurance from my mother and others that I'm an attractive woman. Tall with long wavy blonde hair and, although I have the remnants of a baby belly, I'm not otherwise overweight. I consider my facial features to be acceptable and unlikely to turn milk sour, and I receive compliments on my cornflower blue eyes. Yet, clearly there is something lacking in my persona which would otherwise make me desirable.

I've pleaded with Alan to agree to counselling or sex therapy sessions but he says he won't discuss our private business with strangers. He says he is who he is, and tells me all married couples are the same. He blames my literary choices and movies for putting unrealistic ideas in my head.

"Those books you read and films you watch are pure fantasy," he rebukes.

I disagree. My books are indeed my escape but I deeply yearn for everything I read to happen to me. I know that not all couples are like us. This is why I began looking at the Internet late at night and at work. I know that websites exist, solely centred on pleasure. Uniform Dating is only one such site. I have visited others and am becoming increasingly curious about BDSM. This is truly tapping into the darker side of myself, and I only browse those pages after a glass or two of wine, when my inhibitions are lessened. *Oh, why can't it be me receiving the lashing from the leather belt?*

"Have you had a good day?" I ask, sitting down with a large glass of Claret, having settled Joe in bed and helped him with his homework.

"Same as usual. You?" He sips whisky from his favourite tumbler, not averting his eyes from the television as he talks to me.

"Same as usual. What take-away did you get?"

"Burger and chips. I was going to get Chinese but I noticed last time they've put their prices up— bloody ten pence on the rice. Can you believe that?"

*Ten pence? Who cares, you tight sod?* "Daylight robbery if you ask me," I reply caustically. "How was work today?"

I try to kindle the conversation, partly through guilt at my attempted infidelity today. Alan has worked for the same company, Best Business Solutions, for approaching twenty years showing no ambition, nor desire for promotion. Instead he says he is happy to have a secure job in today's volatile workplace. This conjecture would be credible if he didn't always complain about his job and colleagues.

I.T., he tells me repeatedly, is for younger men nowadays, graduates who aren't even old enough to shave, snapping at his heels leading to insecurity, fuelled by his employer, Gerard, who forever reminds Alan how highly trained and keen the younger generation are. He tells me the only thing that keeps him sane is working with his best friend, our Best Man, Mike. We've talked about trying to pair Mike up with Ruth, but Alan says Ruth would eat Mike alive and spit him out. He misjudges her, but he won't change his mind and anyway, Mike isn't Ruth's type. He has a low opinion of women borne through bitterness since his wife, Patsy, ran off with her personal trainer, taking their son with them.

"Work was shit as usual," he grumbles. "Gerard wants me to go on a bloody course. I told him not to waste his money, no bloody course is going to make me better at my job, but he said if I don't keep up with the new software then he'll find a younger bloke who will."

"I've got my course coming up this weekend, don't forget," I remind him. "Well, not actually a course but a team building thing for businesswomen. The thought of it fills me with horror too, but we have to do these things, Alan. We have to keep abreast of change or fall behind and be trampled on."

"Yeah. Whatever." He drains his glass and burps.

"Charming."

"Better out than in, heard about a bloke who died once from trapped wind." He burps again, and turns up the volume on the television, and so ends our conversation.

# Chapter 2

It's finally Thursday. The time is twelve-fifty and I'm inside the *Value Inn*, waiting for an elevator to take me to the third floor, room 311 where my delectable fire fighter Simon awaits.

I don't think I have ever felt so sexually charged. My new lace panties are damp with my arousal and my heart is pounding. I'm wearing a long navy woollen coat, which reaches to the tops of my black knee length boots. Beneath the respectable woollen façade a scandalously short gold vest dress clings to my curves and allows my breasts to spill forth almost to the nipples. Lace topped stockings are suspended from my newly purchased black suspender belt and garters.

I feel like a whore. I *am* a whore. My entire ensemble was hastily purchased yesterday and kept secreted away in carrier bags in the trunk of my car. Changing at work had been a challenge, but I succeeded in racing from the office to my car without being seen. Here I am now, squirming and tugging down the hem of my dress from beneath the flaps of my coat, my work clothes folded neatly on top of my sensible shoes in a small navy holdall at my feet.

I knock gently on the hotel door as a flake of paint falls away. Three knocks. Wait. Another knock. Our code. The stranger releases the lock and the door opens. There stands a treat to behold, naked except for a white towel, which hangs loosely from his hips and is tied to the side. Broad shoulders taper down to narrow hips with sharply defined pectoral muscles and solid biceps. I lick my lips, thinking all my Christmases have come at once.

"Simon. Hi." I can't think what to say to him, suddenly embarrassed, my face flushing fiercely. I place the holdall and my handbag on the wooden luggage rack next to the door.

He doesn't reply. Instead he's all hot breath and sultriness, as he pushes the door closed, stands behind me and places his fingertips lightly on either side of my neck.

I shiver in momentary alarm, reminding myself how little I know of this man. His fingers slip beneath the lapel of my coat and he pulls it from my back. I outstretch my arms to aid the coat's removal, and he drops it to the cheap green patterned carpet, where it pools at my feet. He's still behind me and I feel the prickle of tiny electric shocks coursing down the trail of my spine.

"Sit on the bed," he commands. I step forward to the queen size bed and sit on the edge, revelling in his assertiveness and keen to comply.

"Wow," I say nervously. "Aren't you the bossy one?"

"Sshh." He puts his finger to his lips. Oh my.

The ache between my legs is becoming unbearable and my breathing quickens in anticipation of what this man will do to me. He saunters with a slow, sexy swagger to where I sit and my stare travels from the trail of dark hair at his perfectly formed upper pubic area to his navel, up to his beautifully sculpted chest, which is matted with course black hair.

This man is a god. I've won the sex lottery, and I intend to spend my winnings during the next two hours before I'll have to leave to collect my children. Guilt surges through me like a tsunami as I think of the family I am betraying, but Simon forces my legs apart with his knee and guilt gives way to lust once more.

Gazing longingly at Simon's ruggedly handsome face, I note that he appears younger than his profile age of thirty-eight, by a good ten years. His youthful looks belie his manly expertise as he sinks to his knees between my quivering legs. He leans forward and his mouth finds mine. His tongue pushes between my parted lips and probes inside my hungry mouth. He bruises my lips with his brutal kiss, and I reach forward and entangle my fingers in his bushy black hair, tugging roughly at the roots until he moans. His hands clutch at my breasts, releasing them from their Lycra restraint. His mouth leaves mine. I'm panting and wanting, pushing his head downwards demandingly.

"Wait," he rasps, as his expert mouth finds my throbbing nipple, sucks and flicks it so tantalizingly slowly.

"I want you *so* badly." I groan. My fingers travel down from the nape of his neck to his back where I glide my hands over the beading sweat that is forming.

"You're so hot, Rosie." He pulls away from my nipple, leaving it bereft, and trails his hot tongue down to my navel, his towel falling away, exposing his lean buttocks and colossal manhood. *Oh, thank you, Lord...he's huge!*

Self conscious, I try to suck in my jelly belly. Extending my arms behind me, I rest back on my hands so my midriff is elongated, and the small folds of tummy fat become less obvious. He roughly pulls off my panties before his tongue continues its journey southward. My eyes close in utter rapture, as his fingers part my cleft and hold me open and exposed. His mouth encompasses my clitoris and sucks before his teeth catch the tip of me, making cry out in ecstasy. Collapsing back onto the bed, I grasp the white cotton sheets as he circles and flicks at my sweet spot with his tongue.

"Your cunt is dripping for me," he murmurs appreciatively, as he slides two fingers into my wetness.

"Oh. Please. Don't stop." I pant at the blissful sensations from the unfamiliar attention my body is receiving. A third finger slides in, lubricated by my juices, and all three of his probing digits massage the sweet bundle of nerve endings deep inside me while his thumb rubs me so exquisitely. I feel myself building, and he senses my imminent orgasm and quickens his rubbing and massaging, thrusting now with his hand, his mouth on my thigh, biting into my flesh. I'm lost in the crescendo of pleasure which ripples and spasms, drenching his fingers in my liquor. As I feel the tremors subsiding, I lay panting on the bed feeling a release which is alien to me in its completeness.

"Holy fuck," I gasp, breathlessly.

"Suck me." The cold instruction cuts through my stupor, and I raise my trembling body from the bed. He's standing before me now, between my legs. His magnificent cock stands erect and hard, the veins along its length throbbing as he thrusts his hips toward my eager mouth.

Sliding off the bed to my knees, I grip the backs of his thighs, pulling his waiting organ to my mouth. He grabs my hair with both hands and forces my head toward his groin. The shiny head of his enormous cock is almost too large. I flick my tongue across his crown and eagerly lap up the salty bead of fluid, which has formed on the cleft of his tip.

"Yes. Take it all, you fucking slut." He forces my head nearer, so his pulsing cock enters my mouth, causing me to gag as it hits the back of my throat. He is so immense but I work him with my mouth, sliding him past my lips, sucking hard and working his root with my cupped hand. His enraptured moans reassure me that I'm pleasuring him well. My head bobs as I work his cock, but my breath catches as Simon pulls sharply on the hair at the nape of my neck, tugging me away from his groin. He slips from my mouth but continues to pull my hair so that I'm forced to stand, aroused, the pain blending seamlessly with the pleasure.

I lean into him and kiss him, seeking assurance that he's pleased with me. Pulling away from my kiss, he grasps my shoulders and spins me around so that I have my back to him once more. Still using the tug of my hair to guide me, he forces me forward over the edge of the bed so that my ass is in the air. Releasing my hair, he moves close to me so that I can feel the tickle of his pubic hair against my buttocks and the hard rod of his penis pressing into my ass. I feel him reach to the nightstand, hear the tearing of foil as he slides a condom onto his hardness. Panic sets in at the vulnerability of my most private cavity but instead, the head of his cock presses into my pulsing vagina, stretching my walls until, with one sharp thrust, I feel him fill me so full that I fear he'll tear me apart.

His thrusts are purposeful and fierce and, in just a few short moments, he cries out my fake name. "Rosie. Oh, shit. Here it comes," and he pumps and releases his load as his sweating torso arches back in frenzy. "Fuck, you're good," he praises as he pulls out, removes his condom and tosses it into the waste paper bin.

I crawl up onto the bed and pull the sheet over my glistening body, feeling suddenly self-aware, exposed but deliciously used. I feel dirty, as though I've been a mere vessel for his climax. *Is this a good feeling or a bad feeling? It feels like both.* This inner conflict is not what I envisaged, and yet it's entirely what I bought into when I began my illicit journey. Hearts and flowers and loving sentiments do not marry with uniform dating and extra marital affairs. Simon takes my hand and pulls me up from bed into his waiting embrace. My arms fold around his waist, cheek pressed to his moist chest. We're both flushed and the hotel room smells of sex.

"Shower with me. I've got to go in a minute," he orders curtly.

"So soon? I have another hour," I say, my eyes searching his for signs of a connection that surpassed sex, yet finding none. Evidently a man of few words, I wonder whether he has much depth but then I remind myself that the purpose of our meeting wasn't for conversation.

The water is cleansing and goes part way to purging the dirtiness I feel within. "Will I see you again?" I ask tentatively, towelling my body dry. He's made no mention of repeating today's sleazy afternoon, which doesn't boost a girl's confidence.

"Yes, sounds good. I'll call you. I've got your mobile number," he promises.

"Only call between nine in the morning and three in the afternoon, please." I'm suddenly concerned that Simon may call when I'm at home.

"No worries. Jealous husband?"

"You could say that." I frown. Alan would kill him. Or kill me, if he found out. *Or would he even care?*

"All right. I'll be careful. It'll have to fit round my shifts, though."

I retrieve my work clothes and fresh underwear from the holdall and dress quickly, screwing the gold dress and slutty underwear into the holdall, boots on top.

"Very prim," he says, watching me while leaning against the wall by the door, towel still draped around his hips. "But I know what a whore you really are, don't I?"

"Isn't that a good mix?" I ask, a smirk curving my lips. "Prim on the outside, whore on the inside?"

"Oh, yes. A very good mix," he purrs.

Buttoning my coat, I take a last look at my surroundings. The bland interior of the economy room does nothing to lessen the cheapness I feel in myself. We kiss briefly, Simon assuring me that he will be in touch in a few days, and I leave.

Sitting alone in my car in the school parking lot, killing the hour until pick-up time, I reflect on the afternoon, mentally flaying myself for being an adulterous slut. The enormity of what I have done overwhelms me and tears sting my eyes.

With the children on board, I suppress the forlorn sobs which threaten to burst forth, dutifully asking them about their day and resign myself to settling back in to my dull life. *What was I thinking? This isn't the answer, Beth.* If I do leave Alan, it needs to be because of his unreasonable behaviour, not because of my cheating. The children would never forgive me if I chose another man over their father and yet, having tasted the forbidden fruit, I'm not convinced I have the willpower to stop myself now.

Alan won't be home for another hour, which gives me time to hide the holdall at the back of my wardrobe, under a mound of shoes. I'll have to launder the clothes during the weekend, hide them amongst the school uniforms. Thankfully for me, Alan never gets involved in laundry duties.

Later, lying in bed in the darkness, Alan snoring

beside me, sleep evades me. My mind runs through today's encounter moment by racy moment. Feelings conflict from relief at not being caught, to arousal at the memory of the hair tugging, from fulfilment to deceit, from elation to despair. I ponder the idea of seeking counselling. It cannot be normal to feel so mixed up. But there is no way I can add more pressure to my schedule, nor can I share these disreputable thoughts with another.

Eight thirty-five. We are even later this Friday morning. Lack of sleep means I am running on zero energy. I shout at the kids to get in the car, forget Joe's book bag, and forget to say goodbye to Alan. *Thank goodness it's nearly the weekend. Except I have to drive all the way to Cornwall for the teambuilding thing.*

Arriving at work, I'm truly thankful for the peace and tranquillity my office affords me. Immersing myself in work distracts me from the jumble of emotions plaguing my mind. Our finances are under strain. The industry is doing well in spite of the recession, but we have to chase the work more than we used to and this requires additional advertising investment. We are fast outgrowing our offices and need more administrative staff. All of this pressure falls upon me, Ruth leading on the operational side of the business. I need to find the money, but where?

In need of a distraction, after three hours of number crunching, I click on the Google search engine. *What shall I search? Hair tugging? Caning? How quickly my mind degenerates!* I'm carried along on a web thread to the dark and lurid world of BDSM. Bondage and discipline, dominance and submission, and sadism and masochism include but a small part of the comprehensive definition offered up by Wiki. It's a whole new world, and yet strangely familiar to me.

*I'm a masochist.* There, I've said it, like an alcoholic at an AA meeting. *Hello, my name is Elizabeth Dove and I'm a masochist. It's been twenty-four hours since I last had my hair pulled and it's driving me crazy. I long for another drink of sadism, but I worry that another drink will lead to a real BDSM addiction. I've got kids, you see, and I'm a respectable woman. Nobody knows I long to be drunk on a good beating. Can you help me quit the habit?*

A BDSM dating site is displayed before me, tempting me shamelessly with free and instant membership. After hesitating and battling with my inner demons for fifteen minutes, it only takes five minutes to create my profile, after which I sit back and stare at the screen with trepidation and excitement. Just two minutes later, three men have viewed my profile—dominant men seeking submissive ladies.

Opening a new frame, I search dominance and submission online for clarification and confirmation that I can call myself a submissive. It seems that I do indeed fit that dynamic sexually, albeit in my fantasies if not in real life. *Beth Dove, submissive slut.* Actually, I'm no longer Beth Dove, technically I am now *rosiesub,* not imaginative but it hadn't already been claimed. The pseudonym enables me to separate my professional and personal life with my sordid desires and alter-ego, lessening my inner conflict.

"Hey, Beth. Are you busy?"

I startle at the intrusion, minimise the opened window on my desktop and turn to face Julie, the temp who is covering a maternity leave.

"No. Not at all," I bluster. "What can I do for you?"

"Ruth asked me to make sure you've signed off the accounts before the weekend. Can I tell her you have?"

"Yes. Nearly done, thank you, Julie."

Alone once more, I click on my profile and see I have unread mail. Intrigued by the name of the sender, *SlaveMaster*, I open the message and almost fall off my chair.

*Girl,*

*Master is interested in talking with this girl, despite the lack of information on her profile. Master is not interested in this girl for curiosity. I have decided I am going to turn you into the perfect slave. You will listen to everything I tell you and provide Master with all of the information I seek. This must be clearly understood by the girl.*

*I expect a reply to this message within forty-five minutes of you reading it. You will include your description, which will be full and detailed. Your description will not be generic and will describe you as you look at this precise moment in time.*

*The girl will also tell Master of her current living arrangements, work, and relationship status and a list of duties the girl will perform. You will reply in exactly 200 words.*

*SlaveMaster*

When I can stop laughing enough to type, I daringly tap a humorous reply.

*Dear SlaveMaster,*

*Thank you so very kindly for your interesting and challenging email. I have my stopwatch ticking down the forty-five minutes, because I am anxious to appease you in this first task, which you have so generously set me.*

*I am tall with longish blonde hair and blue eyes. I am wearing nothing at all because I stripped all of my clothing off the minute I read your message, such was my excitement and eagerness to please you.*

*My living arrangements are that I reside under a bridge, which is exceptionally cold, especially since I am not wearing clothes right now. No sacrifice or hardship is too great to please you, Master. I am fortunate in so far as I have full Internet connection under this particular bridge, thanks to the hot-wiring I did on the nearby streetlight. My years spent in the Women's Remand Prison served me well and I am glad that I studied hard on the electronics course when I wasn't being ravaged by a plethora of lesbian inmates.*

*My relationship status, Sir, is that I am single— technically. I am still married but he is likely to remain in prison for another twenty years unless he makes parole. After the last time he got caught—that wasn't my fault, I genuinely thought I was helping by turning him in—they said they were throwing the book at him. In hindsight I guess I shouldn't have hidden him under the stairs for those two long years. He may have got off more lightly.*

*Sir, I digress. To summarise, I am keen to drink from a dog bowl and lick your shoes until they shine brighter than the sun itself. Just say the word, and I and my thirteen children will be by your side.*

*Yours respectfully, Rosiesub*

Within five minutes, I receive a reply from the jerk.

*Girl,*

*Thank you. Unfortunately, it wasn't 200 words exactly, so I couldn't read it.*

*What a weirdo!* I sign out of my profile and get back to finalising the accounts, in need of some welcome normality. I may be sick, but I'm not that twisted. I wonder when I will hear from Simon, and whether I want to hear from him. I have a husband, healthy children, and a good business. What more could I need?

When we arrive home after school, Joe hands me a letter from his teacher, advising me that Joe has been unacceptably late on three occasions this week and two last week. He asks if there is a valid reason for this tardiness, and offers to meet with me to discuss Joe's progress, or lack of it. I fold the letter and tuck it in my briefcase. I will deal with this on Monday.

By the time Alan returns home from work at six-thirty, my overnight bag is packed for the morning and dinner is ready to serve. We sit, as a family, at the kitchen table. Alan and the children devour the lasagne, while I pick at my food with my fork but eat very little, my stomach in knots.

"Not hungry?" Alan observes.

"No. I think I'm getting nervous about tomorrow. I don't like meeting lots of new people, or doing a long journey alone." I rest my fork on my plate, replete.

"So, who else is going?"

"A bunch of egotistical alpha females I suspect. My idea of hell, but Ruth and I agreed that I'd go. You don't mind, do you?"

He cocks an eyebrow, apparently surprised at the request for approval. "Do what you like." His reply is dismissive and cold.

"Nice to know I'll be missed," I quip.

"No doubt there'll be some blokes there, too," he adds, ignoring my comment.

"Alan, it's a *Women* In Business event. The clue's in the name, *women*."

"Yeah, right. It just seems odd to me." He scrapes the remaining lasagne from his plate into the food recycling bin, and crashes his plate and cutlery into the sink before leaving the kitchen.

"Oh, piss off," I hiss under my breath.

# Chapter 3

Saturday morning, and I have made an early start on the long drive to Cornwall. The Women In Business team-building weekend event. *Why on earth did I put my name down for that? As if I don't have enough to do, I now have to surround myself with alpha females, up to my arse in mud in Cornwall, of all places, where I feel sure everyone drinks cider and is inter-bred.*

Not only that, Alan is clearly convinced I'm making up the whole event and am in fact planning a liaison with another man. I worried last night that he'd found out somehow about Simon, but then assured myself he'd have gone crazy if that had been the case. Satisfied he has no idea what I did two days previously, I made a show of kissing him goodbye this morning and telling him I would miss him.

As I drive west on the A35, the rain sets in. My journey to Cornwall should take three hours and twenty minutes according to Google Maps, and I'm glad that I set off early.

I pick up the M5 and the motorway is quiet. I relish the peace and solitude of my journey. A night away from Alan will be refreshing. I call my mother on hands-free, and have a chat with her. I haven't seen her as much as I should lately and it's good to talk to her. My mother lives only two miles from our house and is a considerable help with the children, for which I'm eternally grateful. She's seventy-four and has lived alone since Dad succumbed to prostate cancer twelve years ago. I make a mental note to treat my mother to a spa day sometime soon.

Mum seemed quiet on the phone when I cut the call and reflect on our conversation. I think about Dad, and by the time I pass Exeter, I'm feeling melancholy.

Turning on the radio, I flick through the channels and settle upon an upbeat tune in the hope of raising my spirits before stopping for a strong cup of coffee and a bathroom visit near Launceston.

The pub I find is a traditional thatched inn, which is several hundred years old and very quaint. As I enter it feels as though one hundred eyes are upon me, all viewing me as a trespasser. I pay for the coffee and a cheese and pickle sandwich, then find a table near the door, feeling nervous. I wish I'd cancelled my booking for the event, not relishing spending twenty-four hours with a bunch of strange women.

Although aware that outwardly I appear to be a competent entrepreneur, I seriously lack confidence and frequently doubt myself. I wear so many hats— mother, boss, wife. The saying, *Jack of all trades, master of none* fits me well. *Who is the real Elizabeth Dove?* I used to love to paint, before the children came along. I used to write poetry. *What happened to that carefree girl? Where and who is the real Elizabeth Dove now?*

I finish my lunch and return to my car feeling

refuelled and ready to face the day ahead.

Shortly before two o'clock, after traversing dangerously narrow country lanes, the satellite navigation system on my dashboard tells me I've arrived at my destination. Indicating a right turn, I drive past a pair of stone pillars on which stand two stone stags, weathered and chipped yet graceful with majestic horns. They look down on me with austere regard. The half-mile drive, lined with dense rhododendron, is staggeringly beautiful. Through the trees I glimpse acres of woodland, which gives way to paddocks with horses and fallow deer grazing. Beyond lies a jagged cliff, falling away to the sea beyond. I'm now driving slowly along the dirt and gravel track toward the most magnificent manor house I have seen. It takes my breath away.

I park next to a sleek white Range Rover, and cut my engine. Stepping out of the car onto the pale yellow gravel, I turn and gaze up at the façade of the enormous house, recalling from the literature sent to me that the main house is seventeenth century.

Taking my overnight bag from the trunk of the car, I walk toward the impressive entrance, feeling more positive about the weekend ahead. It will be therapeutic to have time away from Alan, and this is a pretty cool place to hang out. Above me I notice a 1634 date stone, and a family crest featuring a dragon and shield. The house has a gothic style with stone mullioned leaded windows. I approach a vast arched doorway where I rap heavily on the wrought iron lion head knocker.

The door opens and, expecting a dusty old butler, I'm surprised to see a pretty, dark haired girl ushering me in. The hall has an ornate plaster ceiling and fireplace with carved wooden over- mantel, on which I can see the date 1650. The mottled grey flagstone flooring is softened with ornate rugs in ochre and crimson hues. The walls are adorned with swords, axes, and shields criss- crossed and glinting like metal rainbows in the sunlight, which streams through arched coloured leaded light windows on either side of the front door, that look as though they belong in a church. Each pane is adorned with a glazed image of knights, stags, rabbits, and lions. It's so beautiful that it captures my attention for several moments.

"Stunning, isn't it?" the girl says. "Breath-taking."

"Come on, I'll show you through to the library.

Most of the ladies are here already."

The girl takes my overnight bag from my hand, then leads me through to the library. With dark oak panelling, carved pillars, and yards of dusty books, it has a comfortable feel but not the silence one would expect of a library. The room is buzzing with the conversation of twenty or thirty women chatting in small groups.

Collecting a porcelain cup filled with milky coffee, I begin to introduce myself to a group of four women all dressed like me, in jeans and pale pink sweatshirts with the *Women Mean Business* slogan emblazoned across the front. The four women are all from the same organization, a PR company in London. We make polite small talk and, as one overly bleached blonde tells us about her latest client, I glance across the room. That is when I first see *him* and the room stands still. My breath catches and I feel myself flush.

I suggest that all women have an ideal man locked away inside their psyches. Mine is tall, dark, and handsome with a commanding and assertive demeanour. The man whose gaze I meet exceeds my dreams. He's tall, maybe six-foot-three or four inches and is dressed in blue denim jeans and an open necked blue checked shirt tucked in, the sleeves rolled half way up his strong, muscular forearms. His hair is jet black, yet speckled with silver flecks to the temples, giving him an air of maturity. He has coal dark eyes, framed by black eyebrows sculpted into a serious frown, and the broadest shoulders.

Those shoulders are the kind on which a woman could cry, cuddle, knead, and which would be consummately powerful. I estimate his age to be mid-forties, but it is hard to be sure. As I stand transfixed by his maturity and rakish charm, his head turns and his gaze meets mine across the room. Blushing as a shiver passes through me, I avert my eyes. How ridiculous I must look, a grown woman beet red and trembling like a new-born lamb. I turn away.

*Play hard to get, Beth. What are you thinking? Why would he be vaguely interested in me? I'm a married woman, for Heaven's sake!* I turn back to Bleached Blonde and laugh raucously at a droll story she is telling, then a hand touches my elbow and a spark courses through me. I turn and my cornflower blue irises lock on to his smoky dark hazel eyes with which he studies the plastic name badge pinned above my left breast.

"Elizabeth Dove. Managing Director, Evershaw Dove Recruitment Agency. Very impressive title, *Elizabeth*." His deep, sensual gravelly voice renders me speechless. He uses my full name, which no one has for many years, and the way his lips form the letters, parting to reveal perfect white teeth and the hint of his tongue, makes me tingle. I am lost to him in that very moment. "And you are?" I inquire, trying to sound disinterested and aloof.

"Sebastian De Montfort. Delighted to meet you. Welcome to my humble home." So he is the owner of this incredible house. This man is a mythological deity. He could not be more perfect.

"Pleased to meet you too. It's a beautiful home."

"Thank you, Elizabeth. I look forward to personally showing you around. I'll see you later. Do enjoy the afternoon." He's charming, beguiling, and oh so dangerous.

I'm blushing a deeper shade of crimson as his eyes, deep and serious, fix their gaze upon me and refuse to blink or look elsewhere. He is so intense, so measured and controlled. His hand lingers on my arm, and he holds my gaze a moment too long.

Then, he's gone. I can still feel his touch as he turns to greet a tall brunette in a uniform pink sweatshirt.

"Isn't he delicious," gushes Bleached Blonde. "Delicious. Yes," I whisper.

We are ushered through a glazed door leading

from the library onto a paved terrace overlooking a walled garden where we are divided into two teams. I know we'll be mud running but I really don't understand what this means. I imagine we'll be jogging, or in my case most likely walking, getting very grubby, and having a good gossip and giggle. It comes as rather a shock, therefore, when we are assigned a team coach who is a fearful dragon on whom I feel sure the De Montfort family crest was cast.

The troll uses a megaphone to launch her verbal assault upon us. We're coaxed, bullied, and cajoled into sprinting across the expansive lawns and down the tree-lined driveway. We're ordered to veer off road when we reach a giant oak, and are soon running, tumbling through woodland in a battle to traverse the boggy terrain, endeavouring to beat the other team to the finishing post.

The ground beneath our running shoes becoming increasingly tricky and I feel my right foot slip. Before I can stop myself I am face down in slimy mud and I wonder if this can possibly be any more humiliating. Apparently, it can, as Bleached Blonde laughs mockingly when she passes me. I am motivated to get to my feet. My knee stings, and the right leg of my jeans is torn exposing a raw graze. I wince but refuse to show any sign of defeat or to let my team down. I push onwards, spitting out a mouthful of dank mud. How I survive ninety minutes of this torture is beyond me but I do, and when we break through the trees and back onto the driveway I am immensely relieved until I see the other team already at the finishing post, sipping cognac from paper cups. Damn them all.

I limp behind my teammates, my knee finally saying enough is enough. Laying claim to my cognac, the pitiful glances by the winning team don't go unnoticed and my mood worsens. It's not improved by the further humiliation of De Montfort handing out winners' medals to the other team and losers' medals to my team.

Standing in line, ripped trousers, bloody knee, caked in mud with leaves in my hair and a forced smile on my face, the Adonis places a ribbon over my head, adjusting the medal so that it rests on my sternum. He pauses and regards me, his amused eyes slowly drinking me in, his lips curled in a poorly concealed smirk.

"I realize mud has untold benefits for the skin, Elizabeth, but I do wish you had left a little of it behind."

I could punch his conceited face but I hold back my twitching fist. Thankfully, he moves on down the line and I release the breath I've been holding as fatigue takes hold.

We drift back into the house and locate our bedrooms. Mine is a sizeable room with high, decoratively corniced ceilings. It is furnished tastefully with antique pieces in dark oak. The double bed in the centre of the room is a two-poster with canopy, dressed with a gold damask comforter and matching stack of cushions. At the foot of the bed stands a chaise upholstered in rich olive green fabric on which sits my overnight bag. I unzip it and remove a short cream silk nightgown, draping it over the bolster cushions. Retrieving fresh underwear and carefully unfolding a silver crepe evening gown from the crushed confines of the bag, I lay out my evening ensemble before running a bath.

The hot water feels so good despite the gash on my knee stinging fiercely, and I sink down until the water level reaches my chin and reflect on the afternoon. I can't seem to get Sebastian De Montfort out of my head, with his smouldering eyes and moodiness. *Sebastian* is such a classy name, so much more impressive than *Alan*. I decide I want to find out more about the mysterious man, and this evening's dinner will be the ideal opportunity. I determine to make an extra effort with my appearance. After all, I have all the other women to compete with for his attention.

The hot bath improves my mood and eases my aching joints. I'm excited about the drinks reception and dinner that awaits us, eager to discover more about the mysterious Sebastian. I moisturise my entire body, luxuriating in my sumptuous surroundings and the precious time to myself. My trusty, magic support pants—tragic knickers, as I like to call them—are a struggle to pull up but necessary for a smooth silhouette under my slinky silver dress. Slipping the evening dress over my head, the whisper light fabric falls softly over my hips and ends just below my ankles, cut low at my décolletage.

I pad to the bathroom while reaching behind my back to pull up my dress zipper, pulling out the plug in the bath and then trying again to tug up the zip. The loud gurgling of the draining bath water through noisy old pipework drowns out the sound of the light knock on my door.

I'm standing in the bathroom becoming flustered and hot as the zipper catches in the fabric of my dress, and I lean forward against the washbasin, arching my back in an attempt to free the snagged zip when a figure appears in the steamed-up bathroom mirror. Gasping in shock, I spin around and face Sebastian who is leaning against the bathroom doorframe, arms folded with a smile playing across his lips, his eyes crinkled in amusement.

"Don't worry about knocking, will you?" I scold sarcastically, embarrassed once again at the state in which he finds me—hot, red faced, and my gaping dress twisted and puckered.

"Actually, I did knock, but you didn't hear me. I bought you this." He holds a sticking plaster between his thumb and forefinger and waves it in front of me. "For your knee. Would you like me to put it on for you?" he cocks an eyebrow and is clearly enjoying the spectacle.

"No, I don't want you to put it on for me. I'm a big girl," I retort ungratefully. "But thank you. It was thoughtful of you."

He steps toward me, reaches to my side and places the plaster on the marble countertop next to the basin. The closeness of him makes me tingle and I breathe in his manly scent as he lingers for just a moment, his fingers grazing my bare arm. He hesitates and then places his hand on my shoulder and the touch of skin on skin sends further tremors through my core.

"Turn around," he says, as he pulls my shoulder toward him and guides me so that I face away from him.

"What are you doing?" I ask, my redness deepening and my breath catching.

"Your zip, Elizabeth. Unless you prefer to come downstairs as you are? Those large pants would cause quite a stir I'm sure."

*Could this be any more humiliating?*

His finger touches the small of my back as he tugs at the waistband of my tragic knickers, pinging the fabric against my skin and the mortification is unbearable. *Yes, it can be more humiliating, damn him.*

"Just do the zipper up," I bark at him. "Thank you."

My curtness serves only to increase his enjoyment, and the irritating man sniggers as he releases the fabric and pulls the fastener halfway up, oh so slowly. He takes my long hair in his hand and drapes it over my shoulder before gliding the zip home. His fingers brush the back of my neck as he gently tugs my hair into place. Such tiny touches, and yet the electricity that passes between us is incredible. I feel sure he senses it too. As I turn back to face him he lowers his eyes quite shamelessly to the ample cleavage on display, and only averts his gaze when I tug the fabric up as I tut my disapproval.

"Is there anything else?" I ask.

He crosses his arms again and places a finger on his lips as he stares pensively into my eyes. "I think you'll do. Be downstairs in ten minutes," he replies, and with that, he turns and leaves the room, closing my bedroom door firmly behind him.

I let out a deep sigh. *That went well*, I scold myself.

It is a delicious meal of venison followed by a warm pear tart with cream. The wines are divine and I feel my mood lifting with each glass. Dinner is served by the pretty young girl I saw earlier. In addition there are three other, equally pretty young ladies waiting the table. All are wearing fitted black dresses, which sit above the knee, demure but sexy, their hair tied back into a neat chignon. *Curious*. I make a mental note to ask the handsome but arrogant Mr. De Montfort about his choice in staff. Clearly, he hasn't recruited solely on the basis of curriculum vitae.

I sit through a series of speeches and clap politely when an award is given to the woman seated to my left, who has been judged to be the highest achieving woman in business. By eleven- thirty, the evening draws to a close. Tired ladies make their way to bed, and I sit alone in the now empty dining hall. The lights are dimmed and the remnants of candles flicker on the long elegantly dressed table.

I sip my fifth or sixth glass of red wine, feeling deliciously mellow, and survey my surroundings.

The high ceilinged room is papered in rich ruby damask, and gilt framed oil paintings adorn the walls, suspended from ornate picture rails. Many are of hunting scenes while others are, I presume, De Montfort's long dead relatives. They look down at me with reproachful stares.

The dying embers of a fire still offer a warming glow from the oversized fireplace. I take my glass of wine and sit in front of the fire, my legs curled under me on a deeply piled rug. I close my eyes and imagine I am sitting in my own castle, while my prince waits for me in our bedchamber. I imagine what he will do to me when I retire to bed and a sense of longing encompasses me.

I jump as I hear movement behind me. I turn and look up to see Sebastian De Montfort standing over me. He has a half smile, he is studying me curiously. I am suddenly consumed by a feeling of guilt, at how attracted to him I am, and embarrassment that I am so relaxed in his home.

"Elizabeth, don't let me disturb you, I've been watching you," he says. Before I can stand, he places a hand firmly on my shoulder and tells me to stay seated on the floor.

He pours himself a glass of red wine and sits down beside me, his legs crossed and his right knee touching my leg. I shiver at the touch of his limb through the silky fabric of my silver evening gown.

"Let me see your wounded knee," he demands firmly. My mouth drops open, and I look aghast at him. He wants to see my bare leg. My scuffed sore knee.

I shake my head and tell him it's nothing. I have the sticking plaster on it, and it really isn't painful. He is staring deeply into my eyes, a frown etched across his brow.

He doesn't speak for the longest time and then, when he does, he only says, "Show me."

It is not a request, I realise, he is insistent. I hesitate but he leans forward, gently grasps the hem of my dress and slides the fabric up my legs, above my knees. I'm blushing deeply now, but to my amazement, he kisses his fingers and softly lays his fingers onto the covered wound. I feel a thousand sparks coursing through my body and have an overwhelming and totally irrational desire to feel his fingers on my skin.

"You're flinching. Is it sore?" he asks.

"A little," I reply, although it was the spark from his touch, rather than pain, which made me flinch.

"Are you enjoying yourself?" The conversation is awkward.

"Having a lovely time, yes, thank you."

"You did make me laugh, Elizabeth. You were a picture, covered in mud with leaves in your hair." He has that ridiculous smirk on his face.

"I'm glad I entertain you," I huff. "Be sure to book me next time you need a good laugh."

He leans forward and tucks a loose strand of hair behind my ear. "Your hair is so much prettier without the foliage." He is still mocking me, and I cast him a frosty glare in return, trying not to let him see the profound effect his touch has on me.

"Perhaps if we hadn't been subjected to the wrath of the old bat that led our team, I wouldn't have fallen," I suggest, much to his amusement.

"Old bat?" His eyes are glinting roguishly.

"Yes, old bat."

He throws his head back and laughs, a deep rasping laugh, and I love the way his eyes crinkle. "You're laughing at me *again!*"

"Not laughing *at* you, no. It's a long time since I laughed. You light up the room."

"What a lovely thing to say." I put my hand on his tentatively, and I swear a spark crackles as our skin touches.

He stares at me until I look away. "Come with me. I promised to show you a little more of the house, but it's late. The grand tour will have to wait until another time, but I will show you the heart of the house. Come." He takes my hand, pulls me to my feet, and leads me from the dining hall. For a moment I wish he would take me upstairs and have his wicked way with me, but he leads me past the vaulted oak staircase and through a door into a vast kitchen where flagstones pave the floor and a double range stove forms a somewhat wholesome focal point. I immediately love this room. It feels so homely and welcoming. I imagine laughter and conversation around the refectory style oak table, which sits in the middle of the room. It is indeed the warm heart of the house.

He directs me to sit on one of the two heavy church pew benches, which are placed either side of the table, and he lights a candle, which gives a soft ambient light.

I notice there are no staff around and presume they have finished their duties for the night. He offers me coffee, and puts a heavy copper kettle onto the range to boil. Leaning against the wall, his dark hazel eyes fix on mine. It's so hard to read what is going on behind those darkly lashed windows to his soul.

Feeling emboldened by the alcohol, I decide to interrogate my mysterious host. "Tell me about your staff, Mr. De Montfort. It's clear you haven't hired them for their brains." *Did I really say that?*

"Elizabeth." His repeated use of my full name reminds me of my childhood. "That's a strange question. I like to surround myself with beautiful things. Does that make you uncomfortable?" His answer takes me by surprise but affirms my belief that he beds these women.

"Not uncomfortable. No. However, it seems strange to only hire attractive young girls, unless you expect benefits other than waitressing." It must be the alcohol fuelling my confidence, but I can't stop myself.

He regards me more coolly, and I see hardness in his eyes that I haven't noticed before. "And would it shock you if I did?" he asks.

*What does that mean? Is that, 'yes, I do fuck them,' or 'no, I don't'?* I rarely know when to keep quiet, and I never think before I speak. I simply can't let this go. I want to know more. I match his stare. "Naturally, it wouldn't bother me. I don't know you. I'm simply curious as to how you treat these poor staff of yours, Mr. De Montfort." That told him. *Gosh, how much have I drunk?*

His retort cuts me to the quick. "Firstly, Elizabeth, I am not *Mister* De Montfort. I am Lord Sebastian De Montfort, ninth Earl of Trevissay. You may call me

Sebastian, even though, as you rightly say, you don't know me."

*Oh please, a Lord.*

"Secondly, Elizabeth," he continues, "that poor staff of mine elects to work for me. It may be the financial incentives are considerable, or it may be that I am a fabulous lover, either way it's really not your concern, is it?"

*Geez, that told me!*

"Third, Elizabeth—do you take cream and sugar in your coffee?" A wry smile touches his lips, and I notice it meets his eyes. He could melt me with those eyes.

"I'm sorry, I've no right to pry. I think I've had way too much to drink." I apologise profusely, and the atmosphere lifts a little.

"I forgive you. Actually, it's not as bad as you think. Three of the young women were hired for the event this weekend. Only one lives in permanently." That makes me feel a little better. Why do I care?

"I see." I fiddle with a thin silver bracelet.

"That's pretty." He is by my side now. Admiring my wristlet, he lightly runs his index finger along its circumference, his thumb brushing across my skin as I hold my breath. Abruptly, he resumes his position by the range, taking the simmering kettle from the stove.

"It was a gift from my children last Christmas," I tell him, missing Joe and Bella badly.

Sebastian hands me a steaming cup of coffee and sits on the bench opposite me, leaning forward and resting his chin on his hands. "How old are they?"

"Joe's seven and Bella is seventeen." I sip the coffee gingerly.

"That's quite an age gap," he observes.

"Yes it is. We had difficulty conceiving. Primarily because sex didn't happen very often."

"I see. I'd like to know more about you," he prompts. "Tell me why I see sadness when I look into those beautiful blue eyes."

He takes me by surprise again. He seems so intuitive, and yet I feel angry at his bluntness when he'd been so protective of his own privacy. I consider my reply. "Not much to tell. Married, two children, my own business, busy life."

Upon a frown, his lips form a stern thin line. "Thank you for the brief synopsis, Elizabeth, now please tell me about *you*."

"Everything?" I ask incredulously.

"Everything," he confirms, resting back against the pew, his arms crossed.

I find myself telling this man, this stranger, my life story. There is something compelling about Sebastian. I feel safe, in danger, lustful, but mostly I feel compelled to do as he says. He listens intently without interrupting and with an expression on his face that is unreadable. After I have finished, and my coffee is cold, he sits back and sighs deeply. I wonder if I should have told him about my marriage, my loneliness, and my feelings of rejection. He is not saying anything. *Say something.*

"Why do you stay with him? You deserve to be cherished, Elizabeth." He reaches across the table and tucks a loose strand of hair behind my ear again, and it is such a gentle yet sensual gesture that I blush once more.

"It's not that easy to leave him. I don't think I'm the perfect wife either." Yawning, I begin to succumb to fatigue and the alcohol.

"Just because something is a challenge, does not mean that one shouldn't rise to it, Elizabeth."

"You have no idea—"

"You'd be surprised. However, it's late. You are tired. Go to bed now. When you leave tomorrow morning, I want you to give me your business card and we'll meet again soon."

"Aren't you going to tell me anything about you? I'm not that tired."

He shakes his head. "Not yet. Get some sleep."

He is utterly infuriating yet completely addictive. "Okay," I agree meekly. "Goodnight, Sebastian. Thank you for a lovely night."

Sebastian proffers his hand, which I take in mine. "It's I who should thank you," he whispers. "You are an intriguing woman, Elizabeth Dove. I'm very glad you're here."

"Me too." Still holding his hand, I stretch up and kiss him gently on the cheek. He touches his cheek with his fingertips and closes his eyes. When he opens them I see pain in his eyes, a bleakness that makes my heart ache for him, and I long to hold him tightly and kiss him properly.

"Good night." He steps away, my fingers slip from his, and the moment is gone.

Feeling exposed to him, and regretful, I go to bed. My emotions are jumbled and I scold myself for letting my guard slip. Tomorrow is another day—a line from my favourite movie, *Gone With the Wind*—and it's my mantra now. I'll think about these feelings tomorrow.

Climbing wearily into bed, it crosses my mind that I'm doing as I am told for once in my life. I'm going to bed and getting some sleep because I'm tired and because Sebastian told me to. Sebastian has a manner about him which makes me want to obey him, to make him happy. I realise how refreshing it is for a man to make simple decisions for me. It is truly what I long for, what I need. Sleep comes easily.

My eyes open to a soft golden shard of sunlight on my pillow. Rubbing sleep away with balled fists, I reach for my phone and see that it's nearly seven o'clock. Able to focus now, I gaze at my room, at the dusty splendour of days gone by. Puddled curtains made of a heavy ochre brocade pool on the floor. I don't recall closing the curtains last night, yet they are closed this morning, except for a small parting at the top from where the morning sun steals in to dispel the gloom. I try to recall how much I drank last night, as I massage my temples, my head fuzzy. With a languid stretch and deep yawn, I think to myself that I could get used to waking in a room like this each morning. *Heaven.*

Washed, dressed in a skirt, cashmere sweater, and

knee high winter boots, I leave my bedroom and set off in search of breakfast.

The gaggle of female chatter tells me that my event colleagues are gathering in the dining hall. Looking forward to the peaceful drive home, I take a seat next to last night's top business woman. She is a gregarious character who is large both in personality and stature. Congratulating her on her business achievement, we chat while breakfast is served. She tells me that she received her award following the growth of her online business and I wonder how much she's worth, although I don't like to ask, which is surprisingly polite and restrained for me.

"Love, have you met his Lordship yet?" she asks me. "He's a strange one. Doesn't usually rent out his house for anything, so we are very honoured."

I can sense there is gossip about to spurt forth, and I draw closer to her conspiratorially, hungry for information regarding Sebastian.

"When the Women In Business organisers were viewing venues, this one had just been made available for the first time. If you ask me, he must need the cash, or the company of a houseful of women. Rumour has it that his wife's dead, but he's one for the ladies. They always are, these rich country folk."

I recall the spurious attributes of his Lordship's staff team who served us last night. "I met him last night," I say, and watch her raise an envious eyebrow. "He seems rather aloof and, frankly, I found him to be arrogant."

This appears to whet the woman's appetite for gossip,

and she nods her head in agreement. "Arrogant or not, I bet half the women in this room wouldn't kick him out of bed if given half a chance. He's gorgeous."

This time I am in agreement with her. She shovels a gargantuan forkful of scrambled egg into her mouth. My mobile phone beeps, indicating a text message has been received. Pulling it from my handbag, I see it is Ruth asking how the event has gone. No doubt she'll require a thorough debrief on the whole event, as she'd been disappointed she couldn't attend due to a clash of meetings. I have received no text message or missed call from Alan, or from fire fighter Simon, not that I had expected to hear from either, but I find still find it hurtful. It would be nice to be missed and thought of.

The bevy of irritatingly attractive waiting staff are placing hot plates of full English breakfast in front of us all, and I heartily tuck into the delicious sausages, bacon, and eggs and enjoy two cups of English breakfast tea served in a delicate porcelain cup.

Breakfast finished, our group disperses and begins homeward journeys. I wonder if I'll see Sebastian again, finding myself longing to see him one more time. I can't fathom what it is about that bossy, arrogant, tall, dark, gorgeous man that has me so mesmerized.

I stand in the vaulted hallway and look around, hoping for the opportunity to thank our host and to see him once more, but he does not appear. Seeing the member of his staff who greeted me yesterday, I take the opportunity to ask if he will be saying farewell to us.

"His Lordship has already left to take his morning ride," she tells me. *His Lordship.* It has an old fashioned ring to it.

The disappointment weighs heavily on my mind, but I decide to leave my contact information for him, hoping he will get in touch.

"Sebastian asked me to leave my business card for him." I hand my card to the girl, and she places it on the mantel above the fireplace in the expansive entrance hall. "Please ensure he gets that card, and please tell him that Beth Dove says thank you and goodbye."

With a curt nod, she walks away, her trim figure disappearing through the kitchen door. It strikes me how like a slave she is—timid, pretty, dressed in black, and evidently completely controlled by her boss. I wonder if she is the one who lives here, and a twinge of jealousy takes me by surprise.

As I pull away in my car, I glance in my rear view mirror at the magnificent house. I wonder if I will ever be here again, or see *him* again at all.

# Chapter 4

On the long drive back, my thoughts are filled with Sebastian. I run through what I recall of our conversation in the kitchen, wishing I hadn't opened up to him as I did. My loose tongue will get me in trouble one day, if it hasn't already. I feel so stupid.

I stop for lunch at Exeter, and browse in the large shopping mall. In a lingerie shop, I buy myself the smallest, sexiest set of underwear I have ever possessed. Not for Alan's enjoyment or for Simon's. I have bought them for me. I am going to be a sexier, more liberated me.

*You're changing, Beth. About time too.*

Joe runs to greet me as I close the front door. Putting down my bags, I scoop him in a tight embrace.

"I've missed you, little guy."

"Have you brought me a present?" he asks hopefully.

"No, Joe. Mummy hasn't been on holiday, I've been working."

"Dad says you've been off on a jolly." Joe huffs. "Does he now? Well, Dad's wrong."

Alan is sitting at the computer, under the stairs in the tiny recessed study area, which has space only for a small desk and chair. His eyes remain fixed on the screen as I breeze past him to the kitchen. "You're back," he observes brusquely.

"It would seem so, yes," I reply cattily.

"Good time?"

"Not really. Pretty much as expected. Loud women, lots of mud, draughty old house. How are the kids?"

"Fine."

So ends another conversation. I take my bags upstairs, unpack, and take the laundry, including Thursday's gold dress and underwear, to the washing machine. Deciding on an early night, it seems a good opportunity to talk to Alan about my feelings. We can't continue as we are, both bitterly unhappy.

"Alan, I've been thinking about us."

"I'm tired, Beth." He turns his back to me and pulls the duvet up protectively.

"I'm tired too. Look, please will you reconsider couples counselling? Let's at least try and fix our marriage if we can, before it's too late."

"We've had this discussion countless times," he mumbles. "I'm not going air my dirty laundry with a stranger."

"So, you don't want to save our marriage?" "To be perfectly honest, Beth, no. It's too late."

I've tried. There is little more I can do to help us. With a heavy heart, I lie in the darkness until the first light of dawn when I drop into a fitful sleep.

\*\*\*

It's Monday morning, at the office. Ruth is on the telephone barking at some unfortunate soul. I make myself a steaming cup of coffee and sink down onto the couch in my office, feeling weary and reflective.

"Tell me, how did it go this weekend?" Ruth is standing in doorway. I beckon for her to sit beside me and recount the events of last forty-eight hours. She is horrified at the sound of the mud running, relieved she wasn't able to take part.

"Oh, and I met a man." I drop the bomb and wait for the aftershock.

Ruth raises her eyebrows with a look of mock horror on her face.

"Why am I not surprised?" She sighs, rolling her eyes.

"He was the most frustrating man I have ever met. He had this infuriating way of extracting all my deepest, darkest secrets and yet wouldn't tell me anything about himself."

"Oh, sounds very intriguing. Is he attractive?"

"Ruth, he is seriously *gorgeous!* Tall, dark hair, greying at the temples, and he has the darkest eyes. And get this, he's a *Lord!*"

This instantly grabs her attention, and she lets out a loud, "whoop!"

I quickly put out her flames by adding that, of course, I won't ever see him again, and in any case, he is allegedly a womaniser.

"Aren't they all," she adds, and I have to agree with her. She takes a long hard look at me, detecting the changes I feel.

"I can't recall seeing you like this before, Beth." Ruth knows me too well. "If I didn't know better, I'd say you really do *like* this man. You seem different."

Ruth is right. I *feel* different. I haven't felt this way for a very long time. For the first time in seventeen years, a man is interested in *me*. Not Beth the boss, Beth the wife, Beth the mum, or even Beth the whore, but *me*. I want to see Sebastian again.

"Be careful, Beth," she warns. "If you start something with this man, and Alan finds out—"

"Ruth. It's nothing. I'm not having an affair, but it's nice to be noticed. It's good to feel like a woman instead of a drudge."

"I know, love. I know things are bad at home, but just be careful. You've a lot to lose."

The rest of my week is busy. My days are filled with meetings and running errands for the kids. I barely have a moment to myself.

I've heard nothing from Simon since we met last week, and that only serves to confirm I made a huge mistake. Today, I deleted my profiles on the uniform dating website and the BDSM site. I feel neglected and miserable.

It's Thursday afternoon, and I am putting on my coat to leave my office when my mobile phone bleeps with a received text message. I pick it up from my desk and hurriedly check the message, certain it will be from Bella as I am late collecting her from her dance lesson. I secretly hope it may be from Simon.

***Elizabeth I enjoyed our chat. Meet me for lunch.***

*Sebastian.*

I gasp. It's from him. A sudden tingle traces from my belly and travels downwards. Lunch. Typical man. He's in Cornwall and I'm in Dorset and he wants me to meet him for lunch. While I am relieved the slave girl gave him my business card, I am now filled with nervous trepidation at the sight of his text message.

Reading the message again, I note there are no pleasantries in the text. It's a summons to lunch. I feel resentment building inside me. I am used to being in charge and more than fed up with being taken advantage of.

*Sebastian, thank you for your kind invitation but as you live in Cornwall, which isn't exactly down the road from me, I hardly think I can meet you for lunch. Beth.*

I press 'send'. *That told him*, I think smugly. Then, I am filled with self-doubt. *Why was I so rude?* Too late. The phone makes a whooshing sound as it sends my text. Almost immediately, my phone beeps again.

*How do you know I'm not coming to Dorset on business?*

Oh, crap. I hadn't thought of that. In my mind he lazed around his mansion, only leaving his slave girl to go riding each morning. I text him back.

*So, are you in Dorset on business?*

Again, a swift reply.

*No. Meet me outside your office 1:30 p.m. tomorrow. Sebastian.*

He has my business card. Of course he knows where my office is. The calendar on my phone contains my carefully ordered life, and I note that I have an eleven-thirty meeting tomorrow, with a new client. *Double crap.* That should be okay, though, I realise. If I wrap the meeting up promptly, it is only twenty minutes away.

*What am I thinking? How can I possibly have lunch with that man. But lunch is just lunch, right? It's not as if I'm going to jump into bed with him.* Though, the idea sends that same tingle down my body. *It is just lunch.*

"Hurry up, kids, I have a busy day!" I bellow up the stairs to my children. It's eight-fifteen already, and I need to get going. My mind is full of thoughts of my lunch today with Sebastian.

I check my appearance in the mirror in our bedroom for the umpteenth time. I've tried on three different outfits and settled for the black pencil skirt, white fitted blouse, barely black stockings and black heels. Very business-like, but also a little sexy. The skirt and blouse show off my curves.

Alan eyes me suspiciously as we exchange brief

farewells in the kitchen. "You look dressed up again, going somewhere nice?" he inquires with a discernable hint of sarcasm.

"I have an important meeting with a potential new client," I tell him, quite honestly. "I want to make a good impression. It's a valuable contract."

He doesn't look convinced. "Amazing how many meetings you have recently." He sneers.

"Alan. I run my own business. Of course I attend business meetings. Stop the crap."

"Do whatever you fucking want," he snarls.

A pang of guilt pricks my conscience as I dash out of the front door, scooping up my briefcase and yelling at the children to get into the car. We're late again.

I reach my office at nine-fifteen, having deposited the children at their schools and fought with the rush hour traffic. Ruth is waiting in my office with coffee ready for me. We discuss today's meeting, and she tells me she will be tied up in interviews today. I neglect to mention my lunch appointment, knowing she would be shocked. Ruth leaves my office, and I sit down at my desk and power up my computer. I check my emails and reply to any that are urgent.

Then my thoughts wander to Sebastian. He seems so *dominant.* My curiosity wins out again, and I click on Google search, typing in the word dominant and the words man and woman. The first search heading, "The Truth About Men Dominating Women" leads me to a website which discusses domestic abuse. I hit the return key and select the next link:

***Why every woman wants to be dominated by a man.***

*Dominant men exude power, are comfortable in their own skin and with their own identity. They are never weak and never hesitate, nor do they seek approval from others either in a social situation or in the workplace. Women are attracted to those with power. While most men aim for women with looks, women need a man who is assertive, independent, strong-minded and a leader. Women have a deep- rooted instinct that draws them toward dominant males, and this inner urge cannot be suppressed. It is a part of their very survival.*

My friends and family would consider me to be the leader in my life, upon who so many are reliant, including men. Yet, I can relate to the article, as I'm tired of leading and would dearly love to be led. To have some of the decision-making taken from me would be heavenly. A burden lifted. A cloud dispersed. And yet, to hand over control to another would require complete trust, and I don't know if I am capable of trusting unquestioningly.

My meeting runs smoothly, but I find it difficult to concentrate. I have butterflies in my tummy and a growing sense of panic for so many reasons. I have no idea where we will be going for lunch and, when I get back to my car, I take out my phone and run a search on local restaurants. I wonder if we shouldn't be going somewhere farther away, where there is no risk of being seen by one of Alan's friends or associates. That makes me feel more guilt than ever.

*It's just lunch Beth,* I scold myself. I decide upon a bistro on the other side of town, which has excellent online reviews.

I have time to dash into my office and reapply my lipstick and a dash of perfume, and use the cloakroom before my watch tells me it's one-thirty. I step out of our office building and rest against the wall. It's a cold afternoon. The autumn sunshine takes the chill from the air, but does little to settle the nervousness I feel. My gaze darts from one end of the street to the other and back, scanning the faces of those going about their business, in case Alan is watching me. It's irrational but then Alan has seemed irrational and increasingly antagonistic lately. Ruth's warning rings through my head. *Be careful, Beth.*

Then I see Sebastian. He's walking toward me with a confident swagger, and he's even more gorgeous than I recall. He wears a camel, wool overcoat with the collar turned up and his shoulders look so very broad. He has dark sunglasses on to shield his eyes from the low autumn sun, and I can't tell if he is looking at me but I sense that he is. The familiar warmth oozes through my core and my pulse quickens at the sight of him.

"Elizabeth, so good to see you again," he says as he grips my arms, pulls me closer and kisses me on both cheeks. I am a quivering wreck now.

"It's good to see you too, Sebastian." It is a lame response, but I mean it. It is so very good to see him again. "I thought we could try a French bistro across town," I suggest. "The reviews are very good and— "

He puts a finger to my lips to silence me. "I've booked a table for us, Elizabeth, at a very fine hotel I know. It's twenty minutes from here, and the food is excellent. When you get to know me a little better you will learn to trust my judgment, and you will know that I take the lead in all things. Let's walk to my car."

*What is that supposed to mean?* I wonder. However, I like the sound of that. It's such a refreshing change. Feeling bold, I slip my arm through his as we walk to his car. I am a new woman already. I feel it.

We reach Sebastian's car, the sleek white Range Rover I saw at the house. He holds the door open for me and I climb in, relishing the feel of the leather against my legs. Sebastian starts the engine and we join the flow of traffic.

Sebastian presses an illuminated button on his dash and the car is filled with stirring music, which I recognize to be Pachelbel's Canon in D Major—a beautiful piece in which I lose myself as I gaze at the road ahead. Neither of us feels the need for words as we become absorbed in the music.

Arriving at The Willows Hotel, I am instantly impressed. It's quietly elegant but not pretentious, and I wonder if Sebastian has been here before as he leads us confidently through the foyer and into a small, intimate bar adjacent to the restaurant.

He places a hand on the small of my back. I feel the

sparks again, and catch my breath. He guides me to a large tartan covered couch, and we sit. The couch is aged and the cushions soft, and we sink down together, his leg pressed against mine, his elbow touching my breast. He doesn't adjust his position to put more distance between us. A waiter soon approaches, and Sebastian orders a bottle of Pol Roget.

The waiter pours a little of the champagne into sparkling crystal flutes. It's deliciously chilled, and as I sip the dry bubbles, I feel relaxed with this man. I've misjudged him. There is no hint of arrogance today. He seems jovial and approachable, so I decide to strike now and launch into interrogation part two.

"Sebastian, the other night, in your kitchen...I told you things I haven't told anyone before, and yet I know so little about you. Tell me everything— about your life, work, and your family. Please. You're so mysterious." I wonder how much he will divulge. I'm hoping he won't spring a lover and children on me and, of course, I await confirmation that his poor unfortunate wife is dead.

He sinks further into the cushions, placing his left arm along the length of our seat, so that his hand rests behind my back, making me shiver with the nearness of him.

"There's such a lot to tell you, Elizabeth." He fiddles with the upholstery piping. "I'm very fortunate because I've inherited a title, land, and a wonderful house but I've also inherited a burden of responsibility, and that burden is not an easy cross to bear."

This is intriguing. Nodding, I urge him to continue.

"But, inquisitive lady, you will just have to be patient. I'll tell you more about me, but not now."

*What?* He is indeed the most infuriating man I have met.

"Sebastian," I whine. "I'm not a patient person. At least answer a question for me, please." I am not letting him off that lightly.

He raises one of his dark eyebrows at me, and his arm moves from behind me into a more defensive pose, arms crossed.

I'm pushing my luck, but I press on. "I understand you've been married, and...I think your wife passed away. Oh, gosh, that sounds insensitive, and I don't mean to..." I'm digging a huge crater- sized hole for myself, but again I press on. "I just wondered if you are on your own or if you have a special person in your life." *Shoot me now.* Why didn't I just come out and ask him if he's single and if he wants to come to bed with me, because that's how he will interpret my stupid question.

He's looking at me with a smirk on his face. "Well, now, you speak your mind don't you, Elizabeth? I see you've been listening to gossip, but you're right. My wife Libby did pass away, sadly. To answer your second question, I've many special people in my life but I'm unattached romantically."

I have no idea what he means. He is staring at me as he sips from his glass.

"That's what you mean, isn't it?" His lip curls and he cocks an eyebrow. "Why didn't you just ask if I'm available?"

The champagne spits from my mouth as I choke on his audacity. "No," I counter. "That's *not* what I meant." Recovering my composure, I straighten a cushion and put my glass on the polished table in front of us. "I'm sorry to hear about your wife, truly." I wonder how she died, but I decide to keep quiet and drink more champagne. Thankfully, we are ushered into the restaurant for lunch.

"Come. We'll talk more over lunch." We leave the bar, our hands entwined, and the touch of his skin on mine makes me ache with need.

Over a lunch of sea bass, conversation flows freely. We chat about more light-hearted topics such as my work, and he tells me a little about his house and life in Cornwall. He tells me about the tenant farmers who provide the income to maintain his estate. He looks worried when he tells me that, over the years, the tenants —some of whom have lived on his estate for generations —gradually leave, as farming is hit by the recession and EU subsidy reductions.

He talks freely, but doesn't divulge a great deal of personal or intimate information about himself. He seems a very private man but also a deep thinker, and is incredibly intelligent. Lunch is divine, and I can see why Sebastian chose this place. After coffee, he requests the bill and I offer to share it, but he insists on settling it himself.

"One thing you will accept is that I'll never allow a woman to pay. Get used to it, because it won't change."

*How refreshing.*

As we walk out to Sebastian's car, I freeze in absolute horror. Alan is leaning against the hood of the car, and he looks furious. I feel light-headed and nauseous. He must have followed us. My husband marches towards us, his face masked in fury.

# Chapter 5

His stare is boring into my very soul. If he could kill me with a glare, I would be breathing my last.

"You cheating bitch," he spits venomously. "I thought you looked too fucking dolled up for a meeting, you lying whore."

I want to run, but Sebastian places his hand firmly on my arm and I feel him straighten and tense beside me.

"Stay where you are. I'll handle this," he warns me.

"Who the fuck's this?" Alan shoves Sebastian's shoulder. I step between the two men, trembling.

"Alan, for God's sake. I've had lunch with a colleague, that's all"

He's not listening to me. He's beating his fists against his legs menacingly. "Don't fucking lie to me, you slut."

Sebastian steps forward, pushing me aside so that he squares up to my husband. His face contorts with a rage that far exceeds Alan's, and for a moment, Alan looks scared. Unsure what to do and consumed by panic, I turn and run back into the hotel, wanting to escape.

Tears stream down my hot cheeks as I seek solace in the ladies' cloakroom. I lock myself into a cubicle and sob. I'm so unhappy. I love my children and I don't want my life with them to change but, if I was happy, I wouldn't be having lunch with Sebastian. It's all so confusing, and I feel wracked with guilt, but also angry with Alan for following and humiliating me. My unhappiness, compounded by stress, causes the tears to spill forth as I lean against the cubicle wall.

After a few minutes, I hear the door to the ladies' cloakroom open and the sound of heavy footsteps cross the tiled floor. I see, through my tears, a pair of black shiny shoes beneath my cubicle door.

"Open the door, Elizabeth."

Opening the door, I look up at Sebastian and see his face full of concern and compassion, and this makes me sob again.

He pulls me into his arms and tightly embraces me. It feels so safe, so comforting to be held by his strong arms, my tear stained face against his chest. He puts a finger under my chin and raises my face and tells me not to cry. Alan has gone, and he whispers to me that all will be okay. I want to believe him. He lowers his head and kisses each of my eyes, and then his lips find mine. I kiss him back, passionately and deeply, my mouth hungry for his. Our tongues meet and we taste each other for the first time. I press against him harder, and his arms tighten around me. I feel his hardness against me, and a current of excitement runs down my spine and all the way to my sex.

Our lips part and I feel breathless as my chest heaves. My raw desire for this man shocks and shames me, yet I want more. I want all of him, to feel him inside me.

"Elizabeth, I want you more than I've wanted anyone in my life. I know you want me too," he rasps. "I want to protect you. To take all this away from you."

"I don't know, Sebastian, but...I'm married. Oh God, what a mess." The tears come again.

"Darling, you don't know me yet, but you will. We'll get to know each other. Come." He takes my hand and leads me to the basins where he runs a paper towel under the cold tap and wipes away my tears and black streaks of mascara from beneath my eyes.

The door opens, and an elderly lady enters the cloakroom. She gasps when she sees a man in there, and hastily retreats, flapping disapprovingly. I look at Sebastian and we laugh. Goodness knows what I have to laugh about, but I can't help it, my laughter verges on hysteria.

As we leave the hotel and walk back to Sebastian's car, my gaze darts across the car park, searching for Alan's car, but it's not there. On the way back to my office, I wonder what I'm going to do. *Can I go home?* I haven't technically done anything wrong, and certainly not what Alan believes. The kiss was wrong, yes, but it was not adultery. Will Alan believe anything I say? *What if he boots me out of the house, what will happen to the children? Oh fuck, what a mess.*

Intuitively, Sebastian reaches across and lays a hand on my knee, casting a glance across. "You okay?" His hand moves from my knee and grasps my hand in his. He strokes my palm with his fingertips.

"I'm so screwed up. Shit, Sebastian, what am I going to do? I hate him." I look at him for guidance, but he stares at the road, his expression unreadable.

"You know you've always got a safe place to stay at Penmorrow. You and the children." He looks at me briefly again.

"That's so thoughtful. Thank you." I squeeze his hand, with the realisation that I've misjudged this man, who is caring rather than arrogant.

"I mean it, Elizabeth. Whatever you need, I'm here for you."

"I know you do," I say gratefully, "and you've no idea how much that means to me, but this is something I have to work out by myself. I've made my bed and now I have to lie in it. That's what Mum always says."

Sebastian parks in a space near my office and cuts the engine. For a few moments we don't speak, my thoughts centred on the ramifications of today. He gets out of the car and walks around the car to open my door. He holds out a hand and I take it in mine and step from the car onto the pavement. For a fleeting moment, I feel a spark from his touch until he pulls his hand away, and in that moment I know I can't see Sebastian again—not until I know my marriage is over. The pain from this decision is tangible, and a hard twisted knot forms in my stomach.

"Elizabeth, take my card," he says, handing me a small white card with his name and contact details embossed in gold. "I want you to call me tonight when you get home, to let me know you're okay."

"Actually, Sebastian, I'd rather not call. I need some space to think about my life, and to see if Alan and I can work through our problems," I tell him sorrowfully. Of course, this isn't what I want. I want Sebastian. I need to see him and *more*, but I am thinking now about harsh reality and the implications for my children, the devastation they would feel if Alan and I were to separate.

"I see, as you wish of course. You have my card, and I'm here if you need me." He looks forlorn as he embraces me and kisses my hair. As he gets into his car and drives away without a backward glance, I want to run after him, tell him I've made a mistake, and that I love him. Instead, I walk back into my office with a heavy heart.

Ruth looks up from her desk as I enter our offices. She notices my blotchy face and red rimmed eyes and frowns.

"Beth, love, whatever's happened? Come and sit down. I'll make us a brew, and you can tell me all about it."

"Oh, Ruth, I've had the most amazing and the most *terrible* time," I whine. "I had lunch with the man who owns the house I went to last weekend, and Alan must have followed us. He called me such dreadful names, Ruth, and obviously thinks I've been having an affair."

"Blimey. You mean the Lord? What was he doing in Dorset?" she asks.

"Drove up just to see me."

"Hell, Beth, I could tell you liked him. You're playing with fire, you know. I warned you about something like this happening." After a moment of contemplation, she asks what I intend to do. "I suggest you go home and talk to Alan before this escalates."

"I know you're right, but it's made me realise I don't want my life with Alan. I still want *more,* I want to feel desired and sexy, not just a drudge. I want to be *me*, but I've forgotten who *me* is!" I sob.

"I understand, Beth, I really do," she replies. "Look, I know it's a cliché but the grass really isn't greener on the other side. Give it a month or two with the Lord, and I guarantee he'll be farting, snoring, and boring the pants off you, just like all men. It's all sex and candlelight for the first few weeks, and then wham, bam, thank you, ma'am. And before you know it, you're washing his socks and wondering where the romance went. Trust me! We've talked about this before."

I look at Ruth incredulously, and we both burst into a giggling fit, hysteria rising within me once again. She has the most eloquent way of putting across her point and I do love her.

She brings me a mug of tea, and I go to my office and close the door. There is so much to think about, but I'll face Alan later. First, I need to check my emails and catch up on some work. I wake up my laptop and sign in to my Yahoo account. Immediately I see an email from Alan's best friend, Mike. He was Best Man at our wedding and has known Alan since school days.

*Hi Beth,*

*I've had a call from Alan and he's in bits, love. I'm not sure what's going on with you but, honestly, I've not*

*heard him so cut up before. He's asked me to talk some
sense into you, but you're a big girl, just don't hurt him.*
    *Love Mike x*

Mike has always taken Alan's side but then he would,
he's his best friend. I decide not to answer his email.
Instead, I pick up my things and set off for home. I really
cannot concentrate on work. My head is full of hot kisses
and angry husbands. Alan's car is parked on the drive, so I
know he didn't go back to work this afternoon. Letting
myself into the house and closing the front door, I see him
at the kitchen table clasping a tumbler of whisky. He's
been drinking; that's not good.

"Alan, we need to talk." I sit down at the kitchen table
across from him rather than next to him, wanting to put
space between us. He looks at me over the top of his
glass, which I note is nearly empty. "I know it looked bad
today, but there's nothing going on."

"The kids are fine, nice of you to remember you have
them." He's full of malice. I reach across and pick up his
whisky tumbler, draining the glass. The amber liquid
burns my throat, the alcohol fuelling my confidence.

"Do you know what, Beth? What saddens me most is
that if it's not him, it'll be someone else. I don't make you
happy, and there's naff all I can do about it. I am who I
am, and it's never going to be enough for you." He looks
my in the eye and adds, "I just don't like the bloody
deceit, Beth."

"You have to believe me, Alan, it was just lunch. I've

got enough going on in my life without all this mess. Let's just get on with our lives as best we can for the kids, okay?"

He nods dejectedly, and I can see he's weary, and drunk. I'm surprised, however, to get off so lightly after this afternoon's confrontation. I'm relieved, but deep down, I know I want to see Sebastian again. The deep longing in the pit of my stomach is gnawing away at my insides.

I go to bed early and open a book, losing myself in erotic fiction. As I read, I become the heroine and Sebastian is the lead male. It's me bending over the bed, and it's Sebastian who is pounding into me from behind. As I read on, my hand moves down between my legs and my fingers probe my wetness. I circle my sweet bud with my finger with increasing urgency, and feel myself building, climbing to the release I need.

Drifting into a restless sleep, I'm back at the house in Cornwall. I'm running desperately from room to room and Sebastian is chasing me. He's dressed in black and is followed by the girl. They're covered in cobwebs, and screaming for me to run to the cellar. I wake up with a jolt, bathed in sweat.

# Chapter 6

Saturday dawns upon a beautiful crisp autumn day. Despite the frostiness from Alan throughout the rest of the week, I am determined to make the weekend an enjoyable one for the children. I have heard nothing further from Sebastian, nor from Simon.

Today, we have Alan's parents, Dora and Brian, his sister Sarah and her husband Nathan, and their young twin sons coming to lunch, so I have lots to do in preparation. It's usually an enjoyable time when the family visits, with lots of laughter, although Nathan is a drinker and a little unpredictable.

The roast lamb is ready and the family arrives. Everyone is in good spirits, and even Alan's mood has lifted. The twins are giggling as they jump on top of Joe, and Alan and Nathan are having a chat in the study while Dora helps me in the kitchen. *Happy families,* I muse.

Lunch is delicious and the conversation, and wine, flows. Sarah tells us that she and Nathan are celebrating their forthcoming wedding anniversary next week, and Dora and Brian are babysitting so they can have some couple time.

Alan suggests a very good hotel where they may like to have dinner—The Willows Hotel. I shoot him a look, which says, "I hope you choke on your lamb," but he smirks back at me. It's apparent he has already told Nathan about yesterday, as the two of them share knowing glances. Sarah, ever the diplomat, changes the subject. The digs keep coming from Alan throughout the rest of the meal. It ruins the day and, when the family departs at six, I am simmering with rage.

"You just couldn't bloody help yourself, could you?" I hiss at him while I wash up the dishes. "You humiliated me with all your sniping and made your family uncomfortable. Did you see Dora's face?"

"It's *your* fault! Don't you blame *me*. I've had just about enough of you. Why don't you bugger off with your Mr. Range Rover, and leave me and my kids? You're never here anyway, you're always at work or up to God knows what—"

He's drunk again, and at this moment I hate him more than ever.

I need some space, so I grab my bag, car keys, and jacket and open the front door, unsure as to where I am going, but needing to be alone.

Bella yells from the top of the stairs, "Bloody nice one, Mum. Piss off!" I turn to go to her, to tell her I am sorry she heard her father and I arguing, but she is gone and I hear her door slam shut. Bereft, I leave the house.

I drive to the coast and park my car in the car park by West Way Beach, it being a cold November evening the car park is nearly deserted. I decide to call Ruth and take out my phone from my bag. When I switch it on, I see there is a text message waiting for me.

*Are you ok? S*

Sebastian is so thoughtful, but he's disregarding my request for space. Yet, he seems so intuitive to my needs. I forget about calling Ruth, and instead text him back.

***Things bad at home, thanks for caring X***

His reply arrives almost immediately.

***I'm here if you need me***

His message is brief, but the fact that he cares is comforting. Feeling better, I decide to head home but I erase his messages first.

Alan's watching television when I return, and he ignores me. The children are very quiet. I presume Joe also heard us arguing in the kitchen, and I feel bad about that, I really do. Tomorrow will be a better day. This evening I will spend time with the kids and then take myself to bed and lose myself in the final chapters of my book. If only real life was like that book.

***

The week drags by incredibly slowly. As usual, I'm running the children around to school, activities, parents' evening, and of course working. Each day seems more arduous than the previous one. I haven't received any more messages from Sebastian despite constantly checking my phone. Thursday comes and I'm wading through reams of paperwork on my desk when my mobile phone rings. I don't recognise the number as I answer.

"Beth Dove speaking."

"Elizabeth, it's Sebastian. Can you talk?"

My pulse races and I feel myself flushing. I didn't expect his call.

"Sebastian, how nice of you to call." My voice sounds just a tiny bit too high pitched and desperate. "Are you all right?" he asks. So caring.

"Same old, same old. My day just got a whole lot better with your call," I add cheekily.

"Glad to hear it. I've left you alone, as requested, but I'd like to see you." Technically he hasn't really left me alone as it's only been a few days since his text, but I'm flattered and relieved to hear his voice.

"I want you to come to stay at Penmorrow for a few days. It'll do you good." My stomach does a backflip as the enormity of what he is asking hits me. I would dearly love to go to Penmorrow and spend a few days in bed with Sebastian, though I know that's not actually what he said, but it is my interpretation.

"Sebastian, that would be wonderful, but I can't. I have the children, work, not to mention how Alan would freak out." I am categorically saying no. It's the sensible thing to do. "Although, I could ask Mum if she'd have the kids for a couple of days. She knows how exhausted I am." *Oh, my willpower is staggering.*

"Good girl. Can you make the weekend or is Monday easier?"

*My thoughtful Sebastian.*

"Let me call Mum, and text you back in a few minutes." The last of my self-control dissipates. "And, Sebastian, I've missed you." I am a lost cause.

"I've missed you too. Call me back."

I call my mother. "Mum, it's Beth. I hate to do this to you, but you know how stressed I've been lately. Things aren't good at home and work is manic, so I'd be so grateful if you could please have the kids for the weekend for me? I thought I'd go to a spa for a rest." I hold my breath, ashamed I'm lying to my own mother.

"Beth, darling, is everything okay?"

"Alan's being the same as usual. I wouldn't ask you but I really do need this."

"Yes, I can have them, of course I will, but on the condition that you go to a really nice spa and have a complete rest."

A rest. I'm not so sure resting will be on our agenda. "Oh, Mum, thank you so much. Yes, I plan to go to bed for two days and sleep. I'll drop the kids to you at ten in the morning on Saturday." We chat for a few more minutes, and then I end the call.

*What am I doing?* I wasn't being totally dishonest. I did indeed hope to spend two days in bed, after all.

I text Sebastian, rather than call.

***Mum said yes! I will be with you Sat pm. Can't wait and thank you. X***

My phone pings as a reply is received.

*You're texting. I said call. Plan on having fun.*

He is so pedantic. Plan on having fun? That sounds so deliciously naughty.

Friday passes slowly, and I can't wait for Saturday. I've told Alan that Mother suggested I take a short break in a spa, which is almost true, so that I can recharge my batteries. He actually agreed this was a good idea, but I can see that he doesn't trust me. However, he trusts my mother, and is satisfied that the children will be well looked after. I tell him that I will go from the spa directly to work on Monday, and will be home that evening.

Saturday morning arrives and I rise early, and dress in a warm chocolate colour sweater dress and boots. I pack Bella and Joe's overnight bags and a small suitcase for myself, hiding my new underwear at the bottom of the case along with my favourite perfume and various clothing. I pack my swimsuit out of sudden panic as I am meant to be visiting a spa.

The kids are in the car and, after Alan bids me a curt goodbye, I drive to my mother's house. I kiss and hug my children and mother, feeling a pang of guilt as I do so. Then I am on my way and I haven't felt so excited since I was a teenager. I feel I may burst.

Penmorrow is even more spectacular than I remember. Perhaps because I won't be sharing it with countless other women, it seems even more inviting.

I drive slowly up the tree-lined drive and the

butterflies in my tummy are doing backflips. I park and cut the engine and step from my car. As I take my small suitcase from the trunk, I inhale the salty sea air. It is invigorating and rejuvenating, and my troubles seem a million miles away. I hesitate at the imposing oak door of the austere house, before raising the lion's head and knocking loudly. Stepping back, I expect to be greeted by the slave girl, but instead Sebastian throws open the door. I hold my breath and look at this man, and in that moment I want him more than I've ever wanted anyone or anything before.

# Chapter 7

We don't speak. Instead, he takes me in his arms and hugs me tightly before kissing my hair. He smells so good. I breathe in his manly scent. Taking my suitcase from me, he takes my hand and leads me into the house. I hesitate in the hall but he has a firm, commanding grip on my hand. He puts my suitcase down next to the fireplace in the vast hall, and continues walking and I follow submissively.

Sebastian purposefully treads each stair, still gripping my hand he leads me up the Gothic looking staircase with cast-iron balustrade. We reach the top stair and he leads me to the left, underneath a vast octagonal lantern and down a long straight passageway off which are several closed doors. He stops at the fourth door on the left and turns the handle, pushing open the heavy oak door.

Sebastian stops in the centre of the room and pulls me into his arms. All that I'm aware of is a vast four-poster bed with ornate carving and heavy, dark purple velour drapes.

We kiss then, our tongues hungrily seeking each other's. His lips bruise mine with his passion and I moan with desire, a warm trickle seeping from my sex. I feel his hand press into the small of my back and move downwards, where it grasps and kneads my buttocks. He takes a handful of my hair with his other hand and tugs it firmly. Still our tongues explore each other and I thread my fingers through the short hair at his nape, pulling on it, consumed with passion. He bites my lip and I wince but seek more hungrily.

I feel Sebastian unzipping my dress and, as he glides the zip down, my spine tingles. He slides it off each shoulder and it slithers to the floor. He unhooks my bra and I press my naked breasts against him, my nipples hardening painfully, elongating with the need for his touch. I pull back and lift his sweater over his head and he raises his arms to help me, then I take off his t-shirt and both are cast to the floor.

He pulls me tightly to him and my nipples now pressed against his bare chest, the mass of dark hairs there tickling my skin. His muscles are well- defined and hard as I trace my fingers across his bare chest. He is the most beautiful male specimen I have ever seen, and I am feral with desire for him.

He runs his palms firmly down my back, his fingers finding purchase in the elastic of my panties, which he roughly pulls down over my hips, tapping at each leg to step out of them. Naked and squirming with desire, my juices coat my thighs as I yearn for his touch on my clit and his cock inside me—deep, oh so deep. Pushing my hips forward, I gyrate my groin against his hard cock, which is pressing through the denim of his jeans, screaming to be released. I undo his leather belt and tug down his zipper, my eagerness growing.

"Mmm, so impatient, Elizabeth. You need it, darling, don't you," he murmurs.

A gasp escapes my lips as I take his huge, erect penis in my hand and squeeze it's length, rejoicing at the way it thickens in my hand. It's been such a very long time since I felt so desired, since I could be free to explore my own desires. I can't wait any longer.

He guides me backwards until I feel the hard frame of the bed against the backs of my thighs and then he pushes me hard, down onto the bed so that my ass is on the mattress, but my legs are draped over the frame. He bends and lifts each of my feet from the soft carpet, and I feel my legs lifted, so high and apart, exposing me, opening me wide to his scrutiny and will. He kneels then, placing my legs over each of his strong, broad shoulders.

Arching my back, I close my eyes and wait for what I know will come. His kisses trail moistly on the inside of my thighs.

"Yes, oh yes, higher...go higher." He's driving me insane.

"If you tell me what to do, I'll stop, Elizabeth."

*What? Oh no, don't stop. Please.*

He pauses a moment, to punctuate his point, before his fingers part my labia, the tip of his tongue brushing lightly at my clit. It's exquisite and I relish every flick, side to side, then circling as I throb down there. I tug at his hair, pulling his tongue harder onto me until the full roughness of his tongue is driving me wild, lapping again and again across my clit, circling until I feel my orgasm building. The warm flush builds from my pulsing sweet spot, and courses through my groin to my stomach, my nipples aching, the tremors rocking me, unrelenting. He licks clean my liquor, his tongue tracing a line from my pubis to my navel, to each of my nipples and up to my neck then settles his lips on mine. His tender kiss deepens, the sweetness on his tongue coating mine, his mouth and chin drenched in my juices.

He moves away and lies next to me on the bed. As he does so, he pulls me on top of him and I am looking down into his lustful eyes. He grabs a fistful of my hair again, and I feel him pushing me down.

My lips leave the salty harbour of his neck, trailing pecked kisses over his heart to a downward path that follows the line of his course black curls from taut stomach to his mound of thick manly pubic hair. His erection lengthens in my palm as he expels a hiss.

"Yes. Take me in your mouth. Now." I need no encouragement. My tongue laps the first bead of salty dew from the head of his cock as his manhood slips into my mouth. His hips buck with each teasing suck in hollowed cheek, taking him out and licking his crown, before welcoming his thrusts into my open throat, my hand milking and stroking his shaft at its root. How he moans and writhes, guiding me with his strong grip.

"*Yesss,* that's right. Take it deep. Good girl." His hand is pushing my head down at a fast rhythmic pace until suddenly, he pulls me by my hair with a sharpness that draws a gasp. Maintaining the pressure on my hair, he forces me up toward him then releases his grip. "Ride me."

Leveraging my hips, he guides me into position then tugs me down to be speared by his slick crown. I am so very wet that he glides into me in spite of his girth. My vagina stretches, coating him in my new arousal yet his length is such that I gasp, struggling to take all of him into me. Grinding down hard, he fills me completely and holds me firmly in place, my back arched, head thrown back as I moan in ecstasy.

I've waited so long for this and so I savour every delicious inch of him with a hunger that can't be satiated. Leaning down, my hair tumbles in a curtain over my face as my mouth seeks his, sucking at his bottom lip through panted breaths. Up and down, he sets a gruelling pace, my orgasm building again as his hardness strikes my deep bundle of nerves. Our fingers lace in the air, his moans louder now as he chases his own climax. With a rasped cry, he explodes deep inside me as I too shatter onto him, my orgasm causing my whole body to shudder uncontrollably. Again he cries out, and it sounds like *Libby* but it could be *baby*. The sound is fleeting and I can't be sure. Exhausted, I flop down onto his chest. His breathing is laboured and he's hot and slick against my skin.

"Fuck, Elizabeth, you have real potential."

*What the hell does that mean? Was I good or was I crap with the potential to be less crap?* I'll talk about that comment later but for now I love being in his arms, lying on top of him, my head nestled against his chest, listening to his heart beating strongly. He feels so powerful, so full of testosterone, a real man. *My man?* At this moment I'm glad he chose me, none of the other twenty-five women, but only *me*.

We doze peacefully, and when I stir it's nearly nightfall. The light is fading fast and shadows cloak the room, rendering it rather eerie. As I grow accustomed to the poor light, I take in my surroundings. The room is huge despite the dark, heavy furniture. There is a vast, ornately carved armoire and matching eight-drawer chest upon which photographs sit in silver frames. A carved chaise, upholstered in dark crimson silk, sits on ball and claw feet beneath the mullioned window. There is an enormous chest beside the door and a winged leather armchair is beside a wooden mantled fireplace. It's a manly room lacking a woman's feminine touch.

Sebastian stirs beside me and opens his eyes with a sleepy stretch and yawn before pulling me toward him and planting a kiss on my shoulder.

"Come, let's go and eat. I'm ravenous," he says, climbing out of bed to retrieve his jeans from the tangled mess of clothes on the floor and tugging them on. Taking my hand, he pulls me reluctantly from the bed. "There's a bathroom through there." He indicates a door next to the armoire. "Freshen up and put on the robe behind the door. I'll be in the kitchen." Before I can answer, he turns and leaves. He seems distant, dismissive almost, and I the old feelings of self-doubt creep back. What we did was amazing and I want him to share this with me. I feel so insecure, yet know it's irrational. *I need to get a grip!*

The bathroom is vast and I wonder if it was originally another bedroom. *Bedchamber* is what it would have been called in days gone by. The white enamelled bath sits proudly in the centre of the bathroom, upon grey marble floor tiles, its weight supported by curved black wrought iron legs, with brass ball and claw feet fashioned in the same style as the chaise in the bedroom. I wonder if it is original or a reproduction, but it looks authentic.

There are modern touches, I notice, such as twin basins with glass shelves above each. On one shelf sits a variety of Sebastian's shaving equipment, aftershave, and a comb. On the neighbouring shelf are a selection of female perfumes in glass bottles, Chanel and Christian Dior. There is a bone-handled hairbrush and a silver cased lipstick. I pull off the lid and twist. It is a bright blood red, and I can see it's been used.

The thought occurs to me that these may be Libby's perfume and cosmetics. I wonder if he is therefore keeping his dead wife's toiletries, and if so then it is certainly macabre. If not Libby's, then which other woman could these belong to? Evidently, it's a woman with whom Sebastian is intimate, or they wouldn't be in his private bathroom. This is another thing to quiz him about, and the more I reflect, I wonder also if the silk robe hanging on a hook behind the door also belongs to the other woman.

The warm water cleanses my mind as well as my body. As instructed, I slip on the short black silk robe and tie the belt. It has a single red rose embroidered on the right breast and it feels luxurious and cool against my skin. A shiver travels down my spine as I ponder the provenance of it. Studying myself in the mirror, the flushed, sex- tousled haired woman I see staring back at me, is the woman who has been waiting to be freed for seventeen long years. I blow the vamp a kiss in the mirror and head downstairs to find Sebastian.

A delicious smell greets me when I walk into the kitchen, and I realise that I am ravenous. Sebastian towers over the range, stirring something in a heavy copper pan. I drop a kiss on the back of his neck, my arms encircling his narrow hips as I peer into the pan to see what he is cooking.

"Hope you're hungry, Elizabeth. I make a mean bolognaise sauce!"

"*Mmm,* it smells yummy and I'm starving. I can't think why." I wink at him, and he returns a sexy wry smile.

"Sit." He gestures, with his wooden spoon, to the church pew and I take a seat. The candle is lit and it casts a warm golden glow across the chunky wooden table. I watch him moving deftly about the kitchen, preparing our food with a relaxed competence. He pours me a large glass of mellow red wine of which I take a deep drink, enjoying the warm flush from the alcohol as I watch him work. Setting two dishes of spaghetti bolognaise, spoons and forks on the table, he nudges a small dish of Parmesan shavings toward me.

"You're such a good cook, Sebastian." I flatter him,

and I mean it, as I slide a dish of the tempting food to my place setting and take some Parmesan. "Do you cook for yourself every day?"

"No, I enjoy cooking occasionally, but Scarlett cooks for me. She prepared the meal for the business event. She's exceptional, very capable, and imaginative."

*Wait right there, fella. Are we talking about cooking, or something else?* I bite my lip.

"I just bet she is," I retort without subtlety, but resentment creeps up on me from nowhere.

Sebastian puts down his cutlery and frowns at me. "Elizabeth Dove, are you jealous?" he asks, all innocence and boyish charm.

"Should I be?" I shovel a forkful of bolognaise into my mouth nonchalantly, my eyes firmly locked on my food.

"I don't tolerate jealousy, Elizabeth. I've already told you I like to surround myself with beautiful things."

I sulk into my pasta, aware that his eyes are focused on me. "I'm not the jealous type, Sebastian, I just find it weird that you have a beautiful woman living here, just you and her. Where does she sleep? Does she have staff quarters?"

"I know what you're implying, Elizabeth, and I don't like it. Scarlett works for me, do you understand? And yes, she has her own quarters downstairs." He looks annoyed but, me being me, I persevere.

"Downstairs? In a cellar?" I ask incredulously.

"The cellar, Elizabeth, is probably twice the square

footage of your entire house," he replies arrogantly. "There's an entire network of rooms below us which used to serve as the working hub of this house. I'll show you tomorrow."

"I look forward to that," I say, with trepidation. "While we're on the subject, Sebastian, who do the perfume, cosmetics, and this robe belong to?" I tug nervously at my robe and regard him with suspicion.

His dark brows are set in a frown, his lips a stern line, and the tension between us is now tangible. "They belong to you. Whom did you presume they belonged to? I bought them for you. Scarlett chose them. Frankly, I'm growing tired of your insecurity. Eat."

"I'm not hungry." I pout, my appetite suppressed at the thought of Slave Girl choosing something so intimate for me.

"You'll need the energy. I plan to keep you on the go all night. Now, do as you're told. Eat." He's determined and obstreperous. With a petulant sigh, I push my food around the bowl, managing to swallow a few mouthfuls of the steaming minced beef. He regards me sternly as he eats his food. I'm learning that Sebastian can be stubborn, evasive, and dark. Not qualities I am familiar with or particularly fond of.

Glancing at the wooden clock, hanging by a short rope from an iron meat hook above the range, it's surprising that it's already nearly eight o'clock. I must call the children and say goodnight to them. I push my bowl aside.

"I've got to call the children, won't be long." "Sure, go ahead," he says.

I take my bowl to the sink and leave the kitchen, still feeling moody. In the hallway, I retrieve my phone from my bag and speed dial my mother's number. She's pleased that I called, and asks me how I'm enjoying the spa. Very relaxing, I lie. I tell her that I've spent several hours in bed and have just eaten dinner, and she's pleased to hear this. I feel very guilty.

Joe comes on the line and babbles about Grandma's house and lists the junk food she has fed him. I ask to speak with Bella. Typically moody, Bella has little to say and is eager to get back to a vampire series she's watching. It feels good to talk to them in spite of the shame I feel at my deceit. I end the call with several kisses, saying good night, and I have a deep longing to hold my children and smell their freshly washed hair.

Replacing my phone in my bag, I feel melancholy. When I turn, Sebastian is leaning against the wall, watching me. I presume he has listened to my conversation, which I find overtly intrusive. He cocks his eyebrow and regards me with an expression that is hard to read.

"Lying comes quite easily to you, Elizabeth." His eyes are dark and smouldering. "You have the makings of a bad girl. I like that."

*I bet you do, you weirdo*, I think. My weirdo.

"I have a gift for you, come here," he commands. "For me?" I'm intrigued. I love gifts, but rarely receive them. I go to him, eager to receive my gift.

"Turn around." I do as I'm told, and turn my back to him.

He moves my long blonde hair away from my neck, and I feel a cool cord being slipped around my throat. Fear creeps upon me, but then Sebastian fixes a clasp behind my neck and turns me around to face him. My hands go to my throat and touch a fine silky choker with a bead decoration in the front. His expression has changed, jaw tensed as he stares at the choker. His eyes lock on mine with a faraway expression I haven't seen before.

"You're beautiful," he whispers hoarsely.

"Sebastian, thank you." I rock onto my toes and kiss his full, sculpted masculine mouth with a gratitude that is heartfelt. He closes his eyes and inhales deeply as my lips leave his.

"Come and look." He leads me by the hand to the ornate gilded mirror above the fireplace in the hall and I gaze upon the choker. It is the finest black ribbon. In the centre is a tiny, sparkling diamond surrounded by a cluster of smaller diamonds. It's exquisite, and I gasp as I touch the silkiness of the ribbon and the roughness of the diamonds.

"I can't accept this, Sebastian, it's too beautiful. Simply stunning." A fervent kiss to my neck silences me, and I lean back against him.

"You *will* accept it. In fact, I insist that you wear it when you're with me here. It's a symbol that you are mine."

Something stirs in me and I try to recall where I have seen a similar choker recently but I can't remember. I love it. It's sexy, beautiful, and it's Sebastian's gift to me, so I will treasure it. Of course I won't be able to wear it other than with him, anyway. Alan really would have something to say about this.

"Yes. I'm yours," I reply. "Oh, Sebastian, I love it. Thank you so very much." I'm grinning and feel happier than I have in a long time.

"You're very welcome. You deserve to have beautiful things, Elizabeth. You're a very beautiful woman. I don't think you realise just how incredible you are." My lips find his, and we share a lingering kiss.

"Come with me. I want to show you something," he says, and I follow him into his study. An oversized antique desk sits against the far wall and to either side are three drawers. He pulls open the top drawer and pulls out a large, blue leather bound book. Lifting the cover open, he reveals a photograph album. "Sit down." He pulls forward a dark green, leather button backed chair and I sit forward, eager to see the photos. "You asked about my family, so here they are."

Looking at the first page, I see three black and white photos of an elegant couple and a small boy. In the first, the couple strike a formal pose. The woman is seated and she cradles a baby dressed in a long white gown. The man stands stiffly to the right and slightly behind, and has a hand on the woman's shoulder. The second photograph seems to have been taken at the same sitting, but this time the couple are side by side, and the man holds the infant. The woman is smiling in both photographs, but the man looks stern, stuffy. The third photograph is far more relaxed, the woman seated casually on a picnic rug with a baby who is barely old enough to sit up resting against her legs.

"Are these your parents? Is this you?" I ask, secretly delighted that he's finally sharing part of himself with me.

"Yes, my mother, father, and I. Those two were taken on the day of my baptism. The other was taken at Penmorrow. We used to picnic up by the old oak," he replied.

"You were adorable! Such a gorgeous, chubby little baby."

Sebastian chuckles, turns the page and I see the young Sebastian is approximately three years old in the single photograph. He is standing next to an elderly, frail looking lady and is petting a large golden retriever, which I presume may have been a hunting dog.

"Your grandma?" I ask.

"Yes. My grandmother, Mary, was sick when that photo was taken but she lasted another three years before she died. I loved her. I remember how she used to sit with me by the fire in the Great Hall and tell me stories about the old days at Penmorrow, the parties she and Grandfather held. I think things were very different in her day. There were certainly more staff living and working on the estate. They used to hold shooting parties, and at the time kept a kennel of twelve beagles. I recall being scared of those gun dogs because they seemed always to be barking, and I remember seeing them fed with pieces of raw meat which the kennel hand told me were pieces of naughty boys. Here, this is me when I graduated." He flicks through several pages and shows me a photograph of a fresh-faced young man in a mortarboard hat and gown clutching a scroll.

"Handsome and clever," I tease, and he smacks my behind playfully, sending a tug to my core. "So, where are your mum and dad now?"

"They both died. They were in their forties when they had me. Mother died when she was sixty-two of breast cancer, and my father five years ago after a stroke. That's when I inherited this old pile and my title. Unfortunately, with no heir, it's likely this place will go to my cousin and then my nephew who both live in Australia. I'm sure they'll sell it. Father would turn in his grave if that were to happen."

"Oh, Sebastian, that would break your heart."

"Things change, Elizabeth." He shrugs with a frown. He seems melancholy and reflective, as though the historical weight and expectations of generations of De Montforts rest squarely on his shoulders. I understand now what he meant by responsibility and burden, and my heart aches for my poor Sebastian, who is alone and with the weight of the world upon his shoulders.

"So, you and Libby didn't want children?"

He seems to blanch at that question. Poor Libby seems a taboo subject.

"We tried, but she...had problems. Not physical problems. Mental health problems, and she was always having one treatment or another and children just didn't happen for us."

I feel sad for him, for both of them, but I wonder what kind of mental health problems she suffered from. "Was it depression?" I ask tenderly.

"Depression and a whole bunch of other stuff. I don't want to talk about it." He closes the album and I regret pushing him about Libby. "Anyway, enough of this. Bed!" He playfully pats my ass. A flutter of excitement runs through me. I hope he doesn't mean sleep.

Sebastian turns out the downstairs lights and I follow him up to his bedroom. It's an eerie house. I wonder if it is haunted, and I shiver at the thought. Closing the bedroom door, he turns on the small nightstand lamps, giving an intimate feel to the room. He pulls at the tie of my robe and it falls open, exposing my nakedness, and I feel suddenly aware of my body and its blemishes and imperfections. Even after what we did earlier, I'm not used to intimacy or showing my body, but at the same time I yearn to feel his touch again. He slips my robe from my shoulders and now I am naked except for the choker around my throat. I do feel sexy for the first time in years. Not cheap or dirty, but desired and feminine.

He stands behind me, his arms encircling my waist. Sweeping my hair over my right shoulder he kisses the nape of my neck, his arousal pressing hard against my sacrum. My breath catches, nipples harden, and my heartbeat quickens at his touch.

"Close your eyes." He moves away from me, then returns and I feel silky fabric placed over my eyes and tied at the back of my head.

*Oh, goodness!* He's blindfolded me. This is so erotic, and a first for me. He guides me to the edge of the bed.

"I want you to lie down on your back, Elizabeth. You have to trust me. Whatever I do to you is for your pleasure as well as mine, okay?" I have no idea what he's going to do to me, but right now he can do what he wants. This is so exciting. I do as I'm told and lie back on the bed in total darkness.

"Open your legs," he commands.

Compliantly, I move my legs apart, feeling exposed and vulnerable, yet creamy with desire. I hear him moving in the room but I can't see him. This is beyond erotic. I feel something soft and light tickling the sole of my left foot and then my right. A giggle escapes my lips. The tickle stops, and I fall silent. The tickling sensation travels slowly across the tops of my feet, up my shins, to my knees. It moves to the inside of my legs and travels up toward my thighs. It's unbelievably arousing and soon the light tickle arrives at my sweet spot. I know he's using a feather, and as it whispers over my clit again and again, I cry out but it's unrelenting. The sensation and anticipation increase until the raw and feral need for gratification becomes unendurable.

"More. Give me more. I need to come," I pant demandingly.

"No. Not yet." He stops abruptly, until my ebb subsides, before teasing again and again with this insufferable torture, and I'm desperate for release. The tickling stops and the room is silent. Frustration overcomes me.

"Damn it, Sebastian. Stop teasing me," I cry.

"Patience. You come when I allow you to come." I hear a drawer open and close. I reach for the blindfold but a firm hand clasps mine and stops me.

"Trust me," he whispers in my ear. "This will be incredible for you." Cold metal touches my nipple and I jerk away from it. The metal flicks over my other nipple, which is hard and waiting.

"What the hell is that?" I demand.

"*Shh*. Enjoy the sensation." The coldness is gone from my nipples. I wait, panting. Every fibre, every nerve ending awaits the next sensation. When it touches me once more, it's on my thigh. The coldness drags slowly up each thigh in turn, before pressing hard against my pussy. Pushing harder now, the cool phallus struggles to enter me, but it's too large. I'm frantic, arching my back to aid the passage so that I can be filled, and it's inside me. Gloriously hard, it's thrust farther until the pain almost overwhelms the pleasure. He rotates it and repeatedly drives it against my G spot, and I scream for him to stop, lest I climax without his permission.

"Come for me now. That's right, feel it, baby," he instructs, and I abandon all control as the orgasm courses through my body in waves that don't subside. The tremors continue until he slides the thing out of me, and only then does my body settle. He removes the blindfold and kisses me but I'm spent and confused.

"That was just for you, Elizabeth, but this is just for me now." He turns me over roughly, pulls me onto my hands and knees, and slaps my raised bare buttock with the flat of his hand, so hard that it stings, and I cry out in surprised protestation. Then he's kissing my smarting skin, before holding fast to my hips and pounding into me hard. He pistons into me, faster and deeper, his testicles thwacking against me, until he reaches his own throbbing climax, collapsing over my arched back as he finds his release.

As we lie side by side in a comfortable silence, I begin to dwell on the confusion in my mind. On one hand, I've just had the most amazing sex but, conversely, his roughness and memories of my afternoon with Simon are awakened. The roughness is so erotic, and again, I feel ashamed that I enjoyed the sting of his hand. I have so much to consider, such a disparity between my real life and my experience here at Penmorrow with Sebastian.

"So deep in thought, my love." He traces his lips across my shoulder and pulls me into his embrace.

"What was that?" I croak.

"This?" He reaches over the side of the bed, and scoops up the object of my torture from the floor. He rests on one elbow as he holds it out to me. I take it and feel the weight in my hands. It's heavy and cool in a matte silver finish. Cone shaped, it is wide at the base and tapers to a rounded point, and is so enormous that I need two hands to hold it.

"Holy crap, Sebastian." Wide-eyed, I pass the thing back to him. He drops it to the floor with a loud thud. "That was too bloody much." I'm angry.

"Yes, I agree," he says. "But that was the hardest you've ever come, wasn't it, Elizabeth?"

"Well, yes. But the way you teased me, I was going out of my mind, Sebastian."

"It's part of my dynamic. By denying and then allowing you an orgasm, it's so much more intense when it comes. For you and me. From now on," he whispers against my ear, "you only come when I give you permission. I own your orgasms. Understood?" He kisses my earlobe.

I sit up, *ouch, I'm sore,* and slap his shoulder.

He laughs. "Good shot!" A smirk curves his mouth, he swipes away my hand as it rises to strike him again.

"Who the hell do you think you are?" I yell, really mad now.

"Go with it, darling. You know you want to." He pushes me back against the pillows and tickles me while I fight to push him off. He's too strong for me and soon I'm laughing and giggling when I want to be furious with him.

"Go to sleep, Elizabeth. We'll talk about it all tomorrow. I want to show you the grounds and more of the house tomorrow too."

"Good night, Sebastian, you infuriating, weird, twisted man," I murmur drowsily as sleep envelopes me in her grey cloak.

I dream I'm running through the house and it is dark, so unnervingly gloomy. I can't look back. I have to get out. But a woman dressed in black is gaining on me. Her face is white, almost translucent, and she's screaming at me, "He's mine. You must die."

I slam into furniture, throw it aside. I have to escape. She's coming, she's coming. Oh, so near now. *My God, my God, no...Don't!*

# Chapter 8

The sense of panic consumes me. My eyes snap open, sweat beads my top lip. *Where am I?*

"Hush, you had a nightmare, darling. It's okay, you're safe. You're here with me in bed. It's all over, Elizabeth," he soothes.

My vision begins to clear, but the face of the woman in black haunts me still. I shudder and sit up, turning on the lamp on the nightstand. Blinking, my eyes adjust to the light and all is as it should be. I start to calm down. Sebastian is stroking my back, and yet I can't shake off a feeling of foreboding. Folding me in his safe embrace, we nestle under the covers together until a more peaceful sleep eventually comes.

After a fitful night, the morning ushers in a languid start to the day. Sebastian brings mugs of coffee and we sit up against our feather pillows, drinking and chatting easily. I welcome the domesticity.

"Hungry?" Sebastian asks. "Ravenous," I reply.

He lifts his eyebrow and I know that wicked glint in his eye.

"For food. I'm hungry for food." I laugh.

We are soon washed and dressed and making our way downstairs. On reaching the hall, I stop to retrieve my phone from my bag while Sebastian continues to the kitchen. I text my mother, telling her that I'm fine, to kiss the children for me. I'm missing them. There are no messages from Alan and I make a mental note to text him later, guilt besieging me.

In the kitchen the hired help is cracking eggs into a bowl, and I recognise her as the woman to whom I gave my business card previously. She smiles at me as I enter, but her smile seems disingenuous. The hairs prick on the back of my neck as realisation dawns on me that hers is the face of the woman in my nightmare.

*Don't be ridiculous, Beth. She was on your mind, that's all.*

"You must be Scarlett," I say with a cheeriness I don't feel. "We haven't really been introduced."

I hold out my hand and she shakes it lightly and returns to the eggs. She's dressed in the black slim fitting dress again. I freeze. She's wearing a black choker around her slim throat. Walking nearer to her so that I can see more closely, it's apparent her band isn't adorned with diamonds. Even so, it denotes the same amatory look as mine. Rage and resentment simmer inside me with the realisation that Sebastian dresses his staff as he does his lover. It's bizarre, and in my opinion, unacceptable.

As I sit down on the hard pew opposite Sebastian, my mind tries to make sense of the relationship between them. Seeing her this morning, domestic goddess in his kitchen cooking breakfast, sharing the intimacy of his gift, just confirms my suspicions about their relationship. A knot deep in my belly tightens with the apparent affirmation that I'm sharing my perfect man. I feel used and stupid.

Sebastian is studying me, and when I look at him, he has a quizzical expression on his face. He's presumably detected my sudden change in mood. "Everything okay?" he asks.

"Fine. I'm just not hungry suddenly," I say resolutely, as a plate of scrambled eggs and bacon is placed before me.

"Eat, Elizabeth, then we'll go for a walk."

He cannot command me. I'm not one of his salaried harlots, and I shoot him a frosty glare.

"I'm not a child, Sebastian," I rebuke. "If I'm not hungry then I won't eat." Sliding the plate away from me, I sit defiantly with arms folded across my chest, daring him to push the point further.

"Very well, Elizabeth. We'll discuss this later. Scarlett, fetch our coats." He barks his order to the girl, and I see how she immediately does as he bids.

"Yes, sir." Scarlett leaves the kitchen.

"You'll learn, Elizabeth, that when I ask you to do something it's for your own good. By defying me, you haven't achieved anything other than to be very hungry and to make me cross."

I stare at him, perplexed. He's the most infuriating person, and yet his imposing manner is appealing, masculine, and contrasts so distinctly to Alan. Scarlett returns to the kitchen and passes each of us our coats, which we shrug on. Dressed for the cold winter morning, we leave the warmth of Penmorrow and I prepare myself for the confrontation that seems inevitable.

The cold salty air is bracing and our cheeks blanche from the biting wind. Sebastian proffers a hand, which I take in mine reluctantly, and leads me across the formal gardens and through a wooded area beyond. The trees break to reveal a spectacular rocky precipice and dramatic seascape ahead. We are prevented from nearing the cliff edge by a high barbed wire fence. Standing side by side, we don't speak as we take in the view of the inky blue sea with foaming surf, below.

He breaks the silence. "Why do you stay with Alan?" I don't reply, but he continues, "It's quite obvious you aren't happy."

"I can't afford to go it alone. The business is doing okay, but if we don't expand soon we'll get left behind and competitors will force us out. He doesn't earn much but it keeps us going financially. Mainly, though, it's the children keeping us together. If you had kids you'd understand," I snap.

I know immediately it was a cruel thing to say, and I squeeze Sebastian's hand, glancing at him and noting with regret his hurt expression.

"I'm sorry, that was mean. I know you wanted children, what I meant to say was there's an enormous pressure to play *happy family*. When you have kids, they become your sole focus, or *should*." I realise I'm not exactly putting my children foremost by being here with Sebastian, leaving my husband and children at home and basing my absence on a lie.

"I'm not a father, as you point out, but I should think

your children are astute. I imagine they hear arguments or certainly pick up on the negativity between you."

He has a valid point. Alan and I often forget the children are within earshot when we fight. It's so easy to be entirely preoccupied, and not see the impact we have on others. "He used to make me happy, when we first met," I reflect, "but we've grown apart over the years. I guess our differences just became more evident. I want more. I want him to be assertive. For once, I'd like *him* to take the lead, make decisions, man up and grow a pair!"

"And if he did that, Elizabeth, would he make you happy? Fulfilled? Or would you still want more? From what I sense, he can't give you what you need."

"And can *you* really give me what I need?" I ask shrilly. "Because from what I've seen in your house, you are the very last person to give me advice on relationships, mister."

He looks startled. "What's gotten into you this morning?"

I pull away and thrust my hands in the deep pockets of my coat. "I'm just so confused," I tell him. "I feel like you and I have something special, but then you go and do things that make me feel cheap. It's not normal, Sebastian. Not normal to do what you did to me last night. Not normal to give an employee the same sensual choker you gave to me."

"I see." His dark eyes regard me icily, and the coldness sends a shiver through me. I pull my coat more tightly around me but it offers little warmth against the chill within.

"It doesn't mean anything. She doesn't mean anything," he garbles. "You're overthinking things, Elizabeth. Look, we're getting to know each other and that takes time and patience. You've got to realise, I *know* what you need and you've got to trust me on that." He takes my hand again and this time I don't pull away.

"And what would that be, Sebastian?"

"You need a dominant man, Elizabeth, one who'll tell you what you need to do, in all things. That isn't something Alan can give you. It's not in his nature from what you've told me about him. Not all men are assertive. They rely on their wives as though they are replacement mothers. Men, like me, are born to dominate. We know what we want and how to get it, but we also know what women want and we give it to them, Elizabeth."

"It sounds more like control. Is that what this is about?" I ask weakly.

"Control, yes. I need to be in control and if you don't relinquish control to me, I can't help you. You'll drift along. Stressed. Unhappy. Don't settle for less."

I shudder, not just because of the bracing wind whipping across the sea and lashing at our coats. My emotions are stirred by Sebastian's words, which are so incisive and to which I relate so wholly. "Well, we *are* still married, so I have to make the best of it. Come on. It's freezing. Show me Penmorrow. I'm dying to look around." We walk back toward the house, taking a different route so he can show me the walled garden, maze, and the old oak where he used to picnic as a child.

The grounds are beautiful, with the backdrop of the cliff and ocean. It's the most remarkable place I have ever been, and I feel a sense of belonging here. *If only my life had turned out differently, I could be happy here. I can change Sebastian.*

We explore the house. There are four formal rooms including the great dining hall, study, morning room, and library. All are opulent in their own way, and in spite of the tapestries looking faded, the objet d'art being slightly dusty, there is an ageless charm, which has seen countless generations living amongst these rooms. My mood lifts and the awkwardness of before is forgotten as Sebastian delights in showing off his splendid home. He's like a young boy, animatedly detailing the provenance of his belongings and the history of his ancestors.

I squeal like a child when Sebastian shows me a hidden passageway, concealed by a false bookshelf in his study. I can barely contain my excitement when the heavy door, disguised with painted books, heaves forth. He flicks a light switch on the wall above the first step, takes my hand and leads me through the secret doorway.

"This is unreal," I gush. "So, these big old houses really do have secret passageways. I thought that was just in movies and books. This is so cool."

"Rumour has it, there is a tunnel somewhere under the house, leading to the cliffs, which used to be used by smugglers. They'd haul their loot and ill- gotten gains from small boats and stash it in the cellars, so folklore says."

"Wow. Real smugglers." I am enthralled by the romanticism of his tale.

The steps lead down and curve round out of sight, worn down in the middle of each tread as if Sebastian's servants or ancestors, or smugglers, have been sneaking around via this passage for centuries. I am guarded in case I brush cobwebs, as an arachnophobic, my eyes dart from side to side as I gingerly take each step behind Sebastian, gripping firmly to the rope handrail. Curiously, there are no cobwebs. The steps look to be free of the dust and debris I expected to see and the walls and ceilings are thankfully missing the spiders I anticipate. Clearly, this staircase is in regular use.

We continue downward and to the left of the narrow stairwell, the light becoming dimmer now, my bravery receding as the gloominess encompasses. As we reach the final step, Sebastian flicks another switch and the way ahead is illuminated by the bulb hanging from the coarse, grey ceiling of the long corridor before us. The walls are arched and we walk on seemingly ancient flagstones. Sebastian walks without hesitancy, as though he frequents this passage and knows every inch as well as he knows his living quarters above us. I wonder where this leads.

"Is this where the servants would have worked?" I ask.

"Yes, this would have been a hive of activity years ago." He guides me through a low wooden doorway. The room we enter is small, possibly eight or nine square feet.

To the right is a black wrought iron framed single bed, neatly made with crisp white sheets and a claret velvet throw folded precisely across the foot. To the left is a small washbasin, a dressing table with mirror and on the wall ahead, a wardrobe.

I walk over to the dressing table and pick up a half empty bottle of Chanel No.5 perfume, and I feel Sebastian move behind me. He reaches forward and takes the glass bottle from me. I feel a cool damp mist on my neck as he sprays the sensual fragrance on my skin. He doesn't touch or kiss me but instead he replaces the bottle on the table and leads me from the room.

"Whose room is that?" I probe, knowing that it is probably Scarlett's room and hating him for that. Jealousy is such a bitter pill.

"This is Scarlett's room," he confirms nonchalantly. He makes it sound so normal but I cannot help but wonder what her job description is, should one exist. Is it a prerequisite to share his bed, for example?

We continue along the passage and Sebastian shows me another bedroom, comparable to Scarlett's room, and a small utilitarian kitchen. Soon, we enter a much larger room which appears to be a lounge. Couches nestle against each wall and in the centre, covering the flagstones, lies a huge Persian rug in red, black, and inky blue hues. My feet sink into the deep fibres. It's plush and luxurious, too good for servants' quarters. There are two small wooden chests against one wall, upon which are table lamps. Their bases are black, shiny naked female forms and each has a fringed red shade.

A silk robe lies strewn across the arm of a couch, and I glimpse the corner of a magazine protruding beneath it. I pick it up, staring at the glossy cover and am shocked to see a naked man and equally naked female. My eyes are drawn to the whip he is brandishing and the exposed female buttock waiting to be lashed. She wears a blindfold and is licking her blood red lips, as she appears to be pushing her hips back to meet the waiting blow. "What the hell's this?" I am stunned, yet aroused enough to feel the burning in my sex.

"What do you think it is? Does it turn you on, Elizabeth?" He smirks with a low growl.

"My point is, Sebastian, what the hell is Scarlett doing looking at porn in your home?" I ask incredulously, not yet diverting my gaze from the erotic picture.

"If you're so shocked, why are you still looking at it?" Damn him. He is so infuriatingly right all the time. "It seems to me, Elizabeth, that you're fascinated by that image and..." He moves behind me, reaching around my waist, down my midriff, inside the waistband of my grey woollen skirt. He finds the waistband of my tights, his fingers forcing behind the snug elastic. He discovers the top of my panties and pushes them down, aside, and his fingers travel to my sex.

I gasp as his middle finger slips between my labia, into my wetness. As he leans forward, into my back, his finger pushes deeper inside me, and I push my hips forward to meet his finger, to take it deeper into me.

Moaning now, I close my eyes, lost in the glorious sensation as his finger now pulls out, finds my clit, and slides and slips again and again over my sweet, throbbing jewel.

"You *are* so turned on, aren't you, Elizabeth? Oh my God, you're dripping. That turns you on, hmm?" Still his finger works on me, his other hand now underneath my cotton top, squeezing and pinching at my left nipple through my lace bra.

"You see the whip, darling? The way she wants it? The way she *wants* to be punished by him?"

"Sir, I'm so sorry!" The woman's voice snaps me out of my forbidden moment.

Sebastian withdraws his hand sharply and we spin around to face Scarlett. She is regarding us with a disdainful expression, as though she is disgusted to witness our passion, and I feel suddenly ashamed. Smoothing down my clothes, conscious of my flushed face and dishevelled appearance, I force a smile and replace the magazine.

"Scarlett." He glares at her venomously.

"I'm sorry to have disturbed you both." She is looking at the magazine. "I'm sorry you found that. I should have put it away, sir, please forgive me." She is talking to Sebastian yet she doesn't catch his gaze, instead looking down at her hands as she nervously plays with the tie at the waist of her black dress.

"It's not your fault. We shouldn't be down here snooping," I try to reassure the girl who seems to be a bundle of nerves.

"I'm interrupting. I'll leave." She raises a perfectly plucked eyebrow and I see a smile play across her cherry red lips. She knows what I am. *Adulterer.*

The entire situation is making me uneasy again. The atmosphere between Scarlett and *Sir* is tense. I feel like an intruder, and I'm consumed with the desire to get away from here.

"I'll go, Sebastian," I mumble, looking past him to the door.

He grasps my arm roughly, a look of concern setting his mouth in a firm line and creasing his brow.

"No, don't leave." There is hardness in his voice as he turns to face Scarlett. "Leave us, *now!* And next time you enter a room where I'm clearly with company, you don't interpose, do you understand?"

"Yes, Sir, I...I'm sorry." She looks remorseful, chin down, as she turns and leaves the room.

"This is crazy," I tell him. "I feel like a spare prick in a whorehouse, literally!" My voice is full of venom, and for a moment he looks aghast, then the coldness once again sets across his eyes as his hands ball into fists at his sides.

I run out of the room and into the gloomy passage. Trying to recall which way we had come, I turn left. Disorientated now, I slow to a fast walk but it doesn't look right. I don't pass the bedroom doors. I can hear his heavy footsteps behind me.

"Elizabeth!" he calls. "Come back, this is ridiculous."

I call back to him as I continue on my way, searching for something familiar. "Sorry, Sebastian. It was a mistake coming here. I just need to get home."

Ahead of me is a dead end, just a dark wood arched doorway with iron latch blocks my passage. Looking back over my shoulder, I see that he's close. Reaching out, I press the latch and the ancient ironworks lifts, the door swinging open, and I catch a brief glimpse of the room within. I see tools, lots of dark metal implements adorning the walls of what looks to be a cavernous cellar.

As I strain my eyes to look more closely at the room, his hand thumps against the door and it slams shut.

"Don't go," he rasps. "You're overreacting. Just calm down and come upstairs with me." He commands me as he commands Scarlett, but he's intoxicating, edgy, and the danger only exacerbates my excitement.

His study offers a welcome sanctuary and an air of normality again. We sit side by side on a leather love seat, and he takes my hand in his and rests it on his lap. His voice is earnest when he speaks.

"Since Libby died, it's been so lonely here, Elizabeth. Scarlett...supports me, she's my companion. She looks after me and keeps me sane."

"But if you have her, why do you need me?" I ask dejectedly. Suddenly I feel as though I don't belong anywhere. Not with Alan, not here. I feel lost, cast adrift like a small boat drifting at sea.

"I *do* need you, Elizabeth, more than you appreciate. I know you need me too. You don't realise it yet, but you do. You have to trust me to know what you need. If you go back to him, to Alan, you'll never be happy." He gently tilts my chin so that I'm looking into his eyes, such dark brooding eyes it's impossible to read his emotions. "I know what you need."

He does know me, and right now he seems to be looking right into my soul.

"There's just so much weirdness in this house," I say. "It's not normal, Sebastian, to have that woman here, all sexy subservience. I don't understand why you want me when your needs are probably being met by her."

"I don't force her to stay. She's paid a decent wage, probably more than your staff earn. Yes, she's attractive, but I told you I like to surround myself with beauty. It's nothing more than that. Trust me."

It sounds so lame to me now, when he says this. "Are you telling me she is nothing more to you than a maid?" I ask sceptically.

"There was a time when she was more. A very brief time," he confesses, his eyes hooded and his tone hushed. "I stopped that pretty quickly, but I think she'd like more."

"I see. Is that when you gave her the choker?"

"Yes. She chooses to wear it now. It's not something I've thought a great deal about, but I understand why it would upset you. I'll tell her to remove it."

"It's not just the bloody choker, Sebastian. Don't you see that?"

He runs a hand through his hair, his face pensive.

Looking at him, I question why I'm here. I seem to be adding more complication to my already overly complicated life, which was not my intention.

"Look, Sebastian." I take his hand in mine. "I'm not sure why I'm here, what I was looking for, but...it's not me, this whole *affair* charade isn't me. I've had the most amazing time, really, but now I want to get home and see the kids."

He looks crestfallen. His dark eyebrows knit into a frown, his eyes veiled with hurt and coldness, he pulls his hand away from my grasp. "You don't even comprehend what you need, and you're certainly kidding yourself if you think you can just go back to your *little* life in Dorset with Alan," he says malevolently.

That confirms my decision to leave. He stands on the stone steps to Penmorrow looking remorseful, like a scolded little boy.

"Don't go."

"I have to," I tell him. "I'm so mixed up right now. I'll call you."

We embrace, and I leave. *Goodbye, Sebastian.*

# Chapter 9

The journey home gives me sufficient time to reflect on the last twenty-four hours. The fact that I'm driving home a day earlier than planned is confirmation of the mistake I've made in staying with Sebastian, although I wonder how I will explain my early return to my mother and to Alan.

Fifty minutes into my journey, my phone bleeps to signal a text message. I pull into the next services to pee, and to check the message. It is from Sebastian.

*I wish you hadn't left. Text me when home. S*

I'm strangely relieved to receive his message, reassured that I haven't blown my relationship with him after all I said to him and leaving early as I did. Goodness knows why I care. He's clearly one screwed up cookie. *So am I, though. We are both completely fucked up in our own ways.* I text back.

*Leave me alone please, I need to sort things at home and don't need you complicating things for me x*

His reply arrives even before I pull out of the service station onto the motorway.

**Text me when home.**

*So bloody exasperating.*

\*\*\*

I arrive at my mother's house late in the afternoon. The dark winter evening is already threatening to close in and the stillness in the air signals the onset of the first frost of winter. I park my car and walk up the familiar pathway to my mother's home. It has never been my home, or somewhere I grew up, so I feel no real attachment to this house. It always holds a homely atmosphere, though, and smells of Mum's perfume and lavender soap.

Mum opens the door and ushers me in to the warmth of her home. "I wasn't expecting you until tomorrow, dear, is everything ok?" she asks. So intuitive, she looks at my face and clutches me into her embrace as I crumble, sobbing on her shoulder.

"*Sshh,* whatever's the matter, love?" she soothes. "Didn't you like the spa? Has something happened to Alan?"

Where do I begin? How do I tell her about my lies, my deceit, about Sebastian and his dark life?

"Oh, Mum," I wail. "I've not been to a bloody spa." She looks confused, but I continue. "I've been to stay with a man I met at a business event recently. Oh, God, it's such a mess. I really like him but he's even more screwed up than me."

"I'll make a brew, and you can tell me all about it.

The kids are upstairs, so we won't be disturbed." My mother sits me down and brings me a cup of hot sweet, milky tea—Mum's answer to all crises, despite knowing I prefer coffee. We talk for quite some time about Sebastian but I am careful not to divulge any details about Scarlett or the porn. I tell her that I realized an affair is not for me. I love my kids too much to put them through a messy separation. She seems reassured that I'm not going to run away with this man, and it's been good to talk and get these feelings out.

It's nearly nine o'clock when I pull in to our driveway with Joe and Bella. The lights are on in the front sitting room and I can see the silhouette of Alan watching television. Shutting the front door behind us, I call out to him that we're home. I think I hear a grumble from the sitting room in response, but it may have been the television. I hang my coat on the peg behind the front door and step into the room to see Alan. I'm eager to gauge his mood, as that will confirm whether or not he is suspicious of my whereabouts these past twenty-four hours. I need not have worried as he barely acknowledges me.

Joe still loves his bedtime chats, and I welcome the return to normality. Kissing him goodnight, I turn out the light and check on Bella who is engrossed in Facebook, apparently chatting with a boy. I close her door and leave her to it.

In the sitting room, Alan's watching a documentary on quantum physics. Frankly, I'm amazed he understands the data presented although I suspect he's not paying attention to it. Sitting on the armchair next to him, I try to concentrate on what the presenter is telling me but it's way over my head. I'm restless as thoughts of Penmorrow, cellars, and Sebastian fill my mind until they become a jumbled cacophony of images. Looking at Alan, I can't comprehend how far removed his life is from Sebastian's and I resent my husband for his lack-lustre persona and meek disposition.

Alan picks up the remote control and presses the button to silence the television. Turning to me, I notice a flush in his cheeks and wonder if he's been drinking. Then I smell whisky.

"Where the fuck have you been?" he spits. Astounded and panicky, I look wide-eyed at him and feign an expression of innocence and surprise.

"At the spa, Alan, where the hell do you think I've been?" I counter.

He laughs, a deep, guttural belly laugh, which is not based on humour but some dark sense of irony. "You lying fucking bitch. I know you've not been to a bloody spa. I called every sodding spa on the south coast." He takes a deep gulp of whisky from the crystal tumbler, which I see had been on the hearth next to his feet along with a near empty bottle. "What I don't bloody get," he continues, "is why you came back early. In fact, why did you come back at all. If your life there is so bloody terrible, why don't you bugger off with whatshisname and do us all a favour?" The bitterness resonates through every word he spits at me. He looks so forlorn, and totally defeated, as he eyes me with contempt.

"Alan, I...I don't know what to say." My response is pathetic. I know my fate but am unable to change it. I know we're over, but the guilt I feel, and bleakness of our marriage consumes me, and a tear winds it's way down my reddened cheek.

"Don't bloody say anything. I don't believe a word that comes out of your mouth. I've done everything I can to support you with your business, the kids, this house. I couldn't have done more." He stares despondently into his empty tumbler.

"I know, love. We've just grown apart. We want different things out of life."

My phone bleeps in the kitchen. We both hear it, and Alan huffs in irritation. "Probably *lover boy*, you'd better answer it." He reaches for the whisky bottle and drains the remaining alcohol into his glass, while I walk into the kitchen and take my phone from my handbag.

*Presuming you're home now Elizabeth? You didn't call as I asked. S*

I slip my phone into my pocket and retreat to the upstairs bathroom so that I can reply in private without antagonising Alan further.

*Not replied as just got home, things awful here. Please don't text me, leave me alone!*

The phone whooshes as the message is sent and a sense of relief washes over me, with the knowledge that I have made the decision to end things with Sebastian, at least until such time as Alan and I have talked about our marriage and made rational decisions. I really don't need any more complications. Sitting on the edge of the bath, I stare at my phone screen, waiting for a reply from Sebastian, which doesn't come.

Downstairs, Alan has finished the bottle of whisky and is slurring his words. "So, watcha gonna do now that I know all aboutcha little love affair, huh?" He's very drunk and there is little point continuing this discussion until he sobers up.

"Look, Alan, why don't we get some rest and talk tomorrow. I'll finish work early and maybe the two of us can pop down to the Crown for a drink. Just the two of us. We can talk then." I try to rationalise and calm him but can see the anger bubbling beneath the surface in my husband's face.

"Mum?" Joe has crept downstairs and is standing in the doorway looking anxious. "I heard Dad shouting." He looks at Alan, seeking reassurance that everything's all right, but we both look blankly at him, unable to find words to reassure him.

Upstairs, Joe nestles down beneath his duvet and smiles at my goodnight kiss. Lying next to him on his narrow bed, I listen to his breathing settle as he falls asleep. Gazing at my sleeping son, I wonder what I'm going to do, but then I hear Alan striding up the stairs. He throws open the door.

"I wanna talk to you, *now!*" he hisses. A sense of foreboding crawls through me, starting in the pit of my stomach.

"Downstairs," I whisper, so as not to disturb Joe.

Alan is in the kitchen, pacing across the floor from the table to the sink, I can see the fury in his face and I suddenly feel afraid and unwilling to argue further tonight.

"What the hell's this?" He throws my mobile phone down onto the kitchen table and places his hands on his hips.

I pick up the phone. The screen is black, and I raise my eyebrow questioningly. "It's my phone, Alan. What's your problem?" I ask defiantly.

"The fucking *problem* ish the messages on there." He is now very drunk and slurring his words. "Ish that *Him,* that tosser you were with at the hotel?"

Mentally slapping myself for not locking my phone with a passcode, I desperately think of an excuse to explain the texts but knowing that there is no plausible explanation I can proffer, I opt for the truth.

"It's not what you think, Alan." I try the gentle approach. "I've only seen him once since you saw us having lunch at the hotel. I stayed there last night." Alan's eyes widen as the enormity of what I tell him sinks in, and I fear he is going to have a heart attack.

"How could you do this to us? What about the kids?"

He is swaying now, his fury burning and the alcohol destabilising him. "What the fuck are you playing at?"

I start to cry through humiliation, guilt, and genuine remorse at the distress I've caused my husband. This wasn't my intention. I had merely wanted to do something for me rather than for everyone else, to find myself—the real Beth Dove, whoever she is.

"I don't know. I honestly don't. So, where do we go from here?" My question seems superfluous now as it is evident Alan will not forgive me, and so it seems inevitable now we will separate.

"I'm outta here. Shit, Beth, you can do what you want, but I wanna see my kids."

Sobbing, I go to him, try to hug him, and he receives my embrace with an iron-rod back. To me, the hug is a farewell gesture, and a shrug to our past. All tenderness is lost.

It doesn't take Alan long to throw a few clothes and toiletries into a suitcase. He's leaving me, but before he goes, he kisses Joe's cheek as he sleeps, and whispers something to his slumbering son. Then he knocks on Bella's door. She removes her earphones as he enters her room and turns off her music, then I hear my daughter and husband talking in hushed voices. Shortly after, he leaves our home with a slam of the front door and I feel desolate.

I decide to go to bed. Tomorrow I can worry about what I'm going to do. Right now, I feel exhausted.

# Chapter 10

On Monday morning, Joe is quiet and pensive during the journey to school. Bella refused to travel with us, instead choosing to take the bus, and there had been no point in arguing with her. She has her father's mulishness.

At nine o'clock I arrive at my office, business as usual. Ruth has her head buried in a stack of paperwork but looks up over her reading glasses as I arrive.

"Beth, how was your weekend?" she asks.

I roll my eyes and sigh, giving her a look that says, *don't go there.*

"Coffee, love, that's what you need, and then I want a full low-down on what you've been up to, missy." She has never been the most diplomatic of my friends but she's the most determined, and so she will insist on a full account.

Over coffee, I tell Ruth about my fight with Alan and she listens sympathetically, without interrupting. When I finish, she sighs heavily then gives me a tight hug.

"I'm so sorry you're going through this shit, Beth. He still won't go to couples counselling?"

"Not a hope, Ruth. God knows I've tried and tried. It feels like it's really over."

"I'm so sorry, love. So, if you didn't go to a spa, where *did* you go?"

I tell Ruth about my visit with Sebastian at Penmorrow. She is shocked and, I think, rather disappointed at my infidelity but that soon turns to curiosity, and she's now attempting to extract the finer details from me. "Okay, so you've explained why you went and I kind of get that, Beth, but tell me what happens now? Are you going to see him again?"

"Absolutely not! He's so complex, Ruth. He lives alone in that huge mansion. Oh, not entirely alone, of course. He has a live-in housekeeper who is twenty-something, beautiful and sexy, and he tries to tell me there's nothing going on anymore, that she's just staff. But, shit, she had an S&M magazine. When she caught us in the staff quarters, with the magazine, she looked at me as though I was intruding on her and Sebastian!"

"Whoa, slow down. What do you mean *anymore* and *S&M?* You mean they *were* an item? And you mean the whole bondage thing?" She is enthralled and appalled in equal measure.

"Oh, yes. Whips, the lot, and if she's in to that, and he clearly knew about it, then there has to be something strange going on there. He says they were fleetingly an item, but I'm not convinced. I nearly forgot, he gave me the most beautiful choker." I lift my bag from the floor and fish around to retrieve the choker. I pass it to Ruth who studies it closely.

"Beth, it's rather sexy." Ruth admires the delicate ribbon and is evidently impressed by the sparkling diamond cluster. "Are these real?" She tilts the jewels toward the window and marvels as they sparkle.

"They're real, Ruth. Do you know what the bizarre thing is, though?" I don't wait for a reply. "Scarlett wears a choker too. Tell me that's not weird. They don't have diamonds, but it's the significance of the choker that worries me."

"That's weird, yep." She places the ribbon on the desk. "Beth, just don't complicate things any more than they are. Give yourself some space."

My phone bleeps. I snatch it from my bag and turn my back to Ruth as I open the message, which disappointingly is from my husband.

"Shit. It's Alan," I tell Ruth. "He wants the children on Saturday, and he's staying with Mike. You met him last year at the BBQ. He's a good friend to Alan so I'm glad he's staying with him." I'm also glad Alan hasn't done anything stupid. Mike will help him through this, which in turn, means my anxiety decreases.

"That's good, love. At least you know he's okay," she reassures me.

My phone bleeps again. I swipe my finger across the activating button and it wakes, revealing a message from Sebastian.

*Will overlook your previous message Elizabeth. How are you? S*

Such arrogance. This is a man who's evidently used to getting his own way. I reply to his text message, forgetting Ruth who is eying me inquisitively.

*Sebastian, which part of 'leave me alone' do you not*

*understand? B*

I sign as he does, without affection, laying bare my animosity toward him and his unwanted attention.

"Was that *him?*" Ruth asks, eyebrow cocked.

"Yes. But I've made it very clear to him that it's over. I really don't need the hassle." I sound so sure and yet, deep inside me, I long to be in his arms right at this moment. Dangerous thoughts. He replies swiftly.

*Clearly you're upset. Meet me. We need to talk. I can help you, don't push me away. S*

This floors me because it doesn't fit into the egotistical and insensible pigeonhole in which I've placed him. He wants to help me. "He wants to meet me, Ruth." I hand my phone to her and she glances over the thread of text messages.

"Be careful, Beth. Men can be very manipulative and even more so when they spot vulnerability in a woman," she warns. "I know you well. You will go to him and cry on his shoulder. Then he'll have you in bed faster than you can say 'easy lay.' Trust me."

I look incredulously at Ruth, and we laugh together, a cathartic belly laugh that has us both in tears.

Shutting my office door, I relish the tranquillity. I catch up on work pending, and soon clear the pile of waiting documents and junk mail. My thoughts turn to Sebastian as I remember I haven't replied to his message.

I pick up my phone and compose a message to him.

*Hi, I'm sorry if I was abrupt and thanks for your offer to help, I appreciate it. I don't think meeting is a good idea though x*

As I wait for Sebastian to answer, I fire up my computer and check emails. There's one from Mike, and it doesn't make me feel any better.

*Beth*
*Alan's staying with me for a bit. You've really hurt him, which I asked you not to do. It's not good seeing my mate so cut up. Anyway, he wants me to let you know he's seeing a lawyer this pm and suggests you find one too. He's talking about divorce. Get your shit together!*
*Mike*

I am numb and confused as to why Alan is involving Mike. He probably thinks Mike will be able to make me come to my senses. Also, Alan and I are similar in that we both have only a handful of friends, and only one whom we can call a best friend. Mike is Alan's closest friend. I decide not to reply. Let Alan appoint a lawyer, because our marriage is doomed. My mood deteriorates further but is lifted by Sebastian's next message.

*That's better, Elizabeth! Why won't you meet me? What are you afraid of? S*

I'm afraid of so many things but most especially I'm afraid of myself, and my lack of self-control. I know very well what will happen if we're alone together.

*You! You have a power over me Sebastian and ending up in bed with you is only going to complicate things x*

The message is sent. I sit back in my chair and pick up the book I had been reading before all this trouble arose, certain that reading will take my mind off things. I am immediately disturbed by my phone.

*That's a great shame Elizabeth as I've gone to the considerable trouble of coming to take you to lunch. I'm parked in The Crescent. See you in 10. S*

*He's here? Oh my God, is he a bloody stalker?*

I'm furious. No, that's an understatement. I'm absolutely livid. How dare he *presume.* I've said no to this man, and yet he has the audacity to drive three, four hours to take me to lunch.

Snatching my coat and scarf from the hook, I march out of my office without a word to Ruth who watches me leave with a puzzled expression. Damn him for this. *Bloody sodding men!* I seethe.

The rain of late morning is turning to sleet, and I pull my scarf up to shield my chin from the biting cold. It's a short walk at the quick pace I maintain. Turning left on the street, my gaze darts warily in search of his car while also watching for Alan in case he's spying on me again. I'm becoming paranoid. The now familiar Range Rover is parked behind a blue van, and as I approach, Sebastian becomes visible, talking on his mobile phone. Seeing me step toward his car, he reaches across and opens the passenger door for me. I slide onto the warm leather seat, noticing he has thoughtfully switched the seat warmer on for me.

"Yes, yes, Sunday night, fine. Yes, ready at ten, see you then." He ends his call and turns to face me. Ready to tear a strip off this arrogant man, my arms fold, jaw tensed. "What the hell are you doing turning up here, thinking I'll drop everything and have lunch with—" Before I can complete my sentence, he kisses me. It is a long, hard kiss that I fight for all of five seconds, and then respond to with a hunger and carnal passion that surprises us both.

His right hand strokes my neck, and his left hand is travelling up my thigh. I want this man—need. The more that I tell myself this is wrong, the more I want him. His tongue finds mine and explores my mouth, his teeth catching my lip in his passion. His fingers are pressing into my panties now as he rubs my sex through my thin underwear, all thoughts of admonishing him now gone. His touch feels so good. Abruptly, he ends the kiss, pulls back his hand and rests back into his seat. His eyes are locked on mine in a serious scowl.

"*Mmm,* delicious thank you," he growls. "So, what happened to the Elizabeth who didn't want to see me?" He raises his eyebrow and curls his lip in a mocking smile. I just can't remain angry with this man.

"You're insufferable, De Montfort," I complain.

"I aim to please Mrs. Dove." He smirks. "Put your seat belt on, Elizabeth, I'm taking you for that lunch I promised you." I click my seatbelt into place and he pulls out into the traffic. Soon, we are on the road out of town.

"Where are we going?" I ask, mindful that we mustn't go somewhere Alan may be.

"Wait and see. Patience is a fine attribute. You'd do well to learn some," he says smugly.

We drive for twenty minutes and listen to uplifting music rather than talk, for which I'm grateful. My tension eases with each mile that passes. Soon, Sebastian indicates a right turn, and we pull in to a country hotel, which I have not been to before. It looks lovely, and there are very few cars in the lot, certainly not Alan's car nor Mike's.

Sebastian climbs out of the car and opens my door, and I step out. He takes my hand and we walk into the hotel where a log fire burns in the entrance hall.

"Wait here," he instructs. He approaches the reception desk and chats to the receptionist for a few minutes, before returning to me clutching a small white card.

"Come," he says, and again takes my hand.

He leads me across the hall to a staircase, and it is apparent that we are not dining in the restaurant, but instead heading to a bedroom.

# Chapter 11

I know I should protest vehemently, and yet I follow him as a lamb to the slaughter, my body tingling in anticipation. At the top stair, Sebastian takes the right turn and we pass through an open door, the floorboards creaking as we tread. We stop at the very end, and Sebastian places the modern key card into the lock, which gives, and he opens the door. It momentarily strikes me as odd that such a timeworn hotel should have modern technology.

Stepping into the room, Sebastian pushes the door shut behind us with his foot and he's upon me immediately, pushing me up against the wall next to the bathroom, his breath quickening. He's kissing and nibbling my neck, roughly fondling my left breast, while hitching up my skirt with his other hand.

My arms are around his waist and my hand travels down to his buttocks. I pull him harder against me, wanting him so desperately now. I feel his hand between us and he's unbuttoning his fly. I unbuckle his belt awkwardly, feeling his steely erection through the fabric of his boxer shorts. His suit trousers puddle at his feet. He pushes his boxer shorts down and clumsily steps out of his clothing. His enormous penis falls heavily into my waiting hand. He sucks in his breath sharply as I squeeze my fingers around his length.

"Fuck, Elizabeth." He groans, nostrils flaring, as I

purposefully stroke along his throbbing veins.

He pulls roughly at the tops of my panties with his long, deft fingers. He tugs them down impatiently, and I help him, stepping out of them as they fall to my feet. His hand moves past the tops of my silky hold-up stockings.

"Christ, you're *so* sexy. You're wearing stockings for me. Shit, that turns me on. I have to have you. Now." He lifts me, his hands under my buttocks, and I wrap my legs around his waist while I lean back heavily into the wall. The tip of his hard cock finds the entrance to my hot, wet core. He lowers me just enough to allow the slick head of his throbbing member inside me, and he teases me with it, allowing it to enter me just an inch before pulling his hips back. Suddenly he drops me hard and the length of his shaft drives into me, so deep that I slap at his back, my fingers biting into his flesh.

As he lifts me again and again, up and down onto his burning shaft, my back slamming into the wall. We are oblivious to the world outside the thin, wooden hotel door, lost in our lust. His cock hits my G-spot and just keeps on thrashing against it, my mounting climax sending ripples of orgasmic pleasure from my groin until the waves of ecstasy are coursing through me. A cry escapes from deep within my throat. He pulls me down onto him harder, chasing his own climax. He grinds more slowly now, and I feel the sweat on his skin as my fingers splay and I pull him even more deeply into me. He breathes my name into my hair as the convulsions of his orgasm ripple through him, releasing his warm, creamy nectar into me.

We slide down into a hot, sticky heap on the floor and lay entwined, catching our breath, stroking, kissing, and savouring the moment. When the last embers of our passion have ended, we move to the bed and curl up against the soft pillows. Sebastian closes his eyes and is soon asleep, relaxed. Propping myself up on my arm, I look at him and think how handsome he is with his dark eyebrows, messed up black hair greying at the temples, and a shadow of dark stubble on his face. My gaze travels down to his tangle of dark chest hair, which trails in a thick line past his navel to the bushy mound at his groin. He is so masculine, with an almost primitive ruggedness that I find so sexy. As I study this man intently I am unaware he has woken and is watching me too.

"You like what you see?" His words make me jump, and I blush having been caught staring appreciatively at his body.

"*Mmm,* I like, very much," I purr with a sly grin, and he moves quickly then, flipping me onto my back and straddling me. He pins my arms on either side with his knees and I'm unable to move. He has me trapped. "Sebastian, you're a bully. Let me go!" I protest and laugh simultaneously, but he increases his weight further onto his knees, rendering my attempts to escape entirely futile. "Oh, you like to play rough, do you?" I ask playfully.

"Oh, you have no idea, Mrs. Dove," he replies darkly. "Sure, I like to play rough, and I like my women precisely where you are now—restrained and ready for me." He has a cunning grin and an excited gleam in his eyes. He looks so wicked, and for a moment I am fearful of what he may have in mind for me next, but he kisses my lips and moves off, releasing me. "Another time, Elizabeth."

"Sebastian, you're so kinky." It sounds such a puerile statement. He's has roused my curiosity, and I want to know more. "I've been looking online and I'm kind of curious about all that dominant, submissive stuff."

"And it turns you on," he states knowingly.

"Actually, yes, it does. I guess because Alan's totally disinterested in sex and the least dominating man in the world. It's a contrast to my life," I explain. "It's just that I have to be the boss in every element, all my roles are leading roles—at home, at work. I actually find it very appealing to think that a man might take some of that control away from me, tell *me* what to do for once, not put up with my shit." I laugh.

"Where have you been all my life, Elizabeth?" He kisses me again and tenderly strokes my hair. "I'm here for you now, darling. You don't have to be in charge anymore. In fact, I won't *allow* you to be so around me. Just so you understand that point. I'd go further to say, if you try to lead me, you'll make me angry, Elizabeth." He looks sternly at me and I can sense that he means what he says. This man is used to dominating and asserting his will, and I pity those who try to belittle him. I think he'd make a cruel enemy.

"Have all the women in your life allowed you to dominate them?"

"They *beg* me to, Elizabeth!" He has that sly look

again—raised eyebrow, half grin.

"Is that why you like Scarlett working for you, because she's subservient? Does the power you have over her arouse you?" I'm treading on dangerous ground, but it seems a good opportunity to push him on this as it bothers me so.

"Don't confuse business with pleasure," he rebukes. "I've got the message, I know you find it bizarre that an attractive woman lives and works at my house, but what wealthy, unattached man wouldn't choose an attractive woman to work for him rather than a hag? I don't intend to justify my choice of employees to you again, so the topic is now taboo. Understood?"

"Okay, point taken," I concede. "But you did admit she was once more to you."

"I felt sorry for her," he says, as though that excuses his actions. "It was a low point in my life, and she was there. It was over before it began, and she knows her place. She values her job too much to play up."

"Play up? Sebastian, I've seen the way she looks at you, at us together. Believe me, that woman is in love with you."

"Don't be ridiculous. Change the subject."

"Okay. What was Libby like?" I acquiesce, hoping this next question doesn't also upset him.

"She was the most gentle, beautiful creature ever to walk the earth. Beautiful but complex. She struggled, you know, with many things in life. She was not a strong person. Very highly strung, she'd get anxious, and at the end, paranoid. In the early days when we first met, she was vivacious and spirited. I think not having children was a heavy cross to bear. In the end, she was on all kinds of pills, seeing the best psychologists, but she wasn't rational. Her paranoia grew and she began hallucinating. She imagined all manner of things at Penmorrow, accusing me of various wrongdoings. Then, one day, she just...opted out."

He looks crestfallen, miles away, as if he is reliving those last few painful months and days with his mentally sick wife in that old house. Regretting asking him about her, I try to lighten his mood.

"C'mon, let's have a shower together, then I need to get back to work!"

I jump off the bed, strip out of my clothes, and run naked to the bathroom, giggling playfully and hoping he will come after me. He does not disappoint.

***

The drive back to my office is more relaxed than our previous journey. My troubles have been temporarily put to the back of my mind. I find myself wishing Sebastian would take me back to Penmorrow with him. The idea of running away is tempting, if it weren't for the children.

We kiss goodbye in the car, which is parked a hundred yards from my office, and we agree to text each other later tonight. He blows me a kiss as I turn and walk back to work. I'm late for my three o'clock meeting.

*What was I thinking?* It's such a crucial meeting; there is so much riding on this.

As I rush into the office, shrugging out of my coat, I see the meeting room is already heaving with people talking and sipping coffee. I dash into the ladies cloakroom to reapply my lipstick and dab a little powder over my still flushed cheeks and smooth down my hair, hoping I don't reek of sex. Just in case, I spritz myself with perfume from my handbag.

*Good to go. They will never guess what I have been up to.* I smirk to myself.

"Hi, Beth," my secretary says. "You've got a message from Alan to call him back on his mobile, and Joe's headmaster called. I said you'd call him back after the meeting. There are three contracts to sign on your desk too, please, all urgent. Oh, and Nicky wants to know if she can go ahead and order the new marketing brochures. If so, she needs to know today or the deal ends and the price goes up." She is so efficient, but the strain builds as my workload and personal issues mount on my shoulders once again.

Since the recession hit in the UK, so many firms are struggling to survive. Ours has weathered the storm better than most, but new leads are at an all time low and that is why I had to submit an ambitious tender application for a substantial contract. If we are successful it will mean our projected turnover will double, bringing long awaited growth for Evershaw Dove. Now it seems likely that we will be the preferred bidder, panic has set in as Ruth and I struggle to raise the considerable financial resources required to meet our contractual obligations.

Staffing is our main concern. We will need to increase our HR team, which of course means advertising, training, and possibly larger offices. We will need to increase our administration support team by two full time members of staff. All of this requires a significant injection of cash—money we don't have.

Alan and I have a colossal mortgage already with a second charge levied on the building by our commercial lender, so it's not been possible to leverage any more money against the house. Ruth lives with her mother in her mother's house so, again, that's not a cash source we can utilize. It was therefore an enormous relief when our accountant suggested calling this meeting. He has a network of investors, all eager to squirrel away their funds into our sector rather than seeing it exposed to the perils of hedge funds, shares, and even high street banks, which are now largely owned by the British public. The syndicate is a long established one, he assured us, with one or two 'new boys' who seem keen to shore up their liquid funds.

If this meeting goes well, we will secure the funds needed to grow and finally make some decent returns on this business, after years of hard work. Now, more than ever, I am aware of the need to be independently solvent. If and when Alan and I sell the house, I will be damned before I ask him for money to support me.

Smoothing down my black pencil skirt and straightening the hem of my matching suit jacket, I open the door with a false smile. I schmooze a warm hello, and try to catch the eye of each person in turn as I shake their hands, and introduce myself.

"Elizabeth Dove, how do you do?" I gush with the professional tone I have mastered over the years in business. Shaking the next hand extended to meet my firm grip, then the next, "Thank you so much for coming today."

As I take the next hand in mine, the touch is familiar but before realisation dawns, it is the dulcet voice which fills my veins with ice.

"Sebastian De Montfort. Delighted to meet you, Elizabeth."

I withdraw my hand sharply and, wide-eyed, I stare at him in disbelief and then pure guttural anger at his blatant intrusion into my working life.

*What the hell is he doing here?* Why did he not mention he was invited to attend this meeting when I saw him only half an hour ago?

*Crap.*

# Chapter 12

The room is a sea of faces, all looking at me expectantly. "Mrs. Dove...?"

I snap back to the moment. "Gentlemen, th...thank you all for coming today." I try to recover my composure and professionalism. This is too important to allow him to sabotage my agenda. "In front of you, you will find a presentation pack which includes our business growth plan and forecasts. If I could ask you to please turn to page one, the Executive Summary..."

Everyone shuffles the papers in front of them and locates the page as directed.

"You will find a synopsis of the structure of our company, a statement on our readiness for market, and a brief outline of our growth plans." The room falls silent as the investors study the document. I lead them through the plan and include a Power Point presentation, which they digest. When I have finished, I open the floor to questions.

A portly man of later years and a ruddy complexion raises his hand. "Mrs. Dove—Elizabeth, if we are to invest the monies you require, what share interest are you proposing to offer?"

*None, I just want your money!*

"That's a very good question" I reply out loud. "In terms of return on investment, we feel that six percent annualized interest plus a ten percent share holding is a very generous return. I should add that we would not be offering a Board position, and there would be no voting rights attached to the deal."

"Elizabeth." Sebastian commands my attention. He sits back, arms crossed and a wicked glint in his eyes. He is relishing my discomfort. I stare at him with the coldest, steely glare I can muster. "With all due respect, you cannot expect investors to simply write a cheque for the level of funding you are seeking, and expect them to be happy with a return they would achieve from a high street bank with little or no risk exposure. I personally would require a non-executive Board position, in addition to twenty percent of your ordinary shareholding."

*Oh, I just bet you would, you control freak.*

I am furious with Sebastian for demeaning me in front of these men, and for sowing the seed in their fat little heads about wanting a slice of our company. Well, it's not up for negotiation. *Over my dead body!* This business has pretty much cost me my marriage, my social life, and years of stress. If he thinks I am going to hand it over on a plate, then he is crazier than I gave him credit for.

"Thank you *Mister* De Montfort," I say with more than a hint of bitterness. "As I just indicated, the option of a Board position is not something we would consider at this time."

Averting my frosty gaze from him, my attention returns to the others in the room. "Please remember, gentlemen, that you would be receiving a very healthy *profit* share as well as an attractive interest rate on your investment. That is not something you would receive from your high street bank."

Sebastian looks impassive but raises an eyebrow at me, shakes his head, and writes something down.

I answer questions from two gentlemen, and thankfully these are operational rather than financial queries. Drained, I sit down again as Ruth stands to deliver a closing speech. Looking at the faces of the men, I can't read their expressions in order to guess whether or not they may bite the cherry.

Avoiding Sebastian's gaze, I look everywhere except at him. I'm simply too angry with him, but I feel his stare burning into me, and it takes all my willpower to avert my eyes. Ruth is thanking everyone for attending the meeting today, and for their interest in Evershaw Dove. Soon, I'm shaking hands with them all as they leave, most muttering that they will be in touch, but no firm offers.

Sebastian is waiting behind the last gentleman, who is telling me he will give the matter his earnest consideration. I turn to follow him out, but I feel a firm grip on my arm forcing me back into the meeting room. Ruth has left the room, and I see she's in deep conversation with our accountant, so I am alone with *him*. He shuts the door and leans against it, arms folded and an amused smirk plastered across his face. I let him have it.

"You arrogant, conceited, son-of-a-bitch!" I hiss. "What the *hell* do you think you are doing coming here like this, no bloody warning, making me look an idiot? It's all a game to you, isn't it?" I am on a roll and the venom spills forth. "Oh, it's just fine to turn up here out of the blue, take me to a hotel, and have your way with me, no mention of the real reason you are here which is to bleed my company dry. Oh no, the sex was a nice little added bonus, wasn't it...a little extra for your trouble in driving up here. I...I'm lost for words."

"Have you finished your little rant, Elizabeth?" the patronising twerp asks.

I cannot speak to him. I cannot find any more words to relay how angry I am.

"Because if you have, then please allow me to respond. Sit down."

Staring aghast at him, I cannot believe he dares to order me to sit, so I remain standing with my defensive posture of folded arms, chin in the air.

"Sit," he barks, pulling a chair away from the table, and swishing his hand toward it indicating that I should sit.

I sit, cross my legs and arms, looking straight ahead out of the window rather than in his direction, like a petulant child waiting for a reprimand from her head teacher.

"That's better. I appreciate that it was a shock to see me here, but I knew very well that you would not have allowed me to come had I discussed it with you first. Yes, I did want to see you other than in the boardroom. Although, I have to admit I would rather like to fuck you *hard* over this table right now. But, that aside, I thought we would kill two birds with one stone, so to speak. I had you to myself before the meeting, let's call it due diligence, Elizabeth. Plus, I was then privy to a very interesting business meeting at which a sexy, clever woman convinced me to part with a large chunk of my money and not many people achieve that. Very well done."

My jaw has dropped. I am totally speechless. He doesn't see that this is wrong on so many levels. He wants to fuck me over the table—hard! He is going to lend me the money. *Oh, and he wants to fuck me over the boardroom table.* My mind keeps on returning to that point, and I'm so furious with him.

"Fine" I say sullenly. "Ten percent, and I'll shake on the deal here and now." The cocky little prick will never agree to a reduction in terms, so he will walk away and I shall have won and proven he cannot always get what he wants.

"Ten percent it is." He rises and proffers a hand to shake.

*What the hell?* We shake hands, his grip so tight on mine that I wince. "I'd have gone to fifteen," I tell him smugly after the deal is sealed with a shake, his hand still gripping mine.

"And I, Elizabeth, would have dropped to five percent."

*Damn him.*

He doesn't release my hand, gripping me like iron. He's close to me, and I feel his breath on my neck as he pulls me forward and kisses my cheek. He's clever. Anyone looking through the sound proofed glass would see us shaking on a deal and him politely kissing the cheek of a newly acquired business partner, nothing more sinister. Yet, he's hurting me now, not releasing me, and I start to protest. I pull at my hand but he maintains his hold on me. "Come to Cornwall this weekend, Elizabeth. Drive down to Penmorrow and be with me."

"You really are *nuts,*" I hiss at him, incredulously. "You may be investing in our company but don't for a minute underestimate me and think you are buying *me.* I won't be driving anywhere this weekend. I will be here trying to sort the tatters of my marriage, and if I never see you again it will be too soon."

He releases my sore hand, and I turn, open the door and flee to the ladies cloakroom where I lock myself in a cubicle, and sob with the humiliation and stress of the day.

Ruth is tapping lightly on the door and asking me what's wrong. I open the door and fall into her arms. She hugs me tightly. "Beth you did really well. Don't cry," she soothes.

"You don't understand," I wail. "He's agreed to give us the money for five percent, *damn him.*"

"What? That's fantastic news. Why on earth are you crying? Which one was it? I bet it was that gorgeous black haired Adonis. He couldn't take his eyes off you," she says excitedly.

"Yes, but don't you see...that was Sebastian! It's all about control, he wants to *own* me, Ruth, and now I've agreed to his investment. I've walked straight into his plan and...sold my soul to the *devil!*" I sob.

"Let me deal with him, Beth. To be honest, I would rather enjoy *dealing* with him, he's so sexy!"

I flash her an angry glare at which she blushes.

"Look, we take his money, grow the business, and we need never see him again. He'll receive his money via our accountant and, meanwhile, you get on with your life. Get yourself sorted, divorce Alan, think about yourself and the kids, and don't complicate it further with Mr. Moneybags," she says wisely.

"You don't know what he's like. He won't let it go, Ruth, and he'll be all over our business like a rash. He's a control freak."

"I'll deal with him, Beth. Leave the creep to me. The main thing is we've got our money, so we can go ahead with our plans."

"Be careful," I warn. "I'm discovering just how manipulative he can be."

# Chapter 13

Alan's mobile phone rings as I return his earlier call. He picks up and I can hear the acrimony in his tone.

"Beth. Thanks for *eventually* getting back to me. I've spoken to my lawyer and it seems that, if we can agree things amicably, we can get the divorce without having to incur huge legal bills each and, to be honest, I'd rather we sorted everything as soon as possible."

He tells me I can have the house but he wants his pension and his share of the business, if and when it is sold. He then talks about custody of the children, clearly having written all his terms down before my call, stating the children must stay with him on alternate weekends and two nights during the week plus half of their school holidays.

"Another thing" he says. "You are *not* to have a man back to *my* house at any time, understand?"

I do not counter his vexatious request with the fact that it's also *my* house. Instead, I agree to his terms, which overall seem reasonable. He ends the call by informing me that his lawyer will prepare a draft agreement and then send me the divorce papers. I'm left feeling partly relieved that we have reached an agreement on which to move forward, but also a profound sadness at the ending of our marriage.

I return the call to Joe's school and ask to speak to the head teacher who advises me that Joe will be excluded from lessons tomorrow morning for telling Mrs. Elmore, his history teacher, to fuck off.

*Can today get any worse?*

He will be required to sit in the school library and write a letter of apology to Mrs. Elmore, who apparently has never been spoken to in such a manner before. I somehow doubt that, as I recall her as an irritating, mousy woman with a squeaky voice and cynical attitude. I apologise profusely, and explain that Joe is going through a difficult time at home as his father has left. This news is not met with empathy by the head teacher of Joe's Catholic school. I'm not surprised, but the school needs to know that my Joe has his reasons for being rebellious right now.

Ending the call, I hurriedly sign the waiting contracts on my desk and call Nicky to authorise the ordering of new brochures, figuring we can afford them now we have the investment. That returns my thoughts to Sebastian and his meddling.

*What am I to do with that man?* Never before have I been so subjugated by any man, and I detest the part of me which welcomes his dominance. It's as though I'm two people: Elizabeth Dove the respectable mother and business woman, and some harlot who dwells in my darkest psyche. She wears red lace underwear, a black choker, and bends over saying, "Whip me now, baby!" I can't recall her always being there. Perhaps she's been asleep, and Sebastian has awoken her?

My phone bleeps.

*Hi PARTNER. I hope you keep that boardroom table polished Mrs. Dove. I intend to have you there, perhaps after our next board meeting? S*

He's so obtuse. Partner! He may have wiled his way onto the Board, but he will not be receiving any extra benefits from me anymore. My reply is curt and I hope it stings.

*Mr. De Montfort, Ruth will be your point of contact here, I don't deal with minority shareholders. B*

He is quick to reply.

*Interesting. Hope Ruth has great legs too and likes tables. S*

Insufferable ass. I can't resist a cutting reply.

*I'll be sure to give her the choker! B*

I wait for his reply but my phone stays silent. I'm full of regret then. For some reason he's under my skin and, although I try to despise him, I find myself wanting him even more.

I begin to wonder if this is just escapism, if my life has been so lacking in male affection that I am pouncing upon the first male who shows me attention. Perhaps he strokes my female ego, and I tell myself I'd be better served gleaning satisfaction from books and my vibrating toys rather than suffer the complexities and manipulations of men.

Time to call it a day. It's five-thirty and the kids will be home waiting for dinner, having taken the bus home from school. I hate them having to take the bus, but I had no choice again today.

When I arrive home the house seems strangely empty without Alan. Joe's engrossed in with his games console, blowing apart a zombie, while Bella pretends to complete homework. She thinks I haven't noticed the instant messages on the screen of her PC.

There is precious little food in the fridge so I retrieve a ready-made chicken curry from the freezer. *Defrost thoroughly before use*, the packaging advises. I remove the cardboard, and stab the plastic film lid aggressively with a fork, then toss the whole solid, frozen mass into the oven onto a baking tray and turn the dial to the highest temperature. It's an improvement on most of my culinary attempts. Most food items are prepared using my ten minute microwave rule, and miraculously I haven't poisoned us yet.

The children and I sit at the kitchen table and eat our insipid curry, and I realise I miss the family dinners we used to enjoy around the dining table with everyone talking in turn about their day. The normal activities of living seem so far removed suddenly, and I feel a stabbing of remorse and sadness in the pit of my stomach.

*No good dwelling on the past. I've got to move on.*

Joe's in bed asleep, Bella's gone back to her bedroom, and I'm alone and feeling miserable. I pour myself a large glass of red wine in the kitchen and take it to the lounge where I sink down onto the sofa, exhausted. My iPad is on the coffee table and I pick it up and rest it on my lap, reaching forward and picking up my glass. I wake my tablet and, as the screen comes to life, I take a long drink of wine and savour the warm richness, allowing my thoughts to drift to Sebastian. I can still feel his touch on my skin and see the wicked glint in his eyes when he looks at me.

It's nearly nine o'clock and not too late to send him a message, so I pick up my phone from the coffee table, replacing it with my wine, and send a text.

**Hey, you busy?**

Staring at my phone, I wait for his reply. A few minutes later my phone alerts me to a new message received, but it is not from Sebastian. It's from Alan and he's obviously drunk.

**Hope ur happy Beth ruin our marriage for wot? Never good nuff for you well I want the kids I'm a better bloody parent than you**

His message fills me with dread and anger. A knot in my stomach tightens and, made braver by the wine, I tap a hasty reply.

**_Piss off Alan! You're hardly blameless in our marriage breaking up are you?! As for the kids I hardly think a court in the land would give custody to a whisky soaked drunk!_**

Shaking, I send the message and drain my glass. _If it's a fight he wants, he can bloody have one._

My phone bleeps in my lap, I hesitantly look at the screen.

**_Hey sexy, lovely to hear from you. Still angry with me? S_**

_I'm angry with all men, honey, not just you._

Deciding I've had enough of men for today, I switch my phone off and go to bed without replying.

The next morning, Joe is brooding and quiet when I drive him to school. Bella has insisted on taking the bus again, and I'm unsure as to whether she is angry and blaming me for her father leaving or just showing the first signs of maturity and independence. Chatting to Joe in the car, my light conversation is met with grunts and one-word answers and he is keen to get out when we reach school.

At the office, I have a heap of paperwork waiting for my attention, which I plough through by late morning. Ruth is at a meeting with our lawyer to discuss

Sebastian's investment and shareholding.

My work completed, I wonder whether to bunk off for the rest of the day. Instead I decide upon a little much needed *me* time and welcome distraction. Taking my latest raunchy book from the drawer in my desk, I flick through the chapters until I reach a particularly erotic scene. They are ensconced in a secret room, her hands and ankles bound with rope, and he is applying clamps to her nipples.

*Ouch.* It makes me shudder, and suddenly I'm more curious than ever about this perverse form of sex.

I fire up my computer, and tilt the screen to an angle so no one entering my office will witness my search. There are numerous online pages offering a plethora of deviancy, ranging from torturous equipment, to bondage and sadomasochism dating websites. A forum for submissive women catches my attention. Reading the threads, I recognise many of my needs and desires within those postings. The women talk about dominant men who care for them and ensure they are safe and looked after, yet with the expectation and profound understanding that their submissive meets their every desire enthusiastically and tirelessly, without question or disobedience. The primary attraction for me, apart from the hot sex, is that the woman is not expected or required to be the decision maker or alpha of the relationship.

Reflecting on my own marriage and my career, I can see this is parallel to my own life and realize that I've been craving a significant life change for some years. Perhaps submission is the panacea to my unhappiness and dissatisfaction with my life. This is why I'm attracted to Sebastian. He holds the key to unlocking and freeing *me*.

*Go with it, Beth. Life is short and it's your turn to fly.*

Picking up the phone, I tap Sebastian's number. My hand is trembling slightly and the knot in my stomach is firmly twisting. *Feel the fear and do it anyway.*

Sebastian answers, and his deep sexy voice turns the knot in my stomach to a warm tingling in my groin. He reassures me with his confident tone, listening to me as I dump all my anguish and feelings on his shoulders. He tells me exactly what I so need to hear. My marriage breakdown was not my fault, as it had clearly been on the cards for years, and it is now *my* time to do fulfil my own desires. It's nearly Christmas, he reminds me, and the children will find this year tough because we won't be a family unit. We must come to stay at Penmorrow for the holiday season. He doesn't allow me to interject, assuring me he knows best and I must trust him on this.

My mobile phone rings. Number withheld. I accept the call.

"Elizabeth Dove speaking."

"Sorry, I must have the wrong number." The voice sounds familiar.

"Who are you trying to reach?"

"Rosie. I don't know her surname." It's Simon. "Uh, hold the line, I'll get her for you." I place the phone down in my lap for a full minute, before picking it up again. Changing my voice to a slightly higher octave, I say, "Rosie speaking."

"Rosie, hi. It's Simon."

"Simon, what a lovely surprise. How are you?"

"I'm good. How are you?" The conversation is awkward at best.

"I'm fine thanks. How's work?" *Think of something to say, Beth.*

"Work's good. Not many fires though." *Blimey, he's boring.*

"Well, that's a good thing right?"

"Guess so."

"So, Simon. What can I do for you?"

"Just thought I'd phone for a chat. See how you are."

"How lovely. I enjoyed our time together," I lie.

"Yeah, me too," he says.

"Well, then."

"Wanna do it again?" Simon asks. *And they say the art of romance is gone.*

"You bet." Another lie. "Let's fix something up really soon. I'm busy for the next couple of weeks but why don't you text me some dates, and we'll put something in the schedule." *Like, maybe next century.*

"Yeah. Sounds like a plan. See ya." He cuts the call before Rosie can say goodbye.

At the end of the day, my desk is tidy and I turn out the office lights and put my coat on. My phone pings with a new text message.

**Rosie I can do next Wednesday or the following Monday. Any good? Same hotel, same hot sex. Simon x**

Oh, crap! I tap a quick reply to him.

***Hi Simon, sorry can't make either of those days due to meetings. Will call you. X***

*Don't hold your breath.*

Driving home I scold myself for getting into these tricky situations. There's no comparison between Sebastian and Simon. Sebastian is complicated—*very* complicated—but at least he doesn't have a vacuous void for a brain. I make a mental note to delete the message from Simon, erase him from my life. That thought is forgotten as my mind drifts back to thoughts of Sebastian.

# Chapter 14

The weeks pass so quickly. Each day is a master class of juggling—the children, housework, the business, divorce correspondence. I am utterly and completely exhausted, both mentally and physically.

My mother tries to help as much as she can and is invaluable, as is Ruth. Between the three of us, we somehow manage always to keep the cogs and wheels of my life well oiled and turning. The children have not yet starved or burned the house down on the days I have worked late, thanks to Mother being there. The business has not suffered from my drop in efficiency thanks to Ruth shouldering more than her share of meetings. Life after Alan is bearable.

Alan is not thriving alone. He doesn't appear to be at work very much, and the children tell me after their latest visit with him that he's on leave— meaning suspension. For what misconduct, I have no idea, although I suspect whisky may be involved. Bella tells me he's drinking all the time. When I question her on this, she clams up, loyal to her father. It spurs me to notify my lawyer, seeking a reduction in his access and restricting him from driving our children in case he is under the influence of alcohol.

His fury at the ensuing letter culminates in the mother of all rows on the phone late one night, when he accuses me of being a manipulating bitch who is just like all those other women, and no wonder *Justice For Fathers* were in the news every day when women like me stopped them seeing their kids. There is no reasoning with him, and it leaves me with a steely resolve to continue the restriction, as the safety and welfare of my children seems to be my priority alone, not his.

This new confidence is directly attributable to Sebastian. Our daily telephone conversations reaffirm my decisions and actions, and Sebastian's wise words and practical suggestions prove invaluable in helping survive each day rather than curling up in my bed and closing out the world, as I wanted to do soon after Alan left me.

\*\*\*

Christmas is fast approaching. The children have just two more days before their schools close for the holidays, and I have just two more days to work until the start of my two week period of leave. I can hardly wait. The anticipation of seeing Sebastian again after so many weeks, together with the promise of a much needed rest, are steering me through each day.

Alan vehemently refuses to allow the children to spend the entire holiday with me, and I relent, agreeing that he can have them stay with him for New Year. I decide he is less likely to drink himself into oblivion on New Year's Eve if the children are with him. It also means they can travel to Penmorrow with me for Christmas, and we leave in just four days' time.

Mother is unhappy that the children and I will be absent for Christmas, but she has decided to invite her sister, Aunty Margaret, to travel from Eastbourne and enjoy the festivities with her. They are not close but my mother will nevertheless enjoy her company, and it absolves me from my selfish act of going away. My penance for such a sin was to agree to host dinner for the two of them on the night before we leave for Cornwall, and we exchange gifts over an early turkey dinner at my home before kissing and hugging our farewells and festive wishes.

***

The white carpet of frost glistens on the front lawn and path, twinkling in the early morning sun as I load suitcases and brightly wrapped Christmas presents into the trunk of my car. The children seem in good spirits, chatting animatedly for much of the journey. They seem unconcerned to be visiting a stranger or spending Christmas with him. Instead they seem more anxious to know whether I have bought Joe's latest console game, and Bella's iPad, as demanded on their hastily penned Christmas wish lists, which of course I have.

"Kids, are you excited to be staying in a mansion for Christmas?" I ask, observing the reaction on their faces in my rear view mirror.

"Bella told me it's haunted," replies Joe nervously, "and she said there will be dungeons and secret tunnels and everything."

Bella laughs, "*Belieeever!*" and Joe digs her ribs sharply with his elbow.

Bella yelps and responds with a hefty thump to Joe's leg. I sigh. This is my life these days, but I resist the urge to scream at my children or to dampen my excitement. Instead,I switch on the radio and crank the volume up to drown out their squabbles.

We break our journey only for a comfort stop near Exeter and to share out the hastily made sandwiches, which are in the picnic bag beside me. Fifty minutes later, I leave the arterial road to north Cornwall and am soon navigating the tiny capillary lanes threading toward Trevissey. It's odd, but the smaller the roads, the greater my excitement as we approach the turn to Penmorrow. We soon pass the stone stags, and the children gasp as the grandeur of Penmorrow looms ahead.

# Chapter 15

The car wheels crunch noisily on the gravel, signalling our arrival. As I cut the ignition I see Sebastian approaching from the house.

The children are already out of the car and, as I open my door and step out, the sight of Sebastian embracing Bella and shaking Joe's hand melts my heart. I'm beaming when he walks over to me. He puts his arms around my waist and pulls me tightly into his chest, kissing my forehead. I wrap my arms around him, and I turn my head upwards and plant a lingering, intense kiss on his lips—I'm so very glad to be with him again, having grown to miss him terribly over the last few weeks.

After an eternity of kissing, we become aware of the children, impatient to get on with the business of ghost hunting and exploring the vast house before them. Sebastian opens the trunk and retrieves our luggage, which he carries into the house. The children run ahead of him. As I follow him inside, a feeling of optimism and belonging enfolds me.

*I am home.*

Two hours. The time it takes the children to complete their mission of discovery, after which they find us in the kitchen and regale us with tales of dark shadows and 'really cool' rooms. Sebastian feigns intrigue, then fuels their excitement by telling them stories of an apparition of a grey lady purportedly seen floating along the upper landing and passing through bedroom doors. I laugh and admonish him for telling tales, which will inevitably keep Joe awake tonight.

Sebastian leaves us at three, returning an hour later with the most enormous Christmas tree the children have ever seen. We have a wonderful time adorning the branches with the glass baubles Sebastian retrieves from the attic.

It feels cathartic—to laugh, to be a family unit, to forget Alan and all the negativity which has clouded my life of late. It's Christmas, and I feel safe, my children are happy. Life is good once again.

Scarlett serves a delicious supper of beef wellington with a warm chocolate fondant for dessert and, irritatingly, joins us at the table.

"Beats your microwave dinners, Mum!" exclaims my ungrateful son as he devours his second helping. Scarlett catches my eye, and I note the smugness with which she smiles at me.

***

In the great hall, the last embers of the fire glow, and the last remnant of burning pine spits cinders and crackles. Refreshed from a hot bath and now dressed only in a towelling robe, I'm sitting on the rug with Sebastian, as we did the night we met, gazing at the fire and sipping port. We don't speak but instead relish each other's closeness. The house is quiet. The children are sleeping upstairs, and the only sounds I can hear come from the fire and the grandfather clock in the entrance hall chiming intermittently.

I'm seated between Sebastian's open legs, resting back against his strong chest. I raise the crystal port glass to my lips, finishing the warm sweet liquid and breathing in the aroma of smoky pine, sighing contentedly. He kisses the back of my neck then nibbles at the top of my ear, and I moan at the touch of his lips. "*Mmm,* that feels so good."

"I aim to please, Elizabeth. And how does this feel?" He moves the hair from my neck and traces gentle kisses down to the top of my spine, sending small tremors down my spine to my sacrum.

I squirm and melt back against him harder. It feels so good. He falls back with my weight against him, onto the rug, taking me with him. My glass tumbles from my grasp. His legs entwine mine, and we're kissing passionately, our tongues seeking each other's with a raw hunger. He roughly grasps and kneads my breasts, pinching my nipples until I cry out with the delicious pain. He moves on top of me, my legs now wrapped tightly around his, pulling his hardness against me. I need him so badly. The ache within me is almost unbearable.

My hand moves down to his hardness, stroking the length of him through the course fabric of his jeans. He groans, reaching down to unzip his fly.

His manhood rises, freed from the constraints of the denim. He hurriedly pulls at the tie belt of my robe until it gives, the robe falling open to expose my nakedness. His hand moves between my legs, his fingers probing my creamy arousal, his thumb stroking at my clitoris so expertly. He continues his assault on my clit as I stroke his throbbing member, my teeth catching his lip as the passion of our kiss engulfs us. He sits up, pulling me with him and positioning me to straddle him.

My legs still wrapped around him, I feel the slick head of his cock pressing at my wetness as he grabs my hips and purposefully guides me down onto his shaft. He is pounding into me again and again, as his grip on my hips controls the pace of our movements, forcing me to ride him faster, harder, and deeper. We chase our orgasms together.

The delicious waves course through me as I grind down harder, taking all of him greedily. His breath catches as he finds his own his release, the spasms of his climax shuddering through my core. The strength leaves my body as my climax abates. I sag forward into his arms, not daring to move my hips or legs, wanting him inside me still. Savouring this moment, neither of us moves, and the dying fire throws just enough heat to warm my buttocks and back.

"You're so amazing," I whisper. "This is what I've been missing all these years." At this moment I feel a flood of warm emotion and gratitude toward Sebastian. *Could this be love?*

"You're pretty amazing too, Mrs. Dove," he murmurs as he plants a gentle kiss on my forehead. He strokes my hair as he holds me.

I've longed for this for so long, fantasising and

imagining how good sex could be. I feel almost drunk with contentment right now. Our breathing steadies. My eyes are heavy as I listen to the faint ticking of the grandfather clock mirroring Sebastian's heartbeat and breathing. It lulls me.

My eyes lazily adjust to the growing darkness of the room as the fire fizzles out. *And then I see her.*

# Chapter 16

A shadow at first, it could be the failing light playing tricks on my eyes. But then the shadow moves, the shape of a woman, I'm certain. It moves from its position by the long heavy drapes at the mullioned window and glides silently toward the door. My breath catches.

I sit up and my eyes are wide now, trying desperately to focus. The doorway is more illuminated with the light from the hallway casting sufficient yellow glow upon the shadow to reveal it is not a ghost. It was *her*—Scarlett.

"Oh my God." I gasp. "Scarlett was right here *watching us!*"

His body stiffens. "Where?" he asks, and I detect just a hint of annoyance in his voice, but certainly not the shock that unnerves me.

"Over by the window, she must have been watching us the whole time. When I saw her, she left."

"Don't be ridiculous, Elizabeth," he scoffs. "Why the hell would Scarlett be watching us? Anyway, so what if she was?"

*So what?* Is this another, freaky normality in this house? Voyeurism certainly is not normal, in my humble opinion. I'm furious suddenly, and I want answers from her, as it's painfully obvious that none shall be forthcoming from him.

"I'm sorry, Sebastian, it may be perfectly acceptable to you but not to me. I'm going to ask her what the hell she was doing spying on us."

I get up quickly, pulling my robe tightly around me. I tie the belt firmly, and leave before he has the opportunity to stop me. I exit the great hall and make my way to the kitchen. When I enter, the room is empty.

Instinct takes me to Sebastian's study, and I find the door ajar. I can hear him moving around in the great hall, and imagine that he's hastily putting on his clothes and is sure to follow me. I move through the doorway, which hides the steps to the basement and, flicking the light switch on, begin my descent.

Scarlett's door is closed but I don't bother knocking. I firmly twist the handle and open the door, to find her at the dressing table brushing her long dark hair. She turns as I enter her room, her rosebud lips pursed at the intrusion. "Excuse me, don't you ever knock?" she asks indignantly.

"No, I don't bloody well knock, and I hardly think *you* should be questioning me so bloody huffily, when you just spied on us having sex!" I reply, rage turning my cheeks red now, my hands firm on my hips in a challenging stance.

"Believe me, *Elizabeth,* you've a lot to learn if you find that so disconcerting," she retorts and continues languidly brushing her glossy locks.

"What the hell's that supposed to mean?" I screech. She' still brushing, and I'm tempted to rip out a handful of her lustrous dark hair at this point.

"What exactly upset you? Was it the fact you were watched, or the fact that you were watched doing things you haven't done before?"

I'm horrified by her insolence, but she continues. "Because it seems to me, Elizabeth, that you're ashamed and truly, you have nothing to be ashamed about. It's all perfectly natural."

I take a step back, trying to comprehend what she's saying to me.

"It's *not* natural, Scarlett. To watch two people having sex is absolutely not natural, and I don't think Sebastian is happy at all about you watching us."

"Oh? I think you'll find he's fine about it, Elizabeth. Why don't you ask him?" The blatantly disrespectful harlot has gone too far, and I intend to see to it that he dismisses her ass immediately.

"Ask me what?" Sebastian stands in the doorway, one arm resting on the frame and the other stroking his chin, his expression unreadable. I spin around and beseech him to take action against the tramp.

"She admits spying on us, Sebastian! You have to fire her," I exclaim in exasperation, ignoring his question. His eyes are on hers I notice, not mine, and I click my fingers at him impatiently to snap his attention back to me.

"Admits it, hmm?" He turns his gaze to me now. "Some people find it rather erotic being watched. Does that not turn you on?" he asks, his eyebrow arched awaiting my reply. I'm speechless.

"*Hello?* Am I the only person here who has a sense of decency?" my high-pitched voice enquires, my eyes darting from him to her. Neither of them shows any sign of remorse. Each has a smile on their lips, a *knowing* smile as if they're part of a club and I'm the outsider, not party to some secret handshake or coded language.

Scarlett sighs, puts her hairbrush down on her dressing table, and rises. She's wearing a sheer white night dress made of delicate tulle, the thin straps barely supporting the floaty garment. I can see the dark shadow of her nipples through the fabric, the outline of her slim figure silhouetted by the lamp on her nightstand. She's an ethereal beauty. I feel sure Sebastian has noticed her near nudity.

"Come, Elizabeth." He proffers his hand toward me but I ignore it, shooting him a disdainful glare. I want him to object and hiss at her but instead he continues to hold out his hand to me. He's staring at Scarlett, and at that moment I'm sure that they are still lovers, and it sickens me to my core. Scarlett steps toward me and she, too, reaches out for me. I'm between them both. Each is reaching for me and yet I trust neither. I back away from both, until I feel the cold metal of her bed frame behind my knees.

She reaches me, where I stand, and her arms encircling me. She embraces my rigid body, rendered immobile by the shock of her audacity. Her lips close to my ears, her warm breath against my neck, she whispers, "Everything's fine, sweet girl, you have nothing to worry about. You're here where you belong." She releases me from her embrace and pads barefoot to Sebastian's side where they both regard me with matching smirks. "I think we'll be good friends, Elizabeth. We've a lot in common, more than you think," she says.

"Okay, I get it," I snarl. "It's still going on, isn't it?" I look from one to the other but neither seems to be willing to explain anything to me. Then Sebastian moves toward me and takes my hand, pulling me down with him to sit on the side of the bed. He looks up at Scarlett, and I notice the coldness in her expression as she eyes Sebastian's arm around my waist protectively. She averts her eyes from his.

"I'd rather eat my own eyeballs than be friends with you, lady," I hiss at Scarlett.

Scarlett sighs resignedly. "You need to lighten up. You really do not want to make an enemy of me, trust me."

"Is that a threat?" I yell, harnessing the last remnants of self-control so as not to slap her smug face.

"Enough, you two," he barks sharply. "Leave us, Scarlett. I want to talk to Elizabeth in private."

"Yes, Sir. If you need me, I'll be in the kitchen. I'll make cocoa." She closes the bedroom door behind her, and we're alone.

I chew my lip nervously, unexpectedly self-conscious in his presence, angry and hurt too. I am insanely jealous of the bond the two of them clearly share.

"I want to know," I declare. "If you and Scarlett still sleep together, then I have a right to know, though how you manage to maintain the charade of employer, I have no idea. It's just plain weird, Sebastian, weird and wrong." He's still clutching my hand in his and when I try to withdraw it, he increases his grip.

"We don't sleep together, Elizabeth, I promise you that," he says quietly.

"I don't believe you," I whisper, tears pricking my eyes as my dreams are shattered, as the brutal reality of his betrayal crushes my heart. Then the anger boils within me. "No, I get it. God, I'm stupid. You have free sex with me. Hell, it's probably a novelty for you not to have to pay for it. Shit, I'm so stupid, men are all the same. Why did I think you'd be different?"

He places a finger across my lips to hush me, and turns my chin so that he's looking into my watery eyes. "It's not like that, Elizabeth, and you'll see that if you give me...us...a chance. This isn't about me, it's about *you*. You've been goodness knows how many years living a frigid and suppressed existence and what you'll find here is the panacea to your discontent. You've so many insecurities. Fuck, what has he done to you? You see only the darkness, never the light."

He wipes away the tears, which roll down my cheek, but I flinch at his touch, confused at his aptitude for turning the tables so intuitively, when I am still mad at him.

"I want to unlock your deepest desires and release your inhibitions and frustration, my darling. Think of your time here with me as your time to be who you want to be. No one here will judge you or disapprove of anything you do or say. Equally, you must afford the same courtesy to me, to live as I please and be who I am, without judging me or thinking you can change me. You *have* to trust me. Everything I do, or ask you to do, is in your best interests. Do you trust me?"

"I don't know. I want to, but it's all so far removed from my normal life. To lose control, like you want me to, is so alien to me. I need time. Shit, I am jealous of *her.* You have to understand I've no self-confidence anymore. I doubt myself all the time. Why the hell are you with me?"

He pauses while he digests what I've said to him. "You're my girlfriend, Elizabeth, my *love*. I'll take care of you and the children, and I'll allow you to experience things you've never even fantasised about. You can pass your fears, your insecurities to me to shoulder them for you, and the *real* Elizabeth can be free and unburdened. Now, isn't that tempting?" It is tempting, so enticing, but so wrong. He seems to know exactly how to tap into my psyche, to extract my weaknesses and vulnerabilities and lay them bare in front of me. I find myself aroused by his offer, like Eve wanting to take a bite of the forbidden fruit, aware of the dire consequences, but giving in to temptation regardless.

I've always been one to push boundaries and take risks, never dwelling on the consequences of my actions, nor analysing potential pitfalls prior to choosing a path to follow. It doesn't surprise me how easily I push aside the oddities of this house. My inner she-devil is awakening after a seventeen- year hibernation, and I'm sure there is little that can stop her.

"I don't want to be jealous about Scarlett. What you do when I'm not here is up to you but when I am here, you are only with me. Understood?" *What on earth am I suggesting? It will never be all right for him to be with her, under any circumstances.*

"Only you," he soothes. "There is only you. Anything Scarlett and I shared was superficial and short-lived. I've told you this before. She's a vulnerable girl and sometimes her expectations and romanticism needs to be tempered, and I will do so. She's not a threat to us, Elizabeth."

"She needs to be reminded to respect our privacy. You and she may think it's okay to do all manner of things, but I'm not like that."

He strokes my back in comforting circular movements. His deep hazel eyes are unflinching as he stares into my soul. "We just live a more liberal lifestyle here. Don't judge us. Just know how I feel about you."

"It's bloody perverse, though," I counter. He shakes his head in apparent exasperation before leading me from Scarlett's bedroom.

There is so very much to absorb and think about, but right now, I am exhausted. I'll think about all this evening's weirdness in the morning. It's Christmas Eve and I want my children to have a happy day tomorrow.

# Chapter 17

Christmas morning has dawned. It's a magical vista from the house this morning. It's a bright crisp day, a heavy overnight frost glistens across the expansive grounds, and a scattering of deer stand majestically, like reindeer, across the paddocks.

I wake a sleepy Bella at nine, by which time Joe is excited enough to combust. Scarlett is already busily peeling vegetables by the time we all gather in the kitchen. She and I work together, preparing breakfast of smoked salmon and deliciously creamy scrambled eggs. Neither of us mentions our altercation, and she is particularly friendly toward me.

Certain that her motives are disingenuous, I remain cautious, but refuse to allow her to dampen my high spirits. We all breakfast together, seated around the kitchen table, the children guessing what their gifts may be. I feel more excited than the children. Even when they were tiny, I would be the first to wake, banging noisily about the house to wake them so we could open our presents. Alan was never one for Christmas, preferring to slope off to the pub for a late morning whisky than to share in the festivities.

The Christmas tree which Sebastian bought yesterday gives off a wonderfully fragrant pine scent and the tiny coloured lights twinkle on its branches. At the base of the tree, which sits next to the fireplace in the great hall, is a small mountain of brightly wrapped gifts. I have placed my gifts to Sebastian and the children at the back of the pile, so the children don't snoop.

Scarlett has already put the enormous free-range turkey into the oven to slowly roast, and the aroma from the kitchen is divine.

Mother calls after breakfast and the children and I chat excitedly to her, and end the call wishing her and my aunt a very merry Christmas. I tell her I miss her dreadfully but that we are all having a wonderful time. I make a mental note to spoil her next year to make up for being absent this holiday season.

Next I call Ruth, who is bursting with questions as to how Sebastian and I are getting along. It's difficult to talk openly as the children are beside me but I tell her everything is wonderful and we exchange festive wishes. When I end the call I pass the phone to Bella, and ask her to call her father.

Alan is spending Christmas with Mike. I feel incredibly guilty that our family is apart this year, and wonder how he is coping without the children today. It must be painful for him. He answers his phone immediately and he and Bella chat for a few minutes before she passes the phone to Joe. Alan is obviously quizzing Joe to ascertain where we are, and who we are with, but Joe is far too keen to get on with present opening to talk for long, and he thrusts the phone to me before running off to the great hall.

"Merry Christmas, Alan," I say cheerily. "The kids are

fine and having a great time."

I can hear the hatred in his voice as he replies curtly, informing me that he has nothing to say to me other than he wishes to collect the children on the twenty-seventh of December, which is typical of Alan. I had already agreed with him that Bella and Joe would be with me until New Year's Eve, but there's little point antagonising him more. I will have to curtail my wonderful break with Sebastian, but it really would anger Alan if he knew the children and I were here with another man.

As far as Alan is concerned, we are staying with Ruth for Christmas, and I have already primed the children to back up that story, terrible though it is to make them lie. Not that it's any of Alan's concern, but I want the divorce to go smoothly and uncontested. My life is stressful enough, plus I want to avoid expensive lawyers' fees. Alan ends the call having gained agreement that he will collect the children at four o'clock on the twenty-seventh.

Sebastian is clearly disappointed that we will be leaving early, but we agree not to let it spoil a wonderful Christmas Day.

We open our presents by the fire in the morning room, where Joe has placed small piles of gifts and tells us where to sit, next to our respective present pile. It's such a beautiful room, with golden yellow silk walls, and drapes of matching yellow silk, embroidered with Chinese flowers and birds. Small gold glitter reindeer thread along the mantel and a huge bowl of glitter encrusted fir cones stands by the fireside, with tiny twinkling white lights twisted around each cone.

Joe and Bella are delighted with their gifts. Sebastian gives Joe a remote controlled car, which is soon whizzing around the vast floors of the hallways. Bella unwraps an expensive new outfit by a London designer. Scarlett picked it out online, she tells Bella. *Don't let it wind you up, Beth,* I tell myself.

Sebastian places a long, flat, red velvet box in my hands. Opening it slowly, I squeal with delight at the beautiful gold watch within. "Sebastian!" I gasp. "It's too much."

"Nonsense," he replies. "Nothing is too much for my girl." He places the delicate timepiece on my left wrist and closes the clasp. It's an exquisite Cartier timepiece with a circlet of diamonds framing the dial. It must have cost a small fortune. He grins like a schoolboy, clearly delighted with my reaction to his generous gift.

"Thank you, darling. I adore it and will wear it always." I kiss him hard on his mouth until the children cry, "Eww!"

Placing a small black box in his hand, I whisper, "Merry Christmas, darling Sebastian." His eyes light up brighter than the tree, and I picture him, here in this room as a boy on Christmas Day. I wonder if he was as happy then as he seems now.

Opening the box, he breathes, "Wow," as he slips the silver cufflinks into his palm.

"See the engraving?" I ask, pointing at the intricately turned letter engraved on each of the circular discs. "S and

E. Do you see the tiny heart entwined under each of the letters?"

"I do, darling. Thank you. I will treasure them." We gross the children out again with our kisses.

Present opening complete, we feast on turkey and all the trimmings at the sumptuously laid table in the great hall. Scarlett joins us, which perturbs me, but she's good company although laughing a little too raucously at Sebastian's jokes. She chats animatedly with Bella about fashion and music.

The afternoon is spent playing parlour games and it's refreshingly wonderful to see the children laughing. Sebastian is the perfect host. Later, as we curl up in bed after midnight, I feel content.

"Have you had a good Christmas, Mrs. Dove?" he asks.

"In the circumstances, yes, thank you. It's been wonderful." I kiss his cheek.

"Are we okay?" he asks tentatively.

"We have a lot of issues to overcome, Sebastian. I don't want to spoil today, though."

He strokes my hair. "Hey, I have another Christmas present for you."

"But you've given me the beautiful watch," I protest.

He reaches to the nightstand and pulls open the drawer, retrieving a small black velvet box tied with gold ribbon, and places it in my hand. Enthralled, I eagerly pull the ribbon and open the box. Inside is a breath-taking ring of platinum with two tiny hearts entwined, a sapphire at the centre of each heart, which are the palest blue like glacial ice. Sebastian takes it from the box and places it on the ring finger of my right hand.

"Sebastian, it's beautiful. We both gave each other hearts." I gasp.

"It's not a match for your beauty, darling. The blue of the sapphires is the palest and rarest, the colour of your eyes." Those blue eyes are filled with tears.

"This is the nicest thing anyone has ever done for me. The most precious gift, thank you."

"You are mine, Elizabeth. Always mine and only mine."

"Yes, always yours. This means so much to me, Sebastian." A tear rolls down my cheek, and he brushes it away tenderly.

As I admire the beautiful ring, Sebastian moves the hair from my neck and plants feather light kisses from my earlobe to my shoulder. As tremors course through my body, I give myself to him completely.

***

It's time to leave and, with a heavy heart, I call the children while Sebastian puts our cases in the trunk.

He pulls me into his arms and we kiss deeply, passionately. I can feel hot tears prick my eyes, and I don't want to go. I am going to miss Sebastian and Penmorrow, but I don't anticipate missing Scarlett.

I do hate leaving them both alone together. A knot of pain forms in my stomach.

"Don't cry, Elizabeth. It's been truly wonderful

having you and the children here. It feels as though you belong here. Come back to me soon, won't you?" He wipes my tears away, and his eyes crinkle with an adoring smile.

I kiss him lightly and force a smile in return. "You won't be able to stop me. I've so loved being with you, Sebastian. I miss you already!"

The children come running out of the house across the gravel driveway and Joe throws his arms around Sebastian, who sweeps him up and spins him around before tousling his hair.

"Hey big guy." Sebastian looks down at Joe. "You look after your old mum, okay?"

"Not so much of the *old*," I protest.

Sebastian turns to Bella who seems to have really taken to him, which is rare for my moody teenage daughter. He clutches her in a tight embrace and kisses her forehead affectionately. She blushes.

"Bella Belle." He sighs tenderly. "Remember to watch that smart mouth of yours, young lady, and I hope to see you again really soon."

"Yeah, whatever." She laughs, and as she gets into the car she blows him a kiss and another for Scarlett who has joined Sebastian to say farewell.

"Drive safely, darling," he tells me. "Call me when you get home, and I'll try and drive up next week. Oh, and Happy New Year! I'm sure next year will be *your* year."

He kisses me again, and after I hug Scarlett, I get into

the car and we set off down the tree-lined drive.

I can see them both waving, and a twinge of jealousy passes through me at the closeness they share. The knot tightens in my stomach. I have a long journey ahead, and enough time to dwell on this but also to consider how refreshingly different Sebastian is, and how much I adore him already. Plus, the sex is incredible. I had no idea what a whore I could be!

# Chapter 18

Bella is in a cantankerous mood today, adamant that she does not want to go to stay with Alan at Mike's house. I am losing patience with her.

"You *are* going and that's that! Remember, your father hasn't seen you since before Christmas. Try to give some thought for others, Bella, instead of yourself."

"Get lost, Mum. If he wasn't such a bloody loser, he'd still be living here!"

I slap her face. She catches her breath and puts her hand to her reddening cheek, her eyes brimming with hot tears.

"I *HATE* you," she screams as she runs out of the kitchen, taking the stairs two at a time. She slams her bedroom door behind her.

I switch on the kettle, still fuming but feeling guilty for striking her. I haven't hit her since she was three, and that was a tap on the back of her legs when she threw a terracotta flowerpot at me. She's always been feisty. Takes after me, Alan always said.

Bringing my steaming coffee into the lounge, I check Joe's bag again to make sure he has enough clothes for his stay with Alan. I call up to him to bring down his trainers and another pair of socks, and I hear one of the children running down the stairs. As I reach the door to the hallway, I see Bella, coat on and bag slung over her shoulder, heading toward the front door.

"Where the hell are you going?" I demand.

"I'm going to stay with Chloe from school. It's all arranged, and you can't stop me. I've got my phone and money and I'll be back the day after tomorrow." She slams out of the front door before I can protest or stop her. I throw open the door but she's sprinting up the road and disappears around the corner. I know I have to let her go. I text her immediately and tell her I am sorry for slapping her, I love her, and I ask her to text me when she gets to Chloe's house which I recall is only half a mile away. She doesn't reply.

Alan arrives thirty minutes late, and Joe is pacing the hall impatiently waiting for his father. Alan pushes past me and enters the house. I can smell whisky on his breath.

"Hello, Alan. Did you have a nice Christmas?" I foolishly ask.

"Bloody great," he replies sarcastically. "C'mon, Joe. Get your bag, son. Where's Bella?"

"She's gone off to stay with Chloe. Sorry, but you know how she can be. You...you've been drinking, Alan. I don't think you should be driving, especially with Joe."

He looks contemptuously at me, although I notice his eyes don't focus on mine properly. How much has the man had? I feel panicky, sure now that I don't want Joe in a car with him while he is clearly smashed.

"Look, I'll make you a coffee. Stay and have a bite to eat and then leave a little later," I suggest. His face is full of loathing, and his speech is slurring.

"Typical, so you've poishoned my daughter now. Get

in the car, Joe, itsh unlocked. Beth, you have no bloody right to tchell me what I can and fucking can't do, so leave it."

Joe looks from Alan to me, and at Alan again, unsure which parent to obey. His brow creases as the volatility of the situation upsets him, and his eyes brim with tears. He gauges his father's anger to be more acute and decides to do as his father says rather than antagonise him more. He picks up his bag, and reaches up to kiss me goodbye.

"Joe, put your bag down and go to your room," I order. "Everything's fine. Your dad and I need to talk." Joe does as I ask, red faced with tears tumbling down his cheeks. He turns to go upstairs but Alan grabs his arm.

"Get in the car, now!" he barks.

Alan picks up Joe's bag, and I try to snatch it away from him. I'm overwhelmed with the sudden need to protect my son, my instincts screaming through every cell of my body. Alan shoves my chest, and I stumble back, falling against the hard edge of the stair bannister, knocking the wind out of me.

"Alan, for God's sake!" I shriek, but he seems like a different person—a man I don't know, not the man I've been married to for seventeen years. Joe is sobbing now, and the next thirty seconds are a blur.

Alan pushes Joe through the open doorway and up the pathway, his bag clutched in his hand. I see them but am powerless to stop them. My desolate boy, shoulders heaving as he cries, is jostled into the passenger seat of Alan's car. I hear the screeching of tires as Alan speeds away. I'm sobbing, huge wracking sobs, which come from my core.

Hands shaking, I dial my mother's number, and when she answers I can barely speak. I have a terrible dark foreboding, which I can't rationalise, but my mother will understand. Only a mother can understand. She soothes me and tells me she is on her way.

***

Call twenty-seven. There's still no answer, just Alan's voicemail message.

*"Hi, you've reached the voicemail of Alan Dove. I'm sorry I can't take your call, but leave a message. Cheers."*

I try Mike's mobile and landline numbers again, and am about to hang up when he answers.

"Mike, thank God. Look, Alan picked Joe up nearly two hours ago and he was drunk. I know he's probably stopped off for something to eat, but I'm worried. He was pissed again."

"He's not here, Beth. Did you two fight?"

"Yes. But only because I wouldn't let him drive Joe when he'd been drinking. He reeked of booze, Mike. Look, can you call me the minute they get there, please?" I end the call.

My mother calls the accident and emergency department at the local hospital, but thankfully they've had no traffic accident victims admitted this evening. I try

Bella's mobile number, wondering if Joe or Alan have been in touch with her, but she curtly replies she hasn't seen or heard from Alan and doesn't care if she never sees him again, 'the dick.'

I waste no time admonishing her. Instead, I decide to drive to Mike's house in case Alan and Joe have arrived. As I grab my coat from the hook by the front door, my mobile phone rings. It's Mike.

"Beth, love, there's been a terrible accident."

# Chapter 19

Mum holds my hand as we sit in the family room of the Accident and Emergency Department at The Lakes General Hospital. It's a stark little room with peach walls, 1980s floral border and pastel striped curtains. Mum and I sit together on the hard green sofa. A plastic cup of water has been thoughtfully placed on the battered old teak coffee table in front of me, next to the obligatory box of tissues and untactful leaflets on becoming an organ donor. I take a tissue from the box and blow my nose, my cheeks hot with fresh tears.

It's been forty minutes now and there is still no news of Alan and Joe. All we know so far is that Alan's car collided with a tree, and it took the fire crew over an hour to cut Alan and Joe free. It took paramedics another twenty minutes to stabilise both prior to the journey to hospital. The emergency helicopter could not be diverted, due to it already attending an accident near Dorchester. All this information serves to increase my sense of panic at the severity of their condition.

My phone pings and I look at the text message on the screen. It's Sebastian, wondering why I haven't called him to say I arrived home safely. I type a brief message back telling him about the accident, that I will call him later. My phone immediately vibrates as Sebastian calls me. I leave the room to answer, but a nurse shoots a disapproving look at me, so I exit through the automatic doors to the ambulance loading area and burst into tears when I hear Sebastian's voice.

He has such a soothing, calming tone as he assures me that the doctors will be doing all they can to help my boy, and he's certain Joe will pull through, as he's such a tough little guy. Sebastian sounds genuinely concerned, and choked up too, and I am so grateful for his support. I long to feel his strong protective arms around me. Just listening to his comforting voice makes me calmer, and he tells me he is on his way to me.

"Beth!" My mother bursts through the automatic doors and grabs my arm. "The doctor is looking for you, *come on!*"

I cut the call without saying goodbye, thrust the phone in my coat pocket, and follow Mum back in to the family room where a tall, wiry doctor dressed in blue scrubs is waiting for me. He tells me to sit down, and I want to scream.

"Joe?" My voice is barely audible.

"Mrs. Dove. Beth. My name is Doctor David Sutherland. I'm the registrar on duty, and I've been leading the team looking after your son and your husband. As you know, Joe and Alan were in a very bad way when they arrived here. Each had a Glasgow Coma Score of just three. This means that, in essence, their brains were not functioning. You must understand they were both in the front seats of the car and both took the full force of the impact head-on. I only say this so that you understand how difficult it has been to try to reverse the damage that was done. I have to tell you, Beth, with deep regret, that we have not been able to save either Joe or Alan."

My mother wails from somewhere in this cold miserable little room. I can't absorb what the doctor is saying to me. The room starts to spin and I hold on to my mother's arm to steady myself.

"Immediate CT scans showed considerable fracturing of the skull in Joe, and unfortunately Alan sustained a ruptured aorta on impact. Neither will have been in any pain. Mrs. Dove, Beth, I and my team are so very sorry for your loss."

My world falls apart.

# Dark Bonds

## Janey Rosen

# Chapter 1

Deep inside me a fierce torrent of bubbling, salty sea is rising from my belly, like a tsunami within my core. It is crashing through my chest, into my throat and it spews forth from my lips as a gurgling, explosive scream. I scream again but this time no sounds comes forth, the tide has ebbed and all that is left is the taste of the salt. I realise the salt is vomit and a nurse is holding a cardboard bowl under my chin while she strokes my back, comforting me. But there will never be any comfort in my world again.

I gently hold my son's limp hand in mine. It's a tiny white hand, icy cold, the fingernails a blue grey. *I need to clip his nails. They are too long; he'll be in trouble at school with nails like those and I don't want the teachers to think I'm not a good mum. Yes, I need to clip those nails.* I gaze at his face but it's not the face I know. It's not my son, and yet they tell me this lifeless shell is my boy. He's swollen, all of his face is puffy and blotchy and he's so very cold. I need to keep him warm, so I climb onto the narrow bed beside him and wrap my body over his, my arms tightly around him and my leg across his small body. He still feels icy cold. I stroke his matted, crusted hair and sing him the lullaby I used to sing to him when he was small.

> *Little man is tired he's had a busy day. And now it's time for him to go to sleep,*
> *So pack up all your worries,*
> *Little man has had a busy day.*

This time, when I sing to him, he doesn't giggle and snuggle down under the duvet. Instead he lies still and cold under the crisp white sheet and my mother is telling me to stop, that I have to let him go, kiss him goodbye. But he's already asleep, I tell her. We have to be very quiet because he's exhausted and needs his rest and then he will get better but my mother is sobbing and saying, "He's *gone*, Beth. He's gone, love."

I close my eyes and see myself in the hospital bed with my baby boy. He is still covered in vernix, and he's crying with his tiny chin quivering. I hold him to my breast, and his hungry cry is hushed as he suckles from me and I wonder at this perfect tiny child in my arms. Then I look down at the tiny infant and instead of his warm pink skin against my breast he's mottled and dead and the salty tide is swelling inside me again.

It takes the nurses and my exhausted mother three hours to part me from my son. I want to see Alan, I tell them. They say it's not a good idea, but I shake free of their hands and their sympathy and run from room to room until I find him alone behind the final curtain. He's just a shape beneath a white sheet but I know it's him. I'm shocked and sickened when I pull back the sheet to reveal the broken shell of my husband, but pity and sorrow gives way to the stronger beast within me. *Fury*. As I stand beside his fractured body looking down on this man, I want to kill him. If he wasn't already dead I would kill him with my bare hands—*a life for a life*. His life for my son's.

I'm shaking now, violent shudders over which I have no control and my hand takes on a life of its own, avenging Joe for what this man did to him. I strike Alan. It's not my hand now, it's a tool which is working entirely independently of my body as it slaps Alan's distorted face, and it pounds his crushed chest with blows from its tightly clenched fist and a guttural feral roar erupts from my throat. The fist is stopped and I'm grabbed and held and I try to break free so that the fist can continue to mete its punishment, but the arms hold me so tightly I can't move and a voice commands me to stop.

As I regain awareness and self-control, I know that I'm in Sebastian's arms, and my legs give way beneath me. He catches me and lifts me and I'm carried away.

# Chapter 2

Joe and Bella are playing in the sand on the beach, and the sun is shining. Bella is burying Joe up to his neck, and Alan and I are laughing as he wiggles his toes, before Bella can cover them with the sandy pile. The sand turns darker, and it becomes soil and his toes are not wiggling any more. I tell Bella to stop.

*Enough. Let Joe get out now or he'll catch cold in the ground, Bella.* Now the beach is a graveyard, and Alan is putting more soil on Joe's head. I'm running to Joe, but as fast as I run his muddy grave gets farther away, and now Alan's pushing damp soil into Joe's mouth and he can't breath and I can't run any faster.

I wake up sweating and panicking, trying to adjust my eyes to the bright daylight which fills the room. Sebastian is beside me stroking my hair and hushing me, telling me it was a bad dream, everything's okay. But it's not okay. My son is gone, and so is Alan whom I miss, love, and despise all in equal measure.

My mother appears in the doorway to my bedroom and lays a tray on my bedside table. "Try a little porridge, Beth dear, please. Just for me, okay?" She looks haggard and spent and I realise I have been selfish not caring for her, and for Bella who both must be hurting dreadfully.

I ask where Bella is and Mum tells me Sebastian went to fetch her. She's here, in her room, but she is in pieces, bless her. I've been dozing, I'm told, since the doctor prescribed a sedative for me and the whole night has passed. My mouth feels dry and my tongue is coated in a foul tasting gunge. I take a mouthful of the porridge and enjoy the comforting warmth from the creamed oats. Then I give my mother a long hard hug and tell her how much I love her and she sobs and tells me she loves me too.

Bella cuts the call on her mobile phone as I enter her room, and we sit on the edge of her bed. I can see she's been crying. Her eyes are red and puffy and scrunched up tissues are strewn about her room. I pull her into my arms and hug her close, afraid to let her go as she sobs against my shoulder.

"Shh, it'll be okay, darling," I soothe, not believing what I tell her. Nothing will ever be okay again.

I pull on jeans and a baggy sweater, not caring about my appearance or my matted hair. Everything, even eating and making conversation, seems a pointless exercise today.

Alan's parents have been to see Alan and Joe at the hospital mortuary, and are coming over at eleven this morning. I dread facing them. How do I console two people who have lost their son and grandson when I am consumed by my own loss and have no capacity to sympathise with others?

Sebastian is sitting in the lounge, in Alan's chair, reading The Times. He jumps to his feet and hugs me tightly when I come downstairs. His face is full of concern for me and I feel so thankful that he is here, but also aware that Alan's parents will be arriving soon and it would be extremely tactless for Sebastian to be here when they arrive. As intuitive as ever, Sebastian picks up his coat and heads off elsewhere for a couple of hours.

Dora walks up the garden path supported by Brian, both looking frail and desolate, followed by Alan's sister Sarah and her husband Nathan—a bleak and forsaken group for whom I feel an overwhelming sense of sorrow and compassion. I meet them on the doorstep and Dora crumbles into my arms followed by a sobbing Sarah. Nathan guides our forlorn huddle into the lounge and goes to the kitchen to make a tray of tea while Brian sits grimly in Alan's armchair. After a few minutes our group regains composure and Nathan returns with a pot of tea, jug of milk, and five mugs and proceeds to pour the steaming brew.

"Sugar, Nathan!" Brian barks. "Hot sweet tea. That's what the doctor ordered. Hot sweet tea for shock."

Nathan nods and returns to the kitchen to retrieve the sugar. We all accept a mug of the compulsory hot sweet tea regardless of whether we take sugar.

"Terrible business, Beth," Brian states glumly. "What I don't understand is why this happened, eh?" He's glaring at me with an expression full of accusation and blame and I can't meet his pained stare.

"Thing of it is, in my view, if you hadn't kicked our boy out he'd be here now with our little Joe instead of… lying on that bloody trolley in that bloody morgue." His voice grows to a shout and startles us all. Dora sobs again.

Nathan, standing next to Brian, puts his hand gently on his father-in-law's shoulder. "Come on, Brian, mate… it's not Beth's fault. She's as cut up about this as the rest of us. Now's not the time."

Brian shrugs off his hand, gets up and walks out of the room. We hear him opening the kitchen door and exiting into the back garden.

Alan's family stays for an hour, until Brian comes back into the house, and informs us all that they're leaving. I have talked with Dora, Sarah, and Nathan about undertakers but Nathan tells us that we have to wait for Alan and Joe to be released for burial as, he says, there will be an autopsy. This news fills me with horror and the knot in my stomach clenches tighter with the dread and pity I feel for my two loved ones who face such an undignified ordeal after all they have been through. We all hug goodbye, except Brian who gives me a curt nod, and we agree to call each other when we hear from the hospital. We will then meet again to agree on funeral arrangements.

Feeling drained and totally spent, I sink down onto the sofa and close my eyes in the darkness. I hear Sebastian return and hear him talking quietly on his mobile phone in the kitchen. "Scarlett you've done well. You'll be rewarded when I return." What's she done that's so incredible?

The next few hours are a blur to me. A Detective Inspector called Pete Chambers and family liaison officer, WPC Laura Viney, visit in the early evening and ask questions about Alan's car. I give them the number of the garage, which maintains our cars and they make notes of everything I tell them, which unnerves me. For some reason they make me feel as though I'm under suspicion for the accident, so I go to great lengths to explain to them the events leading up to the crash.

I tell them about Alan's drinking and his mood swings, our arguments and Alan's departure from our family home. They nod sympathetically and scribble in notebooks but I am glad when they leave. The WPC assures me, as she leaves, that she is there if I need her but it is not yet possible to release Alan or Joe to the family. They will be in touch in due course.

I watch their police car pull away, conscious of the many pairs of net curtains twitching at the windows of the houses opposite ours, and call Sebastian down from upstairs where he has been chatting with Bella until the police leave.

"Darling, I've been thinking, I want you and Bella to come to Penmorrow after the funeral. Scarlett and I can look after you both. Give you some time and space to heal. What do you think?" he asks.

I'm sitting next to him at the breakfast table and I place my hand gently on his knee. "You're so thoughtful, Sebastian. What would Bella and I do without you? I'm just not sure that's a good idea, though. Bella needs to be near her friends and I don't want to leave Mum at the moment. She's devastated. We're all devastated."

His disappointment is palpable and I feel his knee

stiffen beneath my hand.

"Why don't we take it one day at a time and see how things are after the...after the funeral?" I say, tears stinging my eyes once more, and Sebastian drops the subject.

It is the third telephone call of the day. Still the obstreperous woman in the General Office at the hospital will not confirm if the autopsy has been completed, nor when it was likely that my chosen undertaker—the aptly named Heart Brothers—will be able to collect Alan or Joe. I slam the phone down in frustration. Dora is sure to call again this afternoon, and I'll have to listen to her telling me it's now six days since the accident and how it all seems very suspicious to her and Brian.

***

As every day passes, I feel the finger of blame is more firmly pointed in my direction. Brian won't talk to me at all, and the police officer is due to come over again this afternoon. I don't understand why they all seem to blame me. I blame myself enough for everybody. Blame should focus upon my treatment of Alan and our incessant fights. Blame should not focus on my causing the accident. However, in the last twenty-four hours I've also begun to hold myself entirely accountable for Alan's actions, which led to the crash.

If I hadn't been such a bitch, wanting something I couldn't and shouldn't have, been happy and content with my marriage, then Alan wouldn't have been a drinker, and therefore wouldn't have crashed and my baby would be here with me. So would Alan. Could I have lived out the rest of my life with him? I go round in circles, and always conclude that I could not have lived with Alan any longer, but equally I would do anything to bring him back to life.

Sebastian has been wonderful. My rock. He has returned to Cornwall for a few days to attend to matters on his estate and I miss him dreadfully, but life goes on. He has enormous responsibilities, and I'm grateful for the time he's spent with *me* when I needed him so.

At five to four the doorbell chimes and I welcome Detective Inspector Pete Chambers and WPC Laura Viney into my home, hoping my contempt for them is not outwardly apparent. They both have a grave expression on their faces, which increases my anxiety. I seat them at the kitchen table and switch the kettle on.

"Mrs. Dove, thank you for seeing us this afternoon. We realise this is difficult for you," he says without sincerity. "WPC Viney and I have paid a visit to Coldwell Garage. Very helpful mechanic, that Jimmy. Very efficient garage too, I might say. Rare to find a garage which books your next service in even before you've left from your last one."

I'm unsure where he's going with this, so I busy myself making mugs of tea.

"Yes, he says Mr. Dove bought his Ford in three weeks ago for it's MOT and service. Fitted new brake shoes and discs, he says. Checked the steering mount, changed a bald tire, and gave it a damn good check over. Very thorough is Jimmy at Coldwell Garage, Mrs. Dove.

Reassures you, doesn't it, that your car's well cared for and safe, don't you think?"

I see now where he is going with this, and I do not like it one bit. My cheeks are blushing and I spin around on my heels and let him have it, no holds barred. "Just you wait one damn minute!" I bark. "If you're implying there's anything suspicious about my husband's accident, then I will stop you right there! Yes, Alan was particular about his car, bloody anal about it, actually, if you want my opinion. But that doesn't mean he wasn't pissed or that he didn't hit the bloody tree because he was so tanked up with whisky he didn't know what he was doing."

The policeman looks affronted while the WPC shoots him a sideward glance. It is she who speaks next. "Mrs. Dove, Detective Inspector Chambers is not implying any irregularity, but it'd be remiss of us if we didn't investigate the circumstances leading to this tragic accident. It's normal procedure in this type of event to look into all aspects of the deaths, and you wouldn't thank us if we didn't do our jobs properly so that you could have closure, would you?"

I'm speechless.

"Also, Mrs. Dove, the sooner we carry out our enquiries, the sooner you can plan the funerals."

That hits me firmly between the eyes. Until now, I have convinced myself that it was normal red tape and inefficiencies, which was causing the hold up in the release of Alan and Joe. Now the delay takes on a far more sinister aspect. "Do...do you think someone tampered with Alan's car?" I ask hesitantly.

I note that the police officers exchange knowing glances again. Pete Chambers replies. "At this stage, Mrs. Dove, it's not clear. I have to say though that foul play is one consideration at this time, and if that were to be the case, it would be a horse of a different colour. I'm afraid it would be a murder investigation."

I meet his stare, unwilling to look away lest I should seem guilty.

"I see," I reply. "I want to be as helpful as possible. Honestly, though, I can't think of anyone who would want to hurt Alan or my Joe."

"I see," Pete Chambers says, in the most unnerving manner. "I thank you for your offer of help, Mrs. Dove, and we'll be sure to be back in touch with you very soon. Very soon indeed, so don't plan on going anywhere for the time being, okay?"

I nod sullenly and the two officers rise, both leaving their tea untouched.

At the front door, the Detective Inspector turns to me, and says, "If you need to call me, or if you have any information for me, here's my number." Handing me his contact card, he leaves.

# Chapter 3

Day eight. It seems like an eternity since I held Joe in my arms and today I'm going to visit him at the hospital, only I will not be taking a 'get well' balloon or a comic when I visit my son. Instead I shall be taking Joe's favourite Manchester United football shirt and his 'snuggly'—a tatty old teddy which I bought for Bella to give Joe when he was born. Snuggly has sat on Joe's bookshelf for the past three years, because Joe is a big boy now. Was. Too grown up for teddies. Too grown up for the Spiderman toys, cars and trains, which have been boxed up in the attic for the past year. Snuggly needs to be with Joe now, to offer comfort to my frightened boy and the smell of home to replace the antiseptic hospital scent.

Sebastian has driven back up from Cornwall and I am so glad he is coming with me. At the General Office we are guided to a private waiting area while we wait for a staff member to collect us. A short, plump mortuary technician appears in hospital scrubs and shakes our hands. He has a well-practiced empathy and gentle voice. He leads us down to the bowels of the hospital to the mortuary reception area, where he politely asks us to take a seat while he checks if Joe is ready.

I'm gripping Sebastian's hand tightly. He strokes my hair from my eyes with his free hand, then kisses me lightly on the forehead. "Be strong, my darling," he whispers.

The plump technician returns and tells us that Joe is ready, and to follow him. My legs are suddenly leaden, and I find it incredibly difficult to put one foot in front of the other. My mouth is dry and parched, and beads of perspiration are forming on my forehead, and I feel as though I can't breathe. A panic attack.

Sebastian is so in tune with me that he immediately detects my fright and steadies me. "Deep, slow breaths, Elizabeth. Look at me."

I raise my eyes to his and focus on what he is telling me.

"Slowly in and slowly out. Good girl. Now, you can do this, darling. I'm here with you, okay?"

The plump man hands me a paper cup of water and I drain it, then hand the empty cup back. Plump man tosses it into a waste bin and opens a blue door. Sebastian and I follow him down an artificially lit corridor. He opens the second door on the right and I take a deep breath as I enter, clutching Snuggly and the bright football shirt under my arm.

It's a beautiful room, quite out of place in this vast clinical building. The walls are papered with an elegant gold patterned paper and the carpet is a deep blue. There are candles, which I can see are not real flame but battery powered imitations. The soft glow is calming and the gentle piped music almost uplifting. In the centre of the small room lies my son. Asleep.

Joe looks so little, it's hard to believe he's seven years

old, nearly eight. He never will be eight now, of course. I lift his lifeless arm and tuck Snuggly tightly against him under his armpit so that Snuggly's head is looking up at Joe. My son now looks even younger with his worn and much loved little bear tucked up cosily with him. I brush my lips over Joe's hair and kiss his forehead, and he smells clean and fresh but it is a very different smell to the usual aroma of apple shampoo I am used to. I stroke his hair gently, but withdraw my fingers sharply when I touch the ridges and bumps that are now mapped across his scalp.

Sebastian kisses Joe very lightly on his right brow and I see a tear tumble down my lover's cheek. "Sleep well, little guy," he whispers, and I crumble into his arms.

# Chapter 4

Day nine, and I am expecting Detective Inspector Chambers and his sidekick once more. I'm growing weary of their visits and increasingly impatient to have Joe released to me. I'm hopeful that today will be the day this happens.

Ruth is with me and it's good to see my dear friend. She distracts me with humorous tales of our staff's antics and does her very best to bring some cheer to our deathly quiet house while we wait for the police officers' arrival. Sebastian left early this morning for an estate meeting at Penmorrow, with the promise of returning in two days time. I miss him already. I was so was glad when Ruth arrived unannounced this morning. Punctually, at eleven-fifteen, the two police officers arrive.

"Detective Inspector, this is my dear friend and business partner, Ruth Evershaw. Ruth, this is Detective Inspector Chambers and WPC Viney."

They shake hands and I lead us to the lounge, where Ruth sits next to me on the sofa while the two officers take the armchairs.

"Mrs. Dove," the detective says.

"*Beth*," I correct him.

"Beth. Thank you. Can you tell me, please, if either yourself or your husband have ever been prescribed anti-depressants?"

The question takes me by surprise. "We've both been stressed, yes. Not depressed."

"So, neither of you have ever taken, or had possession of, a medicine called Benzodiazepine? It may be a pill called Diazepam, Flurazepam, or Chlordiazepoxide?" He reads from his notebook.

I shake my head. "No. We've never been prescribed any of those medicines to the best of my knowledge."

"That's what your GP says too, but I had to check. You never know these days. People can buy all sorts on the streets if they have a mind to. Benzos aren't as widely used these days because of the contra-indications and side effects but some psychiatrists still prescribe them."

I'm astounded and affronted that the officer has questioned our doctor, but I also know that it's his job to be thorough, and anything that will free my Joe from the hospital is okay by me.

"We've...eh, had the autopsy and toxicology reports back."

I'm filled with trepidation.

DI Chambers reads from his notebook. "It seems your husband took a cocktail of alcohol and pills before he died, Beth. But, although they were a toxic dose, they weren't a lethal dose. In a nutshell, the booze and pills didn't cause the deaths of Alan and Joe, but they would certainly have impaired his reactions and judgment. It seems your husband had a few too many whiskies, managed to get some anti-depressants from somewhere, popped a couple then made the very grave mistake of driving. Where he obtained the pills is a line of enquiry the WPC here will follow up. Can't have those sorts of pills rattling around somewhere, if you get my drift."

I wonder if Mike has such medicine at home, although it seems unlikely, as he's a very jovial man. The officer is studying me, and it unnerves me. "I'm sorry, how rude of me. Would you like a cup of tea or coffee, officers?" I ask, looking from one to the other.

"No, thank you. We won't keep you any longer than necessary," the DI replies, before returning to his notebook.

"Okay," I say quietly. "Will you let me know if and when you find out where he got those pills?"

"Yes, will do," he replies, watching me intensely. "The coroner is releasing the bodies, you'll be relieved to know. There won't be an inquest. He's recording it as accidental death."

This news hits me like a tornado and lifts my spirits swirling high. The relief is immeasurable and I can't hold back the tears. The two police officers exchange glances but, although the detective looks uncomfortable by my emotional outburst, the WPC leans forward and lays a comforting hand on my knee. Ruth puts her arm around my shoulder.

The crucial thing is that we can lay Alan and Joe to rest, and my thoughts turn to the Heart Brothers and the call I must make when the officers leave. "So, that's it?" I ask, dabbing at my eyes with a tissue and blowing my nose. "We can bury them?"

"Yes. That's it for now," he replies. "If we hear anything further, we'll be back in touch."

"Thank you. It means so much that we can lay them to rest."

The officers shake our hands as they leave and, closing the front door behind them, I collapse into Ruth's arms.

When Ruth leaves, I call Dora and Brian to tell them the news, and then Sebastian.

"Beth, what a relief that must be for you." His voice is so soothing.

"It means no more waiting, Sebastian. *Finally,* we can say goodbye to them."

"Would you like me to drive back? I can be there by early evening." I'm touched by his thoughtfulness and support.

"No, darling. Go to your meeting. I'm fine, honestly. It's just so good to hear your voice."

"Yours too. Have you eaten?" he asks, concern in his voice.

"No. I can't eat, my stomach is in knots."

"You must eat," he scolds.

"Yes, Sebastian. I will eat. I miss you."

"I miss you too. Let me know what the arrangements are for the funerals. I'll be there—or not. Whatever you think appropriate."

"Will do. I love you." I blow a kiss down the phone to him.

"Go and eat," he says again, as he cuts the call.

# Chapter 5

It was a beautiful and moving service. I could not speak about Joe or Alan to the congregation as I was too emotional, but Nathan, Ruth, and Mike all said a lovely piece about their lives and there was not a dry eye in the church. Now beside my son's little grave, I'm throwing a yellow rose on Joe's small coffin, and I smile ruefully at the bright red colour of the wood and the Manchester United football club emblem painted on the lid. My little football fan inside, in his red football shirt and black shorts and his freshly cleaned pair of football boots, would be proud. He is clutching his Snuggly and a signed photograph of his football team heroes, thanks to the local *Dorset Standard* newspaper. They reported the accident and Joe's love of the team, and subsequently the club sent the photo with a moving tribute written on the reverse to their number one fan. He would have loved to show that off to his friends at school, some of whom had come today with their parents. It was very moving when the youngsters went to the front of the church with their mothers, and each lit a candle for Joe.

I had asked Sebastian to stay away, but I'm missing him and needing him now more than ever, and it occurs to me that I am becoming increasingly dependent upon him for support and company.

Bella has been so strong, but I'm concerned that she's

not letting her grief run it's natural course. She seems more introverted, and even Chloe seems incapable of getting Bella to talk about her father and brother.

My mother has given me the telephone number of a bereavement counsellor, and I make a mental note to call her tomorrow although I suspect Bella will refuse to open up to a stranger.

It gives me great comfort and strength to have Joe's friends and mine, and Alan's family to our house after the funeral, although it's with a heavy heart that I note Brian's absence. He did not utter a word to me in the church, and the arrangements were left to Dora, Sarah, and I to make without his input. Dora says he just needs time. Part of the grieving process is anger, and when he moves past that stage he will see the accident was not my fault. She confided in me yesterday that she had, for some time, been worried about Alan's drinking and she told me that Brian has always liked his whisky and so did his father before him, so it is a family weakness. Not my fault. Why do I feel so damned guilty, then?

"Beth, love." Mike puts an arm around my waist and kisses my cheek. "You know that I'm always here for you and Bella. Alan would've wanted me to look out for his girls." His eyes are red and puffy. He has always been such a good friend to Alan and I.

We are joined by Robert, who used to work with Alan until recent months. Robert tells me he's so very sorry for my loss, and I squeeze his arm and tell him that Alan always talked very highly of him. "Don't know why you two didn't work out, Beth. I guess we all do things, meet new people who we think are going offer us more. Then, you know, the grass isn't greener and all that…"

I'm at a loss to understand what Robert is trying to say to me, and I presume the red wine he's sipping is fogging his brain.

"She was a looker all right, Beth, but not a patch on you, love. He loved you, ya know. Not her, he didn't love her."

I will not calm down. Mike is scratching incessantly at the back of his neck and shrugging, trying to tell me that he has no idea what Robert was referring to. Or whom. Everyone has gone home now but I have demanded that Mike stay behind so I can quiz him further.

"She was a looker. He loved me, but he didn't love her. Who, Mike, who?" I demand, despite the hypocrisy of the situation. After all, I was seeing Sebastian. But that is not the point here. I'm being blamed for Alan leaving, and yet it seems he was enjoying liaisons of his own with another woman.

"Okay, look, he started seeing someone. I only saw her once, Beth, honestly. I don't know how they met, but she picked him up from the house once, in a big four-by-four car and I could see she wasn't at all his type. Younger, you know? Bit flighty and provocatively dressed."

I have heard enough. After the emotions of today, all I want to do is fall into bed and block out the images I now have in my head of my dead husband's betrayal.

# Chapter 6

The last few weeks have been the worst of my life. I can't seem to concentrate on my business, and I'm growing tired of the pitied expressions on my staff's faces at work. One very positive piece of news is that Alan's life insurance company has agreed to pay out on his life policy. This means that in excess of one hundred thousand pounds will be arriving in my bank account some day soon.

It's a cool, crisp Friday morning in late April and I'm at work, busying myself with monthly management accounts. My mind frequently wanders to thoughts of Sebastian and of the wonderful weekends we spend together. In just a few short hours, he'll be arriving, waiting for me after work. He's spent a couple of weekends with Bella and I in Dorset.

I have not been to Penmorrow since Christmas, and that seems a lifetime ago. It just seems easier for him to drive to us, than for Bella and I to face the long journey to Cornwall. Recalling our weekends together leads me to daydream once again about our passionate nights. When I close my eyes I can feel the feather light touch of his fingertips on my skin.

"Hey, you!" Ruth bounds into my office with her insurmountable energy and I blush deeply, hoping she doesn't notice. "I have a fantastic suggestion and you simply must say yes." She has my attention. "With the insurance payment, I want you to take a few months off work. Get entirely away from the business, Beth, and let me run it. You know I am more than capable, so I really want you to bugger off," she teases.

"Where would we go, Bella and I, if we did clear off somewhere?" I ask. The idea of taking a holiday without Alan or Joe was not something I could entertain, and to go away with Sebastian would be incredibly insensitive for Alan's parents and sister, so soon after the accident.

Ruth raises her eyebrow the irritating way she does when she wants to say something but doesn't dare. "It's just a thought, Beth, but why don't you take Bella to Cornwall?" The resulting expression on my face shows the shock and surprise at Ruth's suggestion. "Hear me out," she continues. "You and Sebastian get on really well, he's been a rock for you these past few weeks. I imagine it's pretty laid back down in the sticks and you could do with the company. Why don't you take up painting or rambling or whatever they do down there. Just go away and forget about the business, take some you time."

I shake my head incredulously. She makes it sound so easy, so simple to run away to Penmorrow, but I know how difficult it will inevitably be to convince Bella to leave her friends and come away with me. Although, she has become close to Sebastian and he clearly cares for her. Some time in the country may not be such a ludicrous idea after all. I have missed that old house. I have even missed Scarlett, who sent a beautiful card to Bella and I after the accident.

"You know what, Ruth, my darling friend, perhaps we will go. You must promise to call me regularly and let me know of any problems at work. And don't make any big decisions without me!" We hug, and I'm so thankful for Ruth's friendship. Now I need to think through the plan, and decide how best to approach this decision with Bella.

My mobile phone pings. I glance at the screen and see the first two lines of the message.

*Hi sexy Rosie. You never did call me. How about that 2nd date? Si*

*Oh shit!* I thought he'd taken the hint weeks ago. So much has happened since Simon and I spent an illicit afternoon together, and his message is not welcome. I decide not to reply in the hope that he takes the hint.

***

My packed lunch is open on my desk and I'm busily studying financial information while munching on a chicken sandwich, when my office door opens. "Have you got lunch, Ruth?" I ask without looking up.

"Oh, I've got a feast, Elizabeth." Sebastian leans against the doorframe, arms crossed, drinking me in.

"Sebastian!" Leaping up from my chair, I throw myself into his muscular arms. "Why didn't you call and say you'd be arriving early?" It's *so* wonderful to see him. He kisses my hair and hugs me tightly, not wanting to let me free of his embrace.

"I wanted to surprise my girl. Good to see you're eating for a change," he remarks, as he lifts my chin and gazes into my eyes with a dark, sultry stare. "Plus, I wanted to check up on my investment." Pushing me back at arm's length, he eyes my body with an appreciative sigh and a dangerous look in his eyes.

"Fine," I say haughtily, cocking my eyebrow. "The figures are on my desk."

"Are they, Mrs. Dove? First I'd like to check the figure in front of me. Turn around." I do as he asks, giggling, feeling the sexual charge between us.

His hands slip around my waist, and he pulls me close, my back snug against his front. His waiting erection presses into the small of my back. Grinding my ass harder against him teasingly, he sucks in his breath and cups my breast. "Be very careful, Elizabeth or I may be forced to take action against you which could be construed as sexual harassment," he warns, his voice raspy and sexy.

"I have *no* idea to what you're referring." My innocent butter-wouldn't-melt reply earns me a hard slap on the buttock. "Sebastian. Someone might see us." Aware that my gossip-hungry staff would relish our sideshow, I push the door closed and sit down at my desk.

He perches on the edge of my desk, arms folded, and I can't take my eyes off the vast erection straining against the fly of his trousers. "Eyes on the figures, Mrs. Dove," he says sternly, tapping his finger on the papers beside him.

I reach across to his thigh and my eager fingers trail

up to his rock hard penis, my hand massaging him through the fabric. He's so ready for me. His breath quickens and he's flushed. I reach the pull of his zipper and tug it down just an inch. His hand covers mine and he removes my hand from his lap.

"Mrs. Dove, do you brazenly come on to all your shareholders?" he gasps in mock shock.

"Only the *minority* ones, De Montfort. I want your cock so badly. You have to give it to me, it's in the shareholder agreement you signed." I look up at him through my eyelashes, he's grinning.

"I'll get my lawyer to check that, Mrs. Dove. I don't recall a sexual favours clause."

The door to my office opens abruptly. "Oops. Sorry." It's Ruth.

"Hey, Ruth. Come in." Sebastian plants a kiss lightly on Ruth's blushing cheek. Oh please, she fancies him.

"Not interrupting you, am I?" She can't take her eyes off him.

"Not at all. Elizabeth was just showing me the figures. They look very impressive." He is insufferable.

"Fantastic. Shall we all go through to the Board Room? There's more space in there. I can spread out the forecasts and get you a hot cup of coffee," she suggests.

"Ruth, Sebastian isn't here to go through the forecasts. He's just popped by to say hello, haven't you, Sebastian?" I look from Ruth to Sebastian.

He has a sly grin on his face. *Uh-oh.* "On the contrary, Elizabeth. Why doesn't Ruth show me through to the

Board Room, while you fetch the coffee? Strong. Black. No sugar." I grimace at him. He's playing games. "Ruth, let's go and sit at that vast, expansive table, shall we?" He grabs her hand and leads her from my office, winking at me as he leaves. *I will not rise to it, De Montfort.*

Placing cups of coffee on the blotters in front of Ruth and Sebastian, I take my seat at the head of the table, purposefully putting distance between myself, and my obtuse game-playing boyfriend.

"Thanks, Elizabeth. I have to say, this table's a useful size, isn't it?" He blatantly stares at me, all innocence and innuendo mixed together, as he glides a hand across the polished walnut veneer.

"Very useful, Sebastian—especially for *working* at." I raise an eyebrow. Bring it on. He grins.

"Ruth, I understand you're my main point of contact here," he says, turning to my swooning friend.

"That's right," she replies, a little too eagerly.

"Good. Well then, I imagine you and I will be spending a great deal of time together, working at this table over the coming months." I shoot him a frosty glare, he grins again.

"Will you be taking an active interest in your investment, Sebastian?" Ruth asks, hopefully, as she strokes the length of her pen.

"Most definitely, Ruth. Protecting one's investments and working them *hard*, is the secret to success, don't you think, Elizabeth?"

The Board Room door opens and my secretary

notifies Ruth of a phone call. She leaves us alone, closing the door behind her. I turn to Sebastian and see the supercilious leer he's wearing.

"What the hell are you playing at?" I hiss.

"Why, Mrs. Dove. I *do* believe you're jealous."

"You were flirting with my *best friend!*" I'm furious now.

"Nonsense. You delegated me to Ruth because you… how did you put it? You don't deal with *minority* shareholders. I'm merely complying with your directive."

"You are insufferable, De Montfort."

"Is that so?" He sits back on his chair, playing the end of his pen across his lips, challenging me with his stare.

"Insufferable and an ass."

"Careful what you say, Elizabeth. One more word and I will spank your tetchy ass over this very table." His hand once again glides over the veneer.

Ruth re-enters the room, preventing me from firing back a suitably caustic retort. "While you're here, Sebastian, Beth has something she wants to talk to you about, don't you, Beth?"

I raise an eyebrow, but she nods encouragingly. "I do?"

"Yes, about taking time away from the business. If you'll both excuse me, I've a mountain of work to get through. Sebastian, great to see you." She kisses Sebastian goodbye and leaves us alone.

"That's right," I confirm. "We've been discussing the business, and agree that it's a good time for me to take time away."

Sebastian sits forward, listening keenly.

"Therefore," I continue, "I will be taking a leave of absence of six months. I'm going to get away and take some time to heal."

"You're going away?" There is an edge of panic in his voice.

"Yes, that's right. To Penmorrow. If you'll have us?"

He beams at me as though he's happy enough to burst, relief replacing panic. "What a marvellous idea, darling!" His eyes crinkle as he smiles warmly. "You and Bella can stay as long as you both want. It'll be so therapeutic for you both. Long walks, lazy baths and time to heal, as you say."

"Thank you, Sebastian. This means so much to me. To us both." Reaching across the table, I squeeze his hand.

"We'll take good care of you both," he says quietly.

"We?" I ask warily.

"Scarlett and I. She's been moping around since the accident, worrying about you and wanting to come and visit you, but I told her to be patient and you would soon be there."

Scarlett caring is both heart warming and unnerving, and I can't entirely rationalise my jealousy toward her. I remind myself that she's less important to Sebastian than I am. It also occurs to me that she'll be put firmly in her place as a hired domestic when I'm at the house and, as much as I do kind of like the girl, I intend to let her know that anything that may have gone on between them both in the past is now over.

"It will be good to see her but...*I* will want to look after the house and cook for you. I need to make myself useful, darling. Perhaps Scarlett could take some time off while Bella and I are staying?" I suggest.

He's silent for a few seconds and when he replies it is with a firm and decisive voice. "Nonsense. It's Scarlett's home too. Besides I have plans for you and they don't involve you wearing rubber washing-up gloves, or slaving over the stove. On second thought, if you are only wearing rubber gloves and slaving over the stove perhaps I may reconsider."

He makes me laugh for the first time in weeks. I really *do* love Sebastian's smutty side and familiar tingles ripple through my body. "Well then, your Lordship, I will have to pack some rubber gloves. Though, I have to say, I would prefer to be bent over your kitchen table!"

"*Mmm,* what a lovely thought." He sighs. "But I have far more interesting places in which to enjoy you, Elizabeth."

Sebastian takes my door key and goes back to the house, leaving Ruth and I to finalize our plans enabling me to be absent from the business for some months. Our forecasts look positive, and cash flow is healthy thanks to Sebastian's investment. It's entirely workable for me to leave the business in Ruth's capable hands. We decide on one day per week for a telephone meeting so that I can be updated with any difficulties or challenges at work, and we draft a memo to our staff team notifying them of the news that Ruth will be their only point of contact until further notice.

I suddenly feel free. It's such a liberating feeling after years of toil and stress building our company and trouble-shooting. For the first time in years, it feels as though I'm truly doing something for myself rather than for others. I just need to convince Bella of the merits of going away with me to Cornwall. She needs a break as much as I do. The pain of our loss is a black cloud, hanging over us daily.

On the way home from work, I stop at the shopping mall and treat myself to half a dozen expensive pieces of casual country clothing plus a very sexy set of lingerie which will be my treat for Sebastian. I giggle to myself imagining the skimpy garments worn with rubber gloves while I wash up.

It feels good to get home and I realise, for the first time in months, I feel more positive. *Excited* even. I'm keen to talk with Bella about my plans immediately so I shrug off my coat, hang it on the hook by the front door and climb the stairs to Bella's room. In my haste, I forget to knock and instead open her door and enter my daughter's bedroom.

"Don't you ever knock?" she asks curtly. Sebastian lies sprawled on Bella's floor.

# Chapter 7

Leaning into a beanbag, Sebastian clutches the control for Joe's Xbox, cursing at a game on the TV screen. He glances at me fleetingly as I enter. "I'm beating your daughter's ass on *Zombie Killzone*," he tells me distractedly, concentration etched across his face.

"You went into *Joe's* room?" I ask incredulously, the intrusion of that fact sinking in.

"Mum, don't bust his balls," Bella snaps.

"I didn't think. I'm sorry," Sebastian says, pausing his game, crestfallen.

Bella glares angrily at me. "You can't keep his room like a fucking *shrine,* Mum!" she barks.

"Hey, watch your smart mouth, young lady. Don't talk to your mother like that," Sebastian cautions.

"How *dare* you talk to me like that, Bella!" I snap, and my daughter blanches at my reprimand, her eyes brimming with tears. "*Nobody* goes in my son's room. Do you understand me?" Feeling myself losing control, I take deep breaths and try and rationalise my anger. It's grief, Beth. Calm down, take deep breaths.

"Mum, I'm sorry. I miss him too." We hug each other tightly as I smooth her hair and kiss away her tears.

"Want to come and help me cook?" I ask her.

"What's for dinner?" Bella wipes her nose with her sleeve.

"Your favourite. Pasta and meatballs," I reply, and her face lights up. I'm relieved that she seems to be regaining her appetite as she barely ate for the first two weeks after the accident and even now only picks at her food like a small bird.

Sebastian continues playing with the games console while Bella and I work together in the kitchen making meatballs. Bella puts down the spatula she is using to mix the beef and turns to me. "Sebastian asked if we'd go and stay for a while at Penmorrow."

I'm astounded. Primarily, I'm shocked that he would discuss our visit without checking with me first. At such a sensitive time in Bella's life, it's my place to broach the subject with my daughter, not his.

"I've told him we'll go, Mum. Well, I'm going regardless of whether you are." My astonishment now rests like a leaden weight around my shoulders. "I thought you'd be pleased." She sulks.

"I *am*, darling. I'm just a little surprised that Sebastian discussed this with you before I've had the chance to talk to you first, that's all. I'd like to go, I really would. In fact that's why I came in to your room—to talk to you about it. I've taken time off work, as much time as we both need, and we can leave as soon as I've had a chance to talk to Nana. Please don't mention this to her, she's been through enough. We all have. I'll suggest she comes to stay in Cornwall for a weekend soon, okay?"

"*Sick,*" my daughter replies.

In my day we would say 'that's nice,' but teenagers

today insist on saying 'sick.' It's such a weird world we live in now.

"I suppose we'll have to wait for me to finish my last exams?" she asks with a frown. In my haste to speed ahead with our plans I'd overlooked the fact that Bella has five exams to take in May. She's hardly studied and, quite honestly, I've not been of clear mind since the accident and therefore have not pushed her to do so. We agree to wait another month so that Bella can finish her exams and therefore her secondary schooling. The delay also gives me time to spend with my mother, which eases my conscience at leaving her.

Bella's clearly besotted with Sebastian. Using this opportunity to talk to her about her feelings seems a sensible approach to air my concerns. "Bella, darling, I know you *think* you love Sebastian, and that's really wonderful. He's a kind and generous man but, please, don't see him as a replacement for Dad. I just worry that you may see him as a father figure at a time when you're very vulnerable. It's totally understandable that you'd feel that way. I…I just don't want you to expect too much of Sebastian, okay?"

She looks genuinely affronted. Her mouth is gaping and a mist of anger clouds her eyes.

"*For fuck's sake*, Mother. I certainly don't think of him as a new daddy. *Jeez!*"

"*Language!*" I exclaim.

Having had this conversation with Bella doesn't reassure me that my daughter won't end up getting hurt.

After dinner, Sebastian clears the plates while I languish in a hot bath. Closing my eyes and enjoying the sting of the hot water on my skin, my worries begin to soak away and the pain of grief, deep inside me, lessens just a fraction.

Sebastian makes love to me for hours, with a leisurely exploration of each other's bodies, kissing and licking every inch of skin.

As the first blush of sunrise lifts the shadows in the room, I wake to feel his leg draped over my hip as he spoons me. Feeling hot, but reluctant to disturb him, I lay still, listening to his breathing, and feeling safe and loved in his strong arms. Contented sleep envelopes me once more.

Hitting the mute button on my alarm, I kiss Sebastian's bare shoulder and he stirs, pulling me down and kissing my neck. "*Mmm,* good morning, sexy," he croaks sleepily.

"Hi, sleepyhead," I purr.

"It's Saturday. I have the whole weekend to use and abuse you, Mrs. Dove," he promises.

"Delicious as that sounds, De Montfort, I have a hair appointment at ten. I'm going to have to leave you and Bella for an hour, is that okay?"

He plants a tender kiss on my nipple and I'm lost to him again.

\*\*\*

My hair is styled differently. My usual curls have been straightened. The new sleek look frames my face nicely. "God. You look *amazing*," George, my hairdresser, coos.

"You're a miracle worker. Thank you."

"Hope you've got a hot date tonight? Sorry, Beth. I didn't think," he apologises, remembering when Ruth last dragged me in, reluctantly, for a blow dry before the funeral.

"It's okay, George. You know what? I am going out tonight. Why waste this hair-do?" I say cheerfully, careful not to mention Sebastian, lest he thinks me callous dating after my husband's death.

"*Wow!* You're *beautiful.*" Later on, Sebastian admires my new look with that wicked glint in his dark eyes that does untold things to me.

"Wanna take me out on a date tonight?" I ask flirtatiously.

"Oh, I want to do a *lot* of things to you right now." He slaps my backside and pulls me into his arms.

The restaurant is buzzing. Fortunately, we have a table booked, and we are shown to the only vacant table, at the back of the dimly lit French bistro. Sebastian slips my black satin jacket from my shoulders and pushes the chair in behind me as I sit. He's looking delectable in smart black tapered trousers and crisp white shirt, unbuttoned enough to show the dark matting of hair on his upper chest. At my request, he's unshaven so that I can enjoy the friction of his stubble on my pussy later. Sebastian selected my dress for our date—a knee length, chocolate brown slip, overlaid with lace. It clings to my curves and exaggerates my cleavage.

The waitress brings the menus and takes our drink order, her eyes drinking in Sebastian's sexiness. I cast her a poisonous scowl and she leaves us, swaying her hips seductively as she goes. *Nice try, sister. He's mine.* Turning back to Sebastian, my fingers toy with the ribbon of my diamond choker. It's the first time I've worn it since the night he gave it to me.

"I know what you're doing, Elizabeth." He growls darkly, his finger running across his top lip.

"Do you now?" I pout, my lips moist and sticky with the lip-gloss I stole from Bella's room earlier.

"Mrs. Dove, be *very* careful who you play games with," he warns. My stockinged knee touches his and I run the toe of my killer heels under his trouser leg and up his shin.

"Games, Lord De Montfort? Whatever do you mean?" I scoop up my evening purse, push back my chair and rise, leaning forward provocatively so he gets an eyeful of my ample breasts.

"Where do you think you're going?" he asks, eyebrow cocked.

"Powder room. I'm going to go into the cubicle, touch myself through my panties, remove them and bring them to you. *Wet.* I'd like you to think about that while I'm gone."

"I see. Don't make yourself come, Elizabeth. You know I'll be very angry if you do so without my permission." His mouth is set in a stern line, his eyes dark and foreboding, daring me to disobey.

With a flick of my hair I totter off in search of the ladies cloakroom, without a backwards glance, but I feel his eyes burning into me. *I'm playing with fire.* Five minutes later, I return. As I pass him and take my seat, my pink lace panties are dropped into his lap. He hides them in his fist and brings them to his face, closing his eyes and breathing in my scent on the lace.

"*Fuck*, Elizabeth do you have *any* idea how hard I am?" I reach under the table and brush my fingers over his erection, which grows even harder with my touch. "Did you obey me?" he challenges.

"Yes, but you seriously owe me later."

Taking my mobile phone from my purse, I wake the screen and show the image to Sebastian.

"You took a photo of your pussy for me. I approve. Perhaps that will lessen your punishment later," he says.

The waitress returns, putting down warm shells containing Coquille St Jacques. The aroma of parsley and garlic is divine. Placing my phone down on the table between us, I pop a scallop into my mouth and savour the delicious creamy taste.

My phone pings, signalling a new text message.

***Still waiting for your ansa. Let me know when you want my cock ;-) Si***

Sebastian sees the message at the same time as I do. I curse myself for not changing my settings on my phone so that text messages are invisible until opened. It's too late. His jaw sets, his lips snarl, his eyes are dark and threatening.

*Oh, fuck. Fuck. Fuck.*

# Chapter 8

His voice is edgy, cold and menacing. "Do you want to try and explain this?" I feel icy cold, panicky. *Do I lie? Worth a try.*

"Must be a wrong message. I mean, sent to the wrong person," I reply feebly.

"I see." He picks up my phone and rises from his chair.

*Oh shit, he's leaving me.*

"Wait here. *Don't fucking move.*" He holds my frightened stare for several seconds, daring me to move one inch, then turns and strides out of the restaurant. Like a deer caught in the proverbial headlights, I'm consumed with fear. Deciding to defy his instruction, I wait until he's out of the door and follow.

Sebastian stands on the pavement, his feet apart in an aggressive stance. My phone is clutched to his ear. *Crap, he's calling him.* "I'm going to say this once. Only once. Do. Not. Ever. Contact. This. Number. Again."

There's a pause.

"You're not understanding me. If you ever contact this number again, you are a dead man. *Now* do you understand? Good." He cuts the call and spins round on his heels. I have never seen him look so angry. His eyes meet mine, and the burning black coals cut through my soul.

"Sebastian, let me explain."

*Slap!* The sharp sting to my face, delivered by his large hand, drives all the air from my lungs as tears spring to my eyes. "*Sebastian,*" I gasp.

He puts his finger to his lips to silence me and clenches his fists, sighing deeply. At that moment, I see the pain in his eyes and it breaks my heart. "Come with me." He takes my hand and leads me back into the restaurant. *What the hell?* Seated back at our table, the waitress fusses around our table, clearly concerned that we might have been 'dine and dash' customers. "Is everything all right with your food?" she asks Sebastian.

"Fine. Yes." He flicks his hand to dismiss her and spears a scallop with his fork.

"*Talk to me,*" I beseech him, my hand rubbing at my smarting cheek.

"I don't want to hear your excuses, Elizabeth. You are *mine.* If you *ever* do this to me again, it will be the worse day of your fucking life." His words cut through me like a knife. "I will never share you. Is that clear?"

"Yes," I whisper.

"Good. Now eat."

That evening, he takes me brutally. The loving intimacy of last night is lost in the savagery of his lust tonight. He is reclaiming what is his. I let him do this to me, taking my punishment in the hope that it will restore Sebastian to me. *I am his.*

# Chapter 9

Two weeks pass and I have spent quality time with my mother who is trying to be upbeat about Cornwall. I can see the pain in her eyes though and know she is going to miss Bella and I terribly when we leave. It's the second week of May. Just two weeks until we leave for Penmorrow, and Bella is taking her final exam on Monday.

Sebastian hasn't mentioned Simon again but has been cooler and more reserved on the telephone. I'm missing him so. I hope that I can prove my loyalty to him during the summer at Penmorrow, and restore his trust in my fidelity. Feeling in higher spirits today, I call into the office to surprise Ruth and the team for an impromptu visit. I find a parking space several blocks from the office, but even the long walk doesn't dampen my mood. I stop at a bakery and buy a large bag of freshly baked donuts for my staff. Sauntering past the window of Chic Shoes, my attention is drawn to the most beautiful, but painfully high-heeled red shoes. Sebastian would adore these shoes. They are saucy and daring, and I simply have to buy them.

Staring at the shoes, I notice a reflection in the plate glass. It's a pale-faced woman standing directly behind me, and I turn with a start. The woman appears to be in her late sixties, has limp badly dyed auburn hair with grey roots and is dressed in navy blue trousers, teamed with a green, loose knit jumper, both bearing stains. She is staring at me, dark shadows beneath her eyes, and I presume she's a vagrant seeking spare change for a meal. I reach for my purse and retrieve two pounds. I hand it to her but to my surprise, she regards the proffered money with disdain and shakes her head.

"I know who you are," she whispers.

"You do? Um, I'm sorry, do I know you?" I ask hesitantly.

"You're his *latest woman*." My eyes widen, and I feel the hairs stand up on my arms and my scalp prickles. For some reason I can't yet fathom, the woman looks familiar but I can't place her. I raise an eyebrow enquiringly and take a step back, putting a little distance between the woman and myself. "Elizabeth Dove. No, dear, you don't know me but we have a mutual friend. Scarlett."

"Scarlett at Penmorrow?" I ask, the confusion apparent in my voice. "How do you know Scarlett? And Sebastian?"

She regards me with a cold stare, her lips now twisted into an insolent smile. "Scarlett was good to my daughter...*so* kind. She tried to warn me. I didn't listen to her. If only I'd listened. But it's not too late for you." Her eyes take on a wildness, darting from me to those around us in the street.

I begin to take her seriously, realising that she is no longer the vagrant and I'm no longer an arbitrary stranger selected randomly in anticipation of gaining a few coins for a meal. "How do you know about me?" I need to understand how this woman found me and what her connection to Sebastian is. "How did you *find* me?"

"Scarlett. She writes to me, you know? She's a good girl. What that monster has done to her—and to my dear, lost, daughter—I *can't* let it happen to you too." Her eyes have a glassy vacant look now, as though she is lost in deeply dark thoughts and memories and my pulse quickens as I become increasingly anxious. She continues, "She told me about you. Sent me a photograph she'd found on the Internet. Your business, it's all on the Internet, dear. I'm too old now to understand these things, but she sent me a copy and a cutting from a newspaper about your dear boy and husband. Oh my dear, it pained me so, to see what he's done to you already. Such a *waste,* a young life and a man who had already lost you to him."

"*Stop!*" I command. I can't take in all that she's saying to me. It is too surreal. I feel lightheaded and my mouth is dry. "I don't understand. Are you saying your daughter knows Sebastian?"

"My daughter was *married* to that animal."

Now it makes sense to me. The familiarity of the woman's face, so alike the photograph of Sebastian's mad dead wife. The connection enables me to begin to understand this woman's ranting. Perhaps her madness was hereditary. I'm being unkind, I realise. Grief of losing a child can drive a person mad. I share the loss of a child with this stranger and I scold myself for not feeling more empathy for her pain. "I'm sorry. I don't know your name."

"Christina Travis," she replies forlornly.

"Look, Christina, I'm so very sorry for your loss. Really, I am. Sebastian speaks so fondly of your daughter and...I know they were very happy and in love."

Her eyes widen and a flicker of anger, or something darker, sparks across her gaze but I continue to try to placate her.

"It was dreadfully sad, tragic, that she passed away but you really mustn't worry about me. Sebastian has been *kind* to me, to my family. I'm a good enough judge of character to know that he's not malicious or cruel." Christina puts a hand on my arm, firmly grasping the fabric of my sleeve.

"Why won't you *listen* to me? He's brainwashed you. Just like he brainwashed Scarlett and my precious girl. I'm telling you, *he* caused the death of my girl. As good as *murdered* her. Do you understand? She was beautiful and full of life and then she met him and how she changed. Can you imagine what that was like for me, her mother? To watch my vibrant daughter's life being eroded in the *vilest* way? Can you?" Her voice rises to a shrill pitch and her grip on my arm tightens until I wince. I have heard enough. The woman is demented. I pull my arm sharply from her grip and step farther back from her. She steps toward me, wild-eyed, and I turn and run.

# Chapter 10

Throwing open the door to my office building, I check she's not behind me then lock the door quickly. I stumble to the ladies room and lock myself in a cubicle, and sit down on the toilet seat. My hands are trembling, and my pulse is drumming inside my head and through every vein. Taking deep, slow breaths I gradually avert the panic attack, which is looming, and I try to begin to rationalise what has just taken place. I decide to call Sebastian for reassurance.

"Elizabeth, darling, how lovely to hear from you," he says in his gravelly seductive voice which immediately calms me. "How are you?"

"Not good, actually."

He's silent for a moment and when he next speaks there's a discernable apprehension in his voice. "What's *wrong,* darling?"

"The weirdest thing just happened. I was heading to my office when an older lady stopped me. She looked like a tramp. I tried to give her a couple of pounds. Then…she knew my name."

"Who was she?" he asks quietly.

"That's where it gets really weird, Sebastian. She is. *Was*. Your mother-in-law." I hear Sebastian take a sharp intake of breath and he is silent again for several seconds.

"I see. And what did the mad witch say to you?"

Goodness, he sounds really angry and I wonder whether I should progress this conversation.

"She warned me."

"About?" His tone is sharp and my anxiety returns, fearful of Sebastian's volatility.

"About *you*," I say boldly.

"Did she now? What exactly did the poisonous old bat say?" He demands venomously.

"That you…as good as murdered her daughter." As I diffidently recount the claim to Sebastian, I fear the wrath of his response.

"*Fuck it,* Elizabeth. She's a senile old woman who is grieving. You, more than most, will surely understand how the loss of one's child can impede one's rationality. She could never come to terms with Libby's mental illness, so it tipped her over the edge when Libby killed herself. She's always blamed me. Hell, I've blamed myself enough times. That doesn't mean I *murdered* her, for Christ's sake. How about a little loyalty?"

"*Oh no*. Oh God, I didn't believe her. Please don't think I doubted you at all. I told her what a good man you are." Panic rises up from my belly. "Of course I understand, she's just a messed up old lady. What I don't understand, though, is why Scarlett posted a photograph of me to her and a newspaper cutting about Joe and Alan's accident."

"Did she? *Hmm*, well, I shall be asking her to clarify her intentions in that regard. I'm aware she's maintained contact with Christina. She was always fond of the old troll." A giggle escapes my lips at the plethora of insulting names he has for the poor old lady. "I fail to see the *funny* side of this conversation, Elizabeth," he admonishes.

"*You.* You just make me laugh, Sebastian. Am I to assume that you didn't enjoy a close and loving relationship with Libby's mother?" I ask sardonically.

"I think that's a fair assumption. How very astute of you." His reply is sarcastic. I take the cue to change the subject.

"Bella's so excited, you know. It'll be so therapeutic for us both to have time away with you at Penmorrow. She misses you, Sebastian."

"And I she," he replies in a softer tone, his anger abating.

"Oh, and I bought you a present!" I exclaim, excitedly trying to further lighten Sebastian's mood. "I will gift wrap myself in the sexy new lingerie purchased explicitly for your enjoyment, Lord De Montfort," I purr.

"*Mmm*, thank you, darling. What colour is it?" His sexy gravelly voice is back and butterflies dance the Nutcracker Suite in my belly.

"You'll have to wait and see, but I assure you the panties are very sexy and *very* small. In fact there's barely anything to them, just a strip of satin," I tease.

"Do you know how hard you have just made me?" he growls. "Where are you?"

"I'm in the ladies room, believe it or not!" I whisper, conscious suddenly of my surroundings.

"Perfect. What are you wearing?" He sounds

confident and seductive, and I'm aroused. Sebastian has a natural gift of diverting my attention to more carnal matters.

"I have on a blue shift dress and navy heels. I thought I'd dress up a bit as I was coming to the office."

"Take your panties off." His instruction makes me blush and I lean forward and unlock the door to the cubicle, checking through the small gap that I am alone in the ladies cloakroom. All's silent, and I lock the door once more.

Standing, I use my free hand to slide my panties down my legs and carefully step out of them, placing my discarded underwear in my handbag on the floor. "Okay. Panties off." I hear him suck in his breath and then I hear a zipper being pulled.

"Are you touching your cock?" I whisper. I hear him groan and I close my eyes, imagining his long manly fingers stroking his hardness. My sex is tingling and wet.

"Good girl. Yes, I am stroking my hard, *throbbing* cock, Elizabeth, and you are going to make me come by pleasuring yourself. Do you understand?"

"Yes. Oh yes, I understand." I breathe. *Oh, gosh.* This is a first for me and I feel dirty and seedy and deliciously indulgent as I guide my fingers to the apex of my thighs.

"Good. Now do as I say, baby. Hold the phone in your left hand. Take the middle finger of your right hand and run it down from the top of your clitoris, all the way down. Now slide it into your wet pussy. Are you doing it?"

I gasp as I do as he bids. My finger seeks and finds my hot, wet void and I can hear Sebastian's breathing quicken as his pleasure mounts. "That. Feels. *So.* Good," I pant, my sex now on fire as my finger slides upward to once again tease my sweet spot. I am moaning now as I wait for my lover to guide me.

"Baby, yes, you are so wet. Taste it, Elizabeth. Put your finger to your lips and taste your juices with the tip of your tongue."

I do as I'm told, and the sweet taste lingers on my tongue as my fingers travel south once more.

"Tastes good, hmm? My dirty slut. Now circle your clit until you come, baby. I want to hear you." I can hear his rasping breath and his deep guttural moan as he builds to climax. And I'm climbing, my sex throbbing as my hastening fingers bring me to the most intense orgasm, leaning back against the cubicle wall, one leg raised on the toilet seat, my hips thrust forward. The delicious warm tide washes over me and I'm vaguely aware of Sebastian crying out, as he too explodes in harmony with me.

As my body comes down from the crescendo, and I become aware of my senses once more, I hear the flushing of a toilet. *Oh my God.* Someone is in one of the cubicles. Wracked with embarrassment, I quickly cut the call and place my phone in my bag. Sitting back down on the toilet I wait silently until the woman has washed her hands, and then use the noise of the hand dryer to mask the sound as I tidy myself and put my panties on. I listen for the sound of the door closing, before venturing out of my cubicle of sin. As I rinse my hands at the basin, I regard myself in the mirror above. My cheeks are flushed and, when I've dried my hands, I retrieve my powder compact from my handbag and dab a copious application of ivory powder onto my hot skin. A little lip gloss and spritz of Chanel Number Five perfume completes my transformation from harlot to business woman once more.

Clutching the bag of donuts in my hand, I make my entrance in to our offices. It is good to see my colleagues once more, and their eyes light up greedily when they spy their sugary treats.

Ruth swivels around on her chair and claps her hands together happily when she sees me. "*Beth!* Oh my goodness, girl, why didn't you tell me you were calling in? I'd have saved some work for you!"

It's so good to see her again, and we hug before walking together to the kitchen to make coffee.

"I have some gossip for you," she says. "Apparently there was a couple in the ladies room, shagging! Can you believe it?"

My embarrassment is excruciating and my cheeks blush a deep hot red. "*Wow.* I turn my back on this place for five minutes and all sorts of shenanigans go on!" I laugh. "Do we know who it was?"

"No. Absolutely no idea. Apparently Laura heard them at it. She made a hasty retreat so we are none the wiser as to who the naughty devils are. Lucky sods," she muses. "So, how are you? You've lost weight, girl."

"Oh, you know, good days and bad days. I'm starting

to eat more, and at least I can face getting up in the mornings now. Bella seems to be coming out of her more, thanks to Sebastian. He's been a rock to that girl. To both of us."

The sharp reminder of my loss makes me feel melancholy. Sometimes, just for a short while, I have a brief respite from my grief but then it hits me with such a force it physically winds me, and I feel guilty for living my life. For living. My weekly pilgrimage to the cemetery always renews my heartache, and it will be so painful to neglect the graves whilst we are in Cornwall but my mother has promised to tend the flowers and weed the soil in my absence.

"It'll take time, love. Time is, as they say, a great healer. It'll be so good for you both to just get away. That house holds so many memories, Beth."

"I know, Ruth. I haven't been able to go into Joe's room since January. Mum says I should start to sort through his and Alan's things but, you know, I can't because that's like facing the fact they won't be coming home. I've convinced myself that I hear Joe playing his Xbox through his bedroom door. God, do you think I'm going mad?" Hot tears fall down my cheeks and Ruth gives me a tight hug.

"No madder than you've always been, love." Ruth holds me and we laugh and cry together.

***

It's been another emotional day and I'm pleased to kick my shoes off and take my freshly poured glass of chilled Pinot Grigio to the lounge, where I slump onto the sofa and curl my legs up, sipping the cool, delicious wine. I reach for the television remote control and, as I do so, my mobile phone pings with a text message.

*Am I to take it you didn't enjoy our phone sex or did you accidentally fall down the toilet pan and get flushed away? S*

I completely forgot to call Sebastian back after I so abruptly cut his call. I blush as I remember how close I came to being exposed as a shameless hussy. He must think me terribly rude, and not in a good way. My thoughts turn to our conversation prior to the phone sex. He was so dark and almost intimidating in his response to my news of meeting Christina. Beth, you would be furious if someone accused you of murder, I think reproachfully. I tap a reply to him, emboldened by the wine.

*So sorry darling. Nearly caught in the act by Laura at work! It would have been my reputation down the toilet pan! It was very naughty but very hot. You are a bad influence on me ;-) xxx*

His reply arrives almost instantaneously.

*I don't recall you needed much encouragement Elizabeth. You haven't experienced 'naughty' yet. Trust me. S*

*Wow.* I have no idea how he has such a stimulating effect on me but I find his hidden innuendoes highly erotic. A smile plays on my lips as I reply.

**Am I to assume then, that you have far naughtier things lined up for me? You are B.A.D. By the way did you talk with Scarlett? Xxx**

I just bet he didn't.

**Scarlett apologised. Yes.**

*And?*

**What does that mean? That she was sorry she sent information about me to Christina or that she was found out? X**

Sebastian's reply is curt. **Drop it Elizabeth.**

*Drop it? Are you kidding me?* But, I sense this is now a taboo topic—at least for this evening. I make a mental note to raise this with him again when I'm at Penmorrow. I can't resist one last quip back at him. He really does bring out the child in me.

**Consider it 'dropped.' For now X**

He doesn't reply and I switch my phone to silent for the remainder of the evening.

# Chapter 11

It may be my imagination, but Sebastian is still a little prickly toward me. Two more, long weeks have passed since my encounter with crazy Christina and my first glimpse of a sterner side to Sebastian, and it still plays on my mind.

I haven't seen Sebastian for nearly a month and although I miss him dreadfully, I'm apprehensive as Bella and I load our bags into the trunk of our car. There's no discernable difference in the way Sebastian is with me, except that his calls and text messages are more infrequent and it surprises me that he hasn't been to visit. Whoever said 'absence makes the heart grow fonder' hasn't met Sebastian.

My mother's embrace is a tight, lingering body-hug and our tearful farewell brings with it a crushing wave of guilt in the pit of my stomach. She looks older, frailer today—a slight figure in a floral skirt, which hangs from her hips. She wears a pink cardigan, with her usually tidy hair hanging limp. As we part, I place a small envelope in her hand. She looks perplexed as she gently peels it open. She removes the pretty card and smiles at the picture of the chocolate box cottage. "Looks just like Grandma's cottage, where I grew up, dear," she reflects. Opening the card, she silently reads.

*Darling Mum,*

*Thank you for all you've done for Bella and I over the past few terrible weeks. Without your strength and love I simply couldn't have survived. Please don't think that Bella and I are leaving you. We are simply a heartbeat away. Please come and visit us. We will be home by Christmas. I love you so much, Mum.*

*Your Bethy xxxxx*

"*Oh, Beth.*" She's crying again. "I love you too. Just make sure that man is good to you both, or he'll have an angry old lady to deal with."

"He'll be good to us, Mum. You'll come really soon, won't you?"

"Just you try and keep me away, dear." She wags an arthritic finger at me.

Bella and I kiss and hug my mother once more, and get into the car. As we pull away from the curb and join the traffic my mother waves.

As we near Penmorrow, I feel a dark sense of foreboding. What am I doing? But it's too late to turn back.

I kiss Sebastian as I step from the car and I can tell he's missed me too even if he doesn't say it. "Oh my God. I've missed you so much," I tell him.

Bella jumps from the car and throws herself into his arms. He embraces my daughter tightly.

"Hey, young lady. You've gotten taller!" He exclaims.

"I've got heels on." Bella shows Sebastian her

unfeasibly high, hot pink platform shoes and he cocks his eyebrow.

"Tall and grown up I see," he observes, stroking his chin as he studies Bella from head to toe.

"I am grown up. I'm nearly eighteen. *Jeez.*" My daughter the 'adult' makes us snigger, and our amusement is enhanced by the sight of Bella trying to run but only managing a teeter, as she spies Scarlett waiting for us on the steps to Penmorrow. Our new home, albeit temporary.

"Scarlett. How lovely to see you again." I kiss her cheek lightly. "I hope you don't mind a couple of house guests."

"On the contrary. I've been really looking forward to you coming. It will be lovely to have some female company at last!" She looks happy to see Bella and I, but I detect a hint of apprehension in her voice as though her words belie her true feelings. *She's annoyed because she no longer has Sebastian to herself,* I think, perhaps harshly.

Sebastian takes our bags to our rooms and I follow Scarlett to the kitchen where she fills the kettle and places it on to the stove to boil. Sitting down on the familiar church pew bench at the oversized oak kitchen table, I study Scarlett as she busies herself setting out cups and saucers and spooning tealeaves into the white bone china teapot. She looks slimmer than when I last saw her. She is really thin, her hip bones prominent beneath her uniform black dress and I wonder if her weight loss was intentional or rather as a result of unhappiness.

"Tell me how you've been, Scarlett. How is Sebastian and the house? It seems an absolute age since I was last here."

She takes the whistling kettle from the burner and pours the boiling water into the teapot, places the kettle down and turns to face me. She is pale. "Oh, you know. Same old, same old here, Beth," she states with a sigh. *Wow, she really is unhappy.* "Sebastian's fine. He's been in London much of the time on business so I haven't really seen very much of him."

This is news to me. He hasn't mentioned London and I feel affronted that he didn't call in and see me en route. I know Sebastian has an investment advisor and stockbroker in the city but I can't imagine that either would require so much of his time. For the first time, it occurs to me how little I know this man. I decide to push for more information. "What was he doing in London?" I ask lightly.

"He doesn't tell me, Beth. I know he has friends in London so it may be that he visits them. They stay here too sometimes, so I'm sure that's what he's doing. Seeing *them*."

"I see. Do the friends visit him here frequently?" I probe further.

"What friends are these?" Sebastian asks curtly. Scarlett is startled by Sebastian's presence in the kitchen and I notice she blushes.

"Scarlett was just telling me that you have been to see friends in London. I'm surprised you didn't call in and see me." I am pouting and I can't help it.

He eyes me cautiously and then turns his steely gaze upon Scarlett. "I didn't realise that you were my social secretary, Scarlett." His words sting and she lowers her gaze and hangs her head immediately, studying the floor. "Serve the tea. That is, of course, if you wouldn't mind doing the actual job for which I *pay* you."

I feel mortified that he's talking to the poor girl this way. It is unjustified but I hold my tongue for fear of facing his wrath myself. Scarlett places the china teacups and saucers on the table in front of me and pours the tea. The rattle of the lid on the pot alerts me to her trembling hand and then I see an angry red weal around her wrist. It is a circular wound, which looks as though she has worn a red-hot bracelet.

"Scarlett, your *wrist!*" I gasp. "What happened to it?" She nervously places the teapot back on the stove, and pulls her sleeve down her arm to cover the sore welt.

"It was a careless accident, wasn't it, Scarlett?" Sebastian prompts. "Silly girl burnt it on the stove. Leave us now, Scarlett. I want to talk with Mrs. Dove." So formal. Scarlett, still blushing, leaves the kitchen.

"You're very tough on her, Sebastian," I scold. "It sounds as though she's been pretty much running things at the house while you've been partying in London."

"I see. I feel now would be the perfect time for us to establish one or two house rules."

I raise my eyebrow at him in surprised defiance. My parents were the last people to lay down house rules and I do not take kindly to Sebastian doing so now in adulthood.

"First, kindly remember that Scarlett is a salaried employee of mine and, as such, is not a new best friend with whom you may gossip." My jaw drops in astonishment. "Secondly, no familiarity with my staff. I prefer that she and my estate workers refer to you as Mrs. Dove. Also, I have interests that are varied and diverse and these interests may take me away, or I may indulge them at Penmorrow. I hope that, in time, you will share these interests. Do we understand one another, Elizabeth?"

"Well." I am almost, but not quite, speechless. "I think you've made yourself *very* clear. In fact I'm wondering what the hell I have let myself in for, coming here to stay with you." My skin prickles and my face is red with rage. I look at Sebastian and see a steely resolve in his dark hazel eyes, his eyebrows knitted together to form a scowling snake. He regards me with both hands planted firmly on the table as he leans across, intimidating me. I will not back down.

"You are here, *Elizabeth*, because this is where you belong." What the hell does that mean? "You have belonged here since the first day I saw you, covered in mud if I recall. You were beautiful then and even more so now. You're here because you need me, and I you." *Need? Not love?* "And you're here because you want me to take care of you and give you what you desire, deep in your core, Elizabeth."

He has straightened and is walking slowly around the table toward me. In his black jeans and uncustomary black t-shirt he's an image of sexy badness and despite my anger, I feel the familiar tingles in my groin and I tense my thigh muscles, clenching them tightly together. I part my lips to utter a sarcastic quip in return but he is behind me and his hands are caressing the back of my neck, sliding down to my throat. He sweeps the long hair from my back, across my right shoulder and I feel his hot breath on the back of my neck as he trails kisses around to my left earlobe which he takes between his teeth and nibbles hard.

I arch my back, turning on the wooden pew. His mouth is on mine then, his tongue probing mine. I rise from my seat, turning to face him, resting up on my knees to meet his kiss. His hands run down my spine and his fingers probe beneath the waistband of my cotton trousers, down to the cleft of my buttocks and down farther until he grasps a handful of my ass and squeezes hard so that my breath catches.

My mouth is on his hard now, the stubble on his face grazing my skin. Our teeth grind against each other's as our tongues fight a fierce battle. My hands are in his hair, tugging, entwined in his black messy locks. His hand cups my breast and then moves down and finds the hem of my sweater. Moving beneath it, I feel his fingers moving up to my bra, forcing the cup upward. He kneads and tugs my nipple until I feel that I may come here and now.

Sebastian pulls away and I moan in frustration. He

comes around the pew and then he is lifting me up onto the enormous oak table, sweeping aside the china cups, ignoring the smash of crockery upon the unyielding flagstones. My ass is on the edge of the table, which bites into my buttocks, my legs are around his waist, gripping him with my knees, longing for him to enter my yearning wetness. Stepping back, he unzips my fly and roughly pulls down my trousers and panties. He turns and pulls off each of my ankle boots and tosses them behind him, pulling off my lower garments in one fluid movement. I am naked and exposed from the waist down, my legs forced farther apart by his rough hands. I hope that Bella and Scarlett are busy elsewhere as I am powerless to stop what Sebastian has started. The only conclusion I want is the orgasm I so desperately need.

"I *need* you…" I pant. I grip the edge of the table as I ease myself back onto the hard wood, lost now to my desire.

"Oh, be careful what you wish for."

My swollen clit is going to combust, but he kneels, his head between my thighs and I know that his sweet rough tongue will gift me release. My clit is left wanting. His mouth is not upon me. I'm getting so frustrated, unable to hold back a cry of disappointment and impatience. He nibbles, bites at my thighs so sharply that I'm forced to push his head away roughly. Standing now, he's looking down at me, his eyes burning with what—*Desire? Control?* He forces down the zip on his jeans, unbuckles his belt and pulls it from his waistband. *Oh crap, what's he going to do with that?*

Lust succumbs to fear as I watch him over me, strong and powerful and grasping the leather belt in front of him. "Sebastian, Bella could walk in. Or Scarlett. Let's go upstairs to your bedroom." I am aware of the impropriety of our surroundings, and the risk of being caught further dampens my arousal.

"Then I'll be quick. Stop talking."

Who the *hell* does he think he is to speak to me this way? Inwardly seething, I sit up, my eyes locking with his dark coals and his cocked eyebrow dares me to defy him.

"I see how it is, Elizabeth. You want to play hard to get?"

"No." I'm worried about getting caught, and he's freaking me out.

With a deep, frustrated sigh, he puts his shoulder against the far side of the oak dresser adjacent to the door, sliding the heavy furniture across the doorway. "There. Are you satisfied now?" He ambles sultrily back to his position beside me.

"Yes. Thank you." I reach out and grab his biceps as I try to stand. He sweeps both my hands away and holds them in a firm grip with his left hand, his right hand encircling my wrists with the leather belt.

"What the *hell* are you doing?" Fear gives way to anger. This is no longer sensual or consensual.

"Trust me, Elizabeth. You have to learn to trust me. You're not in control now. You relinquished that when you came here." He raises my bound wrists using the belt, and gently pushes me back down onto the table. Pushing his boxers down, he moves between my open thighs. Lifting my head from the table, I see his organ standing erect and vast, and I gasp as his hardness presses at the entrance to my sex, lust consuming me once more. He's leaning down over me, his chest hair lightly tickling my nipples. His left hand holds firm my strapped wrists. *This is so wrong, so sordid, and yet so divine.*

He forces himself deeper and deeper into my pulsing wetness and I close myself around him. He's hitting and rubbing my sweet spot deep inside me, then sliding out and repeatedly thrusting up into my core while his right thumb rubs at my clit, faster and faster, and I am building. Tipped over the edge of the precipice of pleasure, I feel the waves of my orgasm coursing through my body, every muscle contracts and it carries on building, not dissipating until I cry out for him to stop.

As my orgasm diminishes, my body prickles with unbearably heightened sensation. Still he pounds into me hard on the edge of the table, my legs firmly grasping him to me, pulling him in deeper. His breath is quickening and I look up at him above me. His eyes are tightly closed, his expression one of carnal lust and dark despair and he comes with a guttural moan as I feel him pulsing inside me. He flops forward onto me, hot and sweating and spent. I stroke his hair as his breathing settles and tell him I love him. *His silence is agonising.*

# Chapter 12

I stare aghast at the plethora of dresses, skirts, and silk garments hanging in the antique wardrobe. "Sebastian. All these clothes, where did they come from?"

"Do you like them? I asked Scarlett to pick out one or two new pieces for you." He's lounging on the chaise, long legs stretched out, crossed at the ankles, regarding me and gauging my reaction to his extravagance.

"I don't know what to say. When will I have the opportunity to wear these?" My eye is drawn to a full-length crimson taffeta gown with black sash and black lace underskirt. Taking it from the hanger, I hold the exquisite dress to me and spin, feeling how the crisp fabric rustles as I turn.

"Put it on." Sebastian runs a finger across his top lip, his eyes burning as he observes me.

"You'd like your own fashion show?" Raising my eyebrow at him in recognition of the dark look I know so well now, I let the dress fall gently into a taffeta puddle at my feet and slowly, teasingly, remove my clothes down to my underwear.

"Take it *all* off," he commands. "I want you to feel the taffeta against your breasts. Feel how it rubs your nipples."

"Certainly, Sir," I goad.

"*Sir?* You're learning fast, Elizabeth." The hint of an approving smirk flashes across his face.

Naked, I step into the centre of the dress and pull the fabric up and holding it to my body, pad over to Sebastian, turning and indicating for him to fasten my dress. It's a strapless gown with fitted corset, flaring out below the black sashed waist, the stiff folds of fabric supported by the unyielding black net beneath. Standing, Sebastian takes the black laces of the corset in his long fingers and pulls sharply. Catching my breath, I hold in my waist to aid the fastening as he pulls tightly with each lacing.

"You've lost weight," he remarks, and he's right. I haven't regained my appetite fully, since I lost Joe and Alan.

"Do you like the slimmer me?" My waist seems impossibly small in the dress as he pulls me in even tighter, my hands on my hips to help him. He's fastening it so forcefully that I fear the seams may give.

"*Fuck*, Elizabeth, you have *no* idea how sexy you look. Yes, I love your figure, but don't lose any more weight. I like my women curvy."

"Which women would these be, Sebastian?" I ask haughtily. He responds with a sharper tug on the cords.

"You know what I mean," he mutters irritably.

"Enlighten me." Not intending to let this drop, I attempt to turn and confront him. He prevents me from doing so by pulling the cords of the dress in the opposite direction to my rotation, rendering me immobile.

"*Stay still*," he snaps.

"You haven't answered me," I whine.

"No. I haven't. I'm not indulging your insecurities." He finishes his task with a knot and a bow and I'm at last free to face him.

"Don't you think that perhaps those comments exacerbate my insecurities?" Hands still firmly on my hips, my eyes lock fiercely with his. He holds my stare, mirroring my stance.

"Go, and look at yourself in the mirror." He indicates to the full-length gilded dress mirror, which rests against the wall adjacent the bathroom door.

"Don't think this conversation is over, *Mister*," I warn petulantly as I do as he bids. "Oh my God. I look like a vamp!" I exclaim as I regard my reflection, turning from side to side. "What did you do with my waist? It's as though you have eradicated all evidence of two pregnancies." It's truly a miracle. I love it, yet it isn't me.

"You're a stunning woman," he admires, standing behind me now, his hands resting on my hips.

"But when will I wear this? It's so...so...*over-the-top*."

"You'll wear if for your fortieth birthday party next month." He kisses my bare shoulder, sending shivers through my body.

"Sebastian, I don't want to celebrate my birthday," I protest. "Not without...without my Joe here. It feels wrong." The pain of grief, occasionally giving me periods of reprieve, returns as a hard fist to my stomach.

"I know, darling," he soothes, tucking a strand of hair behind my ear and kissing my neck. "It will be good for you. To have the party to plan will take your mind off your terrible loss. Trust me." His muscular arms encircle me comfortingly and I lean back against him, savouring the support both physically and emotionally.

"You're right, I need to carry on. Sometimes, though, it's just too hard. It seems pointless without him. So *empty*."

"We have Bella to consider. She needs us to be strong, Elizabeth. Even when you feel like giving up, you must remain focused on her. In time, the pain will ease. Then, one day you realize that you don't feel guilty for living. You just enjoy your memories which you keep forever." I turn and hug him tightly.

"Thank you, darling. You make me feel so protected. You make sense of all the madness. You turn the dark to light." His fingers tilt my head so that his mouth finds mine and our kiss is fervent, needy.

He breaks away, his breathing quickened. "I don't. I turn the light to *dark*." He has such a lost, desperate forlornness about him at this moment it takes my breath away.

"That's not true," I whisper. "You're a good man." His eyes search mine as though desperately seeking the truth in my words.

"God. How little you know me."

A knock at the bedroom door is followed by Bella's entrance before we can call to enter.

"Hey, guys." She breezes in. "Eww. *Gross*. Put him down, Mum!" I scowl icily at my daughter's intrusion.

"Was there something you needed?" Pulling away from Sebastian's embrace, I'm aware that Bella is staring, open mouthed, at my dress—at me.

"Oh. My. *God*. Look at you." Unsure if this comment is appreciation or disgust, I fold my arms defensively.

"Doesn't your Mother look divine?" Sebastian purrs.

"She looks like a…a *whore*." My heart sinks and my confidence plummets. Bella has her hand over her mouth in mock horror.

"*Bella!*" Sebastian snaps angrily. "Apologise at once."

"It's just so not you, Mum," Bella is shaking her head to enforce her harsh judgment.

"Bella. This is a present from Sebastian. It's *he* you should apologise to." Fury and hurt build in equal measure and I reach behind me, to find the ends of the cord so that I can remove the gown.

"I'm sorry. It's just…I've never seen you look like this, Mum. When would you wear it?" She's staring at me, wide-eyed.

"Your mother is going to wear this gown on her fortieth birthday. If you go to the wardrobe in your bedroom, Bella, you'll find that you too have a new gown. Albeit yours isn't quite as slutty as you seem to think your mother's is."

Sebastian's tone is reproachful and Bella lowers her eyes away from his frosty glare, remorsefully. "I'm sorry, Mum. I guess you look kind of cool. I really have a new dress?" She perks up, meeting his eyes once more. "Can I go and see it now?"

"Go." Sebastian waves her away and she runs excitedly to her room.

"You handle her well," I praise, admiring his firm manner with my wayward teenager.

"She's nearly a woman. She needs to learn discipline," he replies sternly. "I'm going to see that she has some boundaries." He notices my concerned expression and quickly adds, "It's for her own good. Trust me."

"I *do* trust you," I say firmly, hiding the glimmer of doubt I feel.

Over dinner, our mood is improved and conversation jovial. Sebastian and Bella tease each other mercilessly and it warms me to see how close they have become. Talk turns to my party and I'm eager to find out more. Bella gushes excitedly about her new dress. "What sort of party shall I have?" I ask him, excitedly. I'm thinking high-end dinner party with a handful of guests.

"We're having a masked ball," he states. He doesn't cease to surprise me.

"I don't know enough people! I only have Ruth and a couple of the girls from work. Mum. She wouldn't feel comfortable at all at a masked ball."

He raises his hand to silence me. "Any other reasons you can think of not to do this?" he asks sarcastically.

"Well, no. I don't want to seem ungrateful," I add apologetically, seeing the hurt in his eyes. "It will be a wonderful party. I can't wait." I smile broadly and the darkness on his face lifts immediately.

"Good girl." He's smiling too. "Leave the guest list to me. You just need to discuss the menu and decorations with Scarlett." He nods across to Scarlett who is busy spooning apple pie and custard into bowls. She nods agreement without catching his eye.

"Scarlett, it will be such fun," I say with more conviction than I feel. "Let's sit down together tomorrow and brainstorm some menu ideas."

"Yes, that's fine, Mrs. Dove," she says meekly. It seems so wrong, Scarlett referring to me so formally, but Sebastian insists and I'm starting to fear his wrath when I defy him.

"Whom shall we invite?" I ask Sebastian, presuming he has already drawn up a guest list. He doesn't disappoint me.

"It's all in hand, Elizabeth. What two roles have I given you?" *I'm not a damn child.* I bite my lip.

"Yes, okay. Menu and decorations." I roll my eyes.

"Correct." *He can be so obtuse.* "I have some friends coming from London and you may invite Ruth. Not your mother."

"My mother is coming to my fortieth birthday party. End of discussion," I say bravely. He raises a single black eyebrow at me, warning me to push the point further, which of course I do. "No mother. No party." My brow arches even higher than his. *Stick that in your pipe, Mister.*

"We'll talk about this later." His clipped words are a veiled threat and I know I've gone too far yet am determined to win this argument.

"There's nothing to discuss later. I'm very clear on this. It's my birthday, so I should have input in to my guest list."

"We will talk about this later."

"*Fine!*" I hiss, pushing my plate away from me like a petulant child, knowing how he abhors me saying fine or whatever.

"*Fine?*" he echoes, incredulously.

"Yes. *Fine.* You are such an ass."

Scarlett drops a bowl, which shatters, making me jump.

Sebastian puts down his knife and fork, and it's clear he is bristling. His black coal eyes are boring into me. He pushes back his chair so that it scrapes noisily, across the hard slab flooring. I've gone too far, and he's furious. He holds out a hand. "Come with me, please, Elizabeth." It's not a request. I take his hand, trembling with excitement and fear. *Why does it turn me on so, to make him mad?*

"Certainly, dear." I smirk sarcastically at him.

His brow cocks again and his eyes are smouldering, sinister. He takes my hand in his and squeezes. *Ouch.* My wedding ring bites in to the skin on my left ring finger. He leads me from the kitchen, closing the door behind us. *Holy crap. Where are we going? What's he going to do to me?* Wishing I could learn to tame my mouth and temper my insolence, I allow myself to be led to face his wrath in private. We cross the hallway and enter his study. He evidently wants a quiet word with me, to reprimand me away from Scarlett and Bella. I'm thankful that he doesn't scold me further, in front of my daughter and the hired help. He leads me through the study toward the cellar door. Hesitating, my hand pulls in his as I come to a stop at the top stair.

"Why are you taking me to the cellar?" My eyes are wide with fear as I'm unable to predetermine his actions.

"You are going to learn not to defy me." Pulling me with a sharp jerk, we start our descent. With each step, my pulse quickens.

# Chapter 13

Passing Scarlett's room, we continue, Sebastian's grip on my hand now painfully smarting as I continually try to withdraw. "Stop struggling. Trust me," he barks menacingly.

*Trust you?* My mind is full of fear and increasingly dark thoughts. "Maybe I'd trust you more if you didn't bloody well *hurt* me." Furious now, anger replacing fear, I stomp along matching his pace.

"I wouldn't have cause to bloody well hurt you if you'd cut the smart mouthed attitude." He looks at me briefly before easing the pressure on my hand.

"Sebastian. Where are you taking me?" I ask wearily, my pace slowing, Sebastian matching mine now.

"Wait and see, we're nearly there." He's grinning now, anger temporarily forgotten. He's apparently eager to reach his intended destination and I wonder what awaits me.

We progress past Scarlett's living area. I glance sideways at the lamp lit living room, remembering the only time I have previously been there, when Sebastian and I had been caught in an amorous encounter by Scarlett.

Onwards we march, the corridor familiar. I recollect where this passage leads. We enter the room with the tools, which I discovered when I first stayed at

Penmorrow with Sebastian. When I had stumbled upon this room, he had slammed the door shut, but not before I caught sight of the implements and ironwork which adorn the walls. We didn't speak of that room again. Now I curse myself for not having revisited the strange scenario I'd witnessed.

He flicks a switch as he kicks the door closed behind us, the latch clicking into place, restricting my exit. The bulb flickers and then illuminates our surroundings. Releasing my hand, Sebastian stands with his back against the rickety door. The room looks untouched for centuries, the implements hanging from large meat hooks on the wall are of dull metal, some rusted. Others look new, shining in the artificial light. There are no windows. The walls are of grey cobbled rock, held in place with ancient mortar while the ground beneath our feet is dusty cobblestone. The wall to my right comprises a wooden grid of shelving holding countless bottles, each lying on its side—some dusty, others look newly placed.

"A wine cellar?" I ask, taking in every detail of the chamber.

"Wine, yes." He's leaning back, arms folded, with a mischievous expression on his face.

"What are you up to? Why have you bought me down here?" His grin widens and his expression darkens.

"Come with me. I'll show you." He swaggers over to where I stand and, placing a hand on the small of my back, he guides me forward through the chamber. There is a low-beamed oak door set in to the far wall. He turns a key and lifts a heavy iron latch. The door creaks open revealing a dark space beyond. The light switch is on the outside of the inner chamber and when Sebastian flicks it down, a dull yellow light is cast into the room. Stepping tentatively forward, my eyes behold the sight before me.

"What the hell *is* this place?" I gasp. The room is circular and the walls and floor are made of the same stone as the neighbouring room. The ceiling is lower, with wooden beams running horizontally across and tied in to the aged mortar. A six-inch diameter metal hook protrudes from the central beam. In the centre of the small spherical room and directly below the hook, is a circular bed. "My God," I'm astounded at the bizarre and unexpected sight. "Where did you buy such a bed?" I can't take my eyes from it. It has no visible frame, simply a sumptuous mattress on low base, covered with a gold satin sheet. Plump cushions, in place of pillows, are heaped in a deliberately neat pile to one side.

"I had it made to my design," he replies, proudly. "It had to be made in two halves because the doorway is so narrow. Getting it down the cellar steps was an entirely more difficult challenge," he adds.

"But *why?*" This is too weird, what am I doing here?

"Why is the bed here? Or why did I bring you here?" His breathing is heavy and his eyes sultry. He's clearly aroused by my discomfort.

"Both," I whisper. "What is this room?" Finally averting my gaze from the bed, I notice the Moroccan inspired floor cushions placed around the bed. The one little table against the wall is covered with a mosaic of tiny blue, black and gold tiles and holds a candle and incense sticks, which explain the sweet heady scent although they aren't burning now.

Sebastian's hand remains on the small of my back and his fingers begin to trail up and down my spine. "Do you know why I bought you here?" he murmurs into my ear, his breath hot on my neck.

"To prove what a weird freak you are?" He tenses, but I continue. "There was no need, I know what you are."

"Precisely because of comments such as that, Elizabeth." His hand moves down to the waistband of my trousers, fingers probing beneath the fabric to the cleft of my buttocks. I squirm at the intrusion of his touch. Withdrawing his hand, he replaces it on my upper back and pushes me gently forward so that I step toward the bed.

"Not here, not *now,*" I warn him. "Bella will be wondering where we are, we just disappeared."

He sits on the edge of the bed and pulls me down beside him.

"And Scarlett has served dessert. We're being very rude, Sebastian." He puts his finger to my lips.

"Stop talking and listen to me." He removes the finger from my lips, and I'm silent, waiting for him to explain this weirdness, looking only at my hands in my lap.

"Go on." My voice is hushed, full of trepidation.

"That's better. I need to explain to you what I am. *Who* I am." He has my attention now. "You know that

I'm assertive, yes?" He waits expectantly for my reply.

"Yes, you can be assertive…and bossy."

"Bossy? Wrong choice of words. I'm dominant, Elizabeth. I am a *dominant*. Do you understand what that means?"

*Sadism. Masochism. I've seen it all on the Internet. That's you? Wow.*

"I think I do," I reply. "Sebastian, you're wanting me to be submissive, aren't you?" He's nodding, his expression blank, unreadable. "I see. And this room is where you do your dominance thing?"

He shakes his head, rolling his eyes. "Not as such, but it's a room I'll bring you to often. I want you to familiarize yourself with this room, Elizabeth. It's a room you will come to either love or despise. A room of pleasure and pain."

*Pain? Torture?*

"Don't look so worried," he says. "When you give me attitude, then I shall bring you here and the pain will exceed the pleasure. However, there will still be pleasure but it'll be mine, not yours, so don't misunderstand the purpose of this room."

*Is he crazy? I can't comprehend how he can so comfortably fit the two things together—pain and pleasure.* I'm aroused though, and can't understand why that is. I should run and yet, here I am. "So, are you saying that you will hurt me here?" I ask meekly.

"I'm saying that I will punish you, Elizabeth, until you learn the consequences of displeasing me. However, to clarify, in turn you will want to please me because the pleasure you'll receive here will be immeasurable." *He's so calm, so sure of what he wants and expects from me, but I don't think I can be what he wants me to be.* "Look at this differently." He steeples his fingers under his chin and frowns in concentration. "You need a dominant man."

"Why do I?" I interject, and he scowls at me.

"Don't interrupt. You need a dominant man, Elizabeth, so that you can be freed from the pressures and stress of your life. You've struggled for years. You've been married to a weak man and you've compensated for his weakness by becoming the patriarch of your family. The time has come for you to defer to me in all things, so that you can rediscover who Elizabeth Dove really is. Give yourself to me, and you'll find a freedom which is unimaginable." He pauses and looks me in the eye. His words strike a chord. *He's very astute.*

"You know me too well, Sebastian. If I'm totally honest with myself, I am tired. I really am. It would be heaven to have a strong man to tell me what to do, agreed. But, and it's a big but, I've never been told what to do and I'm not sure that I'd be very good at taking orders or being submissive."

"Would you like to try?"

"What does it entail? Can we talk about the punishment aspect? What do you mean when you talk about pain?" This is a huge worry for me.

"Nothing you can't cope with. To begin with, you will undoubtedly defy me and be a pain in my ass." He's smirking at me. "Therefore, I'll ensure that you have a pain in your ass, probably by flogger or crop."

"You'd beat my backside?" I ask, wide-eyed. *Oh, why does that send a tingle to the apex of my legs?* Crossing my legs, I squeeze my thighs together, which doesn't go unnoticed by Sebastian, who smiles knowingly.

"Yes," he confirms. "It'll smart, but it will be bearable. You'll be punished when you're disrespectful toward me or break the rules. I won't *enjoy* punishing you, Elizabeth, and you won't enjoy it either. I'll always explain the reason I'm punishing you so that you understand not to break the rules again. There will be other times when you'll be whipped, or chained, purely for my pleasure, not as a punishment. You will enjoy making me happy and that, in turn will make you happy."

*This is all so confusing.* "Are you going to punish me now?" Remembering how riled he'd been in the kitchen over dinner, he will no doubt take me over his knee right now. *I hope?*

"No, I'm not. Don't focus on the punishment. In general, what I will impart to you will be discipline. I will transform you not only into what I'd like you to be, but what I believe will enhance you as a person, Elizabeth. I want you to think about what I've asked of you. If you commit to this, then I expect to see a change in you immediately—and any slips in your behaviour will be punished from now on. There are many other aspects of this that we need to discuss too. For example, you don't cross your legs when I'm in the room." *What the hell?*

"That would be because…?" *You're a loony control freak.*

"Because, as my submissive, your legs are open to me at any time and by crossing your legs you are signalling they are closed to me. You are closed to me. That is unacceptable." His eyebrow is cocked again, daring me to challenge him.

"I'll try to remember. What else?"

"You avert your eyes when we're in this room or the outer chamber. You don't look me in the eyes." *Weirder by the second—outer chamber? The wine cellar?*

"Isn't that a little extreme?" Scarlett doesn't look him in the eye. The thought jars me. *Are they lovers? Is she his submissive? Or have they been in the past?* It seems certain to me that this is the case, and I intend to get to the bottom of this in due course.

"No, Elizabeth. It's normal procedure that submissives do not look their Master in the eye. By averting their eyes they are showing their Dom that they are subdued and subservient and showing respect. I'll cut you some slack, however, in the rest of the house. Down here it's a different story. Understand so far?"

"Most of it," I say quietly. I'm shocked and turned on in equal measure. "I'd like to try, Sebastian."

"I knew you would," he states coldly, arrogantly. "It may put your mind at rest to know that the mantra in this lifestyle is safe, consensual, and sane. We'll discuss safe words another time."

"Why are you like this?" I wondered what happened

to him in the past to make him this way.

"It's who I *am*, who I've always *been*. Since I was a young boy, and used to be turned on by watching the school bully in action." There's a distance between us now.

"Was Libby submissive?" I ask. He blanches and I see his eyes darken as I steal a glance at him.

"Libby couldn't handle it. Couldn't handle *me*," he replies sharply, his voice full of recrimination. "You're different. Not as fucked up as she was." *Christ,* he's talking about his late wife with such malice. *Maybe it's you who fucked her up.*

Rising abruptly to his feet, he holds out a hand to me. I take it in mine, and follow as Sebastian leads me from this bizarre little room. I pray that he won't hurt me; I have suffered enough pain. As he turns the key in the lock and we leave the inner chamber, I have a feeling that nothing is going to be quite the same again.

# Chapter 14

Blinking, my eyes adjust to the early morning light which streams through the folds of the heavy velour curtains. I'm hot. Sebastian is spooning me, his leg lying heavily over my hip. It takes me a few seconds to realise that I'm not at home. I'm at Penmorrow and everything feels different. *I feel different.*

Thoughts of last night's bizarre experience whoosh back into my head. I need some air to clear my head and some time to myself to think through Sebastian's proposal. *Proposal!* It couldn't be further from a marriage proposal. *Be his submissive, his slave? Lose all sense of being me? But then again, maybe he's right. Perhaps this new role will enable me to start living again. Isn't he all the things Alan wasn't? Self-assured, confident, sexy, attentive, handsome, rich, bossy, weird. I need some air.*

Rolling gently away from Sebastian, his leg flops onto the sheet and he stirs. Don't wake up. He turns over and his slow, shallow breathing tells me he's still asleep. Standing by the side of the bed, in the dappled light, I admire my handsome man. *My Master!* Even while sleeping, his black messed up hair, speckled with grey, his wide chiselled jaw and muscular arm and back send sparks coursing through my body. My head fills with an image of being pinned beneath his powerful body, unable to move, entirely at his mercy. The sparks intensify. *What are you doing to me?*

Sebastian wakes and sits up, rubbing the last remnants of sleep from his eyes. Those sexy, dark eyes which pierce through mine and look directly into my soul. I avert my gaze and look down at my hands.

"Hey beautiful. Good morning," he purrs sweetly. So at odds with what I now know him to be.

"Good morning. I'm sorry I woke you," I say contritely.

"What time is it?" He's reaching for his watch on the nightstand. "Jesus, Elizabeth, it's only six-thirty. Can't you sleep?"

"No. I wanted to take a walk to look at the sea, get some fresh air. Go back to sleep." Reaching across the bed, I plant a light kiss on his bare shoulder. He growls sexily and before I can straighten up, he grabs me around the waist and pulls me down onto the bed. His mouth finds mine and his kiss is forceful, his hand moving to cup my breast. I'm naked which is how Sebastian requested I sleep last night. My nipple hardens instantly under his touch.

"Mrs. Dove, I do believe you're pleased to see me this morning," he murmurs as he rolls my nipple between his thumb and forefinger.

*Mmm, you have no idea…*

He pushes the duvet away from him so that it falls to the floor in a heap. My gaze travels down his body and I hungrily view his erection, which has risen up proudly to bid me good morning.

"Lord De Montfort, I do believe you are pleased to see me." My hand encompasses his hardness. He inhales sharply as I touch his scrotum and squeeze firmly.

"Are you trying to *unman* me, Mrs. Dove?" He grasps my wrist and removes my hand and, in one swift movement, he has me pinned beneath him on the bed. He straddles me with each of his knees restricting one of my arms so that I can't move. Like a trapped animal, my eyes dart around, trying to think of a way to wriggle free. "Don't even think about it, darling," he warns, his mouth set with a smirk, his eyes burning with desire and power.

"Sebastian. I wanted a walk. Alone." I'm wriggling beneath him and my knee comes up, involuntarily, to nudge him sharply in the back. He sucks in his breath, an initial look of shock turning to a much darker expression now. *Oh fuck. Oh fuck.* "I'm sorry!" I exclaim futilely. He's simmering, about to explode. What have I unleashed?

"Oh you will be," he growls.

"I said *sorry.*" My apology is that of a child, and he's grinning now—a wicked smile reflecting something much darker than humour.

"I do believe you've just broken the rules, Elizabeth," he hisses through his smirking mouth.

"Rules? I recall only a couple of rules being imparted to me last night and neither covered escaping from or kneeing you." *Oh, Beth. Learn to keep your mouth shut.*

"And yet *another* rule broken. Keep going. It's such a treat to be able to punish you so soon after our arrangement has begun." His grin widens.

I'm still trapped beneath him, only now he lifts his knees and grips my wrists with his strong hands, his body heavy, skin glistening with a film of sweat. I smell his power, his masculinity and have never felt as vulnerable as I do right now. *Fight or flight, which shall I do?* He takes that decision from me; in one fluid movement, he sits back onto his heels, pulling me up by my arms as he does so. Swinging his legs around, over the edge of the bed I find myself heaved across his lap, my legs on the bed, my midriff across his lap and my upper body hanging down toward the floor. In this position it is impossible for me to break loose. *Holy crap! What's he going to do to me?*

"I told you last night that I would explain why I am going to punish you." His voice is stern, cold and detached. "So that you understand what it is you have done to displease me and so that you know not to do it again," he continues. "So, Elizabeth, do you know what you have done wrong?"

"I told you I wanted to go for a walk. It's not my fault you rugby tackled me on the bed," I reply, and clearly that is not the answer he was seeking.

He sighs, loudly. "Number one: you fail to talk to me with respect. Number two: you fought to get free from me. Number three: you kneed me in the back, causing me pain. Number four: you didn't ask me if you could go for a walk. Do you understand that none of those behaviours are commensurate with submission?" His voice still cold, his words spoken in a monotone and dictatorial manner.

"Yes," I hiss back at him, the blood now rushing to my head.

"Yes? Yes *what?*" Double crap, now the venom has returned to his voice. I've made him madder than ever.

"Yes, Sir. Now can you please pull me up? My arms are going numb and I've got blood rush," I whine.

"You don't seem to be grasping the point I am making so I will *demonstrate* my point instead." He twists on the bed so that my legs fall to the floor and my upper body now rests on the bed. Better.

"Thank you, *Sir.*" The sarcasm in my voice is met with a further sigh.

"Because you have to learn cause and effect, and clearly you can't understand these verbalized, I'm going to deliver six hard slaps to your beautiful behind. You will count after each slap. When I reach six, you will apologise and mean it." I wriggle but he has me firmly pinned, my buttocks exposed. I feel a plethora of emotions—humiliated, angry, fearful, aroused, and the arousal shocks me. I feel like laughing but also crying.

*Slap.*

"Count, Elizabeth, or I'll add six more."

"One." *Ouch!* That stings. How humiliating.

*Slap.* "Two."

*Slap.* "Three." I bite my lip, hard.

*Slap.* "Four." I'm going to cry.

*Slap.* "Five. Goddam it, Sebastian."

*Slap.* "*Aagh.*" That was harder than the rest. *That*

*really hurt.*

"Number six was in response to your cursing after number five. Cause and affect, Elizabeth. You've forgotten my apology?"

"I…I'm sorry, okay? I'm sorry." I sob.

"Sorry what?" *For fuck's sake, I'm sorry I ever came here.*

"Sorry. *Sir.*" I sniff, wiping my nose with the back of my hand as he helps me to sit on the bed beside him. I don't want to be near him. I want to run away from him. This is the monster I fled to in my quest for peace after all I've been through losing my son and my husband. *What have I done? I've brought Bella to this house. It's not just me, I've done this to her too.*

The worst thing of all, that I'm most ashamed of, is that I was aroused. Of course, that was before it hurt. Before he so callously beat me, so coldly, for something so trivial. *I need to get away. Where will I go—home? To my house, which holds such painful memories?*

"Penny for them," Sebastian says, handing me a tissue from the nightstand. I don't want to talk to him. *Hell, if I say the wrong thing, he'll beat me again.*

"I'm going to get dressed and I need that walk." My voice is little more than a whisper. My buttocks are smarting; it's sore sitting down. "Is that okay?" I ask as an afterthought.

"Yes, it's fine. I'll come with you."

"No. Thank you, but I need some time alone."

He's quiet, pensive and so difficult to read.

"Elizabeth, don't hate me." His voice is reticent, gone is the dominance, replaced with insecurity, remorse?

"I don't *hate* you. I just don't *understand* you, why you'd want to hurt someone you care about—presuming you do care?"

He takes my hand in his and strokes my palm. "I care more than you know. That's why I want you to trust me with this. Everything I do, I do for your own good. In time you'll see that." He's more deluded than I gave him credit for.

"I *don't* see that. I see you abusing a woman who is vulnerable, who's been through a traumatic five months and who came to Penmorrow as a place of safety. To find peace and tranquillity. Instead you've turned it into something sordid and dark." Wiping the tears from my eyes, I stand and walk to the chaise at the foot of the bed, removing the bathrobe, which is strewn across, and shrugging it on.

"We need to discuss your feelings, Elizabeth. What you feel is normal. You're learning and some of the lessons are hard, painful, but you've not yet experienced the pleasure and the sense of freedom. Give it time. Give *me* time, let me lead you." He stands and paces over to me, reaching for me, but I step back toward the bathroom door.

"I'm going for a walk. Please, just leave me. I don't want to talk about it anymore," I plead.

"*Fine.*" He rakes his hands through his hair, seemingly at a loss to know what to say to me. "You've got thirty minutes until breakfast. Please be back by then."

"You're still telling me what to do!"

"Half an hour." He turns and, grabbing his robe from the hook behind the bedroom door, he leaves the room. Aghast, I collect my clothes and lock myself in the bathroom. I have no intention of returning in thirty minutes.

# Chapter 15

Freshly bathed and wearing jeans and a long sleeved t-shirt and pumps, I make my way to Bella's room. Sebastian has allocated Bella the room in which I stayed for the *Women In Business* team-building weekend last winter. It was my first visit to Penmorrow, where I met Sebastian, and I have fond memories of that room. It's a beautiful room with antique half tester bed and gold damask comforter, and fabulously high, corniced ceilings. It's too grand for a teenage girl to appreciate, especially Bella. Knocking, I enter and am pleased to see that she's awake, busy on her tablet.

"Mum. Good morning, what's up?" She can see that my face is blotchy from crying.

"Oh nothing, just missing Joe," which is of course the truth but not in its entirety. "I thought I'd take my daughter out for breakfast." I smile, belying my feelings.

"I miss him too, Mum. Is Sebastian coming with us?" she asks hopefully.

"No. I thought it would be nice to have some mother-daughter time. It's been ages. Maybe after breakfast we could hit the shops, that's if we can find any out here in the sticks."

"Sounds like a plan, Stan. Let me get dressed and I'll meet you down in the kitchen." She climbs from her bed and pads to the bathroom, scooping up black leggings and a gypsy top from the floor as she passes. "Give me five minutes."

"I'll wait here for you." I do not want to face Sebastian in the kitchen, knowing there will be hell to pay if he knows my plans have changed and don't include him. *I don't need his damned permission.*

Bella and I manage to leave Penmorrow without being seen. Thankfully, Bella hasn't realized we are fugitives on the run—albeit for a couple of hours. The drive to Padstow takes fifteen minutes and is a spectacularly scenic journey. The narrow lanes wind through tiny hamlets and past acres of woodland and the smell of the sea is always just a breath away. It's picture postcard perfect. The village is sizeable for the area. We park outside the largest of three pubs but it looks closed.

"Damn, it's so early." I glance at my watch and realise it's still only eight-fifteen. Spotting a newsagent across the road, I venture inside and ask the aged proprietor where we can find an eatery for breakfast.

"Come with me, lover," he says, in his broad West Country dialect. Pushing me back outside the shop door, he points to the far end of the high street, if one can call it that. "Go a yonder up there and you'll find Dick's Transport Café. He'll be open and 'e does a cracking breakfast pasty." He scurries back into the shop and slams the door behind him. I wonder if we have in fact, been teleported by time travel machine back to the nineteenth century.

Dick's Transport Café is as salubrious as its name

infers. Sited on the fringe of the town and adjoining the only petrol station, it is a grey 1960s stone box with plate glass windows through which it's impossible to see due to the copious burger posters tacked on the glass. Bella hesitantly pushes open the door, rolling her eyes as she takes in the shabby interior.

"Come on, darling, I'm sure the breakfast pasties are to die for. *Literally!*" I joke.

"Take a seat, lovelies, I'll be with you in a tick." The young waitress indicates a table by the window and we each pull out a pine chair and sit, resting our hands on the green gingham plastic table cover which is sticky under our skin. I wince, as the hard wood is unforgiving on my tender buttocks.

"Mum, you take me to all the best places." Bella laughs. "Do you think everyone in this town is related?" she whispers.

"Interbred, for sure." I giggle, just as the waitress appears at my side.

"Ready to order?" We haven't even looked at the menu but I suspect it comprises copious quantities of cholesterol.

"Do you have any breakfast pasties, please?" I ask, hoping she'll say no.

"Two breakfast pasties. Yes. Mug of tea with that?" *Wow, this place gets better.*

"Perfect, thank you." I can't look at her or I will laugh. Her ample bosom sits at waist level and I'm sure she tucks them into her panties.

"Ketchup's on the counter if you want it," she adds helpfully, before she and her breasts sway off to fetch our food.

"Hilarious." Bella chuckles.

The only other customer puts his grease covered plate on the counter and bids a cheery goodbye to Big Boobs, before leaving, dragging along his flea bitten dog. The bell above the door jingles as he goes. The tinkling bell merges with the ring tone of my phone, which I don't immediately hear.

"Mum, your phone's ringing." Bella pushes my handbag across to me and I fumble around, finally retrieving the mobile phone as it stops ringing.

Sebastian, missed call. *Oh crap.* He's going to be mad at me. Why does that thought turn me on? I'm so cross with him. My phone beeps.

Sebastian, new voicemail.

I put the phone to my ear, first turning down the volume so that Bella can't hear the undoubtedly shouted message.

"Elizabeth. I see your car's gone. Call me immediately." His voice is clipped, anger tinged with anxiety. *He can stew,* I think, let him worry then maybe he'll realize how wrong he was in smacking me.

"Who was it?" Bella asks.

"It was nobody. Wrong number."

The breakfast pasties are surprisingly delicious, the warm flaky pastry crumbling onto our laps as the scrambled egg, onion, bacon, and melted cheese leave a greasy sheen around our faces. We devour it all, washed down with mugs of milky tea. My phone beeps just as I replace my paper napkin on the table next to it.

*If you don't call I will presume you've had an accident and will come looking for you. Why did you take Bella? S*

Touched at his concern but still angry, I delete his message.

"Mum, you should call him." Bella frowns at me. "Have you two had an argument?"

"No, love, of course not. He's just a bit possessive so I wanted some time out that's all."

She doesn't look convinced.

"I can't go through that again, Mum," she warns, and I know that what she fears is a repeat of the rows between my late husband and I.

"Don't be daft, Bella. Sebastian and I just need a little time to adjust to being together. We've not seen each other much over the past few weeks and have never lived together like this. Just give us time. You know I adore him."

"I adore him too," she replies, with a faraway look in her eyes. "He's quite possibly *the* most perfect man I've ever met. When I get married, I want to meet someone just like him." She has a teenage crush on him. How does he have this affect on every woman he meets? It's because Sebastian is the archetypal alpha male—tall, dark, and handsome with chiselled features and a commanding demeanour. He exudes power thus women feel he's a protector. Conversely, no woman is safe from this predator.

"Keep the change." The waitress regards the ten-pound note in her hand and grunts unappreciatively before removing our plates and mugs. The bell jingles and I turn my head absentmindedly to see who's entered. My mouth gapes open as my eyes lock with Scarlett's.

# Chapter 16

She takes a seat next to me and plays with the cuffs of her black dress, nervously.

"Scarlett. What are *you* doing here?" This is clearly not a coincidental meeting. "He's sent you to find me?" I ask incredulously.

She nods her head meekly. "He's very worried, Mrs. Dove. He wants you to come back immediately. He's worried about Bella too."

"For heaven's sake, call me Beth. I'm enjoying breakfast out with my daughter, am I to be a prisoner at Penmorrow?" I huff irritably. Scarlett fidgets on her chair, but doesn't reply.

"Mum, it's nice that he cares. Didn't you tell him we were going out?" Bella looks at Scarlett who shakes her head, affirming my apparent crime of non-disclosure.

"No, Bella. I'm a big girl and don't need permission to take my daughter out for breakfast. Scarlett, do you want a cup of tea or breakfast?" Scarlett shakes her head again.

"Fine. When you get back please inform Sebastian that I'm taking my daughter shopping and we'll be back before lunch." Scarlett's brow lifts, her eyes widen, presumably in shock at my audacity in defying His

Lordship.

"He won't be happy if I don't go back with you," she cautions. "I thought you'd take me home."

"How did you get here?" It dawns on me that Sebastian must have driven her here. Turning my head sharply toward the expansive windows, I peer through a gap in the posters. The road is quiet. One or two locals are walking their dogs, newspapers clutched under their arms. Passing traffic is light. Shopkeepers are putting A-boards on to the pavement opposite. Then I see him. He's leaning against the lamppost, his lower half obscured by a parked car. Arms folded, he's staring directly at me and, from what I can see from here, he's not happy. Scarlett is right.

"Come on, Bella, we're leaving." Picking up my handbag, I march out of the shop without a farewell to Big Boobs. Scarlett and Bella scurry behind me, trying to keep up. Reaching my car, I hesitate and look across the road where Sebastian is watching me. *He's amused!* I'm astounded. His lips form a crooked smile, his dark eyes reflecting his glee at my displeasure. He thinks he's won. Scarlett is climbing in to my car and he presumes, therefore, that I'm complying with his instructions to return to Penmorrow. Ignoring my passengers now aboard, I march across the road toward him. His amusement turns to surprise as he unfolds his arms and places them on his hips, eyebrow cocked.

"Mrs. Dove. How was breakfast?" He has that dark, wicked glint in his eyes now, as I invade his personal space in an attempt to square up to him. I'm so close to him, my breath catches as his rugged good looks completely disarm me. *Fuck, you are so sexy...but I'm very, very mad at you.*

"Your Lordship. What a surprise to see you here." The sarcasm in my voice serves only to raise his eyebrow almost to his hairline. My neck is craned back so that I can look him in the eye. He seems to tower above me even more at this moment so I rise up on to the balls of my feet in a futile attempt to match his height.

"It seems your phone isn't working, Elizabeth, so I thought I'd come and find you. Call it protecting my assets."

*What the hell?*

Rising to the bait as always, I push my shoulders back and scowl at him in the most menacing way I can muster to which he laughs, a deep belly laugh.

"Oh, Mrs. Dove. What *am* I going to do with you?" His arms encircle me and he pulls me tightly to his chest and I can't push away, despite trying very hard. He plants a tender kiss on my hair and it's no good. I'm a lost cause, melting into his arms, breathing in his masculine scent as his muscular grip locks me tightly to him. "You haven't quite grasped the finer details of submission, have you darling?" he chastises.

"Well, you haven't quite grasped the finer details of mutually respectful relationships, have you, Sebastian?"

He sucks air through his teeth and his muscles are taut now. I'm so close to him, his erection is pressing against my navel. *Here in this sleepy town? What will the locals say?* My face blushes deep rouge.

"Home." He releases me from his embrace and pushes me back at arm's length, smirking at my enflamed cheeks. "We'll need to revisit discipline, Mrs. Dove. Later."

*Bugger. That's not good.*

"What fun," I tease. "I may see you at home, I may not."

Wriggling from his grip, I dart back to my car giggling like a naughty schoolgirl. Casting a glance back at him as I slip in behind the wheel, I note that he's shaking his head and running his hand through his hair. As Bella, Scarlett, and I navigate the winding roads back to Penmorrow, I reflect on what it is about him which brings out the devil in me. *Hopelessly under his spell, I'm a lost cause, loathing his punishments but craving him fiercely. I am a mess of contradiction and he is an enigma.*

"Are you scared of Sebastian?" I ask Scarlett, observing her pale face in the rear view mirror.

"Of course not," she proclaims far too emphatically. "I respect him. There's a difference."

"Well, I think he's amazing," Bella coos.

Scarlett is wearing the choker around her neck again and my eyes alternate from the road ahead to the choker. "Why are you still wearing that choker?" My question takes her by surprise and her slender fingers play with the ribbon.

"Lord De Montfort gave it to me," she says apprehensively. "A while back, for my birthday. It means a lot to me."

Didn't he ask you *not* to wear it now? I'll confront him about that later. Mine is in my suitcase, and he hasn't mentioned the fact that I haven't worn it for him.

We arrive back at Penmorrow, Sebastian's car not yet here. In the kitchen, Scarlett makes a pot of tea and then busies herself with laundry duties while I wait for Sebastian to return.

By seven o'clock in the evening, Sebastian has still not returned and I know it's to make a point. He can be so childish. Scarlett is preparing dinner, basting a chicken, and Bella is setting the table.

"Just three places, Bella," Scarlett tells her.

"Three? Aren't you eating with us this evening?" I ask.

"Yes, if that's okay. His Lordship won't be dining with us tonight."

"What?" This news hits me like a sledgehammer. "Where is he?"

Scarlett replaces the chicken in the oven and wipes her hands on her apron. "He called me this afternoon to say that he's having supper with friends tonight. He won't be back until late." She has a knowing smile, clearly delighting in keeping this information from me all afternoon. Leaving the kitchen and taking my mobile phone from my bag, I seek the privacy of Sebastian's study and call him. The ringtone is cut short and sent to voicemail. I redial. It again goes unanswered, so this time I leave a message.

"Sebastian. It's Beth. This is not funny, why don't you

grow up? Enjoy your evening."

I cut the call and turn my phone off. Two can play at that game.

***

Dinner is eaten in silence. Bella detects the frosty atmosphere and retreats to her room without dessert. Taking the opportunity of being alone with Scarlett, I pour us both a brandy before confronting her. "I've got to ask you this. What's with the choker? Please don't say it was just a birthday present."

"Why don't you ask Sebastian?" She's being evasive.

"I'm asking *you.* He's not here."

"I'm sorry. I'm not permitted to discuss it with you."

"What do you mean, you're not permitted?"

Scarlett drains her brandy in one gulp.

"Beth, I'm not your enemy. You've got a lot to learn here and it's not always easy," she says. "We have to trust Him to guide us, he'd never do anything which was not in our very best interests, you know."

I gulp down my brandy and pour another, topping up Scarlett's glass again. The alcohol burns my throat and enflames my confidence. "Have you *slept* with Sebastian?" I need to know. She stares coldly into my eyes as she again empties her glass.

"No, Beth. I haven't *slept* with Him." She's lying; I can tell. Her cheeks are flushed and her bravado false.

"So, you haven't actually slept with him. I'll rephrase the question, have you had *sex* with Sebastian?" She pours another brandy, averting her gaze now and the inability to look me in the eye confirms my suspicions.

"You need to ask Him that, Beth. Please don't ask me anything else. I care about you. We need to look after each other." She fidgets nervously with the stem of her glass.

"Do you *love* him?" she asks quietly.

"Yes. I do." The realisation that I have come to love and rely on Sebastian only occurs to me now. "I *really* do." She's silent, tears glistening in the candlelight as they fall down her cheeks.

"Oh my God, you love him too, don't you?"

There am I, consumed with envy at the thought of a sexual relationship between them…when she loves him. *Does he love her?* While I am lost in the torturous thought that the man I love could be anything other than true to me, Scarlett slips away, gently closing the door behind her.

# Chapter 17

It's been years since I rode a horse. Scarlett suggested that I ride Zariya, a steady mare. Paul, Sebastian's stable hand, looked a little troubled at my choice but saddled her up compliantly.

She's going easy on me as we gently trot across the expansive grounds. It's still early. The sunrise is spectacular, the sky a spectrum of inky blue, crimson, and violet. The beauty of the dawn contrasts starkly to the pain within me. When I woke this morning, I reached across for Sebastian but he hadn't returned. So I find myself riding one of his horses as he rides so often at dawn, to feel what he feels and to see the beauty that he sees.

"*Go on, girl.*" My confidence is returning. Tightening the rein and squeezing my outside leg, Zariya responds by quickening her pace, and as she picks up a canter I let my seat rest heavy and push her forward. It's exhilarating. Soon, we reach the ancient oak where Sebastian used to picnic as a child. Pulling Zariya up, I dismount and pat her sweating flank. She snorts and nudges me before turning her attention to the grass under hoof. Still clutching the rein, I catch my breath and look back across the meadow, beyond to the manicured lawns and finally rest my gaze on Penmorrow, the austere structure softened to a golden stone in the early light. Sebastian's Land Rover is drawing up to the house.

Zariya whinnies as I mount her once more, her nose dipping to find more grass but I pull sharply on her bit. I need to see Sebastian, to gauge how he is with me, to hear him tell me that he loves me, and to know that he doesn't love Scarlett. The hiss of my crop against Zariya's flank produces the speed I require and our canter turns to a gallop as she senses she's on a homeward run. Out of my comfort zone now, I pull on her rein and lean back in a futile attempt to slow the speeding mare. Confused by my rusty horsemanship, the poor horse misreads my intention and continues at speed toward the house. I pull sharply on the inside rein and squeeze my inside leg in an attempt to slow her but she turns sharply and I'm slipping. My feet lost to my stirrups, I slide and the ground is rushing at me. My head strikes something with a sickening thump, and blackness envelopes me.

*I'm running through the cellar, the darkness alive with watching eyes. I can't see who's there but feel their piercing stares. A whip cracks and the lash tears at my buttocks, splitting the skin apart and Sebastian laughs a guttural roar. My hands are tied, the rope chaffing my wrists and I'm forced to watch Scarlett take Sebastian in her mouth. Again and again she sucks and devours him while he writhes against her hungry mouth until he's screaming her name in ecstasy.*

*"Why can't it be me?" My voice is a whisper, but I can't cry out. I try again louder, "Why can't it be me?" They can't hear me but I scream to them, "Why are you doing this to me? I. Love. You!"*

*They hear me now and turn in unison in my direction. We are all in the chamber of pain. They are on the circular bed, and I am chained by the wrists from the hook above them. They look up at me, goading and laughing while she grinds down hard on his cock, riding him while I sob above them.*

*"Scarlett. Oh Fuck, Scarlett. Darling Scarlett."* His voice is soothing now, drifting in and out and then the darkness comes again.

The throbbing in my head is making me feel nauseous. I try to open my eyes but the brightness of the light is too harsh. I can hear Sebastian talking, and he sounds frightened. He's such a strong man. Why does he sound so scared?

"It's okay, darling. Not again. *Fuck,* not again. I can't lose you. I'm with you. *Oh fuck*, I'm so sorry, Elizabeth."

I try to reach up to touch him, soothe him, but my arms are heavy and my head hurts. I need to sleep, then the pain will go. When I open my eyes, he's beside me, his head in his hands. I don't recognise the room. Everything looks different.

"Where am I?" My voice is weak, my head aching. He clutches my hand and moves to sit on the edge of the bed.

"Darling. Thank God. You're in hospital, Elizabeth. You came off Zariya, you stupid bloody fool. What the fuck were you doing riding her?"

"You didn't come home. I wanted to ride, to feel close to you. You were so distant."

He brushes my lips lightly with his. "I could fucking kill Paul. What the *hell* was he thinking, putting you on Zariya?" His eyes are burning, rage and concern etched on his face.

"Don't be mad at him, it's my fault. Am...am I going to be okay?" I reach up to my head and I feel a bandage and thick wadding to the right of my temple.

"You're fine. You have concussion and a nasty gash. You can come home tomorrow. The doctor says you need to rest for a few days and the stitches will come out in a week. I was *so* worried."

He loves me. The thought warms me and lifts my spirit.

"Bella's here, darling. You gave her a fright too. I'll go and get her. She's grabbing a coffee." He rises and leaves the room. Taking in my surroundings I see that I'm in a private room. It's basic but comfortable, like a budget hotel room. A pretty blonde nurse enters and picks up a clipboard from the end of the bed. She puts a cuff on my arm and pumps it tight.

"Hello," she says. "Welcome back. You had quite a sleep after your nasty fall. How's the head? Need some pain relief?"

I give her a feeble smile and tell her my head hurts.

"Not surprised, love. I'll fetch you some Codeine and perhaps a drop of Oramorph to help with the pain. Blood pressure's fine. You should be able to leave us tomorrow."

Sebastian returns with Bella in tow. The nurse's mouth gapes as she looks up and sees him. Blushing a deep crimson, she flutters her eyelashes unashamedly at him. So, he has that effect on all women. *Take a hike sister, he's mine.*

"How's she doing, nurse?" he asks in his sexiest voice, clearly aware of her reaction to his damned good looks.

"Oh. She's doing just fine," she purrs, now a deeper red still. "She mustn't exert herself," she adds. His eyes light up and his lips curl into a seductive smile.

"I'll be sure not to jump her bones until at least tomorrow then, nurse," he replies playfully. Frowning and tutting, the nurse makes a hasty exit and Sebastian's attention returns to me.

"Sebastian, you shouldn't tease. You know what you do to women. You're so mean."

He's grinning at me, all innocence and charm.

"I don't know what you're talking about, Mrs. Dove. I'm going for bite to eat in the café. I'll leave you in Bella's capable hands. Get some rest." He blows an exaggerated air kiss and leaves Bella to keep me company. So tired now, my eyes close as my daughter curls up in the chair at my bedside and I drift into a welcome sleep once more.

My daughter is holding my hand and I squeeze gently. "Mum. You okay?"

"Bella, love. I'm fine. Sorry. I must have drifted off."

"That's okay, you've only napped for a few minutes. How's your head?" She touches the bandage gently.

"I've felt better," I tell her. Hearing her sniff, I crane

my neck so that I can see her. She's crying. "Bella, darling. Don't." She takes my proffered hand in hers.

"I thought you were going to die." She sobs. "I couldn't bear to lose you…after Dad and Joe. I'd be all alone, Mum.

"Oh, Bella. I'm not going anywhere," I soothe. "God, I've been *such* an idiot." Tears are pooling in my eyes and Bella dabs at them with a tissue before blowing her nose.

"No, you haven't, Mum. It was an accident. The bloody horse should be shot and used for dog food, if you ask me." She smiles, as do I. "Sebastian's been so worried, Mum. He's really feeling guilty about not coming home last night. You two need to sort yourselves out. You're like a couple of kids. Shit, Mum, you're nearly *forty* yet you act like a bloody teenager," she scolds.

"Yes, Mum," I tease. "Was he really worried?"

"Shit, *yes!* Scarlett's been here too. She bought you a few things in a bag. She's been upset. They've been having a cuddle to comfort each other. She was crying and everything."

A cuddle? My subconscious screams. I need to get home. The sooner Scarlett realizes that I'm not putting up with her shit, targeting my man, the sooner she will hopefully resign and leave Penmorrow.

"I want to go home," I try to sit up but a wave of nausea washes over me and I fall back onto the pillows.

"Tomorrow, Elizabeth." Sebastian is standing beside the bed, scowling down at me. "Take the pain killers the nurse left for you and then sleep. It's nearly midnight. I'll be back at eight and we'll go home if the doctor discharges you." Leaning down, he kisses me on the cheek as though I'm an aged aunt he's visiting in a nursing home.

"Kiss me properly." My plea is needy and he leans down once more, this time delivering a firm kiss on my lips.

"Sleep. See you in the morning." He leaves the room as Bella blows me a kiss and follows him out.

Sebastian arrives promptly at eight the next morning and we wait together for the doctor to discharge me. My headache is easing and I'm keen to go home to Penmorrow.

"All looks fine, Mrs. Dove, but expect to have quite a headache for another couple of days. No exertion. You must rest." The doctor puts away his pen light and my eyes adjust to the daylight.

"I'll make sure she's well looked after," Sebastian assures the doctor as he takes my overnight bag and my hand in his. Sebastian's car is parked near to the hospital entrance and he helps me in, being careful to shield my injured head with his hand as I slide in to the passenger seat.

"Thank you for caring," I say as he drives us home.

"It's my job, Elizabeth, one which I take seriously, and actually quite enjoy," he says with a sideways glance. He's smiling and he reaches across to squeeze my knee.

"You won't scold Paul, will you?" I ask. "It's not his

fault I rode Zariya. I stupidly thought riding a horse was like riding a bike. Once you've mastered it you are always competent. I should have had some lessons before riding out on my own." He pats my knee.

"Elizabeth, you always think you know everything." He sighs. "Perhaps now you'll defer to *me* a little more. You're very vulnerable and the sooner you accept that, the safer you'll be."

I sit and think about this. Having always considered myself to be a strong and independent woman, it's quite a revelation to hear that he perceives me as being weak and vulnerable. He must be right, I reflect, or I wouldn't have had an accident nor would I have come to Penmorrow to be cared for by him. It's quite a challenge to accept that what I have believed to be true about myself for so many years is in fact a façade, a cloak of falsehood in which I have wrapped myself tightly for nearly two decades. "I think you're right," I murmur.

Sebastian strokes my cheek with the back of his hand as he studies the road ahead. "Yes, I am right. So, what has this revelation taught you, Elizabeth?"

"That I need to trust you more," I reply contritely.

"Good girl."

"One question, please, Sebastian."

He glances fleetingly at me. "Go on."

"Scarlett intimated that you and she have—how shall I put it—had a *relationship*."

He withdraws his hand from my knee and clenches the steering wheel, his mouth now set in a stern line.

"Before you castigate me, I'm not asking you to divulge anything about your past with her. I need to know you're not with Scarlett now. Tell me you don't have *sex* with her anymore." He slows the car and pulls to halt. The wheels scoot up on to a grass verge. Cutting the engine of his Land Rover, he swivels in his seat to face me. His eyes are burning and he looks menacing. *Crap, his mood is so changeable, so mercurial.*

"We've been over this before," he says in a cold, clipped voice. "What *is* it with you? Why are you *so* fucking jealous of my fucking housekeeper?" He bangs his fist against the dashboard and I flinch at his volatility.

"Sebastian. Calm down." I hold my hands up to him, palms outward in a conciliatory stance. His tantrum is making my headache worse, and I wince at the pain.

"You see?" His voice rises. "You see what you're doing to yourself? This is what happens when you doubt me. Nothing good comes from defying or challenging me, Elizabeth, and the sooner you except this fact, the happier we shall both be. Do you understand?"

"Yes," I whisper. "I'm sorry. Please just take me home. I'll try to change. Please don't be mad at me, it's only because I *love* you. I don't want to lose you. I've lost Alan and Joe. I can't bear to lose you too."

He cups my face with his strong hands and kisses me tenderly. "Well then, you need to do as I say," he says, more softly now. He doesn't tell me he loves me but I know that, deep down, he does.

***

It feels good to be home. Sebastian insists I go straight to bed and Scarlett has thoughtfully prepared our room with a jug of water, glass, and magazine on my nightstand. Settling back on the pillows, I scoop up the magazine and open to the first page. A folded piece of white paper falls on to my lap. Opening it, I see it's a note from Paul, Sebastian's stable-hand.

*Dear Mrs. Dove*

*I'm very sorry that I put you on Zariya yesterday. It was stupid of me not to check your skills were a suitable match to the horse I chose. Please forgive me.*

*I've greatly loved my job at Penmorrow and will miss it so much, but I understand Lord De Montfort's reasons for asking me to leave. I wish I could stay but I can't. I wish you a speedy recovery and once again apologize for your fall.*

*Yours sincerely,*

*Paul*

Furious, I step gingerly from the bed and grab my robe from the chaise. My head swims and I clutch the bedpost to steady myself. How dare Sebastian fire Paul when the accident was not his fault. Sebastian is in his study, engrossed in estate accounts. He looks up when I enter without knocking.

"What are you doing out of bed?" His tone is frosty. Marching over to his desk, I slap the letter down on top of his papers. He glances down at the letter, his eyes skimming the words and his expression dark. "*And?*" He cocks his head to one side and lifts a heavy brow, his arms folded across his chest as he rests back into his chair.

"Paul's not to blame. I can't believe you've fired him. It was Scarlett who suggested which horse I should ride," I state incredulously.

"I'm sorry, Elizabeth, remind me when I engaged *you* as Estate Manager."

My head throbs and my temper soars.

"Be reasonable." My voice is shrill. His eyes are locked on mine, burning like black coals, daring me to challenge him further.

"Reasonable?" He laughs. "As you were reasonable, taking my horse for a jolly little run when you evidently don't know its ass from its hoof?"

My hand reaches up to comfort my pulsing temple but I wince when I touch the bandaged wound.

"Get to bed," he snaps, rising from his chair and moving around the desk toward me. "Right now." He takes my arm and leads me upstairs and I don't protest. I really don't feel well.

The rest of the day is spent eating chicken soup and sleeping. When I wake fully, the room is in darkness. Reaching across the nightstand, I flick the switch to the bedside lamp and it casts a golden light about the room. Sebastian isn't beside me. The clock on his nightstand tells me that it's one-fifteen—the early hours of the morning and he's not here. *Where is he? I feel panicky. Alone.*

Shrugging on my robe and slipping my feet into my slippers, I pad down the landing to the top of the stairs. All is silent except for the steady ticking of the grandfather clock in the hall below. The hall is illuminated by a table lamp as I carefully descend the stairs, holding fast to the banister. The kitchen door is closed but I see a light from the gap underneath. Twisting the handle, the door creaks open. Sebastian and Bella are deep in conversation.

"Mum, you're awake." Bella sounds relieved.

"Darling, sit down, I'll make you a cup of tea." Sebastian stands and walks to the stove where he places the kettle on the burner.

"What are you talking about?" I ask, staring at Bella, so demure in the candlelight.

"Bella's been regaling me with tales of her childhood," he interjects.

"Have you, Bella?" Still staring at her, she nods in agreement.

"Yes, I was just telling him about the time I was on the Girl Guide camp and Joe insisted on staying too. He cried and stamped his feet until you and Dad gave in and said he could stay as an honorary girl. He was such a *brat.*" She smiles at the memory. That seems a lifetime away, I reflect. How I miss Joe.

"Why are you both up so late?" I ask Sebastian, who's adding milk and sugar to a china mug.

"Just spending quality time together, darling." He turns to look at me, his demeanour gentle—so changeable.

"I'll be up in a moment. I'll bring your tea up. You get back to bed." It's an order, but I stand fast.

"I'm not tired, I've been sleeping all day," I protest.

He pauses, a teaspoon in his hand and the kettle whistling. "Okay. Sit." He nods to the old church pew on which Bella sits but I take a seat on the pew opposite Bella, so I face her across the oak refectory table.

"It's good that you are both getting to know each other." My words belie the envy I feel at their closeness.

"Your mother called," Sebastian says, "and Ruth. They wanted to know how you are and send their love."

"How did they know about the accident?" I ask him.

"I called them both," Bella replies, shuffling in her seat. "I thought they'd want to know. We were worried about you. Grandma says she will come and see you soon."

The hot sweet tea helps to wash down my pain medication and I welcome the relief they give almost immediately. Feeling drowsy again, I return to bed, leaving Sebastian and Bella to their cosy chat. Thirty minutes later I'm aware of Sebastian slipping into bed beside me and I snuggle back against his chest, drifting off to sleep once more. The nightmares come again, the same as before. Always, I'm in the chamber of pain and Scarlett is fornicating with Sebastian while I watch.

# Chapter 18

Two weeks have passed since my accident and I'm fully recovered. My scar is healing nicely and the headaches have stopped. Sebastian has treated me as though I'm a porcelain doll but, to be frank, I'm starting to seriously crave the rough, sultry Sebastian. Two long weeks without sex is making me restless and short tempered and I wonder how he can survive celibacy when his sexual appetite is usually insatiable. I decide to reward his patience tonight.

Scarlett and Bella are taking a bus to town, to watch a movie and have dinner together as she's missing her friends back home in Dorset. Sebastian and I have the house to ourselves, and I have an evening of delicious erotica planned.

It's four o'clock and I decide to call Ruth for an update on our business, Evershaw & Dove. It's so kind of my business partner and friend to afford me time away to heal after the death of my son and husband last winter. I'm feeling rested and happy. It was the right decision to come here. Sebastian was right. I just needed to trust in his judgment and let him take care of me.

"Ruth! How's it going stranger?"

She squeals when she hears my voice. "Beth! *O.M.G.* It's going brilliantly. We've two new contracts and our bottom line is way up on this time last year. How's life in the sticks? Are you all healed up now? How's your head?"

"Yep, I'm all healed and happier than I can remember. Sebastian's been a dream, he's been taking care of me . Killing me with kindness!" We laugh. "Ruth, you are coming to my fortieth birthday party, aren't you?"

"Try and stop me! I can't wait. You said it would be a masked ball so I've been trawling on the internet, trying to find a suitable creation to wow all the men. I've bought *the* most divine mask, Beth. Covered with bling, it's so me."

"Wow, it sounds stunning. Don't look too sexy or Sebastian will be after you," I warn facetiously.

"No worries on that score, he adores you," she says. "He's been taking a keen interest in his investment. Calls once a week for an update on the figures and I always get an update on my buddy in return."

This is news to me. Although Sebastian invested in our company at a time when we needed the funds, he rarely mentions it to me. We end the call promising to keep in touch. Both of us are excited about the ball, now just three weeks away.

While Sebastian runs Bella and Scarlett to the bus stop, I dash upstairs to change my outfit. Slipping out of my jeans and tee, I spritz myself in Desire and retrieve new lingerie from my drawer. *Scanty Panties, you are so sexy.* I giggle as I carefully slip on the whisper of black lace. Instead of a bra, I select a black boned basque, which has been concealed beneath a pile of sweaters in my wardrobe. It's tight and eventually I have to tug it around bringing the hook and eye fasteners to my front, so that I can hook it closed before twisting it back the right way. Black sheer stockings are fastened by suspenders, which stretch down from the edges of the basque. Gazing in the full-length mirror, I'm in awe of the slut who gazes back. *You are irresistible, you whore.* My feet slip into unfeasibly high black stilettos and I'm ready to cook. I can't actually recall any TV chefs in such apparel.

Tottering across the unforgiving flagstones in the kitchen, I light the pillar candle on the table and check on the progress of the duck, which is crispy and the aroma delicious. You are a domestic goddess. I grin smugly as I hear the heavy front door slam shut, signalling the return of my prey.

I quickly perch on the edge of the table, legs akimbo on the church pew, resting back on my arms so that my breasts spill forth above the confines of the boned corset. I pout my glossy red lips and listen as the footsteps of his boots near the door. I can feel the moistness in my panties as my core tenses in anticipation of his reaction. The brass handle turns and the door pushes open. He stands in the doorway, shock registering on his face, rapidly replaced with a carnal, animalistic desire as he absorbs the scene before him.

"*Fuck.*"

*I think that's a good reaction.*

"You like, Sir?" My slickly glossed lips form an O and my tongue licks at my top lip provocatively.

"Oh, I like very much. Fuck, what have you done to

yourself?" He prowls around the kitchen, drinking me in from every angle, his eyes narrowing darkly. His breathing is laboured and the bulge at his crotch signals his arousal.

"Dinner will be served in two minutes. Please take a seat." Sliding off the table as elegantly as my attire will afford, I indicate a pew. He doesn't take his eyes off mine as he ignores my request. Instead, he swaggers toward me, hips thrust slightly forward, making the bulge appear even more pronounced. God, I want him, right here and now but I'm going to make him wait. All part of my cunning plan. Turning my back on him deliberately, I sashay to the stove, scoop on the oven glove and bend forward, legs apart and straight, and peer in at the duck.

"You shouldn't have done that, Elizabeth," he growls sexily as he moves behind me.

I thrust my backside farther as I reach in to lift out the sizzling tray. He waits until I put the tray down on the hot plate before reaching between my thighs, his fingers pressing against the damp lace. I gasp at his touch.

"If you play with fire," he whispers in my ear, "you are likely to get burnt." His lips brush my ear sending a shiver down my spine. He reaches round me and, taking the oven glove, removes the food from the hot plate, placing it on the marble worktop. I'm about to protest that the food will get cold and spoil, when he takes my hand and spins me around to face him. He looks so hot, all menacing testosterone, and I'm yearning for him with every fibre of my body.

"Come with me." He leads me from the kitchen and I think we are going upstairs to bed. Instead, he marches me through his study. The cellar. This means only one thing—the chamber of pain. He's pulling me so firmly by the hand that it's difficult to navigate the winding stone steps. I keep my free hand on the cold stone wall as we descend.

"Sebastian, slow down," I pant, heels clicking on the worn steps. He maintains his pace and we're soon approaching the first door to the inner chamber. He lifts the latch and pushes the rickety door open. Pulling my hand sharply, he urges me into the wine cellar. He kicks the door shut so that it nearly catches my hip and I quicken my pace. At the small oak door to the far end of the wine cellar, he turns the ancient key and, oh Lord, we are inside the Chamber of Pain. He takes a box of matches from the small mosaic table and lights the incense sticks and candle, casting a warm glow on the grey cobbled walls.

"What do you have in mind for me here, Sir?" My breath catches with anticipation. He's circling me predatorily, his eyes never leaving mine.

"Kneel on the bed." He points to the centre of the circular bed. I stay where I am, challenging and defiant. A smile plays across his lips as his eyes darken. "Kneel. *Now.*" He points again. Again, I defy him, and he shakes his head slowly, sucking in his breath. *Fuck*, he looks really mean and I'm so turned on by the unspoken threat. Before I have time to see him coming toward me, he has my arm gripped behind my back and, forcing me to turn away from him, he pushes me down over the bed by pulling up on my wrist painfully. He delivers a hard stinging slap to my right buttock.

"*Ouch*, you pig," I squeal.

"Pig?"

A second slap whacks across my left buttock but I can't move without causing pain to my arm. *God damn him!*

"Apologise," he says coolly, politely.

"Sor-ry," I hiss at him. This evidently isn't said with sufficient remorse as a third slap whips across my right thigh.

"*Ouch!* That bloody well stings, Sebastian." *I want more!* It's the most erotic experience because I know he wouldn't truly hurt me. He loves me. He'll take me so far and then know the limit to my punishment. I feel sure.

"Are you sorry, Elizabeth? Because the palm of my hand is eager to deliver another smack to your insolent backside." He pulls me up and releases my arm, which I rub briskly to restore the circulation.

"Yes, Sir, I'm genuinely sorry." I smile angelically, and he laughs but his eyes don't smile.

"Good. You're learning that your defiance *will* be punished. Shoes off. On the bed." His breath comes quick as he unbuttons his shirt, revealing his muscular chest covered with thick course black hair and I long to run my hands and tongue across it. He sees me eying him hungrily but clicks his fingers and points to my shoes. I slip them off and move obediently to the bed, resting back onto my heels.

"Excellent," he purrs as he shrugs off his shirt, letting it fall to the stone floor. He moves to a wooden chest, which had been hidden by a large floor cushion, and lifts the lid. Reaching in, he pulls out a length of rope and turns to face me with it, pulling it taut between his fists. My eyes widen at the sight of Sebastian's naked torso, jeans slung low on his hips revealing a hint of pubic hair. The way he is gripping the rope...I'm trembling with desire and carnal lust.

"I need you *so* badly." A moan passes my lips as he places a foot up on the bed and tugs my hair, forcing me to stand.

"I know you do, my little slut, but you have to be patient," he admonishes, kissing me hard on my glossy lips. He pulls back and places his thumb on my mouth. Wiping hard, he smears the gloss from my pouting lips before kissing me brutally again, and I respond by forcing my tongue in to meet his. He breaks away and his jaw sets as he grabs my left wrist and then my right, slipping the rope around them both and knotting it tightly. He pulls the rope upward, lifting my arms above my head, looping then knotting it over the metal hook above the bed so that my arms are suspended from the low overhead wooden beam. My breasts rise up and break free from the restraint of the basque, nipples erect and throbbing for his touch.

"So beautiful." He trails a finger down my throat, down between my breasts and onwards to the top of my panties. Slipping his finger beneath the lace, he finds my quivering clitoris, rubbing it so exquisitely that I cry his name, as my climax is merely a single stroke away. He stops abruptly, leaving me wanting. "Fuck, you're dripping for me."

"Stop teasing me," I whine.

Ignoring my plea, he turns his attention to my suspenders and with a flick of his fingers he frees my stockings. Returning to my panties once again, he grasps the delicate lace between his thumb and forefinger, slides them down to my ankles and I obligingly step from them. Parting my legs, I wait fervently to receive the oral pleasure I feel sure will follow, but he shifts from the bed and returns to the wooden chest.

"What are you doing?" I can barely contain my frustration but he seems oblivious to my needs.

"Elizabeth." He turns, and sees that I'm scrutinising him. "Please remember the rules. You do not look me in the eye. I'll let it go on this occasion but next time, avert your eyes or you will be blindfolded in here. Understood?"

"Yes, Sir." Lowering my eyes, I see that he's holding a length of red fabric. "What's that for, Sir?"

Sebastian again climbs on the bed, standing before me, and the fabric is coming toward my face. "This is a gag which I'm going to tie across your talkative little mouth and secure behind your head. Before I do, we need to agree a signal that you will give me if you want me to stop."

"Stop?" I ask nervously. "What will you do to me?"

"Whatever I want to do. That's the point, Elizabeth. We will have a safe word, which you'll use when not gagged, but it's only to be used if I exceed your pain or pleasure threshold. When I say that, I mean really exceeds it. I'm going to push some boundaries with you and I don't expect you to cry wolf."

"Oh." My imagination is running wild.

"Simply say STOP. If you're gagged, as you will be shortly, turn your head left to right twice indicating NO and I'll stop."

"But—" He gags me before I can continue, the red silk trapped between my lips and knotted behind my left ear.

"Ah, that's so much better." He grins. "Now I'm going to feed that hungry pussy."

Retrieving something from the chest, which he conceals behind his back, he resumes his position on the bed. I look down to see what he has, but he looks up and I look away compliantly. Something cold and hard is pressing against my labia. My eyes widen at the shock of it.

"Open your legs wider."

I do as he bids, and the object presses harder, deeper until it penetrates me and entirely fills my hot aching vagina and begins to vibrate deep in my core.

"*Aagh*..." I can't speak or beg to climax, silenced as I am by the constraints of the silk.

"That's good, isn't it? That's right, take it all, good girl." His other hand grabs a handful of buttock, his fingers probing between the cleft. Just one finger probes deeper, finding my most private place, and I squeeze to block his intrusion but he forces the vibrator forward against my G-spot and, involuntarily, my back arches.

"*Aagh...*" My futile protest serves only to encourage him and his finger penetrates my anus. He withdraws, then pushes again while the vibrator continues its assault. I'm bucking and writing as the tremors of ecstasy, stronger than I have ever known, course up my spine and radiate to my limbs. I'm so completely filled, and the sensation so intense that I can't bear it. The pulsing doesn't stop, the waves growing stronger, and I'm biting down on the gag, head thrown back and still he thrusts faster, deeper until I can't take any more, one orgasm merging with the next until, abruptly, he stops. As he withdraws his finger and vibrator, the hypersensitivity is too much. Over-stimulated, I pull against the rope, which bites into my wrists painfully, causing me to struggle more.

"Stop. Let me take the rope off the hook." Sebastian tugs at the rope until it slips from the hook and I crumble, exhausted, at his feet. My arms are leaden and my wrists sore. I wait for him to untie me, but he doesn't.

"On your knees," he growls. I am spent and can't cope with any more stimulation, but if I turn my head left to right, then I'm conceding defeat, weak and pathetic. Falling at the first hurdle. I do as he says and move to my knees, bent forward onto my elbows, my ass rising to receive more from him, reluctant and tingling. I hear his zipper and the sound of his moan as he releases his erection, and my quivering pussy responds once more. The head of his cock slides easily inside my wetness and I push my hips back to meet his thrusts, which are brutal and hurried. He takes a fistful of my long hair and tugs hard, raising my head, as he pounds into me, quickening his pace, his breathing laboured.

"Fuck. You. Are. My. Whore." He climaxes with a cry as he stills and pulses inside me. When his frenzy abates, he pulls me back into his lap and kisses my hair, removing the gag and rope. He holds me and nuzzles the back of my neck. "You're *mine,*" he whispers, "*always mine.*"

*Yes. I am yours. But what are you doing to me?*

# Chapter 19

Whoever is knocking on the front door is impatient. The grandfather clock in the hall has just chimed nine, too early in the morning for visitors.

"I'm *coming*," I call, irritated that Scarlett hasn't yet risen. Again, the lion's head knocks heavily on the iron mount. "All right. Wait." Throwing the door wide, I nearly expire with shock, for Ruth is standing on the step clutching an overnight bag. "What the hell?" I gasp as my dear friend folds me into a tight embrace.

"Surprise!" She squeals.

"Oh my God. What are you doing here?" When the shock abates, I'm thrilled to see Ruth and pull her by the arm, into the house.

"I miss you, Beth, and I've been so worried about you, what with the accident and then radio silence. I thought I'd surprise you. I left at dawn, and here I am."

I usher her through to the kitchen and place the kettle on the stove.

"Wow." She whistles. "What a pad. He really is rich, this tall dark stranger of yours." She takes in the ancient kitchen with copper pans and the view of the stables from the stone mullion window.

"It's not a bad old shack, bit droughty but it does me okay," I tease.

"Where is he, then?" Ruth places a cushion under her

behind before settling down on the pew.

"Sebastian's riding. He likes to ride most mornings unless he has an estate meeting, and since he fired the stable hand he has to saddle his own horse." I hand Ruth a mug of coffee and take a seat opposite her.

"Why'd he fire him?"

"Because he blamed Paul for letting me ride on Zariya, the mare who threw me. It wasn't his fault. It was Scarlett who suggested I ride that particular horse, but once Sebastian gets an idea in his head there's no reasoning with him." I sip my coffee contemplatively.

"He's a prick." She scoffs.

"Ruth!"

"Sorry, Beth, but you've hardly been in touch since you came here and that's not like you so I presume his Lordship has you under his thumb." She glances at me over the rim of her mug and receives a scowl in response.

"Sebastian's been very good to Bella and I," I rebuke.

"Did I hear my name?" Bella bounds in to the kitchen, her face lit up at the sight of her Godmother. "Ruth! Oh my God, when did you get here?" She plants a kiss on Ruth's cheek, and she responds with a pinch to Bella's.

"Cutie Pie! Whoa, when did you grow up so much?" Ruth admires Bella who is dressed in tight black leggings, high brown rattan mules and a leopard print dress. She twirls gracefully and Ruth wolf whistles approvingly.

"Do you like my new clothes? Scarlett chose them with me. You should see the dress Sebastian bought me for my birthday ball," Bella says excitedly.

Taking Ruth's hands in mine, I beamed. "I'll show you *my* gown, Ruth, it's amazing but very daring so don't be shocked."

"Love, there's nothing you can do to shock me these days." She laughs.

"Come on, let's go and find a room for you. You can take your pick. There are eleven spare rooms!"

She's clearly impressed. "Shit, Beth, I'll have to stay eleven nights and try them all."

Skipping from room to room, we giggle like children. After Ruth has viewed all eleven bedrooms, she chooses the smallest. Located in the rear of the house, it has a spectacular vista.

"It's fabulous, Beth, I love it. Just look at that view. I can see the sea." She presses her nose to the glass and marvels at the distant swell.

"Come on, I want to show you our room." I tug her hand and lead her down the passage to our bedroom. She whistles once more when she sees the opulence.

"You like?" I grin.

"I like!" She nods vigorously as I carefully retrieve my crimson gown from the armoire. Holding the gown against my curves, I sway so that the heavy taffeta rustles and Ruth's eyes grow wide as she looks me up and down.

"*Wow.*" She sighs. "It's gorgeous. Very slutty, but bloody gorgeous." She runs the back of her hand across the crisp fabric with a look of awe. "You lucky cow. I'd love a dress like that but I don't think such a dress would love me."

"Try it on, Ruth." She shakes her head but I'm insistent so she complies. Slipping out of her jeans and sweater, she steps gingerly into the pool of taffeta. I help her to pull up the gown but she is a size larger than me and it's a struggle.

"It's too tight," she protests as I tug at the laces behind her.

"Hold still, stop wriggling." The dress is on. Ruth is barely able to breath.

"Look in the mirror." I indicate the full-length mirror and admire my friend from the bathroom doorway.

Neither of us is aware that Sebastian has entered the bedroom. "What the *fuck?*" He growls. We both spin to face him in unison, equally stunned by his interruption.

"Sebastian, hi." Ruth shuffles to him, kissing his right cheek then his left, her ample cleavage straining against taffeta and threatening to entirely spill forth. He eyes her assets unashamedly, before indicating with his finger that she should spin for him. She obliges and he smiles appreciatively.

"Don't mind me, you two," I snap, jealous of the attention he is affording my friend's curves.

"Darling, you didn't tell me Ruth was coming," he says, remembering I exist.

"I didn't know. She wanted to surprise me."

"Sorry, Sebastian. I hope it's not too inconvenient my turning up like this. I wanted to see Beth. It's been too long. I'm sorry I'm wearing her dress, I'll take it off." She reaches behind her back in search of the laces.

"Sebastian, why don't you go and put the kettle on. I'm sure Ruth would like another coffee. Let her get changed in private." He can gauge from my voice that I'm not to be messed with and slinks off, taking his sordid smirk with him. I slam the door shut, nearly catching his heel as he exits.

"Hey, careful!" he shouts.

"Hey, careful yourself!" I retort.

"I heard that," he bellows, and I feel sure he'll make me sorry later.

When Ruth is dressed, we go together to the kitchen where Scarlett is making a pot of coffee. She turns as we enter and eyes Ruth suspiciously.

"Scarlett, this is my dearest friend and business partner, Ruth Evershaw. Ruth, this is Scarlett, Sebastian's housekeeper." The two women size each other up before Ruth breaks the frosty silence.

"Scarlett. Lovely to meet you," she proffers a perfectly manicured hand to Scarlett, who shakes it weakly.

"Nice to meet you too, Mrs. Evershaw. Do you take cream and sugar in your coffee?"

"Yes to both, please, dear." Ruth sits on the pew next to Sebastian who is studying the newspaper and I take a seat opposite him. He looks up when I sit, his eyes fixed on mine with a steely gaze.

"Elizabeth, you very nearly took my foot off when you slammed the door." He rests his chin on his steepled fingers.

"*Really?* I'm so sorry, Sebastian, I suspect a draft must have caught the door and caused it to slam." My brow lifts as I see his mouth twitch up in a smile. His eyes remain cold, dark, and menacing, sending a shiver down my spine.

Scarlett catches her breath and when she places coffee cups in front of us, her hands are shaking. I glance at her and see the apprehension on her face. She shakes her head as her gaze darts to Sebastian and back to me. I mouth 'what' to her and she indicates again to Sebastian before scurrying from the kitchen. Ruth is staring at me, a quizzical look on her face and I shrug my shoulders before sipping my coffee.

"Elizabeth?" My attention returns to Sebastian. "If we do indeed have drafts, then I'll have my estate manager take a look in case we have a maintenance issue. Or perhaps it was a ghost."

"Ghost? Oh, yes, perhaps it was." I nod. "Ruth, the house is reputedly haunted. A lady is supposed to walk the upstairs corridors, so if you hear any footsteps in the night, it's probably her. That or mice."

"Oh, shit. I'm not going to sleep a wink tonight, now that you've told me that," Ruth says, wide-eyed. "Scarlett looked like she'd already seen a ghost. She's so pale. Quiet sort, isn't she?"

Ruth addresses me but Sebastian replies. "She's a good housekeeper, but yes, she's a quiet little thing. Gets anxious about the most trivial things."

"She doesn't look well, Sebastian," I say.

"Nonsense. She's fine." He drains his coffee and bangs his cup down on to the table. "I wish you wouldn't pander to that girl, Elizabeth. I don't have to remind you that she's the servant and when you indulge her as you do, it undermines my authority and confuses her."

"Sorry," I say contritely. "She just seems subdued. Does she have any family? I never hear her talk of anyone."

"She has a father, who has dementia, I believe. I seem to recall her telling me that he's in a nursing home in Cumbria. Don't think she's seen him for years." Sebastian stands and places his cup in the sink then returns to kiss me on the cheek. "I'm going to Exeter to meet a friend. I'll be back late so you two girls eat without me this evening. Enjoy your girly gossip and I'll see you tomorrow, Ruth." He kisses her cheek and I watch him leave. He's so hot, dressed in jeans and a black shirt, but the sight of him leaving fills me with a primal longing.

"Miss you already," I call to him, but he doesn't hear me.

Ruth leans back and folds her arms. "Well. There's a very peculiar dynamic going on between you two," she observes. "Want to tell me what it's all about?"

"It's just that he's not used to sharing the house with anyone other than Scarlett." I want to tell Ruth of my concerns regarding Sebastian's feelings toward Scarlett but I'm unsure of her reaction. I want Ruth to continue to support my being here, and I know that she will judge me harshly if I voice my concerns. She is my only close friend, though. She knows what I've been through and I need to talk to someone. It's eating me up inside. The trust I felt for Sebastian is diminished, and yet I wonder if I'm imagining a relationship between them through my own insecurity. Hell, I've got to say something. "Ruth, I think maybe I'm going mad, or jumping to wild conclusions, but I wonder if Sebastian and Scarlett are still lovers."

She narrows her eyes and purses her lips as she considers what I have said. "Okay. What have you got on them?"

"Nothing tangible. It's just a *feeling* when I'm around them. When they're together. I feel like I'm intruding, as though there's some unspoken conversation that I'm interrupting. Do you understand?"

She nods, and sighs deeply. "I have to say, Beth, it's not a normal set-up here. She's a beauty and I'd be concerned if my boyfriend was sharing this bloody romantic old house with someone like her, especially since he's already admitted they had a fling once."

That doesn't make me feel any better.

"Have you ever caught them? You know, *at it?*"

"God, no. It's not that. It's a look. A glance they share. The way he treats her. He's very dominant, Ruth. She's very subservient. Submissive, even." My voice trails to a whisper. I've said too much.

"Where does she sleep?" Ruth asks, seemingly oblivious to my discomfort.

"Downstairs in the basement. She has her own room. Anyway, enough of Scarlett, let's go shopping." My calculated change of subject succeeds in distracting Ruth, whose face lights up at the mention of shopping.

"Isn't it all farmers markets and organic veg shops here?" She laughs.

"No! We actually have clothes shops. Albeit they mostly stock waxed jackets and wellington boots." I giggle.

Ruth and I happily peruse the only local boutique. It's quite a revelation for Ruth, who anticipates the shop bursting with cloth sacks and mop caps, but instead delights in finding a collection of current designer pieces. She selects a rather conservative skirt and cardigan while my eye is drawn to a black cocktail dress.

"You look lovely," I tell her, as she pulls back the curtain in the small fitting room opposite mine.

"Honestly? It's not too frumpy?" She tugs at the pale blue cashmere sleeves, which sit an inch too short on her long arms.

"Not at all," I lie. "Perhaps a size bigger?"

"This is a sixteen. I'd rather die than wear an eighteen!" she proclaims disdainfully.

I shrug my shoulders in exasperation, sweep the curtain to my cubicle closed and change in to the skimpy slip of black fabric. It's a snug fit and I note with satisfaction how slimming it is. *Mirrors never lie, right?* I whoosh the curtain aside and twirl for Ruth.

"I hate you, Beth Dove. When did you get so disgustingly thin?" She stands with hands on her hips, a look of awe and annoyance quite evident.

"Not intentionally. I just haven't really got my appetite back after…after the accident." The memory flows unwelcome through me, seeping like molten lava through venous rivers until my entire body is consumed with burning sorrow. I shouldn't be shopping, shouldn't be laughing, shouldn't be—

"Come on. Snap out of it. You look bloody magnificent in that dress." Ruth intuitively knows to lighten the mood and her words succeed in dissipating the darkness within me.

"Sorry. I almost forget, just for a short time, and then it hits me harder than ever. I can be taking a bath and think I hear Joe knocking on the door asking if dinner's ready. Or I hear the television and expect to see Alan in his favourite armchair."

"It takes time, love. You did the right thing coming to Cornwall. It's a different pace of life here. Just make sure you keep yourself busy so you don't have too much time to dwell and mope, okay?"

"You're right, and thankfully I have my birthday party to plan. In fact, I need to catch up with Scarlett and see if she knows who's invited."

"Don't you know?" Ruth asks incredulously.

"Nope. Sebastian says it's all in hand. All I'm allowed to do is plan the decorations and food. Well, Scarlett is organizing the food. He says Mum can't come."

Ruth's mouth gapes. "You're shitting me?"

"I wish I was, but no. I kind of get where he's at. It's for younger people and I guess he's thinking of Mum and how it isn't her scene." I rub the back of my neck and contemplate a milestone birthday without my mother.

"Hey, you're moping again. You need to buy that dress and then we need to go and eat lunch."

The Buttery is a traditional Cornish cafe, with floral print cloths, real teapots and books on folklore for sale. It has a charm and timelessness which is appealing. Ruth and I take a seat at the table in the window and order pork and cider pies and a pot of tea. My phone bleeps and I retrieve it from my bag. It's Sebastian.

*Plans changed, won't be home tonight. See you tomorrow, have fun with Ruth. S*

"Ruth, look at this message." I pass my phone to her, and she reads with disdain.

"Where the hell's he gone?" she asks.

"Absolutely no idea. I intend to find out though." I tap out my reply.

*Thanks for letting me know. Where are you?*

I refrain from ending with my customary kiss. He replies immediately.

*Dinner with friends and looks like a late one. Probably boozy so don't want to drive. S*

I'm furious and also humiliated that Ruth should

witness him treating me this way, so I shield my phone with my hand so that she can't see his message to me. "He's being sensible," I say unconvincingly. "Drinking with friends and doesn't want to risk driving. I'm pleased about that."

She nods in agreement but I can see she's unconvinced. I tap a hostile response.

*Not sure I'll be home either. Ruth and I going clubbing in Exeter.*

I press send and wait for the irate riposte. I don't wait long.

*Are you deliberately trying to antagonise me? I expect you home and will call the house at 10pm. S*

"What a bloody cheek. He can go out, get trashed and not come home but I'm expected to be home like a dutiful wife? Talk about double standards."

Ruth looks puzzled. "We will be home, Beth," she says.

"That's not the point."

*And if I'm not home?*

Nerves knot in my stomach as I send the message.

*Try that shit and see what happens. If you want to*

*see me angry, carry on. S*

*Oh, fuck. He's seething. Damage limitation time, Beth.* **I'll be home. Take a chill pill** *x*

My phone pings. New message from Sebastian.

**Chill pill?? Hmm. Not a very good submissive are you? Will deal with you tomorrow. Will still call at 10pm. S. (ps I note the kiss on last message – better!)**

The familiar butterflies in my stomach beat their little wings, as I contemplate the punishment Sebastian will mete out tomorrow. Our pies arrive, small clay pots of steaming comfort food, which lift my mood considerably.

\*\*\*

I open the second bottle of Chateauneuf-du-Pape and slop it in to the glass tumblers. I feel sure this isn't how such a fine wine should be served but they were the first glasses I found and they hold a copious volume, which is a major positive. Ruth and I are very cosy beneath her feather duvet, having decided to share a sleepover in her room tonight. This had been hastily decided while we were in the Great Hall after a delicious dinner of nachos with cheese, it being Scarlett's night off, when we heard a thud in the hall. Both being brave, we had clutched each other's hand and investigated only to find no cause of the thud.

At this point, we had grabbed two bottles of wine, our

tumblers, and pitched up the stairs—Ruth making ghostly '*woo*' noises and I squealing like a banshee. So, here we are, telling ghost stories to ensure neither of us sleeps at all tonight and getting delightfully drunk. When we drain the last drops of the second bottle, we can no longer suppress our weariness and Ruth is asleep and snoring shortly after. I gently pull the duvet up to her chin and watch her sleep, thinking how blessed I am to have such a true and wonderful friend. I creep quietly from her room and return to my own bedroom, preferring to sleep in our bed with Sebastian's scent on my pillow.

His jacket is strewn on the chaise and I scoop it up, hanging it carefully in his wardrobe. As I do so, I notice a red glossy card protruding from the inside pocket. Curiosity compels me to retrieve it. It is an invitation, and I'm intrigued, Sebastian having made no mention of a party other than my own. What I read turns my blood to ice.

# Chapter 20

The invitation is to Sebastian alone, written in gold italic script.

*Lord Sebastian De Montfort*
*Is cordially invited to attend the 8th Annual Fetish Feast with Charity Auction*

*On Saturday 2nd June 2012*

*At*
*Girling Hall, Brook Lane, Camelford, Cornwall*
*7pm until late*
*Entrance strictly by invitation only*
*RSVP*

Tonight is the second of June so this is presumably where Sebastian has gone.

*Fetish Feast?* I am devastated. I know he's into domination, but to be part of the scene, or whatever it's called, takes his kinkiness to a whole new level. Now I question his fidelity, his love for me. So many lurid thoughts course through my mind along with rage and hurt. I have to call him, but my phone is downstairs in the Great Hall and Sebastian was calling at ten o'clock. The bedside clock reads eleven forty-five. I race, in panic, downstairs—oblivious to ghosts and ghouls—and snatch my phone from the table in the Great Hall. Five missed calls, and two text messages.

*Called as arranged. Where are you? S*

*Oh you are in SUCH deep shit. I'll see you in the morning.*

Contemplating whether to call him, I decide instead on the cowardly approach and type a text message.

*Sorry phone was downstairs. I've been home all evening which is more than I can say for you. Hope you're enjoying the FETISH FEAST!! You're in far deeper shit than I!*

I hesitate before pressing the send button, but my anger wins out. Clutching my phone, I retreat to the sanctuary of the kitchen and immediately feel calmer in the warm womb of the now seemingly bleak house. I make a mug of cocoa and sip at the milky froth, staring at the phone which affords me no comfort with its silence.

I'm startled by a shadow silhouetted in the doorway. Scarlett glides to my side and lays a gentle hand on my arm. I stare up at her, a vision almost ethereal in white muslin nightdress, her long dark curls cascading over her shoulders.

"I'm sorry to disturb you, Mrs. Dove," she mutters

quietly.

"You're not disturbing me, Scarlett. Please call me Beth."

"Can I join you?" I nod and indicate for her to sit. She makes herself a mug of cocoa before seating herself opposite me at the table.

"Is everything all right?" She notices the tear running errantly down my cheek, reflected by the candle, which burns between us.

"Everything's fine."

"It's clearly not," she observes. "Far be it for me to interfere in matters between yourself and his Lordship, but I genuinely hate to see you so sad." She reaches a pale hand across the oak slab and I grasp it tightly, appreciating the tactile gesture.

"He's at a bloody *fetish* party," I hiss, raising my gaze to hers to gauge her reaction.

She doesn't flinch. "I see." She pauses just a moment. "He only goes once a year, Beth. I've been with him. It was two years ago and I can assure you that it isn't nearly as perverse as you might imagine."

I cock a cynical brow and take another sip of my cocoa.

"Mostly he goes to meet old friends. Like-minded people who share the same passion."

My brow rises further at the word. "*Passion?* I presume you mean in the literal sense of the word?"

"He wouldn't be unfaithful to you, Beth. If that's what worries you, then you need to understand his Lordship better. When he possesses a woman, he commits fully and assumes that responsibility wholeheartedly. That's not to say he isn't a hot blooded male. We both know what he is."

My jaw falls slack but I remain silent in the hope that she will confess what I have long suspected. She doesn't disappoint.

"You need to know, Beth. He will be so angry with me for telling you, but I care about you and see the way you look at he and I, so full of questions. You deserve the *truth.* When I moved to Penmorrow, five years ago, I was destitute. I had run away from an abusive home. Not my mother, you understand. My father was an alcoholic and used to beat me. My mother was too weak to protect me or even to acknowledge his mistreatment of me. It took a great deal of courage to pack my suitcase and walk away, but I did it." She pulls back her shoulders and I glimpse the steely resolve, which had gone unnoticed before.

"I took a train to Exeter. It was the first train running when I arrived at the station, and I always felt a draw to the West Country. I had romantic visions of the peace and tranquillity I thought it would offer. Anyway, I arrived and checked in to the first hotel I could find, having just enough money for one night. I asked if they needed any staff but they had a full quota for the season. I was *beside* myself, Beth. I remember sitting at the bar with a glass of water, bereft and wondering how I would eat, where I would live. Then this tall, handsome, mature man approached me. He bought me a drink and we talked. He was so commanding, so insistent that I tell him my story and he listened intently. When I'd finished, he promised me that he would help me. He offered me a job here. That man, *my saviour,* was Sebastian."

"I see." My hand still in Scarlett's is now hot and moist from her firm grip. I withdraw and clutch it around my now cold mug. "So, you came back with him to work here. I understand that and admire his gallantry in offering a hand to a young woman in distress. When did he first take advantage of you?"

Scarlett expels a deep breath and slumps uncomfortably against the hard wood of the pew. "He didn't take *advantage.* I gave myself willingly to him. You have to believe me when I tell you that it didn't happen for a long time. His wife was still alive, but she was ill then. He didn't force me. It was a natural progression and almost an extension of the role in which I was working so diligently. Subservience brings with it a security and protection, which I hadn't known before. I felt appreciated and needed, and I drew great pleasure from pleasing Him. In return, I helped Sebastian regain the passion and fulfilment which had been devoid in his marriage. I put no pressure upon him, no demands, I was simply here for him to take what *he* needed and allowed him to vent his frustrations when her Ladyship deteriorated."

The confirmation of my suspicions brings scant comfort but I can at least comprehend what drew them together and held them inextricably tied. That does not, however, excuse such an arrangement continuing now that

Sebastian is in a relationship with me. "And *now?*" I ask guardedly. "I'm not stupid. Or blind. I see how you two are together and can only assume that nothing's changed between you."

"It has, Beth. He's changed. Before, when her Ladyship was alive, he was tender with me. He always had another side to him. He liked to dominate me, instruct, and guide me. When she died, he increasingly became more aggressive in his demands. He would humiliate me. And that was fine, to a degree…but it was almost as if he began to despise me. I'd try so very hard to make him happy with me. Whatever he demanded, I'd comply willingly. On one occasion, he told me I'd not cleaned the house properly. He left me chained in the chamber for twenty-four hours. I had to pee in a bucket. It was so humiliating. He bought food and water, but left them just out of reach."

"Oh my God. He's a *monster!*" I cover my mouth in horror as I try to comprehend what she tells me.

"No, Beth. He's not a monster. He was beside himself with grief, and guilt. He was sorry afterward. He said I was so good to him and that he appreciated my loyalty."

"Why did you let him do it to you, Scarlett? Why didn't you *leave?*"

"Everything he's ever done, I've consented to. He plays the dominant master so well, but I've seen the vulnerability behind those dark eyes. He's like…a lost boy. If I say no to him, turn my back on him, he'd have no way to challenge the demons. They would simply ride him hard, straight to the pits of Hell."

"*Stop!*" I implore, bringing the flat of my hand crashing against the surface of the wooden table. "You talk about him as if…as if I don't know him at all. You're describing the man I love as though he were someone I don't know. Answer me one thing. When did it stop between you, or is he still *fucking* you?" My voice reaches a high-pitched crescendo of realisation and panic, as I spit the words venomously at her.

Scarlett retains a calmness and serenity that is totally at odds with my animosity toward her. She fingers a stray curl, which has tumbled across her cheek, and meets my gaze, her eyes sorrowful behind inky lashes. "It's not all about sex, Beth."

A shocked laugh catches in my throat.

"No, we don't have sex," she continues. "Not since his Lordship first took *you* to his bed. You meet that need now, not I. What you don't fulfil is his need to express his frustrations, his exertion of power and a channel by which to exorcise his demons. *I* still meet that need in Him." She looks triumphant and at this moment I realise that Sebastian is actually meeting a need in her to be vilified and degraded in order to feel better about herself.

"What does he do to you now?" I whisper, barely audibly.

"Nothing that I don't deserve," she replies, a smile playing on her lips. "Nothing sexual. When I don't please Him, he rightly punishes me. When he is anguished, I allow him to vent that anguish upon me but it's never sexual. You have to believe me."

"What I don't understand is, what *good* is there for you in this treatment?" I ask incredulously.

"What good? I have a home of my own. I belong like never before. I'm *needed*. I'm *happy*."

"But he treats you no better or differently from your own father…"

"Worlds apart, Beth. My father couldn't have cared less if I died. His Lordship would be heartbroken if I died. My father didn't need me, he just needed the comfort of whisky. His Lordship tells me every day how much I'm needed. Appreciated. So, you see, everyone benefits from this. You have a man who adores you, who shares your bed, but you are spared any subjection to his dark side." She crosses her arms across her barely concealed breasts and regards me closely.

I consider what she has said and wonder if it is I who is deluded rather than her. "Actually, Scarlett, I have seen the dark side of him and I rather like it, if you're referring to the chamber. I find his dominance appealing. I know him better than you give me credit for."

She smiles warmly. "Good. Then we are all content, aren't we?" She rises and places her mug in the ceramic butler's sink, and faces me with an air of arrogance that sees my temper coursing. I stand and pull back my shoulders in an attempt to match her stance.

"I'm warning you now," I hiss. "You leave him alone. Remember you are just an employee and I can get you *fired* at any time. Got that?"

"I think you'll find you can't." She shakes her head emphatically. "Beth, you misunderstand me. I'm not your enemy. I'm a friend for you here. We're kindred spirits, you and I. Both love the man in different ways and both owe him a debt of gratitude."

"I don't want to hear any more." I gasp at her audacity and cringe at her asceticism. "I've seen the marks on your wrists. Your...*frailty*. There is absolutely no way I'm living with a sick bastard or subjecting my daughter to it. We've been through enough. In the morning I'll be going home, we both will. Now, if you don't mind, I'm tired and I'm going to bed."

I leave the kitchen without a backward glance, refusing to allow Scarlett a glimpse of the river of tears threading down my cheeks. Damn him. Damn him to hell.

# Chapter 21

The sun is streaming through the window and I shield my eyes from its glare with my forearm. I stretch and slowly awaken, recollection of last night's events hitting me squarely in the stomach. Sebastian. Scarlett. Ruth. Leaving. I sit up, rubbing the remnants of a fitful sleep from my heavy eyelids. That's when I see the long legs stretched beside me on the bed. They are clad in black denim and are crossed at the feet. I turn to face Sebastian who is propped up on pillows, arms folded. His eyes, burning coals, which penetrate to my very core, offer no warmth, nor tenderness. His mouth is set in a stern line with no smile playing on his lips. *Damn, he looks sexy in a black t-shirt, all rippling biceps and meanness.*

"Sebastian." It's more of an exclamation than a welcome.

"Elizabeth." *Fuck, he looks furious.* I'm furious. I'm ten thousand times more furious than he has a right to be.

"I'm leaving today." I wait for his reaction but he stays silent, scowling at me without good cause to do so. "Are you going to say something? *Anything?*" I fist the sheets in annoyance, meeting his stare.

"What do you expect me to say, Elizabeth?"

He can be so taciturn it's infuriating. "How about, please stay? I'm sorry for lying to you about where I was last night. I'm sorry I fucked my housekeeper and beat seven shades of shit out of her, and took advantage of her when she was so vulnerable. Or you could bullshit me some more. It's your choice, Sebastian. What's it going to be?" I'm losing control at this point, on the precipice of hysteria.

He adjusts his position on the bed and runs a languid finger over his bottom lip. His black brow arches, in apparent surprise at my outburst. "Well, that's quite a list, isn't it, Elizabeth. How about, instead, I ask you what the fuck you think you're doing interrogating Scarlett? Or shall I touch upon the total lack of fucking loyalty that you're demonstrating? Or, we can discuss the fact that you couldn't even follow a simple fucking instruction to take my call at ten last night? Had you of course done so, I would have told you where I was, and that the purpose of the evening was to raise money for charity. And mind your fucking language."

"My fucking language?" I repeat in disbelief.

"Precisely."

"Fuck. Bugger. Shit." I challenge him with my profanities. His lip curls in amusement and this serves to infuriate me more. I raise my hand, the palm speeding toward his face to deliver a slap but he grabs my wrist just as my palm meets his stubble rough jaw. He twists my wrist back painfully, and he's strong. I can't free my hand from his grasp. "*Damn* you, Sebastian." I hiss at him, which evidently heightens his amusement.

His eyes light up with that wicked glint I have come to recognise and be aroused by. "Now, now." He laughs at me. "Play nicely." He has me in an arm lock and, as much as I'm struggling, he holds me fast, pinned to the bed. In one swift fluid movement, he throws a leg over and restrains me, a knee pinning down each of my arms. Like a wild animal, I buck and toss but am rendered entirely immobile by the bulk of him. "Are you going to play nicely, Elizabeth?" he asks sweetly, ignoring my protestation.

"Get. Off. Me. You ass."

"No, Elizabeth. That's not nice. Apologise and beg me to please release you."

"Over my dead fucking body, creep," is apparently not the correct response. He increases the weight upon my arms so that I keep still, to ease the pain.

"Dear, oh dear. I think we need to revisit the definition of submission, darling girl." He slaps my face. The shock of the sting brings tears to my eyes.

"I *hate* you," I spit.

"I hate you, *Sir.*" He leans forward, his lips brush mine, and I turn my head to the side in defiance.

Again he pushes down on my arms. I wince and weaken.

"Okay. I hate you, *Sir.* Now get the hell off my bloody arms before you break them," is apparently also wrong.

He slaps my face again. This time he follows the slap with a gentle kiss to my smarting cheek. Never having been struck to my face by a man before, this comes as a total shock. Each slap sends unexpected tremors of arousal surging through my body. It's strangely liberating and fuels a fantasy I have long secretly harboured; there is such a primeval rawness to it. *Christ, I really am as sick in the head as him*, I reflect fleetingly, as he continues to kiss my stinging cheek. He leans over me and whispers in my ear. "Say you are sorry and beg me to please release you."

"I'm sorry. Okay?" It pains me to apologise but my arms have pins and needles as the circulation is impeded.

"Properly," he whispers.

"I'm very sorry, Sir."

"Thank you and I believe you genuinely are."

"Now let me go, my arms are going numb."

"Ask properly."

"*Please* will you release me?" You bastard.

"Of course." He immediately shifts his knees from my arms and I raise them above my head, clenching and unclenching my fists, restoring the blood flow. I touch my sore cheek and feel how it still smarts, wondering how I will explain a bruise to Ruth and Bella. "The redness will fade," he says, reading my mind.

He straddles me still, and I look up at him above me. Familiar stirrings at the apex of my thighs come unwelcome. I'm too mad at him to find him sexy. Yet, his hair is messed up, his broad shoulders and wide frame loom above me, bearing down. As if, again, reading my mind, he grasps the hem of his tee and tugs it off over his head. I hold my breath as I admire his manly powerful form and I want him with a carnal, raw desire. I feel my sex throb and grow slick in anticipation. His lips find mine and his kiss is brutal, his teeth biting at my bottom lip until I wince, sure he's drawn blood.

"Fuck, Elizabeth. Why do you fight me? Why won't you give yourself to me willingly?" He breathes into my ear before nibbling the lobe. I instinctively reach for him, my fingers raking through his hair, tugging at the roots as I pull his head to my neck, needing his kiss, his passion.

"I don't know." I sigh as his lips brush my neck, his fingers on my throat, my breast, pinching at my nipple until it throbs and grows taut. "I know I love you but you're one fucked up guy."

"Not so fucked up, Elizabeth. I'm what you need, darling. I can give you everything. Give yourself to me completely and unquestioningly." His fingers trail down past my navel to the hot aching bundle of nerves between my open thighs. My back arches as I thrust my groin up toward his probing fingers. He parts me and two fingers slide unhindered and slick from my arousal. He finds the secret place within me that he knows so well and strokes it again and again until I feel the crescendo building, taking me to the edge. Still he kneads and beckons in precisely the right way, his thumb rubbing my clitoris, and the waves of orgasm course through me as I clench his fingers tightly within me. At this moment all animosity toward him is forgotten.

"Oh God, Sebastian," I cry. "I want to be yours."

"You are mine. Only mine," he soothes. I reach for his zipper, still trembling as my orgasm dissipates.

"I need you."

"I know, baby." He pushes his jeans down his thighs and positions himself between my legs, the velvety crown of his erection finding my wet, swollen opening. He pushes his hips forward so that the head of his cock enters me. My hips rise to take the rest of him but he pulls back. "No. Slowly." He slides the pulsing head inside me once more and I feel his warm pre-cum on my labia. One forceful thrust and he fills me to my end. I gasp and clutch him deeper still with my legs around his waist until he is inside me to his very root. His thick pulsing cock throbs against my hypersensitive nerves. He lies heavily on me, his thickly matted chest slick with sweat against my breasts.

"Tell me you love me," I implore.

"You know I do," he pants, not saying the three words that I need to hear. "You. Are. My. Soul. You. Will. Never. Leave. Me."

He thrusts with each word and then faster still until I feel him climaxing, his body tensed, his jaw set, and a deep growl reverberating from his throat. He holds me then, so tightly to him as though he knows that with his next breath I will be gone. I stroke his damp, dark locks of hair as his body presses heavily upon me and I know in my heart that I can't leave him even if my head screams caution.

\*\*\*

Bella is cooking a full English breakfast for all of us. The kitchen is in total disarray, eggshells litter the granite worktops, and bacon rind snakes around the tea canister.

She's wearing grey sweat pants and a white vest, which is stained with egg yolk, and is dancing to a tune on the radio as she works. I admire the freedom my daughter has, free from the complexities of relationships and adult problems. She's coped so maturely with the loss of her father and brother that, at this moment, I'm filled with love and admiration for her. She spins on her bare heels and meets my presence with a beaming grin.

"Mum! I didn't see you there. I'm cooking us all the most amazing breakfast. It'll be scrumptialicious!" she exclaims excitedly.

"It smells divine, sweetheart." I flick off the bacon rind and place tea from the canister in the teapot. "I hope you're going to clear this mess up," I scold, good-humouredly.

"Nah, Scarlett can do it," she quips.

"What can I do?" Scarlett enters the kitchen behind me, dressed in her uniform black dress looking svelte and in good spirits.

"Clean up after me." Bella winks at her and Scarlett shakes her head disapprovingly.

"Good morning, Mrs. Dove," she says boldly, as if our conversation last night didn't happen.

"Scarlett," I say curtly.

"Will his Lordship and Mrs. Evershaw be joining you for breakfast?" she asks.

"No, he's gone for a ride. Mrs. Evershaw is still asleep," I reply frostily. "It will just be Bella and I." *Meaning you're not welcome to join us.*

As Bella and I tuck in heartily to bacon, scrambled eggs, fried bread, and mushrooms, my daughter talks animatedly about her upcoming eighteenth birthday, just a week after my fortieth. Her best friend, Chloe, is organising a night out for Bella, who categorically refuses to let me organise a party for her. I agree to drive Bella home to our house in Dorset three days after my own party. We will stay together at the house and I will use the time to catch up on work, realising how much I'm missing my staff at Evershaw Dove Recruitment. Ruth and I have worked tirelessly to build our personnel agency and it's hard for me to be away from it all. Since Sebastian invested money in our growth plans, we are financially secure but I still like to oversee things.

"It'll be a sick birthday, Mum." Bella snaps me out of my daydream.

"If you mean it will be a wonderful birthday, then yes, I'm sure it will be fantastic, sweetheart." I smile. "Talking of birthdays, I need to find the guest list Sebastian has drawn up for my own party."

I leave Bella to clear away the breakfast dishes, and go to Sebastian's study in search of my guest list. His twin pedestal antique desk is cluttered with paperwork and I decide to make myself useful by tidying his papers, inwardly criticizing Scarlett for not doing the task herself. I begin by taking punches of papers and shuffling them in to neat piles. I notice the top drawer is partway open and the temptation to snoop is just too strong. I slide the drawer toward me and scan the contents. An old brown leather address book grabs my attention and I retrieve it, thumbing through the first few pages.

*Christina Travis*
*The Old Bakery*
*4 Portland Crescent*
*Padstow*
*01613 4489099*

Christina Travis, Sebastian's mother-in-law. I recall my encounter with Christina when she followed me to work and warned me about Sebastian. She claimed that he brought about the death of her daughter, Sebastian's wife Libby. I remember the way she implored me to be careful lest 'what he did to Scarlett and Libby' would happen to me also. Initially I had put her ranting down to the grief of a bereaved mother, but now I see how Scarlett has changed since I first met her. The thought occurs to me that I need to see Christina again. I have to know what really happened to Libby. I pick up the telephone receiver on Sebastian's desk and dial her number.

# Chapter 22

The Old Bakery is a charming cob cottage, which would not look out of place on a biscuit tin or chocolate box. Set on the outskirts of the fishing harbour of Padstow, it has a wonderfully tranquil, seaside setting.

As I walk up the path toward the front door, I admire the thatched roof, eyebrow windows, and skewed architecture. The fragrance from the jasmine, which frames the porch overhang, is heavenly. Christina Travis welcomes me in to her home with sincere warmth and invites me to sit in a floral armchair in her cosy living room. When I last saw Christina, she resembled a destitute old lady but today she is smartly attired in a cream blouse and pale green skirt, a string of pearls at her throat. Her mood seems temperate as she fusses in the kitchen preparing a tray of tea and biscuits. "I'm so glad you telephoned me," she calls from the kitchen.

"Thank you for agreeing to see me today," I call back, admiring the comfort of her home. On the side table next to me, a small photograph in simple gold frame catches my attention. I pick it up and study the snapshot of a carefree and beautiful young lady with long golden hair, sapphire blue eyes, and a dimpled smile.

"That's my Libby." Christina places the tray of tea down on to a footstool before seating herself on the armchair beside mine.

"She's lovely." I smile. "How old was she when this was taken?"

"Twenty-five. She hadn't met Sebastian then, that's why she looks so happy." She sighs forlornly.

"Do you mind talking about her?" I ask hesitantly. "I understand it must be painful."

"Not at all, dear. On the contrary, it's refreshing to be able to talk about her. She didn't have many friends at the end, so there really aren't many people I can remember her with." Christina pours the tea into delicate pink china cups. "Sugar and milk, dear?"

"Just milk, please." Christina hands the cup and saucer to me and offers the plate of biscuits. I take a custard cream, placing it on my saucer. A large ginger and white striped cat saunters into the room and sniffs at my shoes before eyeing the milk jug hopefully.

"Mummy will fetch you a saucer of milk, my darling Tigs." She scurries to the kitchen and returns with the promised treat, which the cat laps greedily.

"You have a lovely home," I say. Christina looks delighted and justifiably proud of her cottage.

"It's very small but it suits Tigs and I well enough. Tigs, or Tiger as he's is actually called, was Libby's cat. He was quite the mouser at Penmorrow. Heaven only knows how many mice infest that big old house, now that Tigs has left." She puts a custard cream in her mouth in one piece and chews noisily. I nibble mine and sip the tea.

"Could you tell me about Libby? I'd like to understand a little more about her illness, if it's not too painful for you to talk about."

"Let me start at the beginning, dear. It's important that you understand how Libby was before she married *that* man. Then you will believe me when I say that he caused her death." She rises from her chair and crosses the room to a pine dresser, from which she retrieves a leather bound photograph album, placing it on my lap. "Open it, dear. It's full of photographs of Libby from childhood through to adolescence. Then it has wedding photographs and, at the end, photographs of their last Christmas together. You look closely, dear. Tell me what you see. Take your time."

I place my teacup down on the side table and lift the heavy bound cover of the album. The photographs on the first three pages are black and white images of an adorable baby girl. She is happy and plump and clearly cherished by her parents who tickle and cuddle her for the camera. The following pages hold colour photographs of a young girl with page-boy haircut and dated clothes. The snaps show holidays and birthdays and a young Libby as ballerina at a school production. "She's so cute," I murmur.

"She is, isn't she?" Christina removes the tea tray and retreats to the kitchen, and I swear I hear her sniffing back tears. Libby's graduation photograph shows a now elegant young woman, beaming as she clutches her scroll with proud parents on either side of her. Turning the page, a grouping of family and friends clap as Libby blows out twenty-one candles on her birthday cake. I flick through the subsequent pages, noting how Libby is indeed blossoming into a vibrant and beautiful woman.

"She's lovely," I call out.

"Was. She *was* lovely. Carry on, Elizabeth, please." Christina enters the room once more and sits quietly. Tigs jumps on to her lap and she strokes him languidly as he purrs contentedly. The wedding photographs hit me firmly in my belly and twist at my gut. The happy couple beam at the camera, family and friends showering them in confetti. She wears a full white gown with tiny waist and full skirt, her veil tossed back exposing fair ringlets cascading over her left shoulder. He is looking adoringly into her sparkling eyes and she returns his loving gaze. It hurts me to see the evidence of their love, jealousy coursing through me unashamedly.

"Such a loving couple." I run my index finger gently down the image of her dress, the burning envy causing a bitter taste on my tongue. *You're jealous of a dead woman, Beth. Get real. He loves you now.*

"Oh, they were, granted. They had a fancy wedding at the church in Trevissey, then a fabulous reception at Penmorrow. Her father pulled out all the stops. Nothing was too much for his baby girl," she recalled, fondly. "His parents were long gone, of course. He had a cousin who flew over from Australia for the wedding, and the only other guests on his side were his estate staff and a few friends."

"I haven't met any of his friends yet," I mumble, more to myself than to Christina. "He's throwing me a fortieth birthday party in two weeks time, so I guess I'll meet them then."

"Yes, he likes his parties. Libby told me about a few of them."

There are no photographs after the wedding pictures, until the last page. Glued in the centre of the page is a snapshot taken at Christmas. My hand instinctively covers my mouth as I stare, shocked at the image of an emaciated woman, seated next to a glum-looking Sebastian. Her head is bowed, though her hollow eyes look up to the camera wretchedly. "Oh my God." I gasp in horror.

"You see, dear? You see the change, now?" Christina reaches forward and rests a hand on mine. Looking into my eyes, she sees the tears, which have misted my vision.

"Yes," I whisper. "I'm so sorry, Christina. I see what you mean. But why? Why did this happen?"

"All was fine for the first few months of their marriage. He was always very domineering, but her father thought that was a good thing. He was old-fashioned, you see, said a man should be the boss of the household. Libby used to tell me he was firm with her, but then… then I started to notice bruises, such as on her wrists. She couldn't sit down one day. She was right here in this room and tried to sit in the chair you're in now. I remember she winced, put a cushion under her bottom, and when I asked her what was wrong, she said haemorrhoids were causing her pain."

"And you don't think that was true?"

"No, Elizabeth. Scarlett once told me what he used to do to her. We went round there, and I even called the police but of course, Libby told them she was fine. Said her husband liked to indulge in a bit of kinkiness, that was all. Police said there was nothing they could do, she consented and it wasn't abuse. I know it was abuse. My daughter wouldn't consent to being treated like that. She was bought up properly, and knew right from wrong."

"But why didn't she leave?" My question seems hypocritical, as I know full well what the sting of a slap feels like and yet I haven't left him. I wonder then, if Libby was initially aroused by Sebastian's dominance as I am. Christina appears to read my mind.

"It's all very well," she says indignantly, "women today wanting to experiment in all this sex business. But they don't realize that if you give a man like Sebastian an inch, he'll take a mile. He takes advantage. He's a sexual predator. Libby's always been a romantic girl. She just wanted to please that man in any way she could. In my opinion, he saw her weakness and vulnerability and he used it to turn her into the passive, compliant *toy* he wanted."

I close the album, feeling a plethora of emotions— empathy toward Libby, poor weak woman that she was, and guilt for feeling that I am somehow stronger than she. My mobile phone rings in my bag I retrieve it and decline the call from Sebastian.

"She felt she was failing him," Christina continues. "She told Scarlett she couldn't be what he wanted her to be and that sense of failure depressed poor Libby. I took her to the doctor and he prescribed pills for her anxiety,

Benzodiazepines. They were no good for her. I tried to bring her here, make her well again, but she wouldn't have it. She said her place was with him." She spits his name with such venom that I truly believe she thinks he killed her with his bare hands.

"She wasn't well, Christina," I say gently. She straightens her back and regards me pitifully.

"He's got you under his bloody spell already, hasn't he? I *knew* it. Goddam that man to hell."

"Now, wait a minute." I match her ramrod posture. "I have seen nothing but kindness from Sebastian and am certainly not the sort of woman to put up with anything less than a mutually respectful and honest relationship." It's almost true. Dominance in itself does not a murderer make. "The only person who is under a spell at Penmorrow is Scarlett."

Christina nods in agreement. "You're right, that girl is besotted with him. I've tried so hard, as I did with Libby, to warn her but she's just like my daughter, she won't be told. That's why I've kept in touch with Scarlett, so that I can keep trying. I couldn't forgive myself if anything happened to her and I hadn't tried my best."

"Did you know that Scarlett and Sebastian used to be lovers?" I ask. Christina takes a moment to consider what I have said.

"I've suspected it, Elizabeth. The signs were the same. Why do you stay with him? What is it about him that enthrals and captivates women regardless of how he treats them? Besides his charm and money, of course."

"I don't want to discuss that with you." I feel uncomfortable now. Something is gnawing at me and I can't fathom what it is. It's something Christina has said and it's bugging me. "I'm going now, but I want to thank you for being so open with me. It means a lot that I've been able to fit another piece of the jigsaw of Sebastian's life." I stand to leave, picking up my bag and holding out my hand to Christina.

"If you want to add more pieces of his jigsaw, I suggest you talk to his friend, Marcus. He's known him since childhood and he can tell you about Sebastian's childhood which does, in part, explain why he's like this."

"Marcus? Where can I find him?" Sebastian has not mentioned Marcus. How strange that he should neglect to mention such an old friend.

"I've got his address somewhere. Give me a moment." She returns to the dresser and takes a notebook from the drawer. Thumbing through the pages, she finds the information and scribbles it hurriedly on a blank page, which she rips out and hands to me.

"Thank you, Christina. I'll talk to him, and I promise all is well. Nothing's going to happen to Scarlett or to me, so please try not to worry." She takes my outstretched hand and squeezes rather than shakes it.

"Take care, dear. Remember what I've told you. You've got a daughter, haven't you?"

"Yes, Bella. She's nearly eighteen," I confirm, wondering where she's going with this.

"Then be careful for her, if not for yourself."

"Thank you, I will. Goodbye, Christina."

"Goodbye, sweet Elizabeth."

She closes the door, and I walk back to my car, closing her white picket gate behind me. My phone rings again. I hesitate before declining Sebastian's call once more. Then I dial the number for Marcus.

# Chapter 23

Marcus answers on the third ring. I feel nervous and foolish calling a strange man I've never met in order to question him covertly about my boyfriend. "Hello." His voice is very nice and that spurs me on.

"Oh, hello. You don't know me. My name is Elizabeth Dove. Beth. I understand that you are great friends of my partner, Sebastian De Montfort." I stammer and sound like a lunatic but he immediately puts me at ease.

"Beth, hi. Sebastian's told me all about you. It's great that you've called. Is this about your fantastic party?" He serves up the perfect motive for my call, and I'm grateful for that.

"Yes, that's right. I'm hoping you and err…"

"Becky."

"Yes, you and Becky can come?"

"We wouldn't miss it. We're both itching to meet the woman who's stolen Sebastian's heart."

*Stolen his heart?* Oh, how that lifts me.

"Great. Well, I look forward to meeting you both too. I did wonder if I could perhaps meet up with you sometime? I'd like to get to know Sebastian's greatest friends and the party will be a blur. You know, champagne, masks, hardly a great way to get to know people," I babble.

"Sure. Tell you what, why don't you and Sebastian

come for dinner this Saturday night? Becky's a great cook. I'm sure she'll rustle up a treat for you guys."

*Dammit, I want to talk to you alone.*

"Perfect," I say cheerily. "We'd love to. What time would you like us?"

"Seven-thirty would be good. We'll see you then."

We say polite goodbyes and end the call. *Shit.* Now Sebastian will know I've called him, and I won't be able to get him alone.

\*\*\*

Driving home to Penmorrow, I reflect on my visit to Christina. What was it that she said, that rings alarm bells in my mind? Benzodiazepines. With a rush of realisation, I remember what was playing on my mind. After Alan and Joe's accident, the police officer, DI Chambers, had said the toxicology report showed this same drug in Alan's blood. Why would Alan and Libby have been taking the same tablet? I tell myself that thousands of people must be on that same drug. It's simply a coincidence.

DI Chambers had told me the drug would cause drowsiness and this, combined with alcohol, had caused Alan to crash the car. I still don't understand how he obtained the pills apparently without a doctor's prescription. If Libby was on the same medication, it's possible that her lethargy and frailty were exacerbated with the tablets she was taking. In essence, this may have been a circle of destruction for her. She was already depressed and anxious, and the pills made her listless. This, in turn, made her more depressed. *Doctor Beth, psychiatrist extraordinaire*, I muse. It's all starting to make sense to me now, and begins to exonerate Sebastian.

When I arrive home, Sebastian's car is in the drive but he's not in the house. Bella is on her laptop in Sebastian's study, chatting online with Chloe, and she grunts when I say hello. Ruth is in the morning room watching television and she looks up as I enter.

"Hey, stranger. I was worried about you. Where have you been?" She mutes the sound and looks at me expectantly.

"Hi, Ruth. I'm really sorry to have left you alone this morning. I had something to attend to, and you were still asleep when I left, but I did push a note under your door." She looks as though she wants details, but then thinks better of it and pats the seat next to her. I sit down, putting my arm around her shoulders.

"Yes, I read it. Rather cryptic, it just said you had errands to run. Anyway, I've been enjoying some me time. It's been so great to be here, Beth. It's such a shame I have to go back. It's been a flying visit."

"It's been so wonderful having you here, Ruth. Are you sure you have to leave today?"

"Yup, someone has to run that business of ours. Did you know Sebastian's coming to the AGM, the week you're back for Bella's birthday?" She cocks a perfectly sculpted brow when I shake my head.

"No, he didn't tell me. I didn't think he had the right to attend. Doesn't he need to be invited?" I ask, irritated at his intrusion.

"Beth, he's every right to be there. He's a shareholder. He has legal rights. Why don't you want him there?"

"He interferes, Ruth. He's bloody annoying in the boardroom, as well you remember."

She laughs and gives me a hug. "You two are hilarious. It's worth every minute of him being there for the entertainment value alone."

I slap her knee playfully. "Fine, but if he says *one* damn thing to irritate me, I'll have his ass thrown out. Agreed?"

"Agreed." We both laugh.

"Speaking of Sebastian, where is he?" I remember the rejected calls. No doubt he's once again mad at me.

"He showered and changed after his ride, then said he was going to look at the deer enclosure. He said something about the fencing. Why don't you go and find him?"

"Yes, I will in a moment."

"Beth, he's divine, isn't he? If you ever grow tired of that man, then cast him my way. I'll quite happily accept your sloppy seconds. Those smouldering eyes, and the way he swaggers, it's enough to make a girl's toes curl."

"Ruth!" I exclaim in mock horror. "He's my boyfriend. You can't say things like that."

"Girl, believe me, looks like his should be censored."

\*\*\*

With wellington boots on, I hike across the lawns and over the deer park in search of Sebastian. It's a glorious day. The sun is warm and I've changed into tight blue jeans and silver vest top. I feel fit and sexy and hope to distract his inevitable bad mood by baring my flesh. The sun beats down on my bare shoulders and, my hair clipped up, it kisses the skin on the back of my neck. On a day like this, it feels good to be alive, especially in such a spectacular setting. The deer chew at the lush grass until their awareness of my approach sees them spring away effortlessly across the grounds.

I view Sebastian across the park, knocking a post into the ground with a mallet and decide to sneak up on him by skirting across the enclosure, behind him. As I get nearer, the sight of him wearing only khaki combats, muscles bulging, sends a tremor to my sex, which instantly grows slick in anticipation. I tiptoe the last five yards and place a gentle kiss on his hot, sweaty back. He jumps, dropping the mallet on his foot. "For fuck's sake!" He hops from foot to foot and snarls at me. *Oh, fuck. That's really improved his mood, Beth.*

"Shit, I'm so sorry, Sebastian. I wanted to surprise you. Fuck it, are you okay?"

"Mind your mouth," he shouts, pulling off his work boot as he hops to keep his balance, but falls straight on his ass. *Oh, fuck.*

"Oh God. I'm so sorry." I can't help laughing at the sight. As much as I know this will make him madder, the hilarity of the situation tickles me.

"*Funny,* is it?" he barks. "I'll show you funny, lady." He staggers to his feet, wincing as he puts his injured foot to the ground, and hobbles in my direction.

"Sebastian, you're injured." The laughter won't stop, much as I want it to, knowing it's inappropriate.

"Come here." He lunges for me and catches hold of my belt, pulling me sharply by the waist until I'm pressed against him. His muscular arms wrap firmly around me, his chest, misted with sweat, pressing against my breasts, causing my nipples to instantly harden at the contact. "Still funny?" he purrs, his nostrils flaring, dirt smeared across his rugged jaw.

I kiss him, my lips hungry for his, my tongue forcing entry to his mouth. His hands move down to my ass and he squeezes hard enough to make me thrust forward against his erection, which presses on my navel. My arms encircle his strong frame and my nails dig into the bare, moist flesh of his back. We kiss passionately, our tongues battling, our teeth catching each other's lips. His right hand moves down farther, his fingers sliding down the central seam of my jeans until he reaches the apex and pushes against the constraints of the denim, making me wet with desire. "Are you wet for me, Elizabeth?" he whispers in my ear.

"Dripping," I rasp. "Are you going to do anything about it?"

"Topping from the bottom, as ever, Mrs. Dove." He looks so hot. His breath comes fast and heavy, as he looks roguishly at me through long inky lashes.

"No, Sir. I wouldn't dream of it." I gasp as innocently as I can.

"Hmm, you don't seem too contrite, Elizabeth. Kiss

my toe." He releases me, to the annoyance of my voracious pussy. He points to his bare foot, the big toe now red and swollen.

"Kiss your *toe?*" I echo, incredulously.

"She can hear but she clearly doesn't understand," he quips, still pointing at his wounded foot. Evidently irritated by my reticence, he clicks his fingers in front of my face and cocks a brow, a smile playing on his lips.

"You're so hot, De Montfort, do you know that?" The attempt at distraction holds no sway with the man who cocks his brow higher still. I kneel before him but maintain eye contact.

"Don't look me in the eyes, I'm not happy with you. Kiss it better." He clicks his fingers again and points once more to his toe. I gingerly lean down and place a light kiss on his inflamed toe.

"Good girl. Now take it in your mouth," he instructs. I do as I'm told for once and take the sore tip of his toe between my lips tenderly, afraid to hurt him more.

"Suck it gently."

Following instruction, I take the entire toe in my mouth and gently suck. He pushes me down farther. He groans and I'm unsure if with pleasure or pain, or most likely both. It's so demeaning and yet so erotic, my arousal causing a river between my legs. My nipples struggle against the confines of my bra. He tugs at my hair clip, raising my head. His toe, wet from my saliva, slips from my mouth.

"Put that mouth to better use now, my little slut." He

unzips his fly and his heavy penis flops forward, standing proud from his combats, inches away from my mouth. "Suck me," he commands. "Make me come and take all of it in your mouth. Do not spill a single drop, do you understand?"

Before I can answer, he thrusts his hips forward so that the crown of his cock touches my lips, a single drop of his nectar already waiting for me. I lick the salty droplet and circle the velvety soft head with my tongue. He groans and his fists clutch my hair, which breaks free of the clip, tumbling down my back.

"Good girl. That's right, take it all in your mouth, Elizabeth."

I have no idea if we can be seen from the house and, right now, I don't care. My greedy mouth wants all of him. I hollow my cheeks and cover my teeth with my lips as he thrusts forward to the back of my throat. I clutch the backs of his thighs, sucking and licking in earnest as his hips set the rhythm, fucking my mouth. The prominent veins along his length pulse as he reaches his climax, and he stills my head as he spills forth, emptying his creamy orgasm so fast that it makes my throat burn. I struggle to swallow but he holds me fast. When I have licked him clean, he allows me to stand and kisses me tenderly. I'm panting now, my own desire to climax unbearable but to my utter dismay, he pulls up his fly. "Good girl, you did well. Now leave me to finish my work."

"What?" My sex is throbbing with the need to have him fill me, and yet I'm being dismissed.

"Punishment, Elizabeth. No orgasm for you. Now do as I say and go back to the house, and no playing. If you make yourself come, Elizabeth, I will not allow you to climax for a week. Now, off you go."

I pout and sigh but there is little point arguing. He's made his point and I set off back to the house, extending my middle finger behind his back in frustration.

*** 

It's mid-afternoon and time for Ruth to leave but, sad as I am to see her go, I look forward to her returning for my party. She hugs Bella and I tightly before saying goodbye to Sebastian. "You take care of her," she warns, good-naturedly. "Don't forget the AGM after the party. You need to be on your best behaviour or I'll tan your backside."

I groan at her audacity, but thankfully Sebastian takes it in good humour and gives her a tight embrace. "Oh, I think I'd like to see you *try,* Ruth," he teases as he lets her go. My dear friend has no idea of the irony of what she just said. I grin and wave as she drives away. Sebastian puts an arm around my waist as we walk back to the house.

"So, you're going to be interfering in our business again, De Montfort?" I shake my head disapprovingly. He smacks my behind, a wicked smile playing on his lips.

"I am now."

"Bloody great. Control freak."

"Mrs. Dove, I do believe I need to take you back to the chamber and step up your submissive training.

Where's your choker?" he asks darkly.

My fingers move to my bare throat and I blush deeply. *The choker? Oh crap!* "It's in my bedside drawer. Take a chill pill," I quip. His hand drops from my waist and he runs his hand through his hair in exaggerated exasperation.

"A chill pill?"

I glance sideways at him, butterflies throwing fits in my stomach. Double crap! I should learn to hold my tongue. His eyes are burning embers, hooded and menacing. He points to the front door.

"Chamber. *Now.*"

"Only if you can catch me," I call as I run for the door.

My breath comes in short pants as I pin myself flat to the wall, behind the door to Sebastian's study. I hear his heavy footsteps on the flagstones of the hall. My skin prickles with excitement and anticipation. I'm yearning to be caught but enjoying the delicious game of hide and seek.

"Come out, come out wherever you are…" His voice is close by. I squint through the gap between door and frame and see the toe of his boots. The hairs on the back of my neck stand proud and I hold my breath. I wait a full minute and peek again, the boots now gone. Another minute passes with my eye pressed to the gap. Where the hell has he gone? I now desperately want to be caught but, as the game goes on, so the fear of his reprisal deepens.

As quietly as a mouse, I tiptoe to the edge of the door

and peer around it. There is no sign of Sebastian in the hall, nor can I hear him. Treading lightly through the doorway and into the hall, there's still no sign of him. Where are you? I creep gingerly forward; he grabs me from behind and I jump clean out of my skin, screaming as his hands encircle my waist, clutching me firmly to him.

He's behind me, his hot breath on my neck, my back pressed into his front. "Sebastian!" I pant, my body on fire at his touch.

"So, you want to play games." He breathes in my ear. "When you play with the big boys, you need to prepare to get hurt, Elizabeth." The threat lingers in the air as he releases his grip on my waist and takes my hand firmly in his. "Chamber. Now." *Holy fuck!*

# Chapter 24

He slides the bolt across the heavy old door to the outer chamber in the basement. I glance toward the closed door to the inner chamber but he makes no move to take me there. He's pacing, regarding me silently from the corner of his eye, like a tiger. I tremble as I stand in the centre of the ancient room. "What am I to do with you, Elizabeth?" he murmurs.

"Let me go?" I whisper. His eyes narrow and he grins mischievously.

"Oh, I don't think so," he purrs. "I need to take your training back to basics. Teach you the principals of submission. Head up, but lower your eyes when I look at you," he barks.

I dip my gaze and study the flagstones compliantly. He continues pacing. I glance up through my lashes and see him stroking his stubble covered chin, looking so very mean but oh so sexy. He catches me watching him covertly and sighs deeply before striding toward me, only stopping when the toe of his boot touches the tip of my pumps. Casting my eyes downward I see the military style work boots, feet apart in a wide stance. His hands are planted firmly on his hips.

"Kneel." He clicks his fingers in the most derogatory way and points to the floor at his feet.

"Here?" I ask.

"Here. *Now.*"

I do as I'm told and kneel uncomfortably on the hard stone floor, my arousal now cresting, making my apex slick with desire.

"Keep your head up. Lower your eyes, Elizabeth," he instructs again. "Peek at your peril. Do you understand?"

"Yes," I whisper.

"Yes *what?*"

"Yes, *Sir.*"

"Good girl." He seems genuinely surprised at my acquiescence as he moves away and disappears from my limited view. Resisting the temptation to cast a sly glance to see what he's doing, I think better of it and instead listen intently. I hear the sound of metal, or perhaps heavy wood on stone, something being slid across the floor, then the sound of the boots returning to me. From behind, he places a blindfold over my eyes and ties it firmly at the back of my head. *Oh goodness, this is so hot.* Immediately, my remaining senses kick into overdrive. Sounds amplified, the smell of his perspiration, the smell of my own, the feel of the course fabric that rubs my eyelids as they continue to blink beneath their constraint.

Sebastian places something across my mouth and panic sets in as he pulls down my lower jaw, opening my mouth wide to accommodate a spherical ball. It's seemingly attached to a leather strap that he takes behind my head, my hair catching in the buckle as he fastens it tightly. I gurgle my protestation as my tongue fights against the suppression of the plastic ball. *Christ, he's gagged me.* I'm out of my depth; I can't say my safe word. He senses my panic and plants a tender kiss on my forehead and strokes my bare arm sensuously.

"Be calm, darling," he soothes. "At any time, you can stop me by turning your head left to right, left to right. Nod if you understand."

Relieved, I nod.

"Good girl. Now, nod if you consent to continue. Remember I would never put you in danger. Safe, consensual, and sane are our buzzwords. Understand?"

Again, I nod my consent. *Am I crazy? What the hell am I consenting to?*

"Excellent." He grabs a fistful of my hair and tugs it sharply, raising me to my feet. Standing unsteadily and feeling vulnerable but hyper-stimulated, I wait patiently. Again, I hear him moving. When he returns to me, he slides my vest top from each shoulder, carefully lifting each arm to remove it, so that it now sits around my waist. My nipples strain against my bra, swollen and needy. He unclips the fastening of the bra and removes it. I now feel exposed, naked from the waist up, nipples erect and throbbing for his touch. He skilfully unbuttons the fly of my jeans and in one fluid movement, slides the jeans, vest top and my panties down to my ankles. I think I sense him squat in front of me. I feel his firm grip on my ankle. I reach out and find his muscular shoulder and I grip tightly for stability as he lifts my left foot, removes my pump and slides off my remaining clothing. He repeats the action with my right foot. My breath comes in short, fast pants and I fear I could orgasm just by his touch alone such is the height of my arousal.

He moves once more, placing a hand on my elbow, guiding me gently forward. I'm afraid I will fall but he intuitively puts an arm around my waist and leads me— *where?—to the bed, in the inner chamber?* He stops after just a few paces. *What next?* The anticipation is almost too much. He releases me and I stand exposed and vulnerable, entirely at his mercy. I hear the sound of wood creaking. My remaining senses heightened, sound amplified, and feel the press of his hand on the small of my back, urging me forward. I reach out but he clasps my left wrist and rests it on a curved wooden rest. He does the same with my right, and pushing my head down, makes me bend at the waist and lean forward. I fear I'll fall, but he places a guiding hand on my shoulder as my throat finds curved wood on which to rest. *What the fuck is he doing? What is this?*

The sound of creaking wood once more precedes the feeling of something closing down on top of me, enclosing my neck and wrists in wooden holes. Realisation slams at my belly as it transpires that Sebastian has me restrained in stocks. No amount of wriggling or stamping my feet in annoyance brings about my release.

"My naughty wench is in the stocks," he mocks in a deep, gravelly voice.

I momentarily ponder using the safe signal, my inner conflict of desire versus common sense leading me to delay long enough for Sebastian to place a strategic finger on my sacrum.

"What am I to do to such a *wicked* slut?" He runs his index finger languidly down the cleft of my buttocks, and my hips thrust back to meet him as he reaches my most private puckered place. The touch is gone in an instant. "So keen, so willing to take your punishment. Such a good girl…and yet such a *bad* whore."

His slick tongue travels down, his large hands parting me, saliva trickling down so delectably to the forbidden place his tongue now probes. I strain against the wooden bonds, moaning into the gag, protesting at the degradation, encouraging, begging but still he persists at a leisurely pace. Warm juices trickle unbidden down my thigh, my sex engorged and wanting.

Listening, all I can hear is the quiet lapping of Sebastian's tongue against my flesh. He stops abruptly, leaving me sighing and writhing. I hear him moving and feel cold gel being rubbed around and into my anus. *He's going to take me—there!* I try to turn my head but the wood bites into my neck.

"Keep still," he instructs, but my eyes are wide as I bite down on the hard plastic, my buttocks clenching. He parts me again and something hard and slick presses against my anus; it's unrelenting and I resist its intrusion. "Relax for me, Elizabeth. Trust me."

I try, feeling utterly humiliated and yet so desperate to be filled. I release my muscles there and the thing slides in deeper. It is the most intense yet stimulating sensation, making me gasp and my ass pushes back to aid its passage.

"Good, good girl. Take the plug. That's right, so good."

*A butt plug! I've read about those but oh my, I had no idea they feel so hot.*

With a final push, he drives it home until my ass is entirely full. I squirm at the ripples of pleasure it causes, clenching and unclenching my internal muscles until the tremors building take me almost to climax. Completely blind and mute, my senses concentrate only on the pressure within my rectum. The thing begins to vibrate subtly, a gentle purr deep within my core, which drives me wild so that I'm pulling at my restraints, my hips circling in time with the pulsing within me.

"Don't come." He moves behind me. *Please, please, take me, make me come.* My words are unspoken; muffled grunts are all I can emit. "From now on, your orgasms are for your Master. I have absolute control over them."

Soft, feather light tickles travel down my back, from shoulder to shoulder and down my spine. Again and again the multi-tendril softness drags over my sensitive skin.

"Feel the flogger, sweetheart. Feel how nice it is? Soft deerskin, so gentle and tickly, isn't it?" he says.

Whip. It smarts, oh fuck, it smarts. He lashes my buttocks again and again, lightly first then thrashing harder so that the bite of the leather brings tears to my eyes, which soak into the fabric of the blindfold. I need to safe word. This hurts.

"What's the matter, my little slut? Not so foul-mouthed now are you? Remember, you can use the safe sign at any time and I'll stop."

All I need to do is turn my head—left to right, left to right—and the torture ends, this pleasure, this forbidden delicious torment.

With one hand, he pushes the plug deeper into my core, and with the other he flicks at my skin with the flogger. Between my legs so that it stings at my pussy, my thighs, my arms—all are assaulted by the soft yet unyielding leather.

It's too much; tears sting my eyes, the frustration of the climax withheld, my senses on fire, the frenzy he's driven me too, it's all too much. I decide to safe sign, but the sting stops abruptly. The vibration continues but that is ecstasy. He grips my hips and he's kissing my back, his lips brushing my sore skin, murmuring how good I have been, how proud he is of me. *Tell me you love me.*

I hear a zipper, then his erection presses against my soaked vagina and, with one powerful thrust, he drives his cock in to my very end. Again and again his hardness strikes and rubs at the bundle of nerves deep inside me. "Good girl, that's right. Come for me hard, baby."

My fingernails dig painfully into the palms of my hands, my neck strains against wood, my teeth bite on plastic, the tremors build and build until the orgasm so desperately needed erupts in a million pieces, then radiates through every sinew of my body. My back arches and I'm shuddering so badly that my legs grow weak.

His breath quickens as he continues to pound me, his hips grinding as he thrusts deeper still. I hear his breath catch as he reaches his own glorious climax and he stills as his warm semen spurts.

"Fuck, oh fuck *yes.*" He folds forward against my back, his skin slick with sweat, his chest hairs tickling my over sensitive skin. "Fuck. I love you, Elizabeth."

*He loves me! Oh my God, finally he tells me he loves me.* It's taken a beating and degradation for him to say it, but he's said it and the pain no longer matters.

Sebastian peels himself from me and removes the plug, leaving my muscles there quivering. The creak of the wood signals a welcome release from the stocks and he helps me to stand, my back and neck aching, my wrists sore. He unfastens the gag and carefully removes the ball, before untying the blindfold. I blink as my eyes adjust to the light. My lips feel numb and my legs weak. I feel lightheaded as though the blood is rushing to my head and the room spins.

Sebastian scoops me up in his arms, unlocks the door to the inner chamber and lays me tenderly on the circular bed. The satin sheet gives cooling relief to my smarting skin and my shoulders heave as sobs escape my lips. He lies down beside me and gathers me in his arms.

"That's right, Elizabeth, let me have your tears. I'm so proud of you. You've made me *so* happy." He soothes me, and strokes my cheek as the tears flow, moistening his chest. "Don't hate me, though, Elizabeth. Christ, I can't bear it if you hate me."

"I…I don't h-hate you," I sniff. "I love y-you."

"And I love you, darling. I love you so very much. That you would give yourself to me, as you have, makes me love you more deeply than you can ever imagine." His voice calms me as he pulls the silky satin over my weary body and I sleep.

\*\*\*

I open my eyes and for a moment, I wonder where I am. I find comfort in the womb like surroundings of the chamber. Rolling cautiously onto my side, ouch it stings, I face Sebastian who is lying on his side, staring intently at me.

"How long have I been sleeping?" I murmur drowsily.

"Only an hour or so. I've been watching you. Did you know you talk in your sleep, Elizabeth?" A smile plays on his lips. I trace my index finger along his lower lip and he kisses it lightly.

"What did I say? What an absolute freaking *pervert* you are?"

He smiles warmly, and it lights up his whole face when he smiles like this. I wish he would do that more often. "Actually, Mrs. Dove, you told me you loved me again. It's becoming a habit."

"A good habit, or an annoying habit?" I play with his bottom lip, and he bites the finger playfully, making me giggle. I like playful Sebastian.

"A very good habit. It's understandable. I'm pretty lovable." He bites harder, then takes my index finger into his mouth and sucks hard on it. Delicious shivers prickle my spine and I climb on top of him, wincing at the sting of my buttocks as I straddle him. We kiss deeply, passionately as my eager pussy rubs against his erection. This time, I take him—my pace, my terms.

By the time we emerge from the vaults of the house, it's nearly eight o'clock at night. Feeling remorseful that we haven't fed Bella, or indeed paid her any attention today, I set out to find her. My daughter is sprawled across her bed listening to music when I enter her room. She tugs out the ear buds and scowls at me. "Where have you been?" she asks.

"Sorry, love, Sebastian's been showing me his wine cellar. He's quite a collector of fine wines. It's fascinating." The lie makes me blush guiltily.

"Cool, well, it would be nice to see more of my mother at some point. Must be a bloody interesting cellar," she says pointedly.

"Fair point. We'll be back home soon so you can catch up with your friends. I know it's been a bit boring for you but the rest is doing us both good."

"Whatever." She replaces the ear buds and dismisses me with a sarcastic wave. I make a mental note to spend more time with my daughter tomorrow. She's had a tough few months and it can't be much fun being holed up in this big old house.

"Why don't you see if there are any discos in the area?"

She rolls her eyes at me disdainfully. "Are you still here?" she asks loudly over the music drumming through her buds. Sighing, I leave the petulant teenager and take a shower.

Sebastian is in the great hall with Scarlett. She is setting the table for dinner while he sips a gin and tonic, resting back on a dining chair.

"Dinner will be ready in ten minutes, Mrs. Dove." Scarlett is so damned efficient; she puts me to shame and she knows it.

"You shouldn't have cooked, I was about to do it," I say sulkily.

"Elizabeth. How was your shower?" Sebastian eyes my damp hair and tracksuit bottoms, slippers and baggy tee. His expression is impassive; he's so mercurial I can never predict his mood. "Sit down. Drink your gin and tonic, no ice, slice of lime. Just how I like it." He nods toward the table setting opposite him where my drink awaits. I note he has prepared the gin how he likes. I prefer ice.

"Thank you, very thoughtful." I sip the not cold enough aperitif and welcome the relaxing effects of the gin.

"You've been quite the busy bee, haven't you?" He's regarding me darkly, his index finger circling the rim of his glass. Oh crap, what have I done now?

"Oh? Have I?"

"You have, yes. Visiting senile old ladies, telephoning my friends. Goodness, I don't know how you find time to fit in so much underhandedness in one day." He cocks an eyebrow at me, as he does when I'm in trouble, which is frequently it seems.

"And you would know all this because…" I lower my gaze from his and study the lime in my glass.

"Because you don't do underhandedness very well, clearly."

How the hell does he know all this? I'm guessing Marcus called him, but how does he know about my visit with Christina?

Scarlett scurries off to the kitchen, leaving me to face Sebastian alone.

"Please be a little more discreet, Elizabeth. You are fully aware that Scarlett is in touch with Christina, so you should have considered that Christina would of course impart your entire conversation to Scarlett. Which she did and Scarlett then informed me."

What? The interfering witch. Wait until I get Scarlett alone later. I cast him a scowl and open my mouth to protest, but he raises a hand to silence me.

"Don't interrupt. Don't you dare look me in the eye."

I close my mouth and look down at my glass, now devoid of gin.

"Uncross your legs."

Obediently, I do so. *Damn him, he's so bossy.*

"Your actions today have embarrassed me, Elizabeth. Not only that, you've demonstrated a callous absence of loyalty and very poor judgment. What the hell were you hoping to achieve by going behind my back in this way?"

Fidgeting with glass, I try to think of an appropriate excuse for my meddling.

"You will answer me. *Now.*"

# Chapter 25

Nervously, I fidget in my chair considering how to best phrase my answer. "I just wanted to find out more about Libby, about you. I hardly know anything about you, not really anyway."

"I see." He strokes his finger across his bottom lip. I can see his sullen expression as I tentatively peer up through my lashes.

"Do you think it unreasonable that I would expect you to come to me if you wish to know about me? Eyes down."

"You said I only had to avert my eyes in the chamber," I retort grumpily, my eyes lowered again.

"You haven't earned the right to look me in the eye. You say you want to be submissive, Elizabeth, and yet at every opportunity you defy and betray me. How can this relationship work between us if the very foundations of *trust* aren't there?"

I hadn't thought of it like that. *Do I trust him? Perhaps not; maybe that's why I'm a terrible submissive.* "I have to trust you too, Sebastian, and when you keep secrets from me, I lose respect for you."

"Respect, Elizabeth? Who is the man whom has given you respite from the shit going on in your life? Who was there for you when you life was in tatters? Who held you when you cried after Joe and Alan?" He spits the words venomously. "Who has offered you *everything*, to take all your worries from your shoulders? Who is liberating you so that you can find your true self? Answer me, damn it."

"You, and you don't need to remind me about the accident. There isn't a day that goes by that I don't torture myself or miss Joe. I know you were there for me. I don't honestly know how I could have survived without you." My voice is a whisper. His words sting. It's a low blow to bring the accident into the argument.

"Correct. *Me.* Have I not, then, earned the right to be respected? Have I not proven myself to be the man you need? Well?"

"Yes, you have. You are the man I need. Can I say something, please?"

He sighs. I glance up fleetingly. He is massaging his temples, strain visible on his gorgeous face. "Go on," he says curtly.

"I went to see Christina because I wanted to know what happened to Libby, but also because of Scarlett. She told me everything, Sebastian."

"Did she now?" he mumbles sullenly.

"Yes. It's confusing for me. I wanted to get the full picture before talking to you about it all. Scarlett's really changed, and Libby changed too. I felt that Christina would be able to tell me why, from a more distant perspective."

"I see. Go on."

"She showed me photographs of Libby, how she used to be, and then how she became."

"When she was married to me, you mean?"

"Well, yes."

"So you immediately blamed *me* for her demise." He sighs deeply. "And the old bat will have painted me as the devil personified, of course."

"No. I don't know. It got me thinking about how you are, your dominance, and why you're like that. She suggested I speak to Marcus because he's your oldest friend. I knew you wouldn't be happy about it, but I needed to piece the jigsaw together and so I called him."

"I know you did. He called me immediately after you'd called him. I understand we're having dinner with them tomorrow night."

It's hard to know if he's still angry with me. His lighter tone is probably deceptive.

"You planned to interrogate my friend in the hope that he would spill forth some dark secret which would explain why all the women in my life are fucked up?"

*Yes.* "No, of course not. I just want to understand you better. I need to understand your relationship with Scarlett better too."

"What, exactly, is your understanding?"

"According to her, you and she had a relationship, it's over now, but you still punish her."

"Is that what she told you?"

"Yes. Is it true?" *Please say it isn't true.*

He chews at his bottom lip as he considers his reply. "Yes. It is, but I've been pretty screwed up in recent years. We had a very brief fling, but that was over before I met you. She's a mixed-up young lady, Elizabeth. Don't believe everything she tells you."

Right on cue, Scarlett knocks lightly on the door.

"Come," he snaps.

"Dinner is ready, can I call Bella and serve?" She tentatively peers around the door.

"Yes, yes. Our discussion is over. Serve dinner."

It's far from over, I reflect. For now, though, we will outwardly enjoy a peaceful dinner with Bella and store the discussion for another time.

\*\*\*

Joe and Bella are playing in the sand on the beach, and the sun is shining. Bella is burying Joe up to his neck, and Alan and I are laughing as he wiggles his toes, before Bella can cover them. The sand turns darker, and it becomes soil and his toes are not wiggling any more. I tell Bella to stop. Enough. Let Joe get out now he'll catch cold in the ground, Bella. Now the beach is a graveyard, and Alan is putting more soil on Joe's head. I'm running to Joe, but as fast as I run his muddy grave gets farther away, and now Alan's pushing damp soil into Joe's mouth and he can't breath and I can't run any faster.

"Elizabeth, wake up!" Sebastian's voice tears me from the graveyard and I open my eyes, startled. "You were having the nightmare again, darling." He kisses my lips tenderly and brushes a damp curl from my cheek.

"It's the one on the beach again." Shuddering as the last remnants of tormented sleep ebb away, I curl up in Sebastian's arms, seeking his protection and reassurance.

"It's over, darling."

"It'll never be over," I whisper.

"Come on. It's a beautiful Saturday morning. I'm taking my girls out for a treat. Get dressed and meet me downstairs in twenty." He ruffles my hair and springs from the bed.

"You know I hate surprises. Where are we going?" My mood lifts marginally. It will be lovely to take Bella out—a real family outing. Family. Fighting against the negative thoughts, I do as I'm told and get up. When dressed, I wake Bella and, with some coaxing, she complies and grumpily gets up and dresses.

Sebastian drives us to Padstow. It in indeed a beautiful day, as we travel down the hill to the harbour. Bella and I marvel as the sun shimmers on the sapphire sea, giving the impression of a million crystals sparkling on the swell. We park up outside the National Lobster Hatchery.

"Come on, we're going to explore." Sebastian links arms with Bella and I and we giggle at his boyish excitement as we enter the hatchery. It's fascinating, and even my sulky teenage daughter appears enthralled as we glimpse the marine laboratory. "Local fishermen bring in pregnant female lobsters," Sebastian tells us. "They rear their young here in captivity so they have the best chance of survival, away from predators."

"How sweet. Then they're boiled alive and eaten," laughs my sardonic daughter.

"No, Bella," Sebastian corrects. "Then they're released back into the ocean. Then they're caught in lobster pots, boiled alive, and eaten." I swipe at him with a visitor brochure but he catches my hand and tickles me unrelentingly, encouraging Bella to join in until we all double over with cathartic laughter.

Leaving the hatchery, we drive down to the harbour and park next to the quay which is bustling with tourists. Some are watching fishermen preparing a plethora of boats of varying sizes, others are ambling past the galleries and gift shops. Sebastian leads us into a café and we enjoy a delicious brunch of Cornish pasties and coffee. "This is such a lovely day. Thank you, Sebastian." I smile.

"You haven't had your surprise yet." He grins at Bella and I mischievously.

"What are you up to?"

"Come. We're going fishing."

The Lady Martha takes us to sea, cutting through the foamy swell. We don't venture far from the rocky shore. Our skipper, Bob Tanner, is a jovial man with sun-kissed skin and a booming voice. Sebastian has chartered the vessel for four hours, which is hopefully enough time to snag some mackerel.

"What do you think of her?" Sebastian calls from the angling platform to the rear of the smart Evolution 38.

"She's *fabulous,*" I call back, windswept and exhilarated. The skipper is trying to teach me how to 'work' the fishing tackle and rod and it's plain I'm testing his patience.

"Let me do it for yer," he finally says in defeat. Joining Bella and Sebastian, who are both competently casting their lines to sea, I set about trying to fish.

Three hours later we have bass, mackerel, and Bob has snared a four-foot-long porbeagle shark, which he declared was small. Bob produces a cooler containing a basic packed lunch and we ravenously devour every crumb. It's been a wonderful day. Arriving back at Padstow Harbour, we wake farewell to our skipper and walk wearily back to the car.

"Thank you so much, Sebastian. It's been the best day ever," Bella says.

"Not too nerdy, was it?" he teases.

"Not at all. For an old man, you're all right." She play punches his arm, which he reciprocates. It's heart warming to see them so happy and relaxed.

"Mrs. Dove, I think we should get home so you can make yourself look even more beautiful for tonight. I want to see Marcus's face when he sees what a babe I've snared."

"You men, you're so funny. Thank you, darling, for such a wonderful day. I really mean it, it's been therapeutic." On tiptoes, I plant a big kiss on his cheek.

Sebastian pulls up the zip on the black cocktail dress he selected for me from the armoire. Presumably Scarlett chose it, but much as that smarts, it does flatter my figure well. I fasten my choker around my throat and turn to show Sebastian. "You look good enough to eat." He eyes me speculatively.

"Play your cards right, mister, and that's precisely what you can do later," I purr.

He looks striking in charcoal trousers, a white pin-stripe shirt and silver tie. He forgoes a jacket as it's a balmy June evening. Sebastian insists that Bella accompany us. Apparently Marcus has a son, Theo, who is nineteen and he's certain Bella will like him.

"Where do they live?" I ask, as we drive away from Penmorrow.

"Camelford. It's a twenty-minute drive. We should be there on time," he replies. "You'll like their house, it's quite something."

Twenty-five minutes later we arrive at a fine Georgian manor house. It is by no means as grand as Penmorrow, but still impressive. "Girling Hall." The name is familiar. Where have I heard that before?

"Marcus is new money, darling," Sebastian says. "He's a property developer who has done incredibly well. When we were at Plymouth University together, I honestly didn't think he'd ever take anything seriously enough to stick at it. Let's just say he was the playboy amongst us, and not the sharpest in terms of brains."

We draw to a halt alongside a Bentley and exit our car. Suddenly I recall why the name of the house is familiar. Girling Hall was the address printed on the invitation that I had found in Sebastian's pocket, the venue for the fetish party, or 'auction' as he had referred to it. "Oh my God. This is where you came for the auction," I hiss as we approach the entrance, whispering out of Bella's earshot. "So, Marcus is as kinky as you?"

He grins and winks infuriatingly. "Might be. Depends

on the definition, Elizabeth."

"Ass."

"Ass?" He slaps my bottom and shakes his head. "I'll give you *ass*."

Marcus and Rebecca make a fine couple. He is just a little slighter in stature than Sebastian, with an unruly mop of fair hair and a charming manner. Rebecca is almost as tall as her spouse and is dressed elegantly in a cerise shift dress and stunning pink Jimmy Choo heels. She embraces us warmly as Sebastian introduces Bella and I, before Marcus holds me at arm's length, letting his gaze travel slowly up my body in an overtly appreciative way.

"Sebastian, how do you manage to attract such peaches?" Marcus digs Sebastian in the ribs and earns an expletive in return.

"She's out of your league, Marcus, old chap," he mocks.

"It's wonderful to meet you both," I say, nudging Bella who has yet to say hello. "Finally, I meet Sebastian's friends. Rebecca, I love your dress, and those heels are to die for."

"Please call me Becky. Everyone does, and thank you, we must go shopping and do lunch one day, Beth."

"That would be lovely."

"Becky. Drinks, and how's the food coming on?" Marcus sounds so like Sebastian. It's apparent they do indeed share their dominant trait.

"Another ten minutes," she replies. "Come on through, all of you. Let's have a Bellini." She leads the way in to an expansive orangery. Constructed entirely from wood and glass it affords a spectacular view of manicured lawns and box hedging. A crystal chandelier illuminates a white dining table, tastefully set for dinner.

"Theo, darling. Come and meet the beautiful Bella and her equally gorgeous mother, Elizabeth. You know Sebastian already, of course."

Bella and I turn to face a tall, long-limbed young man with shoulder length mop of golden curls and brilliant green eyes. He shakes my hand with a confidence that belies his age, but his eyes are fixed on my daughter who is blushing a furious crimson.

"Very pleased to meet you, Bella." He holds out a hand to her, which she shakes timidly. It's clear that she's as taken with his beauty as he is with hers.

"Why don't you two youngsters go and do something more interesting? Show Bella your recording studio. I'll call you when dinner's ready." Marcus slaps him on the back playfully.

"Want to come and see, Bella? It's kinda cool." He hasn't yet released her hand. Instead, taking a cue from her nod, he leads her from the room.

"He's a handsome young man, Becky. You must be very proud of him," I say.

"We are. Very Proud. He's a talented musician too. Marcus had the studio installed for him for his eighteenth birthday. We keep encouraging him to apply to the X Factor but he said that's not for serious musicians."

"Well, Bella certainly looks smitten already. It's so

refreshing to see her mixing with someone nearer her own age. I think she's going stir crazy at Penmorrow." I catch Sebastian frowning and quickly add, "Of course, she loves it there, but she needs new friends. I hope they get along."

Becky hands flutes of Bellini cocktail to each of us, before regaling us with tales of a recent trip to Venice. The ice cold Prosecco with peach puree is delicious, but goes directly to my head and loosens my tongue almost instantaneously.

"Beth, you wanted to talk to me about something?" Marcus has an arm placed around my waist much to the annoyance of Sebastian, who cocks a challenging eyebrow at his friend.

"No," I counter, "it was nothing in particular. I just thought it would be good to see if Sebastian really does have any friends."

Marcus roars a guttural laugh, while Sebastian turns his eyebrow on me. Keep your hair on, De Montfort, I'm only teasing. "Not sure I'd call myself a friend, more of a long- suffering acquaintance, hey, De Montfort?" he quips. "Come on, Beth, while Becky burns the dinner, let me show you our University photos in my study." He takes my hand and leads me from the orangery before I can protest, leaving Sebastian blazing. "Did you see his face?" Marcus nudges me as he closes the study door.

"He's rather protective of me, Marcus. Don't take it personally, please."

"Beth, I've known Sebastian for more years than I care to recall. I know what he's like, but he doesn't intimidate me. Come here. Sit down." He pats edge of the desk, having seated himself in the sole chair in the sparsely furnished home office. Affronted, I remain where I stand, looking less than impressed. What a pratt. "Please come and sit. You can see the photos better here," he says more convivially.

Following orders, I perch on the hard edge of the desk and study the album he's retrieved from a drawer. "We shouldn't be too long," I say nervously. "Becky will wonder where we are."

"Nonsense, she can keep the dinner warming in the oven. Look—there we are in the student bar. See how weedy he used to look?" He points to a young Sebastian, fresh faced and clutching a pint of beer.

"He was handsome even then."

"Handsome! Girl, you have got it bad." He laughs. It's a fascinating glimpse into Sebastian's past, which enables me to feel that I know him a little better.

"Can I please ask you something?" My finger nervously trails along the edge of a blotter pad.

"'Course you can. What is it?"

"I went to see Libby's mother this week and she suggested I ask you about Sebastian's past. She insinuated there was something that happened to him, which may have caused his…behaviour."

"His childhood. Hmm, I'm not sure I should be discussing this with you, without his permission." He closes the album, replacing it in the drawer, and folds his arms defensively.

"I'm sorry, I didn't mean to pry." My cheeks flush fiercely.

"Look, I don't suppose it will hurt to impart one titbit of information about him. Sebastian didn't have a conventional adolescence. I'm not saying he was fucked up by his parents. For the most part, they were very good to him—top private education, fantastic inheritance. His mother had, shall we say, an anger management issue."

"Oh? What do you mean?" This is intriguing.

"She used to beat seven shades of shit out of him, Beth. The first time I noticed it was when he came back from the first summer recess. He had a nasty black eye, so of course I presumed he'd been in a bar brawl, and I teased him mercilessly. We got drunk in the halls of residency and he told me she'd hit him. His mother. I didn't know him before University, so I can't tell you how long it had been going on, but he hinted she'd always punished him from a young age."

Oh my poor, poor Sebastian. Images of a little dark haired boy being struck by his mother brings a tear to my eye.

"Did he say *why* she'd hit him?" I rasp.

"Nothing he'd done, apparently. She was always the bossy one, used to order Sebastian's father around and it seems, on this occasion, he'd messed up in some way and she took it out on her son. Between you and I, Beth, I suspect that's why he's gone the other way in adulthood."

"Other way?"

"Dominance. Think about it. He's effectively turned

the tables on his mother's actions. It's as if he's correcting the imbalance and putting women back in the position he feels they belong, restoring man's authority in the household."

It all makes sense to me now. "You're right. He's put himself in a position of total control and power so that no woman can hurt him as his own mother did." The thought makes me nauseous. My vulnerable, fucked-up man has, in essence, put a defensive iron cage around himself. It breaks my heart that he should have been subjected to such ill treatment, and it makes me angry for the pain he has suffered and for the impact upon Libby and Scarlett. And me. *What of our relationship? Were the beatings I've taken at his hand really sensual, or something much darker?*

"Don't read too much into it," he adds contemplatively. "He enjoys his dominance, and he's pretty good at it. I shouldn't feel too sorry for him. After all, look at the totty the bugger attracts, hey?"

I want to smack him in his condescending mouth but we are interrupted just in time. "Come on you two, dinner's getting cold." Becky has entered the study and regards our expressions guardedly.

"Did you forget to knock?" Marcus barks.

"Sorry, Marcus. Please, could you both come through and eat. Sebastian looks most uncomfortable. I think he's missing you, Beth. I'll let him know you're coming."

As we walk together to the orangery, I place a hand on Marcus's arm. "Thank you," I tell him earnestly. "I needed to know. Thank you for telling me."

"There is a positive side to all this," he whispers as we near the others at the table. "The sex is fucking amazing if you go with it."

"What do you mean?" I ask, shocked.

"Dominance. Submission. Go with it. He's told me a lot about you. Hope you don't mind." His places a hand on the small of my back and lets it slip down to my right buttock. Glaring at him, I step to the side so that his hand drops away.

Sebastian has witnessed the grope. "Elizabeth. Marcus. How good of you both to join us." He looks mad. His eyes burn darkly as we take our seats at the table. My gaze meets his and I mouth an apology and smile meekly but he narrows his eyes sinisterly. I take the cue and lower my eyes. "Marcus, I do hope you haven't bored Elizabeth."

"On the contrary, Sebastian. We've enjoyed each other's company, haven't we, Beth?"

*Crap. Don't wind him up; he's already wound tight as a spring.*

# Chapter 26

Glancing up at him, I can see Sebastian's mood has darkened still further. He catches my furtive glance and widens his eyes in a menacing stare, causing me to fidget nervously in my seat.

"It's been *interesting,* yes," I reply, hesitantly smiling at Marcus as he fills my wine glass with iced Chablis.

"I've been showing Beth our University photos. She said she didn't realise you were clever," Marcus scoffs.

"Did she now?" Sebastian says icily.

"I said no such thing," I exclaim furiously. "Marcus showed me a couple of photos, but we didn't talk about anything, did we, Marcus?"

"Nothing at all?" Sebastian looks quizzically at me. I take a large gulp of chilled wine and glare at Marcus.

"Nothing at all, no," he confirms, winking at me.

An audible sigh escapes my lips. Just shut up!

"You were gone a considerable amount of time, to have talked about nothing at all," he observes sarcastically, and it's apparent he suspects that Marcus did indeed impart information that Sebastian would prefer remain a secret.

Bella is seated next to Theo, and listens intently as he talks to her. I smile as I see her interact with him, so shyly and demurely, and so unlike my daughter.

The meal is delicious. Becky is a talented cook; her

menu is sophisticated and fresh but avoids the tortured cleverness of high-end restaurants. The entrée of seared scallops in spicy Asian broth are divine and yet are eclipsed by the roast grouse, which Becky serves with lentils and, to my amazement, a chocolate jus. Marcus continually tops up our glasses with perfectly matched wines and, as Becky clears away the table, I'm replete and slightly drunk.

Theo takes a giggling Bella to watch a movie. Marcus ushers us to a comfortable seating at the far end of the orangery. Sebastian guides me to a love seat opposite the sofa on which Marcus sits. He places a hand upon my knee and squeezes gently. "Okay?" he whispers.

"Fine, thank you," I reply, placing a hand lightly on his, relieved that his mood has brightened.

"We won't stay long," he murmurs in my ear and kisses the lobe.

"Look at you two lovebirds. Put her down, Sebastian." Marcus pours amber liquid into four crystal glasses and hands one to Sebastian and I before sipping his own.

"Try this. It's Vin Santo and it's to die for. We picked it up in Tuscany last year."

"Marcus is a wine snob," Sebastian chides as he sips the wine.

"Darlings, wait for these." Becky returns to the orangery and offers a plate of nutty biscuits. "Biscotti almond cookies. I baked them this morning and you simply must dunk one in your Vin Santo," she enthuses.

The taste is quite extraordinary. The creamy honey flavour of the wine complemented by the less sweet crunch of the cookie is heavenly.

"Is there anything you can't do?" I ask Becky with admiration. The woman is a goddess. Looks like one, cooks like one.

"I just like to keep Marcus happy." She smiles at him and he pats her bottom as she bends down to retrieve her glass.

"Christ, she keeps me happy, don't you, darling? And when she fucks up, I make damned sure she learns her lesson and doesn't repeat her mistake. Isn't that right?"

She nods demurely and sits beside her husband who is quite clearly now drunk. "That's right. Marcus is very patient with me and very fair."

"You see, Elizabeth?" Sebastian squeezes my knee again, harder this time. "You could learn from Rebecca. She's mastered the art of submission nicely."

I nearly choke on my Van Sinto, or whatever it's called. "*Sebastian!* That's very personal," I protest, cheeks reddening.

"Nonsense," Marcus roars. "We need to get you to one of our suppers, hey, old boy?" He winks lecherously at Sebastian whose mood is again hard to read.

"It's my party soon," I enthuse, hoping to change the direction of conversation. "I'm so glad you're both coming. I don't think I'll know many other people there."

"Masked ball, eh?" Marcus winks again and I feel like punching his winking eye. I'm feeling feisty.

"That's right. It should be great fun." I drain my glass, only for Marcus to refill it instantaneously. Consciously trying not to slur my words, I turn to Sebastian. "Well, apparently we have thirty-five guests, and I know about a handful of those. We have caterers doing all the food, which is great because I can't cook. Oh, and Scarlett has chosen me a dress. Can you believe that, Becky, another woman choosing what you will wear for your own special birthday party? Oh, and not to mention the fact that she's also chosen the decorations, masks, music and—most probably—the entire guest list." My mouth is now disengaged from my brain and running on autopilot.

"Elizabeth. Enough."

I ignore Sebastian and his vice like grip on my knee. "I wouldn't be surprised if she doesn't choose Sebastian's outfit, wash behind his ears and dress him on the night." A crass peel of laughter escapes my lips, silenced only by a deep drink of Von Snotto. It's making me feel queasy. Hell, I'll finish it anyway.

"*Enough!*" Sebastian barks furiously, bringing a smug smile to Marcus the Winker's face and a 'tut' from Miss Perfect Rebecca.

"Sebastian, she's a feisty one." Winker reaches across and taps my other knee, the one that isn't being clamped in a painful vice by my boyfriend.

"Isn't she just?" Sebastian shifts his position, now able to look at me directly. Oh, he looks mean.

Miss Perfect offers her cookies in an attempt to break the tension and says sweetly, "I always find Scarlett to be so…amenable."

"You do?" I ask incredulously. "Personally, I find her to be irritatingly there. She's always around, with her prettiness, and her weakness, her please-don't-tell-me-off-I'm-made-of-glass-I-might-break, irritating personality. I think Sebastian's too afraid to get rid of her." The alcohol is entirely fuelling my vocal chords at this point.

"Do you mind?" Sebastian asks. At first I think he's talking to me but it's Marcus who replies.

"Please do. Be my guest. I'm just surprised that you've let it go this far." Winker winks again. I glare at him.

My mouth is open in readiness for a quick retort but my hand is tugged sharply as Sebastian, standing, indicates that I'm to follow him. *Oh no. Me and my smart mouth. Where's he taking me?* Leading me away from our hosts and past the dining table, we reach our destination very quickly—the far corner of the orangery. Here, Sebastian places his hands firmly on my shoulders and turns me to face the corner. He's behind me, pressing his body against my back, and I want to protest that now is not the time nor place for seduction, but I think better of it. His lips brush my ear, sending erotic sparks coursing down my spine and an involuntary moan escapes my lips.

"Why have I put you in the corner, Elizabeth?" he rasps, his breath hot against my neck.

Giggling, I reply, "Because you're a dirty bugger but I don't think this is the time or the place, Sebastian."

He sighs heavily and grasps a fistful of hair with

which he tugs my head back painfully. I gasp, not expecting this at all.

"I'll ask you again. Why have I put you in the corner?"

"Are you serious?" I'm now feeling less sure of myself, humiliated at the spectacle we are creating in front of our hosts. "Let me go. You're embarrassing me."

"As you have embarrassed me. You will stay here until I decide that you may rejoin our party. Do you understand, Elizabeth?"

"I'm not a fucking *child*," I hiss.

"No. You're not. You're also not a very good submissive, are you? I've been far too lenient with you so it's about time I demonstrated that your bad behaviour will not go unpunished. Stay there. Don't talk. Not a fucking word." He returns to his seat and resumes his conversation.

The utter humiliation is overwhelming. My eyes sting with tears, which I blink back, determined not to let our hosts witness my shame. *Bella!* If my daughter sees me here, how will I explain that my dominant boyfriend has placed me in the corner, chastised for my conduct? I can't remember ever doing such a thing to my children. Children. Joe. *What have you done, Beth? How has your life turned into such a mess? What was so damned wrong with your old life that you brought about such a chain of catastrophes?* Right now I hate myself with a force that is a thousand times more shameful than any action Sebastian could possibly take against me.

I'm left, standing in the naughty corner for what seems like an eternity, castigating myself for every mistake and foolish action that has led directly or indirectly to my current position in life. By the time Sebastian calls to me, I'm bereft and empty. I want to go home, to my real home. The only positive element is that Sebastian summoned me to join him on the sofa the moment he heard Bella and Theo returning, thus sparing me any further degradation.

Becky gives me a hug, and kisses my cheek. "Well done, darling," she whispers. "Learning is not easy, but do persevere. He's a wonderful man who loves you very much."

Marcus winks at me once more but his expression is softer and therefore I forgive him his annoying habit, relieved that nobody mentions what has just transpired. Even Sebastian is tactile and strokes my back tenderly, smiling warmly when I catch his eye.

"Uncross your legs," he whispers, his hand touching my right leg, which rests over my left. "Good girl," he murmurs when I oblige. *Christ, back off.* I sigh. *Just try and be fucking nice.*

Bella is apparently taken with Theo. The two make a striking couple; both are tall and fair, their humour evidently well matched as they share a private joke. "Theo can drive, isn't that too cool?" she enthuses.

"Too cool, yes," I agree. Bella has not shown any desire to learn and I haven't encouraged her, my fear of cars and alcohol and the inevitability of teenagers mixing the two components fills me with dread.

"If we can tear you two apart, then it's time to go home," Sebastian says. We thank our hosts and after hugs and kisses, bid farewell. It's been quite an evening and I'm glad to go.

\*\*\*

The lights burn brightly in Penmorrow, Scarlett as ever being ultra-efficient has lit the house in readiness for our late return.

"Goodnight, Mum. 'Night, Sebastian." Bella kisses us and turns in for the night, busily texting as she goes. *No doubt already missing Theo*, I muse.

"How do you think that went?" Sebastian asks, brushing a lock of hair from my neck and kissing me lightly just below my left ear.

"I'm still mad at you." I swat at him grumpily but he catches my hand and kisses my palm.

"Not as mad as I am with you, my darling," he counters, his lips curled and his eyes crinkled warmly.

"You don't look mad."

"That's because you've been punished and therefore I don't wish to dwell. However, we need to have a conversation tomorrow, revisiting the premise of submission."

"Let's talk now," I suggest, feeling feisty from the alcohol.

"No. We'll talk in the morning. You need to sleep. It's late."

"But—"

"Bed. We'll talk tomorrow." He loosens his tie and my mood lifts as I admire the spectacle that is Sebastian. His eyes burn with amusement as he notices my admiring stare. His black hair, speckled with grey at the temples, adds maturity to his otherwise youthful looks, a dark stubble shadow across his square jaw and tendrils of hair escaping above his now open shirt collar transform my respectable country gent into a dark, sensual ruffian.

"I'll be up in a minute. I need a glass of water." Aroused, yet mildly afraid, I decide to try and sober up before getting into bed with my mercurial man.

As Sebastian ambles tiredly upstairs, I head for the kitchen where I find Scarlett at the oak table, thumbing through a magazine. She's wearing only a white muslin nightgown, through which her nipples are prominently visible. *Expecting Sebastian, I see.*

"Scarlett." My voice is clipped as I take a glass from the cupboard and fill it from the tap.

"Mrs. Dove. How was your evening?"

"Fine. It's late, why are you still up?" The cool water quenches my raging thirst and begins to clear my head.

"Do you have a problem with me being up? I do live here," she replies pointedly, concentrating on the magazine page, which I see is an advert so clearly not as interesting as she would have me believe. Not interesting enough to prevent eye contact, unless of course she can't face me.

"Yes. You do, but for how much longer? I wonder."

"I'm sorry but what the hell is that supposed to

mean?" She finally raises her startled stare from the page.

"Just that. If Sebastian and I decide to make this stay a more permanent arrangement, then your services won't be required." *Put that in your pipe and smoke it, missy!*

Her expression changes to one of amused pity, and it takes all of my self-control not to wipe the smirk off her pretty little face.

"Just as I thought. His Lordship would *never* send me away. He needs me, just like he did before and just like he always will. I thought getting you here would be good for him. I really did. But you know what?" She spits her spiteful words with venom but I let her continue, keen to see more of the true Scarlett. "You're no better for His Lordship than his dead wife was. She couldn't fulfil him and neither can you."

Stunned at her outburst, I'm shaking with rage. "What the fuck would *you* know about him? All you are to him is a skivvy. A low, weak, pathetic little waif who has the personality of a gnat and the sex appeal of a stick insect." My trembling hands carefully place the glass on the granite worktop, and I grip the edge for stability.

"Is that what you think?" she asks mockingly. "Do you really think he can ever be satisfied by *you?* You wouldn't even be here now if I hadn't stupidly thought that you'd fulfil the 'wifey' role, to provide him with the family I can't give him—Libby couldn't give him. That's all you're here for. Nothing more. You're not needed for anything else, you see. I can meet all his needs other than giving him a child."

The shock of her words is a fist to my stomach. "You're lying," I hiss. "Sebastian loves me. Not because of Bella, or of Joe. He loves me. You just can't handle that because you're obsessed with him, aren't you? Well, let me tell you, lady, when he hears what you've just said to me, you'll be out of here so fast it will make your sick little head spin. So, will you go willingly or will you wait for him to fire your scrawny ass?"

"Poor, bereaved Elizabeth." She sighs, shaking her head sorrowfully. "Your mind hasn't been right since your son and husband died, has it? You messed up your marriage, you screwed around, you threw yourself at the first eligible man who would take you in and then, when I give you the golden opportunity to satisfy his need for a family, you mess that up too."

I slap her face hard enough to sting my palm. "Don't you *ever* talk about my son and my husband again, do you understand? And what the fuck do you mean when you say you 'gave me the golden opportunity?' What the hell did you *do?*"

She raises a hand to her reddening cheek and smiles. "Do you think I'm not used to pain, Elizabeth? Do you think I don't enjoy it? That's what I live for. I'm here to take the pain away from Him—the pain that Libby caused, the pain that infertility caused, the pain that you cause. I was wrong to bring you here. I see that now."

"Bring me here?" I screech. "What the fuck are you talking about?"

"That poor husband of yours. Dear dead Alan. He was

a lousy lay. I have to agree with you on that one. Even so, it pained me, but I did what I thought was right. For *Him*."

*Oh my God. The accident. Did she…*

Movement in the corner of my vision snaps my gaze away from Scarlett. Sebastian leans against the doorframe, wearing a robe.

"Who wants to tell me what the hell is going on?" he demands sternly.

The room is spinning. He's talking. I see his lips move but my ears don't hear what he says. He's walking toward me but it's in slow motion, as though someone hit the slow replay button on a movie clip. *She killed them. Oh my God. She killed them.* The words won't leave my lips, the shocking thought too horrendous to verbalise. His arms are around me and the world goes black.

# Retribution

## Janey Rosen

# Chapter 1

It's daytime. The sunlight is streaming through a chink in the curtains, spilling golden light upon the honey coloured furniture in our bedroom. My head feels muzzy. I'm disorientated, unsure if it's morning and how I got to bed. Recollections of last night stream back with startling clarity, I remember what Scarlett said to me. *Could it be true, or was I so drunk that my imagination ran away with me? Scarlett has many faults, and irritates the hell out of me ... but a murderer? Could she really have slept with Alan? She intimated that she caused the accident which killed my husband and son... but how?* Such dark thoughts, so many questions.

"Ah, you're awake. Good. How's your head?" Sebastian enters the bedroom wearing an expression of dour sobriety. Sweeping my legs aside he perches on the edge of the bed, his features strained and his peppered hair messed up. He's dressed in faded blue jeans and black tee and he looks sizzling hot, momentarily distracting me from my troubled thoughts. He places a glass of orange juice on the nightstand and regards me with a scowl.

"Sit up. Drink. All of it."

Obediently, I heave my leaden body to a sitting position and slump back against the disordered pile of pillows, grimacing as my temples throb. The juice is ice cold and I drain the glass appreciatively, refreshed and glad to rid my mouth of a stale bitterness.

"Did you talk to Scarlett?" My words are but a croak.

He sighs deeply and runs his index finger down my cheek and across my lips, his mood difficult to read as ever. "Yes of course I talked to her. After you passed out in a drunken stupor, I sat talking with her for a couple of hours."

Damn it. Scarlett had time to spin her lies and cover her tracks.

"Did she tell you what she said to me about the accident?" I ask urgently.

"What is your problem with Scarlett?" he quizzes, his finger now trailing down my throat, down still further to the naked valley between my breasts, *so distracting*. My nipples elongate and stiffen as his finger brushes lightly over each, my body acting in total discord to my brain.

"Sebastian. Stop it." I brush his finger away reluctantly but he immediately returns it determinedly to my right nipple, stroking and circling and then pinching it sharply between his thumb and index finger. I try not to react but moan involuntarily, my back arching as he shifts his position, his mouth finding my left nipple. *Damn him.*

"Please. Sebastian stop. This is important."

He sucks hard on my sensitive bud, his tongue flicking over the tip, his fingers continuing to pinch and knead. I grasp his head, my fingers clutching and tugging at his hair, forcing him to take more of my breast in his hungry mouth. I have an urgent, primal need to reclaim Sebastian as mine and erase the taint of Scarlett's words.

Pulling back, stronger than I, he releases my tight grip on his hair, a few strands still clutched in my fist. "I only want you. *Only* you. You'll always be mine. Stop this jealousy." His lips find mine and stifle my protestations, his weight pressing down on me as I slide back down the bed beneath him. He makes slow passionate love to me and it's divine - not kinky nor hurried, nor brutal but an expression of adoration that is true and profound. *I am his.*

I call my mother, feeling a deep need to hear the comforting and familiar sound of her voice. Distracted by Sebastian this morning, I've not been able to have a full discussion with him regarding Scarlett, and last night is weighing heavily on my mind compounding my melancholia and anxiety.

"Beth, love, it's been too long. How are you both?" Those few simple words are calming and offer a small taste of home – of simpler, happier times with my parents when the only complication in life was homework, boys and music.

"Everything's fine. Wonderful," I lie, not wishing to worry my mother with the complexities of my life nor to tarnish the high esteem in which she holds Sebastian. It's not for my mother to carry the heavy burden of guilt, nor the suspicion surrounding her Grandson's death. I simply want to wrap myself tightly in the comforting, maternal embrace that her loving voice offers.

"Will you be home for your birthday?"

"No Mum, I'm really sorry. We're having a few friends over here. I'll be home just after my birthday though, in time for Bella's so we'll all be together for her special day."

"Alright love, I'll keep your present until I see you. Bella's ok, I hope?"

"She's just fine, she met a boy last night – Theo. He's nineteen and has his own car, so he's the coolest boy on the planet in Bella's eyes."

"That's good. You tell her that her old Grandma sends her love and I'll see her soon. Oh and send my love to Sebastian, and you look after him."

"I will. I love you Mum. Very much."

"I love you more."

"Impossible," I say, smiling at the ritual that used to be ours alone when Mum tucked me in at night, as a child. How I long to be in my mother's arms, clutched tight against her breast, her arms an iron fortress impenetrable by evil or harm.

Ruth answers on the first ring. I've walked across the lawn to the rear of the house, to afford me some privacy. I recount what I recall of last night's heated discussion with Scarlett and Ruth listens quietly. When I have finished, she takes a deep breath and considers what I have told her in the measured way that she has.

"Ok, so are you saying that you think Scarlett was seeing Alan and that she was somehow responsible for the accident?" She clarifies.

"I know it sounds far fetched, Ruth, but yes – that's exactly what I'm saying."

"And she caused the accident because she wanted you and the children to come to Penmorrow, to give Sebastian the children that neither she, nor Libby, could give him?"

It sounds so unbelievable when Ruth recounts my story that I wonder if I imagined the entire argument.

"Ruth, I'm only telling you what Scarlett said to me. I *know* it sounds crazy but yes, that's what I'm thinking. I don't believe that Sebastian has ever thought of Scarlett in the way she thinks of their relationship. I think she's seriously deluded, Beth."

"But Joe ... if that's the case, why would she harm Joe?"

"She couldn't have known that Joe would be in the car but I really believe that she's dangerous. She seems to think that she can offer Sebastian everything ... except a family. He's desperate for an heir Ruth, that much is true. The whole estate passes to distant relatives in Australia when he dies. It all makes sense, don't you see – she thinks he loves her, and that the only thing missing is children. An heir."

"Calm down. Let's look at the facts. At the funeral, didn't Mike say that Alan had been seeing someone? You told me that Mike mentioned a woman in a 4X4 car. Could that be Scarlett?"

"Of course it could. Sebastian drives a Range Rover – it could be that she used his car to meet with Alan. She takes his car sometimes to go to town."

"Ok. So, she uses his car, sees Alan and plots the whole thing, that doesn't explain the anti-depressants found in his blood stream."

"Libby was on the same medication. What if Scarlett has those tablets? What if she convinced Alan to take them? He was pretty messed up about us."

"So, the accident happens, you go to Penmorrow with Bella – it's not a son though is it?"

"I know but that doesn't matter. The estate passes to any surviving heir. I think she saw me purely as a means by which Sebastian could have an heir. She's so obsessed with him. What if she thought that I'd come here, to be some quiet little thing who would provide the heir, while she and Sebastian continue as lovers."

"Continue? You mean they have had *sex?* Do you know this, Beth?" Ruth sounds sceptical, I need to convince her that I'm not going mad, that this really is happening.

"She took advantage of him when Libby died, it wasn't his fault. Ruth, you need to believe me. Something isn't right here and I'm really scared. I love Sebastian so much and I know he loves me, he really does. It's her, Ruth. It's Scarlett – she's crazy and she's dangerous... I'm frightened."

"I want you to come home, Beth." Ruth's tone is insistent.

"I can't."

"Why can't you? I'll come and get you if necessary but you and Bella must come home. You've both been through so much, you don't need all this Beth."

"Because if we come home, then Scarlett has won. She gets Sebastian and I can't let that happen, he's the love of my life, I need him."

"I understand," Ruth sooths calmly. "But I want to speak to the police inspector who dealt with the accident. I'll just run her name past him, see if it throws anything up."

"What if he thinks I'm crazy?"

"He'd be right," she jokes. "It will put your mind at rest, leave it with me. Please try not to worry, you've been through so much, this could just be grief you know."

"Do you think so?"

"Possibly, but let's get the cops looking into the bitch, see if anything turns up. Love you my loony best friend." "Love you too. Bye."

"Bye."

# Chapter 2

Sebastian pulls off his riding boots and pads across the kitchen floor in his socks, pulling me into a tight embrace.

"You smell of horses," I protest, pinching my nose.

"Hey, I'm a simple country boy," he purrs.

"Well, country bumpkin, we need to talk." I'm determined that we have this discussion and I'm not going to be distracted by his erection pressing in to me through his jodhpurs.

"Talk? Can't we do something more fun?" He grins impishly and grinds his hips so distractingly, but I will not give in to temptation.

"No. I mean it - we *need* to talk. You side-tracked me this morning. Please sit." I indicate to the pew opposite mine.

"Since when were you the Domme?" he quips with a cocky grin.

"Scarlett," I say and his expression darkens instantaneously.

"Not that again, Elizabeth, give it a rest." He pulls away from me defensively.

"We have to talk about last night, Sebastian. I want to know what you're going to do about her."

He slumps on the pew and steeples his hands beneath

his chin, avoiding my gaze. "Ok, look, I talked to her last night. You were very drunk and the whole thing escalated. She's very sorry if she offended you and I have reminded her of her position here. You'll find her more amenable from now on."

"Do you have any idea of the terrible things she said to me?" I ask, incredulous.

"No and I don't want to know. I'm sure you both said things that you didn't mean and the main thing is that you both move forward from this. It's home to you both so you need to try and get along, is that clear?"

*No! Over my dead body.* "I want you to fire her," I state.

His mouth sets in a stubborn line and he runs a hand through his messy black hair. "I will not fire her. You do *not* tell me what to do, she runs this house and I have no evidence that she's committed any crime nor any misdemeanour, other than upsetting my very drunk girlfriend who, most likely, was equally offensive to Scarlett."

"But ..."

"No, Elizabeth. That's an end to it."

"She's done something, Sebastian. Something very bad, I know it ..."

"Enough." He bangs his clenched fist down hard onto the table, the impact makes me jump. "Scarlett is going to try very hard to get along with you, and I expect you to reciprocate. It starts tonight, she's going to cook a special dinner for us both by way of appeasement and we will enjoy it and be grateful."

"Yes, Sebastian. I'll try," I say with far more conviction than I feel. *I will be vigilant - I don't trust her and yet it's so difficult to verbalise my concerns to Sebastian, he's so controlling ... and so loyal to her.*

"I need to take you back to the chamber, my girl." His mood changes to one of seduction but my thoughts remain preoccupied.

She's baking a cheese soufflé. I can smell the delicious aroma from the Great Hall. Our paths haven't crossed all day, deliberately on my part and I suspect on hers too.

"Go and help Scarlett bring in the entrée, Elizabeth." Sebastian cocks an eyebrow, daring me to defy him. Thinking better of it I head to the kitchen compliantly.

"Good evening, Mrs. Dove." Scarlett wipes her hands on a crisp white apron and smiles demurely as I enter the kitchen.

"Good evening, Scarlett," I mutter sullenly. "Can I take in the entrée?"

She's fussing over the soufflé, wiping the ramekins with a paper towel. "You'll need the oven glove, they are fresh from the range so boiling hot."

I place the soufflé on a tray carefully, noting as I do, the skill with which Scarlett cooks. She is an accomplished chef, although not the tidiest and the mess she is creating makes me smile. *Not so perfect, are you?*

The meal is divine and, much as it pains me to admit it, Scarlett has gone to considerable trouble to produce a feast of cheese soufflé followed by beef wellington. Conversation over dinner is stilted, lacking the easy banter to which we are so accustomed. The only discourse I wish to have is the one topic which is taboo, thus rendering any other dialogue trivial.

"I've given Scarlett the rest of the night off, so you will have to see to the dishes." Sebastian is grinning devilishly.

"Gee, thank you Sir," I say, unable to hide the sarcasm from my voice.

As I clear the plates, he smacks my bottom hard.

"Off to the kitchen, wench. I'll have a brandy ready for you upstairs. Be there in thirty minutes."

The familiar throb emanates from my groin as I wash up the dirty crockery. He has a way about him that makes me take leave of my senses and melt at his touch. I'm still angry, confused and troubled and yet all I want to do is feel him deep inside me.

The plates and pans are stacked neatly on the draining rack and all that remains is to wipe down the granite surfaces. The pestle and mortar have been left on the worktop, next to the herb stand. Placing them in the sink to rinse, I notice that Scarlett has crushed something other than herbs and spices. A white powder coats the ceramic dish. *Don't trust her.* Running my finger gingerly along the surface and placing a little of the powder on my tongue, the mildly bitter taste is unfamiliar. I can't see what she could have crushed – it is curious, and certainly a matter to confront Scarlett with in the morning. Now, though, my sexy man is waiting for me and I don't wish to keep him waiting, especially with the threat of the chamber still fresh in my mind.

In our bedroom, Sebastian reclines naked against the cushions on the bed, sipping brandy, with the beautiful decadence of a Michelangelo painting. He smiles roguishly and nods toward a brandy balloon on the dresser, inviting me to drink. Clutching the glass, but not daring to move to him lest I break the spell of the moment, I instead lean against the wall adjacent to the closed door, and regard the vision before me.

"Sebastian, the last time I drank brandy, I passed out. I was sixteen and we stole it from my friend's parents' drink cupboard."

"I feel sure it won't have been a fine cognac such as this, Elizabeth. Swill the brandy around the balloon, put your nose over it, like this." He demonstrates the technique, making me giggle at the vision of him – stark naked yet giving me tuition on brandy tasting etiquette.

I swill the glass and watch the brilliant, deep amber liquid as it reflects the light from the chandelier above the bed.

"It smells of marshmallows and old wood."

"Taste it," he says seductively.

"*Wow*," I breathe as the fire travels down my throat and hits my belly. "Spice ... caramel ... and fruit. Is that right?"

He's beaming at me. "There's no right or wrong, it's your personal interpretation, but I'd say yes, that's how I taste it too. Finish it."

The fire spreads from my belly to my limbs; the delicious warmth saps my strength and wraps me in fur.

He puts his glass on the nightstand and crawls off the bed, hips swaying he reaches me, and he's all meanness and seduction. *Oh God, what you do to me...*

Pulling at the belt of my jeans, he pulls me toward him and, with the ease of experience, he strips me in a heartbeat, my clothes pooled at my feet.

"Lie on the bed on your back," he instructs.

"Certainly, Sir." Doing as he bids, I lie supine; the fire now burns in my nipples, my apex slick with my arousal. He pulls the belt of my silk robe free where it hangs on the back of the door. *Oh Christ, my desire is palpable.*

With skill he binds my wrists with the silk belt and, pulling my arms above my head, loops the silk through the spindle of the bed frame. My legs part, I am exposed and yearning to feel his torso between my thighs, my breath quickens, my pulse races.

"Fuck me," I plead.

"Fuck me *what?*"

"Fuck me *please.*"

"Fuck me please *what?*"

"Fuck me please *Sir.*" My body writhes in anticipation and with raw need. He strokes his cock languidly, his eyes focused on my erect nipples.

"No." He shakes his head slowly, his hand working his erection more fervently now as he stands beside the bed, the muscles in his arm straining, the blood vessels along his enormous length pulsating.

*What?* "Don't tease me. I need you." I say urgently. My thighs squeeze tightly together now, the sensation between them almost unbearable.

"No. Don't speak. Watch me," he rasps.

His breath catches as he pleasures himself, his eyes now fixed on mine, his skilful hand milking his hardness, which oozes the first delicious drops of nectar down his thigh.  He moves onto the bed, kneeling beside me, so near and yet he doesn't stop working his throbbing member.

"Oh fuck. I'm coming." He quickens his stroke, eyes closed he arches his back, his erection jerking as he spills forth – ejaculating his warm, creamy climax over my

quivering breasts. "Oh yes, *oh fuck*." He expels the remaining drops, which bead upon my belly leaving me bereft and wanting.

A lone tear escapes and runs like a tiny sorrowful river to my hairline. *Doesn't he want me?* A sob escapes my lips as I stare up at the man whom I love more than life itself and who just brought himself to orgasm rather than make love to me.

"Don't cry," he implores.

"Why? What's wrong with me?" the tears flow faster.

He doesn't reply, instead his hand massages his warm semen over my breasts, my nipples slick with his pleasure. His mouth moves down to my sorely neglected folds and he sucks and flicks at my clitoris until I'm screaming his name.

The clock on the nightstand tells me I've slept until ten in the morning and yet I don't feel refreshed. The brandy must have left me with a hangover, I'm so drowsy this morning. Sebastian has left a note on his pillow letting me know that he's gone to London for a meeting and will be back late tonight. He's taken Bella with him for a day out and given her money to go shopping, I suspect she's meant to buy a birthday gift for me but will no doubt spend it on clothes and make-up instead. I'm glad she's having a day away from Penmorrow, it's not good for a young woman to be cooped up in this old house.

My thoughts turn to my party in just three days time. I'm so unprepared for it, I really must check on Scarlett's progress with the food and flowers. Scarlett. What did you do? Perhaps it is grief affecting my judgment, or maybe I imagined our conversation and was more drunk than I thought. The powder...*what are you up to?* Stretching and yawning, I drag my weary body from the comfort of the bed, pull on my robe and head for the kitchen.

Scarlett is making porridge, the aroma from the creamed oats and honey fills the kitchen fuelling my appetite. "Good morning, Mrs. Dove," she says absently as she stirs.

"Scarlett."

The pestle and mortar have gone, opening the cupboard, I see them clean and carefully put away in their place.

"Can I help you with something?" she asks.

"Actually, yes you can. What were you grinding with the pestle and mortar last night?"

She looks surprised, a trace of emotion fleetingly flicks across her pale face–possibly guilt, perhaps something more sinister–but it's gone in an instant, her features now set in a cold stare. "Cornflour and rock salt. Why?"

"It didn't taste like that."

"Meaning?"

"Meaning I don't believe you. You're up to something and I intend to find out what, and when I do you'll be history. Do you understand?"

She glares at me insolently, her mouth agape.

I continue, "and don't think I've forgotten what you said to me the other night, Scarlett. This isn't over, I want you to trust me on this. I have no idea what you've done or how, but you will regret crossing my family."

She returns to stirring the porridge in silence and this unnerves me, I'd expected her to react and protest her innocence, but instead she takes two bowls and ladles the creamed oats before setting the dishes on the table. "I don't know what to say," she sits at the table and tastes the porridge. "We both said things the other night, Mrs. Dove, things that were spiteful and didn't mean. I want you to know that I'd never *ever* do anything to harm His Lordship. You do know that, right?"

Seating myself opposite her, I regard her closely. "I do believe that you would never harm him. What I don't believe is that you wouldn't harm me."

We sit in an uncomfortable silence. The steaming porridge looks so tempting, my stomach rumbles as I play with the spoon set beside the bowl. *It's just porridge, Beth – you've seen her make it. Did she crush anything into it? No she didn't so stop being irrational and eat.* It tastes so good, the warm gloop filling my belly, the honey sweetening my bitter mood.

"Do you want me to leave?" she whispers.

"Yes. I do. Will you?"

"If that's what His Lordship wants, then yes I will. I see how happy you make him, do you know how painful that is for me?" Her voice cracks as tears spill down her high cheekbones, she wipes them away with the back of her hand. "All I've ever wanted is to make him happy."

"I'm sure you did, Scarlett. You were here for him when Libby died and that would have meant a great deal to him, but *I'm* here now. He has a family and it's time you accepted that and moved on."

She rises and scrapes her uneaten porridge into the bin before returning to the table and collecting my empty dish. Suddenly I feel sorry for her, pity is not an emotion that I anticipated feeling toward her but she looks bereft, lost and child like.

"Why don't you stay for the party and then go?"

She lifts her red-rimmed eyes to mine and smiles. "Yes I'd like that, thank you. Let's go over the plans, I've worked hard to prepare the very best party for you, everything's ready."

Yawning, I try and focus on the details of my party

but fatigue grips me and it's all I can do to stay awake.

"Are you sick?" Scarlett looks concerned.

"No. I'm just tired, too much brandy last night. When we've finished going over the timings for the party, I'll grab another hour in bed."

The sun is low and shadows cast over the room create shapes that look like demons. My eyes fix on a demon with a tail, which lurks next to the bathroom door. It is still, just a shadow. No such thing as demons. The demon moves, a flick of its tail, nothing more but it's enough to make me scream.

"What's wrong Mrs. Dove?" Scarlett appears in the doorway, her face etched with concern. I'm sat up in bed now, the demon hasn't moved again but I'm watching it.

*I'm watching you. I'm watching both of you – Scarlett the demon and the shadow demon.*

"Mrs. Dove, are you sick? Shall I call His Lordship?"

"I'm fine. What time is it?" Blinking my eyes very fast makes the tail flick. *Must not blink. Must not blink.*

"Six thirty. You've been asleep for hours, I didn't want to disturb you but if you need something...?"

"What? Where did the day go? I must be sick, I never sleep in the day." My balled fists rub the remnants of sleep from my gritty eyes, which now watch Scarlett. Her eyes glow red. *Demon.* I rub them again. Blue eyes staring back at me. "I saw that. I saw what you did with your eyes."

"I'll bring you a tray of supper, Mrs. Dove. Stay in bed and I'll get you some analgesics, I think you must have a fever, you're hallucinating."

She turns and walks away and as she goes, her tail flicks against the doorframe. The wooden frame ignites where her tail caught it, embers glow and then combust. The burning frame becomes a ball of orange fire, and the fireball rolls across the carpet toward the bed. I can't scream because my lungs are burning, the orange flames are travelling down my oesophagus, melting my bronchioles and even thrashing at my chest with a pillow doesn't extinguish the flames. Reaching to the nightstand, I clutch the glass of water and gulp as though my life depends on it. The flames go out, the pain is gone. *I won. I'm alive. I won.*

There is no fire. There are no demons. Everything is as it should be and Scarlett is placing a tray on the nightstand. She's cooked me an omelette but I'm not hungry.

"You're sweating," she observes. "Here, take these." She places two tablets in my hand and passes me a fresh glass of water before going to the bathroom and returning with a damp flannel. She gently lays the cooling cloth on my forehead and wipes away the beads of perspiration from my hot skin. It feels so refreshing. She lifts my hand to my mouth and helps me to put the tablets on my tongue, her hand cups mine and she raises the glass to my lips. I swallow the pills like a good girl.

"Thank you Scarlett."

"You're welcome. I need to take care of you," she murmurs.

Sebastian tenderly kisses my forehead. My eyes feel heavy as they blink open, adjusting to the artificial light from the bedside lamp.

"Hey, darling. How are you feeling?" His fingers lightly stroke my cheek.

"I'm sick," I reply feebly.

"I know darling. Scarlett told me. I'm sorry I wasn't here for you today."

"That's ok, Scarlett took care of me." The irony of my words is lost on me.

"Scarlett was very worried about you, she sent me a text this evening saying you were running a high temperature, so I came straight back. The traffic was diabolical on the M4, it took us nearly four hours."

"You're here now. Thank you," I smile up at him and run a finger over his pouting lips. "Just seeing you makes me feel better. Is Bella home? Did she have a good time?"

"Bella's fine. She spent all the money I gave her and is busy in her room trying on the plethora of clothes she bought. She's had a wonderful day. We went for lunch together at my club."

"You have a club?" I ask. *Has he mentioned a club before?*

"I'm a member, I don't own it," he chuckles. "It's in Pal Mal – I'll take you there for lunch one day soon. They have some very elegant bedrooms there too," he grins salaciously. "Anyway, you need to get well. It's your party soon."

"I'm feeling better already." *Lies.*

# Chapter 3

It's the day before my fortieth birthday and I have a list of final preparations, yet feel riddled with panic and anxiety, this being the largest social event I have ever hosted. With so many of Sebastian's friends and acquaintances attending I feel the enormity of the task at hand, even if Sebastian and Scarlett have taken over much of the planning. I have to make a good impression on those Sebastian cares about, I need them to like me.

Sebastian is back from his ride early this morning but, even so, it irritates me that today of all days he still went for a ride when there is so much to do. He's in the kitchen munching on toast and reading *The Times*. Clearing up the scattering of crumbs he has left on the bread board I ignore him purposefully.

"Leave that, Elizabeth. Scarlett can do it."

"Scarlett can't do it. She has 100 jobs to do today, Sebastian," I scold, casting the breadboard into the enamel butler sink with a loud clatter.

"I said *leave* it." His tone is not one to counter, he does not like being disobeyed. *Tough. You have no idea the stress I am under today, mister.*

"You seem very laid back, Sebastian. It's fine for *you*, you know everyone who is coming, whereas I feel I'm going to be judged by thirty strangers who all knew Libby and will no doubt be comparing us and realising that you've landed a neurotic crazy lady."

"Which is exactly what you sound like right now," he observes coolly.

"Oh well pardon me for being ever so slightly nervous. I didn't want a sodding party anyway." I know how ungrateful and childish I sound but I'm so tired I have little control over what escapes my lips.

"That's gratitude for you. Come with me." He rises from the pew and takes my hand, pulling me roughly in the direction of the hall. He casts a glance at me, his eyes are narrowed, dark with a steely resolve.

"*Ouch,* leave me alone," I hiss, trying unsuccessfully to retrieve my hand. "Where are you taking me? I've not got time for your games."

"You'll see. Games are exactly what you need, my girl. We are going to relieve some of this stress." *Oh shit. This is not at all what I need. I need to get on with the plethora of jobs which have to be done today.* He is determinedly striding toward his study with me in tow, pulling against him and shuffling like an errant child. When we reach the steps to the cellar I know precisely what he has planned for me and I am not happy about it, not happy at all.

"You're an inconsiderate pig, Sebastian. Do you know that?" Knowing that such words will only be used against me shortly, I plough on regardless. "All you can think about is your dick, when I have so much to do. You are adding to my stress, not relieving it."

"Carry on ranting, Elizabeth. It won't make a jot of difference to me, it may however make it harder for you to sit down."

"Sebastian. You *wouldn't!*"

"Oh. You know I would"

Sebastian flicks the switch illuminating the small chamber, the edge of the circular bed presses into the backs of my thighs. He has locked the door, rendering escape impossible, fanning the flames of anger within me.

He's pacing back and forth, his back to the door, his breath coming in short pants, nostrils flaring like a stallion who has been ridden hard. His long fingers stroke his chin as he decides what to do with me.

"Sebastian...I have to..." Before I can finish, he steps forward, grasping a handful of my hair he pulls my mouth to his, kissing me roughly. Involuntarily, my body responds as it always does, my pulse quickening, cheeks flushing and a warm burn emanating from the apex of my thighs. Abruptly, his mouth leaves mine as an anguished moan escapes my lips. I'm torn–I am totally stressed yet my body is betraying me yet again. I have never before encountered a man who has this effect on me and I chastise myself for being so weak in his presence. Before I can utter a further protestation, he flicks the light switch and we are plunged into inky black darkness. This throws me and I feel utterly vulnerable yet my breath quickens with the thrill of expectancy. I hear his rapid breathing close to my ear, turning my head to my right my lips seek his but are left wanting. Reaching my hands in front of me, I feel for him but his breathing is quieter, more distant.

"Stop playing games." I turn my head listening for sounds, my remaining senses compensating for the loss of sight. I smell his delicious scent. He's close. I hear the swish of fabric falling to the floor followed by the sound of a zipper being pulled. I taste the salty beads of perspiration forming on my top lip. I feel fingertips brushing against my outstretched left wrist, trailing down to my own fingertips and then his touch is gone. "Sebastian. I don't have time for this. Where are you?" *Silence.* Losing patience I take a tentative step forward in the direction I believe the door to be. A hand grasps my left wrist, my hand is lifted up and my fingertips brush against a roughness I know to be his unshaven chin. He raises my fingers a little further, the roughness replaced with the softness of his lips which part. I hear his breath catch as my index finger touches the warm wetness of his tongue. His lips close around my finger, his teeth gently pressing against the pad and nail. My own breath catches, I gasp as deft fingers tug the hem of my top, lifting it above my head, my finger slipping from his mouth, my arms automatically rising to allow the easy removal of the garment. I feel the gentle breeze against my cheek as my top floats past my head to the floor. His hot breath is on my neck sending a shiver down the length of my spine, he deftly unclasps my bra which drops away freeing my aching nipples. I await the touch of his lips on my throbbing buds, instead he unfastens my skirt, sliding it down over my hips so that it pools over my feet.

"Sebastian...please."

"*Shh.*" His whispered rebuke blows warm on my stomach, my abdominal muscles clench as he swiftly tugs down my panties, which join the skirt at my feet. I am exposed, vulnerable, aroused–all thoughts of schedules now gone from my mind, replaced with illicit desires. Never has he been so sensual, so gentle in this room. He traces a finger lightly from my left thigh, upwards past my hip, my side, across to my left nipple. Circling my areola, he traces across my sternum and repeats the feather-light motion on my right nipple, forcing me to arch my back, thrusting my breasts forward I truly believe he can make me climax this way, such is my desperate need. His finger continues its journey down my right hip, to my thigh and crosses to where I need it to be – on my clitoris. Biting my bottom lip, I will him to end my torment, knowing it will take only a moment more of his rubbing to tease from my body the release that I crave. As the first spasm builds, so his finger stills. A cry of anguish leaves my lips, I desperately reach out for him, finding his muscular arms I clutch them and step forward until my nose bumps against his chest, the thick hair tickling my face. His arms encircle me as my tongue laps at his skin, my mouth kissing his chest hungrily. I rock up on tiptoes and kiss his neck then nibble at his earlobe as he clutches my buttocks, pulling me in closer until I feel his erection pressing into my belly.

"Tell me what you need Elizabeth."

"I need *you*. I need you inside me," I breathe, my hands tangling in his thick hair. A growl hails from his throat and in a swift stroke he pivots us, thrusting me hard against the cold stone wall forcing the air from my lungs. He lifts me as though I am a feather, my legs guided around his waist, my thighs squeezing to gain purchase as the darkness disorientates me still. In one swift movement he pins me in place with his muscular frame and bites at my shoulder but the pain enflames the pleasure as he releases me just enough that I drop down hard onto his erection.

"You *bastard,*" I hiss, but the anger is at myself for loving what he is doing to me and at my body for responding so defiantly. My hand clutches at his hair, tugging at the roots so firmly that he curses against my breast, elevates my ass and drops me down even harder onto him. He doesn't speak, nor whisper his love but his lips find mine, his bruising kiss tells me more than words alone ever could. His teeth and his tongue declare his love and the rapturous cry as he empties within absolves me of insecurities and fears. Liberated, my soul is free to soar as I succumb to the momentary release he has given me. Spent and slick, we glide down the wall to a breathless heap on the cobbles.

"Elizabeth," he whispers as our breathing settles. He strokes my hair tenderly, his cheek pressed against mine.

"Mmm?"

"Whenever you see darkness, don't I guide you to the light?"

A little drowsy, but nonetheless thrown by his profound question, I reach for his cheek and stroke it with my thumb. "Yes," my lips lightly brush his, "my world was in darkness after the accident. Your love has been a brighter light than I ever could have believed possible, but ..."

"But?"

"There is still darkness, Sebastian and I don't feel I can talk to you about it."

"Scarlett." He tenses and I feel his jaw set under my thumb.

"Yes. Scarlett. We have to talk about her...I mean really talk." Prising myself from the weight of his body I stand and pat my hand along the wall until I locate the light switch. Flicking the switch down, we both blink momentarily as our eyes adjust to the light. Sitting beside Sebastian on the cold cobbled floor, I take his hand in mine and stroke his palm. "I know how much you care for her and I'm not trying to come between you, you do believe me don't you?"

He pulls his hand away and rakes it through his messy hair, sighing deeply. His eyes are dark coals framed by long black lashes and are etched with pain. "Yes. I believe you. I just..."

"You just what darling?"

"I just don't want to...I *can't* believe that Scarlett would be capable of harming anyone. If it's true then where does it stop?" He pauses, mouth open he meets my gaze, a look of shock on his face, "where did it start...Libby?" A lone tear trickles down his cheek, I wipe it away tenderly with my thumb. He looks utterly lost.

"Oh fuck, Elizabeth."

"I have no idea," I sigh. "I just know what my gut tells me. What she herself told me."

"But you were drunk. How can you be sure of what she said. How can you be sure she wasn't being spiteful? We all say things." My index finger presses to his lips silencing him.

"I can't be entirely sure but I know how she makes me feel. I remember much of what she said, Sebastian, and I know I haven't felt right for a while now."

"You think she's *harming* you?" Pulling away from my touch, he regards me incredulously. "For fucks sake, Elizabeth. *I'm* here. How would she be harming you without me knowing about it?"

Trying to calm him, I soften my tone before the conversation we must have becomes a fight. "I'm just being honest with you. I don't have the answers, Sebastian."

"No you don't–what you have is a bunch of serious fucking allegations which are totally lacking in any substance or evidence." His words hurt but I listen quietly. "You weren't here when Libby was sick. You have no idea what you're talking about. Scarlett was here. She was my rock when my whole fucking world fell apart. Is that someone who is capable of murder?" He rakes his hair again then drags his hand across his jaw.

"I know it hurts you."

"*Do* you? How fucking understanding of you." His profanities shock me but I can see past the anger to the hurt in his dark hooded eyes. Fear. I see fear in his eyes for the first time, my strong Sebastian is scared.

"She's agreed to go. If you want her to, she will leave." He stiffens but remains silent. Sucking in a deep breath I tell him, "I want her to go."

"So she's tried, judged and sentenced just like that?" he spits.

"We don't need her here. I want to look after you. You're *mine*, not hers."

"Is that what this is really about?" His icy stare meets mine, I avert my eyes. "Fucking jealousy?"

"No." Tears prick my eyes. "I'm scared too," I whisper.

My tears dampen his anger and he takes my hand in his. "I would die if you were harmed, Elizabeth. After Libby passed a part of me died too and I didn't think I'd ever be happy again. Then you...tumbled into my life, all muddy and awkward," his lip curls at the memory. "You were the most beautiful thing I'd seen, so complex, so...difficult, yet I *had* to have you."

"And you were an arse," I grin, he chuckles and wipes the tears from my cheeks with his thumb. "So, how do we move forward?"

He bites his lip, when he speaks his voice is tormented. "I have to choose don't I?"

"Yes. You do. Me or her?"

His gaze locks on mine, earnest and sincere. "Then there is no choice to be made. You are mine." I expel the breath I have been holding, relief coursing through my body, I surrender to his waiting embrace.

"It will be okay," he soothes, stroking my hair, kissing my forehead. "I'll deal with it. With *her*."

"I said she could stay until after my party."

"Elizabeth, it's cruel to evict the girl before she has somewhere else to go." I decide not to push him further. Gathering my clothes and dressing silently together I feel we've reached an understanding and moved our relationship forward. Whatever she has done, or not done, she can no longer hurt me or my family. Scarlett will soon be permanently erased from our lives.

Smoothing down my skirt and still glowing in the afterglow of passion, I fetch my handbag from the kitchen. Sebastian is several paces ahead of me. Scarlett is reading the morning paper and drinking coffee at the kitchen table as though she is the lady of the house. Suppressing the torrent of anger rising within, I nod curtly when she peers over her coffee mug at me. Immediately, she springs to her feet and takes two fresh mugs from the cupboard into which she pours coffee from a percolator. I decline the mug she proffers but Sebastian cocks a brow and indicates that I should join him for coffee before running my errands. I acquiesce and sit beside him, sipping the steaming coffee as quickly as the burn will allow lest I must endure her company longer than necessary.

"It's bitter," I complain. "Is it a new coffee brand?"

Scarlett removes the mug from my grasp and heaps a spoonful of sugar, stirring thoroughly and sighing audibly.

She just forgot to sweeten it, she tells me but everything that girl says or does is sinister in my view.

***

The drive to town seems interminably long, the traffic heavy with the onset of early tourists on the narrow roads. They have all the time in the world and no sense of direction or highway etiquette. The florist brings three long white boxes from the cold storage at the rear of the shop, and places them on the counter.

"Tiger lilies. Beautiful vibrant orange blooms, straight from Asia," he purrs in a camp voice, taking a large bloom from a box. "Smell."

Inhaling deeply, my senses are filled with the vision and sweet pungent fragrance of the exquisite flower.

"There is an old legend from Asia about the Tiger Lily," he says. "A Korean hermit helped a wounded tiger by removing an arrow from its body. The tiger asked the hermit to use his powers to perpetuate their friendship after his death. The hermit agreed and when the tiger died, his body became a tiger lily. Eventually the hermit drowned and his body was washed away. The Tiger Lily spread everywhere, searching for its friend." He sighs contemplatively before replacing the lily in the box.

"That's quite a story," I agree. "So sad, that the hermit should die through such deep love for another." The tragedy brings a tear to my eye. *Will I die...through my love for Sebastian? As those I love have died...*

"Hey. It's just a story, my love. Lighten up." He laughs and snaps me out of my melancholy mood. "Soak them for thirty minutes before trimming the stems and putting in vases. Tomorrow, snip them again on an angle and try and keep them cool today. Ok?"

Having paid the florist, he helps me to load the boxes into the trunk of my car.

"Have a fabulous party, my love," he air kisses me goodbye. "Is there anything else?" he asks. "Mrs. Dove?"

"What?" I'm daydreaming.

"Are you okay, my love?"

"Yes. Sorry, I'm fine. Thanks. Bye." I'm so very weary, finding it hard to concentrate, my thoughts centred on love lost.

The house is a hive of activity on my return. The great hall has been transformed into the most fabulous dining room. The long polished table has been extended to seat thirty, with Sebastian and I to be seated together at the far side. Silverware glistens against the crisp linen cloth and crystal glasses sparkle under the light of the vast chandeliers and sunlight which streams through the mullion windows.

"Six can't come."

The silver candelabra are in the shape of deer. One is moving, just very slightly, barely discernable but nonetheless it's moving.

"Elizabeth. Six can't come."

The deer turns its graceful head and blinks up at me from the centre of the table. *You're an adorable little thing, aren't you?* It twitches its cute nose and raises a delicate hoof.

"*Elizabeth.*"

The stag next to the female deer, seeing his mate move, has decided to take leave of his mount too. Silver antlers sway and dip as the stag climbs down gracefully from the candelabra.

"Look at me. Elizabeth."

"So beautiful. Look at that, Sebastian." I point to the stag who stands proud and strong as he sniffs the air. So tiny it would fit in the palm of my hand, and yet so majestic, the stag regards me cautiously. I lower my voice to a whisper. "Don't move, Sebastian or you'll scare him away. Look, he's watching us."

Sebastian is clutching my arms and is shaking me so that my head flops back and forward. His hand snaps across my cheek. I gasp, shocked at the sudden sting.

"He's gone! You frightened him," I cry, my hand rubbing my smarting cheek, my eyes burning with hot tears of frustration.

"Fuck, Elizabeth. Oh fuck. *Stop this.* I can't take this again." He's holding and soothing me with his soft kisses and kind words but it's too late. It's far too late. Moments like that will never come again, the stag will be too fearful to move. Sebastian leads me upstairs, undresses me as though I am a child. He lays me on the bed and pulls the duvet over my body then lies with me, his strong arms holding me until I fall asleep. I feel so safe, so warm. So loved.

Through an impenetrable fog a slight figure emerges–too small to be a man and too distant to identify yet the figure is familiar to me. It moves with the grace of a swan gliding on still waters, white as a swan too it has an ethereal beauty. As it nears me the mop of unruly hair is unmistakable. "Joe! My darling, you're so pale."

"Hello Mummy," he beams at me with his adorable smile. "It's your birthday tomorrow, don't be sad."

"Mummy's only sad because I miss you, little man."

"I miss you too Mummy. I bought you this for your birthday." His tiny hands holds a white feather, he holds it in the palm of his hand, puckers his pale lips and gently blows. The feather floats up into the air where it catches the breeze, twists, turns and rides the draught before settling at my feet.

"Whenever you see the feather, Mummy, I will be there with you. It's my present for your birthday. Do you like it?"

"Joe, sweetheart, I *love* it. It means so much knowing that you are never far away." I keep my eyes on Joe as I reach down for the feather, afraid he will vanish if my gaze leaves his. The feather has gone. My eyes dart to the ground at my feet as panic grips me. "Joe. The feather?"

"Oh Mummy," Joe giggles adorably, "the feather will come back. When I'm near you, then you'll see the feather. Get it?" He rolls his eyes at his mother's confusion but without malice, just utter love for me.

"Have the coolest birthday ever. Save me some cake." Joe fades away and is gone and my heart breaks anew.

"Wait Joe. Don't leave so soon. Come back to me Joe. I miss you, oh dear God I miss you..."

"Elizabeth! Ssh darling, you were dreaming. It's okay, I'm here." Sebastian is stroking my damp hair, his face etched with concern. My eyes blink as they adjust to the bedside light. Sebastian holds me tightly and soon I hear the familiar settling of his breathing as he drifts back to sleep. I remain awake in his arms until morning light, the tears flowing silently until my pillow-slip is wet through.

# Chapter 4

Bella bounds into our room with the girlish excitement of a ten year old. "Happy birthday!" she exclaims. Sebastian swats her behind as she jumps on the bed between us. She plants a kiss on my cheek as my sleepy eyes adjust to the daylight. I must have eventually drifted back to sleep; my head feels muzzy and I still feel unwell.

"It's my birthday? *Already?*" I croak, sitting up.

"Happy birthday, darling, yes it's Saturday," Sebastian confirms. "Scarlett's made you breakfast in bed. You're going to be thoroughly spoilt today."

Turning my head, I can see a tray on the nightstand; there is a plate of bacon and eggs and a single rose stem with beautiful pink bloom. The clock next to the tray, glows 9:32 am in red neon.

"It's my birthday." I say numbly, wishing the day away, irritated by the exuberance of those around me.

"It is indeed. How does it feel to be forty?" Sebastian plants a kiss on my lips and brushes a stray curl from my eye.

"Old," I reply sulkily. "I had no idea that I'd feel *so* old at forty."

"*Ancient,*" teases Bella. "Open your presents." She places three brightly wrapped parcels on my lap and claps her hands together excitedly. Carefully pulling at the tape, I remove the paper to reveal a box. The picture on the front shows two old clockwork ladies and the gift makes me smile just a little.

"You wind them up and they race with their walking sticks," Bella squeals and Sebastian laughs.

"Charming," I sigh, "are you implying I'm one of those old ladies?"

The next gift is a bottle of Chanel No.5 perfume. "My very favourite, thank you darling." Bella proffers her cheek for a kiss, which I give gratefully.

"Open Sebastian's present next," she enthuses. Unwrapping the slim square package, I see Sebastian hold his breath.

"What have you done?" I ask, carefully lifting the lid of the red velvet case. Tiffany & Co. *Oh my God.*

"Do you like it, darling?" he asks hesitantly.

"*Like it?*" I gasp. "Sebastian I *love* it." The necklace rests on cream satin, the diamonds shimmering brightly as the morning sun reflects on each tiny facet. The perfect diamond necklet supports a teardrop shaped ruby the hue of fire and cranberries. Its beauty takes my breath away.

"It belonged to my Grandmother," Sebastian tells me, as he runs his index finger over the satin. "My Grandfather gave it to her as a wedding gift in 1929. I know she'd love you as much as I do and want you to have it."

"Darling, it's too much, you already gave me the choker. But...it's the most beautiful thing I've ever seen."

"Then you haven't looked in the mirror today. It's no match for your beauty."

"*Please,*" laughs Bella. "You're going to make me hurl if you keep this up."

Embarrassed, my cheeks blush hot and red. *He really does love me.*

"Wear it for me tonight," he whispers as he nuzzles my ear. "It will look incredible with your red dress."

"Yes. I'll treasure it. Thank you."

Bella snatches the box from my hands and her eyes widen at the shimmering jewels. "Sick. This is worth a mint."

"Bella," I admonish, "show some manners. The sentimental value is what is important." Bella does look contrite but only fleetingly as she hands back the gift. After a moment or two of contemplation she starts to speak but thinks better of it. I look quizzically at her.

"I just wish...I wish Joe and Dad were here for your birthday." Bella's eyes mist, tucking a lock of hair behind her ear I contemplate telling her about my dream but decide not to, certain that she and Sebastian already think I'm losing the plot. Ignoring the painful knot that twists in my stomach, I plaster a false smile to my lips instead.

"I know, sweetheart. I wish that too but I'm sure somehow they are here with us."

My thoughtful Sebastian breaks the painful silence that follows with a ruffle of both our heads. "Come on, my two beautiful girls need to get their lazy backsides out of bed. Eat your breakfast, Elizabeth. Scarlett cooked it specially. I want you downstairs in fifteen. Scarlett's taking you to the hairdresser for a make-over, her birthday gift to you.

***

Scarlett drives me to my appointment with a hairdresser in Padstow as I'm still feeling weak, unable to rid myself of this virus, or whatever it is making me feel this way *or whoever it is*. Although it's an effort, I intend to make myself look as good as possible today, after all, I'll be meeting many of Sebastian's friends for the first time and want to make him proud of me.

"You have fabulous hair." Tanya is blow-drying me to within an inch of my life. "Shall we put it up?"

"Definitely. It's a masked ball so I'm hoping you can achieve the impossible. Lots of ringlets, and volume. Scoop it up and let some tumble down over one shoulder please." I gesticulate with my hands in the hope that Tanya grasps the concept I'm explaining. She coos excitedly and sets to work with a curling wand while a trainee files and paints my nails in dark crimson gloss.

"*Wow!*" Tanya holds a mirror so that I can have a good view of my hair from all angles. She's done an incredible job. Two glossy blonde curls trail down over my left shoulder, resembling snakes. The snakes twist and turn before slithering under the collar of my pale pink cotton shirt and disappearing beneath the lace of my bra.

"I'm not worried," I reassure Tanya. "They're friendly snakes, they're *part* of me."

*Scarlett looks smug. I hate that the hair salon had told her about my snakes, when she came to collect me. Now she thinks I'm crazy, just as Tanya thought I was crazy.*

*My hair looks good and I won't let Scarlett spoil my day. She wants me to be crazy but I'm not giving her the satisfaction.* We drive home in silence but as we pass the gates to Penmorrow I turn to her.

"About our conversation, Scarlett." Her face pales and she bites her lip looking so damned vulnerable. "You agreed to go after my party. I'd like confirmation that you are going tomorrow? I haven't seen you moving any of your things yet."

Her eyes mist with tears but remain focused on the road ahead. "His Lordship has told me that I can find another job and place to live first."

"He said that, did he?" I ask bitterly. "Well, you and I had an agreement, and that was that you would leave tomorrow. As far as I'm concerned, that agreement still stands. You may think me hard, Scarlett, but there is no point in putting off the inevitable."

"I see, Mrs. Dove. I'll speak to His Lordship again." *Damn her! The minute she weeps to Sebastian he will be putty in her hands. Hopefully I can talk to him first.*

"No Scarlett," I say resolutely, "an agreement is an agreement and I expect you to honour ours."

She turns her head sufficiently to look at me and, fleetingly, I see pure hatred in her eyes before she casts her gaze back to the lane ahead.

"Ruth!" Throwing the car door open even before Scarlett cuts the engine, I race to my friend and hold her tightly. "You have no idea how good it is to see you," I tell her and I mean it. I really do.

"Beth, love. Look at you–you look beautiful. A little thin and pale but stunning as ever. I hate you," she teases. "Happy birthday, love."

"I'm so glad you're here for my party." Linking arms, we walk into the house together. "The caterers are busy making the food and Sebastian's hired staff to set up and wait this evening," I tell Ruth excitedly. "Meaning all we need to do is enjoy ourselves."

"Ah, here's the birthday girl," Sebastian greets us in the hall. "Ruth, darling. How are you?" He kisses both of her cheeks and I note how she blushes. *You still have a way with the ladies, don't you De Montfort?*

"Sebastian. The house looks amazing, it's good to see you've gone to so much trouble for my best girl's special day." Ruth lightly punches his arm playfully.

He arches his brow and grins at her. "She's my best girl too, remember," he replies, pretending to rub his arm better.

"I see *she's* still working here." Ruth glares at Scarlett as she follows us into the house. Scarlett, ignoring Ruth, whispers in Sebastian's ear conspiratorially. I feel the hairs prickle on the nape of my neck.

"Excuse me ladies, Scarlett wants a quick word. Elizabeth, why don't you show Ruth to her room." He turns and heads for his study, with Scarlett scurrying after him.

"Has she said any more?" Ruth asks quietly as we take her bags to the guest bedroom.

"She's agreed to go. I said she could stay until the

party and then she's history."

"Wow, how did you manage that?" she asks incredulously as she glances appreciatively at her opulent room. Ruth places her overnight bag on the floor and takes the dress bag from me, laying it carefully on the chaise at the foot of her bed.

"I've won, Ruth. She can see she's no match for me. Mind you, I'm not sure how Sebastian is really taking it, I'm hoping that's not what she's talking to him about now, she's so manipulative. I don't want her putting him in a foul mood before the party."

"You think she'll try and talk him into letting her stay?" Ruth throws herself down onto the queen sized bed and pats the purple velvet comforter, indicating to me to join her. Adjusting the multitude of cushions and pillows we get comfortable side by side.

"I have no doubt she will try. We have finally reached an agreement about her going after I gave him an ultimatum: me or her. What concerns me is that she'll prolong it, get him to agree to her staying longer with some sob story about having nowhere else to go."

"Stick to your guns, Beth. He's clearly infatuated with you so use that. He won't want to lose you so you have to toughen up and insist she sticks to the agreement and struts her scrawny arse out of here pronto."

"Uh huh, you're right. It's just that he has a weak spot when it comes to her. She plays the vulnerability card and has him wrapped around her little finger."

Ruth frowns, her contempt for Scarlett very apparent.

"I spoke to DI Chambers about her," she says, catching my eye to gauge my reaction.

My eyes widen. "You did? What did you say to him? Shit, you didn't tell me you'd actually spoken to him."

"He asked how you and Bella are bearing up, sent his kind regards. I told him about Scarlett and what she'd said to you. He said he'd try and look at the notes from Sebastian's wife's suicide, and also see if there was anything listed for Scarlett–any previous form–but other than that there's little he can do unless you file some restraining order."

"I've got no *proof* though, Ruth. She'll deny everything and you know how frail and pathetic she looks–hardly your standard murderer. It's my word against hers. I tell you this much, though, I don't trust her, Ruth. The sooner she leaves here the better I'll feel."

"Speaking of which, you actually look like shit, I was being polite earlier." Ruth ducks as my hand swats at her in protestation. "How long have you been unwell?" She places the back of her hand on my forehead and frowns. "You haven't got a temperature, Beth. A virus, you say?"

"I presume so, yes. I've been seeing things–weird things and Scarlett said I had a fever."

"That's strange, you don't seem clammy or sick although you do look pale and you've got big dark circles under your eyes. Anyway, I'm here now and I'm going to see that you enjoy your birthday." She pulls me into a tight embrace.

"Thanks so much," I squeeze her tightly, "what would

I do without you?"

"Elizabeth." Sebastian stands in the doorway watching me, his face bears a grim expression, coal-dark eyes boring into mine. *Crap.*

"I'd like a word. Ruth, lunch is served in ten minutes, we'll see you downstairs in the kitchen."

Ruth looks from Sebastian, to me with an expression which clearly seeks reassurance that I'm okay with that. I nod for Ruth to do as instructed, warmed by her deep care for me. He proffers his hand and I take it in mine as he leads me downstairs to his study, closing the door before seating himself at his desk. His hands steepled, elbows resting on the leather blotter, chin resting on his fingers, he regards me coolly. I inhale his incredible scent as I hover beside him, I have no idea whether he naturally smells this good or whether its manufactured but it should be classified as a highly intoxicating drug. My standing next to him, eyes closed, inhaling him, clearly irritates the hell out of him as he snaps his fingers to get my attention before pointing to the chair on the opposite side of his desk. Meekly I sit. He can be so intimidating when he's in this frame of mind.

"Is this about Scarlett?" I ask timidly.

Something dark flashes across his eyes, his mouth sets in a grim, hard line. "It is. Yes. She's concerned about you, as am I. She's told me about the hairdresser incident, but I will discuss that with you in a moment."

My mouth gapes as I prepare to retort, but he holds a finger up, warning me to remain silent.

"She's also told me that you have asked her to leave tomorrow."

"We had an agreement, yes. Don't forget, she *offered* to leave."

"Because you have made her presence here so untenable, Elizabeth." He runs a hand through his inky hair before stroking his stubble covered jaw with long fingers, he looks so hot when he's mad but I try and focus, although it's hard to read where he's going with this.

"You don't need her," I reply petulantly. "You and I have discussed this and I thought you'd agreed."

"*I* decide what I need, Elizabeth, not you. She's been there for me, through incredibly difficult times. You have no idea. Now I see you...like this...and it reminds me of Libby. Seeing things. Paranoid. Where the hell does it all end? Is it *me?* Is this what I do to the women I love?"

*No, it's not you. It's her–fucked up Scarlett.* "No. God no. You are the best thing that's ever happened to me, Sebastian...apart from my children, of course. I love you so much. I want to be everything you need. I just can't be that while she's living here too. Can't you see that?" Rising from my chair, I step hesitantly around the desk toward him, unsure of his reaction but I receive no protestation. I place my hands on his shoulders and he spins around in the chair, his hands enfolding my waist, he pulls me in close, between his legs.

He nuzzles the soft valley between my breasts, his hands moving down to cup my buttocks. "Fuck I need you so badly," he rasps, "but I need to have this conversation with you."

My hands stroke his hair, pulling his head in closer to my heaving breasts, relieved by his softer tone I decide to use my sensuality to get exactly what I want. "I need you too. Don't fight me on this, please Sebastian."

"We'll talk about it after the party, okay?" He pauses, waiting for my answer.

"But...she'd agreed to go tomorrow." I am trying hard to keep at bay the anger now boiling in my gut. I'm no match for Sebastian when he loses it and I can see he's close.

"I will *not* see her homeless. Now, you've made your point. You've made me choose between you...I love you, but I will not be pushed on this. Do you understand me Elizabeth?"

"Yes. Okay." I acquiesce but she still has to go.

"Now...your health concerns me greatly, as it does Scarlett and Ruth. I have made an appointment for you to talk to a psychiatrist chum of mine for some bereavement counselling."

This news completely floors me. We have not had a discussion regarding his 'psychiatrist chum' and I certainly have not consented to discussing my painful loss with a stranger. My brow furrows and I return to my chair, putting much needed distance between Sebastian and the slap which my palm may deliver to his face at any moment. "Do I have a say in this decision at all? I mean, of course it's absolutely none of my business whom you order me to see...it's only my grief after all."

"Don't be facetious Elizabeth. Trust my judgement on this please."

"So, I'm not allowed to have a virus without you immediately dragging me to a shrink?"

"A *virus?*" He arches his brow and shakes his head in that infuriating way that he has. "Remind me which virus causes one's hair to transform into snakes? I'm fascinated. I'm sure you are a medical anomaly."

"Temperatures can do that," I say very slowly and sardonically as though talking to a child. "You know...you get ill and you get hot and then, when you're really toasty hot, your body makes you see weird things. It's in the medical journals and everything. Look it up. Google it." His hands slap down onto his knees in fury but, as he rises from his chair, I make a swift departure. Reaching the safety of the doorway my confidence soars sufficiently to throw one last punch, "and she goes. Tomorrow. End of."

The kitchen is a scene of utter chaos. Caterers are preparing a four-course feast including pheasant and grouse and the aroma from the roasting foul smells divine. Sebastian leads Ruth, Bella and I through the disarray and out into the garden. It's a glorious June day; the warm sun on my skin is heavenly. Scarlett has prepared a picnic lunch of sandwiches and pastries, which is laid out on a chequered rug on the lawn. It appears that my outburst is, at least for now, forgiven and the conversation is light as we tuck in heartily, crossed legged and giggling like children.

"This sandwich is yours, Mum," Bella says, handing

me a sandwich with the letter E written in indelible ink on the cling wrap.

"Why is that one mine?" I ask, unwrapping the tasty looking snack.

"Because Scarlett's trying to get you well and said guacamole is good for you. She's mashed some up with mayo and herbs, she's really thoughtful isn't she?"

*She's really thoughtful, suspiciously so. What's she up to? Trying to win me over so she can stay, I imagine.* "Yummy. It's delicious, but I can't eat it all."

"Eat. All of it." Sebastian challenges me with his cool stare, eyebrow raised. "You need the energy to get through tonight," he adds, more softly.

"He's right, Beth. Much as I'm jealous as hell of your figure, you've lost weight and are white as a sheet. Be a good little girly and eat your sandwich." She winks at me in spite of the middle finger I extend. Petulantly, I do as I'm told and finish the sandwich.

"A toast to the birthday girl," Sebastian hands us a glass of bucks' fizz - it's delightfully chilled and the orange juice so refreshing. The little champagne bubbles go straight to my head, soon I'm giggling at Sebastian who has a smear of mayonnaise on his top lip.

"Loving the 'tach, Seb," I laugh, placing my finger across my own top lip mockingly.

"Indeed," he sighs, wiping his lip with the back of his hand. "Come on, birthday girl. We need to get you upstairs for a lie down," he stands and helps me to my feet.

"Whoa!" the ground is moving beneath my feet. "I think you're right," I laugh. Ruth and Sebastian take an arm each and magically transport me to my bed, where I marvel at the breath-taking display of dancing fairies that pirouette across the bed canopy above me. They can't see them, but then it's not their birthday.

# Chapter 5

Something shakes my arm. I swat it away and snuggle further under the duvet.

"Elizabeth. Wake up." Sebastian's Grecian God-like face is inches from mine, it's such a welcome sight, I smile and reach for him. "Come on sleepy head, it's seven o'clock. You have one hour to transform yourself into Cinderella."

*Holy fuck! One hour? My hair, my dress!* Crawling from the bed, I pad over to the dressing table and stare at myself in the mirror. My beautiful up-do is in disarray and smears of mascara streak down beneath my heavy eyes. *Major overhaul needed!* "Oh shit," I moan, "I look horrendous."

"I'll get Ruth to help you," Sebastian tugs on a curl and lays it limply over my shoulder. "It won't take much fixing, the pins are still in. Does Bella have some curlers?"

"No, but I have a curling tong, please can you ask Ruth to come quickly?"

Sebastian returns with Ruth promptly, takes his evening suit from the armoire and leaves us alone. Ruth is wearing a robe over her underwear but her hair and make-up are perfect. She looks stunning already, I hate her and love her in equal measure. She fusses over me, first cleansing my face, applying fresh make-up, and then fixing my hair, re-curling the errant curls. Forty minutes later, I am ready to slip into my gown. I have removed my bra and slipped in to new red lace panties and suspenders, which hold up black silk stockings. I feel like a vamp and a flush of excitement courses through me as I anticipate Sebastian's reaction when I strip for him later.

The crimson taffeta rustles as I step in to the gown, pulling it up carefully until it sits above my breasts forming a most impressive décolletage.

"Do you think I should wear a strapless bra?" I ask Ruth, as I assess my remarkable cleavage in the full-length mirror.

"No. *Wow!* You're perfect just as you are." Sebastian purrs. My cheeks redden as I spin around to face him. He looks so hot, dressed in a black dinner jacket, matching dress trousers and crisp white shirt with black bow tie.

"Sebastian. You made me jump."

Ruth fidgets nervously, undoubtedly sensing the sexual charge between Sebastian and I, she scurries off to her room to dress.

"Come here. Let me tie you up." He prowls toward me, his dark brown eyes smouldering, breathing heavily.

*Tie me up? Now?* "I have to finish dressing," I protest.

"Not you, unfortunately. The dress." He grabs me by the waist and turns me so that he stands behind. Grasping the black laces tightly, he pulls each in turn with a sharp tug - it's difficult to retain my balance.

"Stand still," he scolds, his knee pressing into the back of my thigh as he attempts to steady me. "You're too thin. This dress is far looser on you now, that's why I'm having to pull so hard to lace you up."

"Don't you like me in it?" I ask falteringly.

"I'd like you better out of it," he growls. "There," he says triumphantly, tying the black sash. " Go and look in the mirror."

*Holy fuck!* They say that we all have one day in our life when we look our absolute best – usually it's our wedding day. In my case, I have to admit that I've never felt so feminine, so...transformed, as I do this moment. My waist has contracted under the taffeta constraints to a circumference easily encircled by Sebastian's large hands. My cleavage strains upward with the help of the boned corset, my décolletage pale and full.

"Sebastian. I love it. Thank you," I gasp.

He moves behind me, removes my choker and loops the necklace around my throat, fastening the catch at the nape of my neck. The diamonds dance around my throat in the fading sunlight, the redness of the sunset reflecting on the stones. The brilliance of the ruby compounds the effect that the necklace is ablaze with sparkling embers of fire. My fingers caress the enormous gem, so perfectly matched to my crimson gown.

"You take my breath away," he sighs deeply, his eyes burning into mine in the mirrored reflection, his hands resting on my hips. He kisses my bare shoulder, sending shivers tracking down my spine. "Have you any idea how much I love you?"

*He loves me.* My insides do somersaults. *I'm the luckiest woman in the world. If only Joe could have known you for longer, you'd have been such a wonderful father to him.* "I love you too. I know you think I've been a little crazy recently, but I don't mean to be. I *do* love you."

"Hey," he murmurs, "crazy or not, my love for you won't change. Now put on your mask. We need to go down and greet our guests. They'll be arriving any minute." Sebastian takes a gold hatbox from the top of the armoire and carefully takes out two masks. His is a simple silver mask, secured with elastic, which fastens around his head. He looks like the Lone Ranger, I giggle and he pouts. How I love Sebastian, the little boy. Mine is an altogether different mask, it looks antique although I can't be sure if it's old, or treated in a way to give the impression of age. It has a cream ceramic face, ruby red lips and painted Cleopatra style eyeliner with the eyes missing so that I can peer through. Black feathers tumble from the hairline of the mask so that, when I hold it to my face by the elegant handle, it appears I have feathers in my hair – it's very dramatic and theatrical. Slipping on my black *Jimmy Choo* heels, which I suspect was another purchase made by Scarlett, I follow Sebastian downstairs.

Scarlett, dressed in a stunning black evening gown, with simple black diamanté mask, hands us both a chilled glass of champagne as we wait in the hall to greet our first guests.

"You look stunning, Scarlett," I tell her amicably, holding the flute to my lips, behind my mask. *Damn, this mask is going to prove tricky.*

"Not as stunning as you look, Mrs. Dove. I'll fetch the canapés." She's decidedly cool despite the compliment she pays me.

"*Mother!*" Bella calls from the top stair. Spinning round, my eyes catch sight of Bella, gliding elegantly down the stairs in a pale gold long sheath dress which clings to all her curves. *My daughter is a woman. When did that happen?* She gracefully holds a gold mask to her face and holds out her other hand as though she is a movie star making her grand entrance on the red carpet, I have never felt so proud of her as I do at this moment. Ruth follows behind her in gorgeous emerald green 1950's inspired cocktail dress with black mask, her skirts rustling as she dramatically takes one exaggerated step after another, hips swaying.

"Wow," Sebastian breathes. "I thought there was only one belle of this ball. You're both almost as beautiful as Elizabeth."

"*Hey,*" I punch him lightly on the arm. "I think my daughter and friend just upstaged me for that title."

Sebastian indicates to a waiter to bring more champagne, while I head to the kitchen to chase Scarlett with the canapés.

Navigating past the numerous hired staff preparing the feast, I find Scarlett in the pantry. She's concentrating on adding a sprinkling of fresh tarragon to a silver tray of smoked salmon blinis.

"Scarlett. The guests are arriving, please hurry with those," I say curtly.

She turns and hands me a blini. "This one is for you to try, Mrs. Dove."

Taken aback by her consideration, I pop the salmon treat in my mouth and savour the horseradish and crème fraiche. "It's delicious, Scarlett. Thank you. Please bring them through."

There are so many new faces, all hidden by the façade of a mask. Sebastian is the perfect host, introductions are concise and jovial and, on the whole, our guests are delightful. I'm so very weary and nervous, but try extremely hard to remember names and to ensure the waiting staff top up glasses and serve canapés. Marcus and Becky arrive late, blustering in with profuse apologies. Their son, Theo's jaw drops when he spies Bella and the two are immediately inseparable.

"Dinner is served. Please make your way through to the great hall. Masks may be removed for dinner," our butler-for-the-night announces at eight-thirty. The gaggle of guests moves slowly to take their places at the expansive dining table, where white butterfly name cards indicate where they should sit. Sebastian and I take our seats last, I'm feeling tipsy already, regretting the second glass of champagne and pull the tablecloth accidentally when I sit. Thankfully nothing spills and nobody notices, except Sebastian who places a reassuring hand on my knee.

"Don't drink too much," he warns sternly, I roll my eyes at him in exasperation.

"Did you roll your eyes?" he hisses, a smirk playing

over his lips.

"I may have inadvertently done so," I confess.

"I may have to inadvertently slap the eye rolling from your pretty face, then. Later." *Oh crap!* The threat makes me wet with anticipation.

The man seated to my left is telling a tediously unfunny joke to which I laugh politely and slightly too vociferously. Ruth, seated to his left, is then subjected to endless dreary tales and I can hear her sigh, poor Ruth. Meanwhile, Sebastian captivates the table with light conversation and stories about his ancestors whom, by all accounts, were a colourful if debauched lot. *I see where you get your own kinkery from*, I smile.

"Ladies and Gentlemen, please be upstanding for a toast to the birthday girl herself. Happy birthday Elizabeth." The butler urges everyone to their feet and the whole room raises a glass and sings a very out of tune version of 'Happy Birthday' to which I blush hotly.

"Speech!" they all cry in unison.

"Say something, darling," Sebastian prompts as everyone sits.

"No," I whisper. "I can't. You do it." Taking a long gulp of white wine, I try and make myself very small in my chair, hoping the attention will move away from me, but Marcus pings his crystal wine glass with his fork impatiently. Sebastian glares at me, urging me to address the room. *Oh crap. How embarrassing. Whoa, I'm dizzy.*

Standing shakily, I take another glug of wine to steady my nerves and the room falls silent. All eyes are upon me expectantly, except Bella who is staring into Theo's eyes as he whispers something to her.

"I don't know you all," I start, hesitantly. "But Sebastian has told me a great deal about many of you ..."

"It's not true!" a man heckles loudly.

"I'm just so grateful to you all for coming this evening. I hope in time, to get to know you all properly."

The tiny silver stag on the candelabra steps down from his mount and leaps gracefully across the table, landing in a lady's lap. I'm transfixed watching the shiny creature prance about while the lady seems unaware of it. I'm so very grateful that the stag has once again graced me with its beautiful display that I'm rendered speechless. All I can do is to watch in awe.

"Elizabeth." Sebastian's voice startles the stag, who stands stock still, sniffing the air, his ears pricked forward.

"Erm...I was saying...sorry, thank you for the gifts that you've so generously given me and I'll try and write to you all this week to thank you personally."

The stag has returned to the candelabra where he melts back into the filigree base and is still. I avert my gaze away from it. *Concentrate Beth. You're not going mad. You're not going mad.*

"Did anyone else see that?" I ask the room.

Sebastian is pulling me down onto the chair - he looks frosty, his eyes molten. The room is silent. "Elizabeth. Darling. Drink some water."

"I don't need water," I hiss. "I told you not to make me stand up and do a speech."

"You're *drunk* and you're embarrassing me," he rebukes in a low growl.

Polite chatter resumes and the following courses are served without further embarrassment on my part.

Ten o'clock strikes on the grandfather clock in the hall, and we are all instructed to re-mask, then ushered through to the morning room, which has been cleared of furniture and a wooden dance floor laid. The room looks magnificent, the tiger lilies displayed in all their glory in tall vases on pedestals. Swathes of fabric in gold, burnt orange, red and black drape from the ceiling forming an exotic marquee over the dance floor itself.

Our guests, replete and slightly drunk and resplendent in their masks and finery, appear to have few inhibitions and in no time the dance floor is shaking with the moves of the dancers and vibrating with the beat of the live band.

Sebastian is being decidedly cool toward me since I apparently humiliated him at dinner. I decide he is being most disingenuous, it is after all my birthday and he provided the champagne and wine, knowing that it goes straight to my head.

"What a fabulous party," Ruth gushes excitedly. "So many interesting people and I think I've got a couple of leads for the business. Terry and Barbara someone are looking for a senior manager, I've given my business card. Then I was talking to a pompous man called Paul – he said his investment company needs some personnel so he has my card too. It's all good, Beth."

It's difficult to concentrate on what Ruth is saying

because the room keeps shrinking most disconcertingly. I don't recall it being this small. Perhaps because of the tented dance floor it appears reduced, but that doesn't explain why I can physically see the walls moving inward. I grasp Ruth's arm, alarmed at the speed with which the room shrinks.

"Do you *see* that?" I ask her, my eyes wide with fear.

"See what? Beth what's the matter?" She sounds fearful, so she must see it too.

"The room. It's closing in on us. Something weird is going on here. *Fuck*, we've got to get out. Get everyone out before we're all *crushed*." My eyes dart from wall to ceiling to floor, to the people dancing who don't seem to care.

"Beth! Listen to me. The room is *not* shrinking. Do you hear me?" She's shaking me. *Why does everyone shake me, like I'm nuts or something? Shaking me will not make the room stop shrinking.*

The people in masks are looking at me. Staring. Weird grotesque masks made of snakes and blood and amidst them all is Sebastian. He's dancing with Scarlett, holding her close, his lips whispering against her ear, oblivious to the danger, which is befalling us all. *What's he whispering to her? How much he loves her? Fuck them both – let them be crushed!*

"Beth, stop it! You're scaring me. What's happened to you? Is it grief? Oh shit, where's Sebastian?"

She's looking around for him but he's right there on the dance floor. Oh, he's gone. I catch a glimpse of

Scarlett's black dress in the hallway. I need to follow her. Need to catch them together, confront them.

Pulling free of Ruth, I make haste after Scarlett. I feel guilty leaving Ruth in danger but she's a big girl, she can take care of herself. Ruth tries to stop me but I break away, the masks watch me run.

The swish of black satin vanishes through the door to Sebastian's study making it apparent that he's taking her to the chamber. They're moving fast and I'm finding it difficult to keep up, dizziness and nausea threaten to overcome me. Through the study I run, my hip catching on the corner of his desk painfully, and onwards to the steps down to the cellars.

Clinging to the rope handrail, I descend each stone step with trepidation, yet with a steely resolve to finally discover the truth about them. As each step takes me nearer to the chamber of pain, I realise I don't actually want to find them together for to do so would shatter my entire world and compound the loss I have already suffered. Yet, my overwhelming desire to know the truth forces me forward.

The ancient door creaks under my hand, revealing the first chamber–the chamber of pain disguised as a wine cellar–is empty. Onwards to the far door to the smaller, circular chamber, I creep. I hear noises beyond the small oak door, the sound of a cane, lashing across flesh.

My trembling hand is gripping the latch so tightly that my knuckles blanche. My body is clammy, my legs leaden. Taking deep breaths, I try and stave off the imminent blackness that threatens to consume me. *Do it Beth. Open the door. You have to know...*

# Chapter 6

Blackness blurs my vision as the room spins. Blinking rapidly and on the cusp of hyperventilating I take a tentative step into the small chamber. The smell of sweet vanilla incense fills my senses making me nauseous. Candles flicker to my left, casting an ethereal light across the circular bed, over which Scarlett is bent. Her black satin dress is hitched up high exposing milky white buttocks streaked with purple red stripes. Her hands clutch at the red silk sheet, her head is down and she's pushing her bottom up to meet the lashings, which befall it.

"Yes. Oh yes. Harder please Sir. I beg you. *Please Sir*," she beseeches.

Sebastian is looking at me squarely, his arm held aloft, clutching the cane. He's changed his mask and now bears the demonic face of Satan himself and his voice has morphed into a carnal growl.

"Watch us *bitch.*"

Scarlett laughs shrilly. "Don't waste your time with her. She's a crazy spoilt *slut.*"

"Why are you both doing this to me?" Bile rises. I'm going to be sick. "I *hate* you. You've lied to me," I sob, my entire body trembling uncontrollably. The blackness now almost obscures my vision entirely, I can't see him clearly anymore but I hear him.

"You're next, my fucking little *whore.* Lift your dress

and bend over the fucking bed. DO IT. NOW."

"No. No. I *loved* you. You're breaking my heart." My legs give way and I sink down onto the cold stone floor, welcoming the support it gives me. He's pulling me up by my hair. No leave me alone. It hurts. The words won't come out of my mouth. My legs grow weak again. A sharp slap stings my cheek. Down on the cold stone again. Shapes. I can see shapes, greys and blacks against the light. A large black shape is next to satanic Sebastian and I think the shape strikes Sebastian who falls onto the bed. The black shape and a smaller grey shape move to me, the huge black shape scoops me up - it's so strong I feel safe in its arms. I give in to the darkness, my heart broken. I want the darkness to possess me, not wanting this life any more.

Joe's tiny hand strokes my cheek. He's sitting on the bed beside me, smiling adoringly, his expression one of impish mischief.

"Good morning, little man. What are you up to?"

"I've come to see you again Mummy. I've been away to a really cool place."

"Have you darling? What was it like there?"

"Amazing Mummy. Daddy said I had to come and see you because you're poorly."

"That was thoughtful of Daddy, but Mummy's just tired. Mummy's coming to your special cool place very soon, and then we'll be together again. Won't that be fun?"

"No Mummy. I miss you...but you can't come yet.

Daddy said I have to remember to tell you you're not mad. It's the lady. Daddy says it's the *bad* lady. I don't like the bad lady, Mummy. I want her to go away."

"Sebastian *loves* the bad lady, darling. That's why Mummy is going to come to the cool place."

"Daddy says it's the lady. He says it isn't Sebastian."

"I know Joe but grownups are confusing. Know that I miss you so very much. I'm so happy you've come to see me. Thank you darling."

"That's okay. I have to go now Mummy but I'll come back and see you again soon. I liked the picnic you had, by the way. You didn't have my favourite brownies though."

"It was a lovely picnic. Next time I'll make sure there are a dozen brownies just for you."

"Yummy, thank you. Oh and I'm cool with people going in my old bedroom, Mummy. Bella can have my console."

"Are you sure Joe? It's still your room."

"No Mummy. I've got an even more amazing room now. One day you'll see it."

"I'd like that Joe. I'm glad you're happy."

"I'm really happy, but it makes me sad to see you poorly. Get away from the bad lady, please Mummy."

"I will darling. I will. Try not to worry, Mummy's a big girl."

"Bye Mummy." He brushes my cheek with a feather light kiss.

"Don't go Joe. *Please* don't go."

"I have to Mummy. Daddy's come to get me."

"Oh. Okay. Joe ..."

"Yes Mummy?"

"Tell Daddy I'm sorry. Tell him I *did* love him, I just didn't realise it at the time."

"Daddy says he loved you too and try not to worry, just be safe."

The fog lifts sufficiently for my eyes to focus on Sebastian perched on the side of the bed.

"Go away," I plead, pulling the duvet over my head. He tugs it down and peers down at me.

"Elizabeth. Darling I've been so worried. Thank God you're awake, you've been having nightmares and hallucinations." He's now tenderly laying a cool flannel on my forehead. I have a pounding headache.

"You disturbed Joe. How *dare* you."

"Joe's gone darling. You're sick but I'm going to get you the help you need."

"Joe. Was. *Here.*"

"Ok Elizabeth. Joe was here."

"You don't believe me, you think I'm insane."

"No. I think you are missing Joe very much."

"Of course I'm bloody missing him...but he *was* here. I don't care if you believe me or not."

"If you say Joe was here, then Joe was here." He wipes my brow, his eyes clouded with pity.

"You all think I'm mad but I saw the two of you. You and...her. All these months, you've *lied* to me." My voice is laced with hysteria, hot tears tumble down my cheeks.

He looks crestfallen. He leaves the flannel on my head and runs a finger down my cheek, tracing the watery tracks.

"Don't touch me."

"You silly girl," he sighs. "It wasn't me, Elizabeth. You saw Marcus with Scarlett."

*Marcus? Do you think I'm stupid? I know what I saw.*
"It was you," I say emphatically.

"No, darling. It was Marcus. He and Scarlett have been play partners for a long time. Since shortly after Scarlett moved here actually."

"But I *saw* you."

"No. What you saw was Marcus and, I have to say, he's no longer my friend. I understand it's all blurry to you, but you were hallucinating, Elizabeth. Ruth came and found me and together we tracked you down to the chamber. Thank God I got there in time, he was about to force you into a session knowing that you are mine. Knowing that you were sick..." He runs his hands through his dishevelled hair. He looks unkempt, still in his black suit trousers and white dress shirt, open necked, cuffs undone. He looks so forlorn and lost that my heart breaks all over again. "I'm afraid I punched him hard, he spent the rest of the night in A&E with a broken nose. Serves the fucker right."

*Marcus? This can't be true. I saw them with my own eyes.*

"I saw you, Sebastian."

"The man you saw was Marcus. Not me. You trust

Ruth don't you?"

"With my life. Yes. It's *you* I don't trust."

Sebastian takes a step back from the bed as Ruth appears by his side, her face etched with concern - she looks as though she's been crying, her eyes are red rimmed.

"Hi Beth love. What Sebastian says is true. I was there when he hit Marcus. The scumbag had you by the hair and slapped you. If Sebastian hadn't hit him, I'd have sodding killed him, I swear I would."

"Then...am I insane? What's happening to me?" It's all so confusing, Ruth. I keep seeing things...terrible, weird things and they seem so real to me."

*Joe was here and it was so real, was he just a hallucination too? Or did he really come down from Heaven to warn me? Oh God, I hope he was real...but if he was real then I'm truly in danger.*

"You're going to have to see a doctor, Beth. Sebastian and I think that Joe and Alan's deaths are really impacting on you now. You've been so strong...too strong, and not grieved properly. It's grief, we're sure and maybe you need some medication just to see you through this rough patch." Ruth is stroking my hand as though I am a sick geriatric aunt. "You're coming back to Dorset with me for a few days so that I can feed you up and get you better. Okay?"

"I don't *want* pills, Ruth. I've never heard of grief doing this to someone. But we did plan to go home for a few days, it would be nice to see everyone at work, and

Mum. Bella is coming too, isn't she?"

"Bella is coming too, it's her birthday this week, remember?"

"Oh yes. Her birthday," I reflect absently, my mind still focused on Sebastian. "Ruth, do you promise me that Sebastian has been faithful?"

Ruth sighs deeply. "I know what I saw last night Beth. It was Marcus, not Sebastian with Scarlett. Sebastian is a good man, aren't you Sebastian?"

"Positively angelic, Ruth," he grins, winking at me. A smile plays on my lips and a surge of relief courses through my body.

"Though he's into some *seriously* freaky kinkiness," Ruth adds conspiratorially. "I do want a conversation with you about that, but not now."

"I'm not sure you could ever be called angelic, Sebastian, but I am sorry that I doubted you. I love you, it broke my heart to think you didn't love me." My hand strokes his rough unshaven jaw.

He kisses my fingertips as they brush across his lower lip. "I love you with my heart and soul. We do need to get you well though, Elizabeth. I can't go through this again, not after Libby."

"After Libby went *mad*, you mean."

"She hallucinated. She was paranoid. I see the same pattern in your behaviours as in hers before she deteriorated beyond help. I don't intend for you to slip away from me as she did." He kisses my knuckles.

"I think it's Scarlett."

"You think *what* is Scarlett?" His eyes darken, his mouth setting in a firm line.

"I think she's poisoning me." *There, I've said it.* The sinister thought now seems more credible as I think it through. The hairs on the back of my neck prickle, goose bumps form on my arms.

"For fucks sake Elizabeth. She's got a lot of issues, but she's not malevolent. Why the hell would she poison you? You see what I mean about paranoia?" His hands rake through his hair as they always do when he's angry.

"Think about it. She's been insistent on cooking every meal, when she knows I've wanted to cook for you. She's had every opportunity to lace my food."

"*Why?* Why would she want to do that? You're not making any sense. It's irrational." He shifts away from me, coldly.

"Because of *you,* Sebastian," I implore, my voice shrill. "She loves you, or thinks she does, and both Libby and I have got in her way. She told me she only encouraged me to move here for my children...some twisted idea of hers that my kids would become your heirs. Don't you *see?* When Libby couldn't have children, she no longer served a use for you–that's the way Scarlett viewed it. It's always about your happiness, your needs, she's obsessed with you."

"I've heard enough," he barks, rising from the bed. "Go to Dorset. Take some pills and come back when you're rational. I do NOT want to go through this again – listening to the ranting of a lunatic. I've had enough!" He slams the bedroom door as I crumble into Ruth's arms.

"I'm not crazy, Ruth. It is her. I know it is. How do I prove it?" I sob.

"Shh, love," she soothes, "if Scarlett *is* poisoning you, and I'm not saying I agree with you, it's very farfetched, but if she is...well then when you leave here, you will get well. That will prove it. Also, a doctor will be able to tell if you're being poisoned."

"Ok, but take me away today. Please. I'm so scared."

Ruth strokes my back, her voice calm but her underlying concern toward me is palpable. "We can't leave today, love. Sebastian's shrink is coming this afternoon. I think we should let him decide if what you're experiencing is grief-related."

Sighing dejectedly, I move away from her pulling the duvet up to my chin, the sting from her words hurting as severely as any pain inflicted upon me in the chamber. She thinks I'm crazy too. For the first time in our friendship, my best friend doubts me. "I'm not making this up Ruth and it's not grief. Maybe when I'm poisoned to death, you will all believe me."

"I'm not doubting you, love." Ruth closes the distance between us and tucks a stray curl behind my ear tenderly. I flinch at her touch, she pulls her hand back. "What I'm saying is, no-one suffers a loss as profound as yours without some fallout. Grief festers, Beth and it can't do any harm in talking to the shrink so we can at least eradicate grief. That will then leave two possible causes for your hallucinations. One: you have a virus or some hideous brain tumour. Two: you're being poisoned. Simple."

"*Brain tumour?*" I gasp wide eyed. "Shit. Now you're giving me more to worry about. Thanks for nothing."

"It's a process of elimination is all I mean, silly," Ruth rolls her eyes in exasperation. *A psychiatrist. I have to talk to a damned shrink.*

# Chapter 7

I have never had the pleasure of being psycho-analysed before today. My personal view of psychiatrists is that they are all overpaid, dusty old men who are themselves as insane as those whom they treat. This preconception is shattered, at least in part, when I open the door to Sebastian's study. Resting languidly against the oak bookcase to my right, arms folded, is a tall sandy-haired man of about my age. He wears a crisp linen suit with white open necked shirt and pleasant smile which somewhat depletes my anxiety. He proffers a neatly manicured hand, his smile widening to show perfectly white teeth.

"Psychiatrists don't look like you," I gush, my cheeks reddening as his almond eyes crinkle appreciatively at my compliment.

"Apparently they do," he responds as I shake his hand. "Doctor Leo Fairfax. You must be Elizabeth."

I reluctantly retrieve my hand from his firm grasp. "Yes. Elizabeth Dove. Good to meet you Doctor Fairfax."

"Please, call me Leo. Take a seat." He sweeps his hand toward the chair onto which I compliantly perch while nervously biting my nails. Doctor Fairfax wheels Sebastian's leather chair around his desk until it faces mine and sits, his knees inches from mine. Surprised at his nearness, I shuffle back to widen the distance between us, then worry that he may be interpreting my every move as part of his evaluation of me. The doctor evidently notices my nerves and rests back against his chair to mirror my action. "Elizabeth, I want to thank you for agreeing to see me today."

"I didn't have a choice," I mumble. "It was arranged without discussion...so here I am."

"I see," he replies, unperturbed by my rudeness. "Well then, let me reassure you that you don't have to talk to me about anything that makes you feel uncomfortable. We can sit here for an hour and talk about music, the weather or politics. Sebastian will never know."

My eyes widen in surprise. "How much is he paying you for this?" I ask sarcastically.

"A great deal. I'm not cheap, Elizabeth. May I call you Elizabeth?" He's smiling again.

"Yes. That's fine as it's my name." I cross my arms, growing frustrated at the waste of my time and Sebastian's money.

"Thank you. As I was saying...my hourly rate is preposterously high but Sebastian clearly thinks that I'm worth it." He pauses, studying my face but I intentionally give nothing away, maintaining a mask of disinterest. "I'm not some charlatan. To give you a little background on my qualifications, I am a Fellow of the *Royal College of Physicians* and have a Masters in psychology. I've worked as a consultant psychiatrist for some years and specialise in bereavement and associated psychological disorders."

"Very impressive," I huff. "Can you also juggle blindfolded?"

Ignoring my sarcasm, he continues, "I only tell you this so that you know that I am qualified and experienced, Elizabeth, and therefore someone who is consummately professional, so that–if you did wish to explore your thoughts with me–you will know that you can trust the confidentiality and impartiality of our discussions."

"What you mean is, that you won't tell Sebastian what I say?" *Perhaps I can talk to this stranger. Maybe he can tell me what's happening to me.*

"That's correct. Unless you give me permission to do so, nothing that you say to me will be disclosed to Sebastian or to anyone else." His index finger plays along his top lip as he studies me. "Unless of course you confess to committing murder, in which case I am duty bound to share that information with the relevant authorities. Rather like talking to a priest," he chuckles.

"What if I tell you about a murder that I didn't commit?" I ask hesitantly. He doesn't flinch. "Would you also share that information with the authorities?"

"That would depend, Elizabeth. Are you going to tell me about a murder?" His finger stills on his lip, his eyes lock onto mine. My breath catches. *Can I trust him? I have to take that chance.*

"My son and husband were murdered." The relief of sharing this burden is indescribable. As tension leaves my body with each word spoken, so the knot in my stomach unwinds just a little. *I have done the right thing. He will tell the police and they will believe him because he's a professional doctor.*

"It's interesting that you use the word 'murdered.' My understanding is that your son and husband lost their lives in a tragic motor accident." It's a statement rather than a question.

"No. That's what *she* wants everyone to think. Poor Joe. Poor Alan. It was a car crash. Wicked Beth's fault."

"Wicked Beth?" he repeats.

"Yes. Wicked because of what I did."

"Which was...?"

"Cheated. I *cheated* on Alan. If I hadn't cheated on him, he wouldn't have left me, he wouldn't have drunk that night, he wouldn't have hit a tree and he and Joe would be alive today." The doctor nods slightly, encouraging me to continue. "That's not the whole story though, Doctor."

"It's not?"

"No. It's not."

"Are you comfortable continuing, Elizabeth?"

"Yes," I say. "I have to tell you what she said."

"What who said?" He picks up a pen and notebook and writes something on the page. "Please...don't mind me, I just take a few notes for my own benefit. You don't reach fifty-two and have the same memory as a youngster."

"You don't look fifty-two," I tell him, genuinely floored by his youthful looks which belie his advancing years.

"Thank you," he smiles. "I look after myself. A healthy body is a healthy mind. I need one of those in order to help those whose minds are poorly." *Like mine?* I think. He nods to continue once more.

"What Scarlett said. She told me she'd been seeing Alan. My husband. She said she'd slept with him." I try to recall my conversation with Scarlett with clarity but my head is foggy, my thoughts blur until I'm less sure what is factual and what I think she implied. I decide to tell Doctor Fairfax everything in the hope that he can piece together the real from the imagined and conclude that Scarlett did, indeed, murder my family and is trying to kill me too. He listens intently, making notes as I talk. When I have finished, I take a deep breath and hold it as I await his confirmation that Scarlett is a murderer and I'm not insane. He looks up from his notebook and frowns. I exhale dejectedly.

"Elizabeth," he says gently. "Ordinarily, I would have asked you to start at the beginning and explore your childhood. However, as you were eager to tell me about Scarlett, I felt it best to let you continue."

"My childhood has nothing to do with this," I protest vehemently. "I had a happy childhood, got good grades at school, got married, had kids. Insignificant compared to murder, I should think."

"Indeed," he acquiesces. "I've taken on board your concerns regarding Scarlett. I'm not decrying them as inconsequential or unfounded. What I'd like to do now though is to focus on grief, if I may, so that you understand how bereavement can acutely affect your wellbeing...and your reasoning. Losing a child suddenly, is possibly one of the most painful losses that one could experience, Elizabeth."

"No shit, Sherlock," I murmur.

"Yes, truly. I believe that what you are experiencing is what we term 'grief-related major depression with psychosis." He stops and observes my reaction which is one of faked disinterest, my fingers playing with a lock of hair. "It's relatively rare, but it would explain your hallucinations, misplaced anger toward others, tiredness and paranoia, all of which Sebastian tells me you have been experiencing." I want to protest but decide to allow him to continue, the clock on the mantelpiece indicates half his time is up, this will soon be over.

"Bereavement such as yours is a major stress, Elizabeth. Studies link such bereavement to major depression. If I can explain: there are cognitive and behavioural adjustments which the body automatically makes after such a profound loss so that one can reach a comfortable place where happy memories can sit alongside the feelings of loss. In your case, I don't believe these adjustments have been made. Do you understand so far?"

"No, but carry on," I sigh.

"Okay, I'll try and explain. In grief alone, the intensely sad feelings begin to give way to more positive emotions. The sad feelings are still there, but they become less frequent. With major depression and grief together, there can be...more debilitating symptoms such as impaired psychological functioning." He takes in my blank expression with a frown. "Unless treated, it can lead to hallucinations, belief that your deceased loved one is around you, anxiety.   I suspect you have developed delusional thoughts and paranoia because of the trauma that you suffered with Alan and Joe's sudden passing. Do you recognise any of what I have just told you, in your own behaviours of late?"

"Joe came to see me," my whispered words are written down. "He came to wish me a happy birthday. Are you saying that my son's sweet words to me were my imagination?"

"What do you think, Elizabeth?"

"I don't know what to think any more." My eyes meet his and implore him to help me.

"Shall I tell you what I think?" He asks quietly. "I think you would benefit from a course of bereavement counselling. In addition, I would like you to prescribe some medication that will help you in the short term." He retrieves a prescription pad from the inside pocket of his jacket and scribbles something on the top sheet. I say nothing, slumped dejectedly in the chair I accept the prescription and fold it repeatedly until it's as small as I can make it–a tiny square that seals my fate.

He's watching my fingers work. "Do you have concerns about taking this medication, Elizabeth?"

"What ever gives you that idea?" I tuck the small square in the pocket of my jeans and rest my hands in my lap, my eyes meeting his. "In giving me the prescription, you are confirming that I am insane. It all seems so real to me, Doctor. Some of it I don't want to believe, but Joe coming back...it would *kill* me not to believe that. I can just about cope if I think he's happy and that I'll see him again. If that's all in my fucked up head, then it means *everything* is imagined including him. That means I won't see him again. Do you get that?"

"I understand. However, when you're feeling well you'll learn to cope with the separation from Joe. I'm not saying you'll ever stop missing him, but you will start to let in the happy memories and they will balance the sad ones. Please trust me. Trust Sebastian and your friend Ruth. Do this for yourself and for them, and your daughter and mother. Everyone around you *loves* you, Elizabeth but you have to love yourself and get well."

An alarming thought strikes me. "May I ask you something?" Doctor Fairfax nods. "Were you Libby's psychiatrist?" He nods in confirmation. "Did you prescribe medication for her?" I wonder if Libby was indeed mentally ill at all or was Scarlett poisoning her too? It all begins to make sense to me–a clarity of vision akin to regaining sight after a period of blindness. The correlation of our symptoms and Scarlett's involvement, the diagnosis and Libby's eventual demise are all too co-incidental to be wretched misfortune.

"I can't discuss other patients. I have a duty of confidentiality. Why do you ask?" Shrugging my shoulders in feigned indifference I note the momentary flicker of something dark in Doctor Fairfax's eyes. *Anxiety? Guilt perhaps? I struck a chord with him.* A sharp rap on the study door precedes Sebastian's entrance.

"Ah, Sebastian." Doctor Fairfax springs to his feet, the two men shake hands warmly. "We've just finished, you have impeccable timing as ever."

Sebastian leans over me and plants a gentle kiss on my lips. "Okay sweetheart?"

"Peachy," I reply, rising wearily to my feet. "I'm officially nuts and even have a prescription to prove it." He arches a brow as I retrieve the folded paper from my pocket, and wave it between thumb and index finger in front of his face.

Sebastian casts a glance at Doctor Fairfax but he's watching me. "Medication? Is that necessary, Leo?"

Doctor Fairfax nods as he slips his notebook into a briefcase and clicks the catch home. "Elizabeth, are you comfortable with me answering that question?"

I confirm that I couldn't give a hoot.

"Absolutely, Sebastian. It's only short term, but in my opinion will stabilise Elizabeth's mood and address some of the unpleasant...effects she is experiencing.

"Indeed." Sebastian wraps an arm protectively around my waist. "You *will* take the pills, Elizabeth," he commands as though he can read my mind. "I'll have Scarlett collect your tablets this afternoon." I have no intention of taking the pills but nod in acquiescence. My mind is made up. Albeit, my crazy, depressed, psychotic mind according to the professional and my loved ones. I am the only one who knows the truth. No, that's incorrect...Scarlett also knows the truth and I intend to regain my senses with a week in Dorset after which, battle will commence in earnest.

Sebastian waves from the steps of Penmorrow and I leave a little piece of my heart behind. Bella has been very quiet for the past couple of days and I'm unsure of what she thinks; *does she believe her mother is mad or does she too see what Scarlett is doing to me?*

# Chapter 8

It's cathartic to be home. The pile of unopened bills forms a small mountain which is swept aside as I throw open the front door. The house holds its familiar homely smell albeit laced with dust in the air. Ruth carries our suitcases in and Bella bounds up to her room as I fill the kettle.

"Good to be home?" Ruth asks as she hangs her denim jacket on the coat hook in the hall.

"I have mixed feelings," I tell her. Ruth nods her understanding and links her arm through mine.

We drink our tea sat at the kitchen table, the bills now forming a neat pile on the table next to my mug.

"I have to clear Joe's room out."

"What?" Ruth asks incredulously.

"He told me. It's time to let go, Ruth."

"Whoa! Who told you?"

"Joe did."

She swigs back the last dregs of her tea and gently places her mug down before laying a hand on mine. "*Joe* told you?"

"That's right. Joe told me. I don't care if you think I'm nuts, he told me."

"If you say Joe told you, love, then Joe told you." She looks doubtful and sorry for me.

"Ruth, he came to me and said that he's happy where he is, that Bella can have his games console. He also warned me about Scarlett." I stare at Ruth, hoping to gauge her reaction but expression remains unconvinced.

"Don't you think this is part of grief, Beth?"

"No Ruth. I don't. I *know* what I saw and it was Joe."

"If you say so, love." She squeezes my hand as though I'm a total lunatic deserving of her pity.

"I know what I saw. Also I've been thinking, I want to speak to the police officer," I tell her.

"DI Chambers?" She looks confused, unsure how best to handle me.

"Yes. I feel he should be aware of my concerns regarding Scarlett. Maybe he can arrange some blood tests on me to test for poison or drugs."

"Okay," she reluctantly concedes. "We'll call him in the morning. Let's see if there's anything on Scarlett. If not, I want you to let this go. Okay?"

"Agreed."

"In the meantime, we have an eighteenth birthday party to organise tomorrow, so you need to buck your ideas up missy." She winks at me, I force a smile.

Ruth insists on sleeping on the couch despite my offer of Joe's room or sharing with me. As I climb into bed, my mobile phone rings. Sebastian. I press the 'decline' button and turn off the bedside lamp. I'll call him tomorrow. A small box of tablets sits beside a glass of water. Opening the box, I press a pill loose from the blister card and carefully wrap it in a tissue. As I did last night, I go and flush the tablet down the toilet.

***

I haven't slept well. My bed smells of Alan and the house is deathly quiet.

When I call the police inspector at nine o'clock, his secretary puts me through. "DI Chambers, this is Elizabeth Dove."

"Who?" He's forgotten me already. One more accident filed away and cast aside, yet another life shattered.

"Elizabeth Dove. My husband Alan and son Joe were killed last December."

"Of course, sorry, I remember. Mrs. Dove, how are you?" He says hesitantly, so that I'm not sure he remembers me at all.

"Not so good. I just wanted to talk to you regarding a matter I feel is important."

I can hear him sucking on a cigarette. "Go on."

"I know this is going to sound...erratic, unbelievable even, but I think they were murdered and I think the person who did it is trying to kill me."

There is silence on the end of the phone. "Are you there?" I ask.

"Yes. I'm here. That's quite an accusation, Mrs. Dove." He thinks I'm crazy too. "It's coming back to me now, a friend of yours called me recently regarding a woman who works at your boyfriend's house."

Blushing a hot crimson, I mentally curse Ruth for disclosing my relationship status to the Inspector. Lord knows what he thinks of me now, with a boyfriend having lost my husband. "Can you come round please? It's a long story and it's easier to talk face to face."

"Give me thirty minutes. I'll be there." After noting my address, which of course he should have on file, he cuts the call.

My father used to say 'never trust a man whose sleeves are too short.' DI Chamber's sleeves fall shy of his wrists by a good three inches. He's wearing a shabby brown, ill-fitting suit and has a coffee stain on his crumpled white shirt. I wonder if he's married, and if so, why his wife would allow her husband to go to work in such disarray. He has kind eyes though, eyes which have undoubtedly seen all manner of evil and carnage and yet which retain compassion and an inherent trust in mankind.

He has the patient and poised deportment of a long serving police officer who has seen and heard just about everything, and yet who remains infallible and steadfast in his duty. "So you think you're being poisoned?" He repeats, as he sips his sweet milky tea, regarding me over the rim of his cup.

"That's right. I do."

"Have you seen this Scarlett woman ever put anything in your food, or acting suspiciously around you?"

"No. I've never actually seen her poison my food," I say sarcastically, "but she is doing so. I'm *sure* of that."

He replaces his cup on the saucer and rests back on the armchair, his arms folded. It's Alan's armchair next to the fireplace and it seems amiss to see another man seated there.

"I know you don't believe me. Nobody believes me,

but *look* at me. Do you remember how I looked after the accident? Even after the shock? Did I look this frail?" Ruth fidgets next to me and I sense she wishes to speak but tactfully remains silent.

DI Chambers' eyes drink me in. He shakes his head slowly. "No. I don't recall you looking so thin, nor as gaunt as you do today. That doesn't mean that someone is trying to murder you. It could be a delayed and prolonged reaction to your profound loss." His finger plays across his top lip, his eyes unreadable.

"Yes, it could be but I don't think so. I've been hallucinating. Things seem real, terrible visions which come and go, which I didn't have before recently."

"It could still be grief. Or depression," he suggests.

Ruth rests a hand on my arm. "Tell him about the quack's assessment, Beth." When I glare at her, and it's apparent I have no intention of disclosing the psychiatrist's diagnosis, she spurts forth on my behalf. "Beth's been diagnosed with grief related depression and she's on anti-depressant pills now." He nods sombrely and, I'm sure, makes a mental note of this information.

"No. *Yes*. She's right but there's more," I bluster. "She said something too. She told me she'd slept with Alan and that she did something to him. I think *she* caused the accident."

"Wait. Slow down. What exactly did she say?"

"I'm trying to remember but my memory is foggy. I think she said she'd done what she'd done for him - for Sebastian. She said that she bought me to Penmorrow because Sebastian's wife wasn't able to give him children. Don't you *see?* I had children and so I could offer him the heir that she knew he wanted. I think she somehow caused Alan's death–not meaning to kill Joe too–so that I'd come to Penmorrow with the children but now I'm no use to him either. Nor was Libby. I think she killed her too, and now she's trying to kill *me.* You have to stop her." I can hear the hysteria in my voice but am powerless to calm down, panic gripping me as the enormity of what I'm saying hits home.

"The car was scrutinised. It was road worthy before the accident. Are you saying you think she tampered with it?" He frowns as he leans forward, his fingers steeple under his chin.

"I think she poisoned Alan like she's poisoning me and like she poisoned Libby. I think it was the drugs that were found in his body. *She* gave them to him. You have to believe me," I implore.

"Libby De Montfort died from an overdose, it was recorded as suicide. I pulled the file before I came here, but we have no evidence that it was the same drug which was found in your husband's body."

"Yes, yes. It looked like suicide. She's clever, don't you see? Surely you can check if the same medicine was found in both Libby and Alan's bodies?"

"Mrs. Dove, if what you say is true...and I'm not saying I agree with you...if Scarlett is poisoning everyone, where is she obtaining the medication, presuming it is the same medication? We're not talking about over the counter headache pills here."

"I don't know. That's what you need to find out. Can you speak to her doctor? Maybe he's prescribing them for her but she's using them on me?"

He sighs deeply, massaging his temples. "Okay, here's what we do. If you make a formal complaint, I will be able to sanction the police duty quack to take bloods from you and get the lab to run some toxicology tests. In the meantime, I'll make some enquiries about Scarlett ... check into her past, and I'll get a colleague to review the wife's death. How does that sound?"

"Yes. *No.* I can't make a complaint or Sebastian will finish with me for good."

"It's up to you but I'm pulling some serious strings for you here, it's not normal practice to do anything without some evidence supporting your suspicions, but I figure you deserve a little help. You need to help me too though, ok?"

"Ok. I'll do it, I'll file a complaint."

"It's called a TRO – a Temporary Restraining Order. It has to be granted by a judge but its there to protect you if you believe you're being threatened or in immediate danger of physical harm from this woman. I can help you with this, but we'll have to serve it on her, then you will need to file a Proof of Service with the court."

"Does this mean I can't go back to Penmorrow?" That will be the end of Sebastian and I. Dead in the water. I feel sick at the thought of losing him ... I can't lose him.

"Not if she's living there, no you can't. Do you think

you can convince Lord De Montfort to fire her?"

I laugh hysterically. "You'd think so, wouldn't you? I mean ... clearly it will take my *death* to prove to him that she's fucking evil."

He doesn't look shocked at my outburst, but I imagine he's heard worse language than mine.

"Can I ask you something?" He looks serious, his brow furrowed.

"Yes...please do."

"Do you have any reason to believe Lord De Montfort is having a relationship with this woman?" His words hurt like a physical slap to my face.

My cheeks redden. "They had a brief relationship in the past...before he met me. I thought perhaps it was still going on...but Ruth and Sebastian made me see that I was wrong. I know he loves me. Sorry, to answer your question no I don't believe they are having a relationship, I believe that's what she wants though."

"Fine. So are you going to do the TRO?"

"No. I can't. I don't know. Can I think about it?"

"Take all the time you need. Here's my card, call me when you've made your decision but don't leave it too long...if what you're saying is right, then we need to act on this before you go back there."

DI Chambers places a small white card on the coffee table. It bears the police crest and his contact details. "My mobile phone number is on there as well as the out of hours contact numbers. Be sure to call if you need to. Ok?"

"Thank you," I say appreciatively, "I will call. You do...*believe* me don't you?"

"Mrs. Dove. I haven't been a police officer for all these years without keeping an open mind at all times. I can see that you believe what you are telling me therefore I feel it's worth looking into. If nothing else, it will put your mind at rest." As an afterthought he adds, "you may want to see your GP anyway, get some bereavement counselling." His last sentence tells me he doesn't truly believe me. He's not on my side.

Closing the front door dejectedly, Ruth steps out of the living room and puts an arm around my shoulders, squeezing me tightly. "Hey girlfriend," she says more cheerily than I'm sure she feels given my mood. "How about we head into town, pick up Bella's birthday presents and have lunch–it's on me."

"Fine," I reply still melancholy.

"You need some serious girl time."

The shops are bustling for a Tuesday afternoon, office workers clutching fast food and young mums pushing buggies into clothes shops, all enjoying the balmy weather. Bella has written a birthday gift list for which I'm thankful, unsure what an eighteen year old girl wants today. She's far more mature than I recall being at her age. Ruth says she's eighteen going on thirty but, every now and again, she will throw a tantrum or act the fool and remind me that she's still a teen. Clutching a bag of cd's and makeup there remains one gift I wish to purchase, which wasn't on Bella's list. The jeweller retrieves the locket from the window display. Its simple gold heart with a dainty sculpted edge and fine gold chain. "I'll take it," I tell the pretty blonde assistant who carefully places it in a black and gold box and runs my purchase through the till. It's expensive but my daughter is more than worth it.

The wine bar is busy. Several minutes spent waiting for a table are eventually rewarded and we sit by the window overlooking the town square. Ruth orders a bottle of chilled Chardonnay having first quizzed me as to whether my anti-loony pills are okay mixed with alcohol. Of course, I know I'm not taking them but I tell her that alcohol is fine in moderation. The waitress pours a large measure in each glass and notes our order of a platter of mezé. Nibbling on the delicious olives, hummus and breads while we chat is just like old times. Ruth recounts tales from the office and I realise how much I miss my work and colleagues. It feels as though I have been living in a parallel universe for the past few weeks.

"You seem much better, Beth." Ruth comments as she refills my glass.

"Honestly, I feel so much better," I concede. "My head feels clearer and I haven't hallucinated."

"Those pills are doing you the world of good, love. To be honest I'm a little surprised, I thought it would take longer for them to get in your system." She watches me over the rim of her wine glass, gauging my reaction I think.

"Well, it just proves that the shrink knows his stuff. He's clearly got me on the right pills," I'm relieved to see her smile and nod, yet am wracked with guilt at the lies that slip so freely from my mouth.

"Beth, do you really still think Scarlett drugged you? It's just...you're taking your medication, which amazes me quite honestly, yet you sounded so earnest when you talked to DI Chambers this morning. If you believe she's drugged you, then surely you don't believe you're mad. So my question to you is, *why* are you taking the pills?"

My friend is astute. Now, like a cornered rabbit facing the farmer's gun, I search my mind for a way out of this, unsure what to say. I want to tell Ruth that I'm not taking the pills, but to do so is to admit that I've lied to her and Sebastian. It also reveals that I wholeheartedly believe my own attempted murder theory and in turn leaves me open to being accused of insanity once more. It's better that Ruth, Bella, Sebastian and my mother believe that I'm getting well, and to them that means taking the tablets.

"That's a good question, Ruth." And it is. A very good question. "I believe everyone has my best interests at heart, except Scarlett of course, and that you all want me to take the medication and get well. I'm doing it for you all. That doesn't mean I don't believe that Scarlett means me harm. I know what she said to me...it may be a bit foggy in my mind and I can't remember everything, but the intent to harm was clear. I also know she hinted that she hurt my son and husband. I can't just put that to one side and not act upon it. I owe it to them. I wasn't the world's best mother or wife, I see that now and I have to live with the guilt, but I can do this for them–uncover the truth, whatever that may mean."

"You know you have my support, Beth. Whatever you decide to do, I will back you." We clink glasses as we used to do in more carefree times, and recite our mantra, "here's to us, and down the rest of the buggers." Our cappuccinos arrive and conversation turns to my relationship with Sebastian.

"Do you miss him?" asks Ruth.

"Yes. I really do," I sigh. "He's the man I've been dreaming of all of my adult life, if that doesn't sound too corny?"

"Not at all. I see how you are together and, mostly, you're good. *Really* good."

"Mostly?"

"Well you can both be...fiery and hot headed," she giggles. "If Scarlett went...when she goes, I think you two will be just fine. I do want to ask you about the kinky stuff though. *Oh. My. God.* What the hell is that room in the basement?" She licks her bottom lip, awaiting my reply. I know that look, that's the look that tells me she will not accept anything other than the full lowdown on our sex life.

"He's dominant, Ruth, as you know. He's *a* Dominant." I say.

She cocks her head to one side, smirking shamelessly. "Yes, yes, which means he gets to tie you up and beat the shit out of you?"

"No Ruth. Well...not as such. It's not abuse if that's what you mean. His mantra is 'safe, consensual and sane,' so everything we do is based on mutual trust and agreement."

"Hold on lady," she replaces her coffee cup in its saucer and folds her arms. "You consent to him *horse whipping* you, or whatever it is you two do down there? And what about the 'sane' part? Can that really be said of you?" She laughs and I punch her arm playfully across the table.

"Seriously, Ruth. He's opened my eyes to a whole new way of having sex and...I kind of like the way he takes the lead. I find myself needing that from him more and more."

"I get that," Ruth nods, sipping her coffee. "Doesn't it hurt though?"

"It's hard to explain. It's good pain, if that makes sense? Because it's so erotic, I get carried away and the pain becomes...pleasurable. For example when he shoved the butt plug in me..."

Ruth spits her coffee, showering us both in warm brown specks. I still love to shock her. "For fucks' sake, Beth!" She's laughing so hard that it's infectious. We cackle and giggle unaware of those around us. We don't notice the man stood to my left until he coughs loudly.

"Hello Beth." The man fidgets nervously. Still laughing, I turn to apologise for our raucous behaviour, looking up at the man's face.

"Mike. *Oh my God.* Mike Breeze." Best man to Alan and I, his closest friend and... witness to Alan and Scarlett's affair? Mike indicates to the chair beside me and

I nod for him to join us. He leans forward and kisses my cheek and then Ruth's. "How have you been, Mike?"

"I've been okay. It's been tough, without my mate Alan, but life goes on." He orders a double espresso. "I thought you were living in Cornwall now?"

"Yes. No. We're back for Bella's birthday. It's her eighteenth on Thursday. She wanted to go out with some of her old school friends. So, here we are."

"Can't believe she's nearly eighteen," he sighs. "Where does the time go, eh?"

"Indeed," I reply, feeling awkward and unsure what to talk to Mike about. Ruth makes small talk until his coffee arrives. This is a prime opportunity to quiz Mike about Scarlett. At Alan's funeral, Mike indicated that my late husband had been dating a girl who fitted Scarlett's description. Scarlett herself hinted that she had been seeing Alan. There will never be a better opportunity than this to ask Mike about his recollections. "Mike. I hope you don't mind me asking, but there's been something on my mind for some time and I'd like to ask you about it."

"Sure. What is it?"

"At the funeral, you mentioned that Alan had been seeing someone."

He drains his coffee and wipes his mouth with the back of his hand, his eyes narrowed and suspicious. "What's this about? It won't do any good to go over old ground now, Beth. What's done is done. By all accounts you're still seeing that bloke from Cornwall anyway."

"Yes, that's true," I acquiesce. "I'm not blaming Alan,

God knows he had a crap life with me in the end...not that it was all my fault, you understand. However, I have reason to believe that the woman he was seeing, is Sebastian's maid, Scarlett." In a moment of inspiration, I retrieve my mobile phone and open the camera application. Scrolling through the photographs I find one of Scarlett taken at Christmas. "Would you recognise her again?"

Mike nods. "She was a looker. Not the sort easily forgotten...although it was some months ago. He looks at the screen with no hint of recognition.

"Is that the woman Alan was seeing?" My breath catches as Mike squints at the small image. Ruth shuffles nervously in her seat. He takes his reading glasses from his pocket and slips them onto the bridge of his nose, moving the screen away slightly until his vision is sharp enough to focus on the image. It is evident that the woman is familiar to him, my heart skips a beat. This could be the lead I need to see Scarlett condemned. "It's her isn't it?"

# Chapter 9

Mike hesitates before speaking. "I can't be certain, Beth, but it looks like the woman. She's thinner than she was, but then so are you. You bloody women are always changing your hairstyle, losing weight...but yes. I'm fairly certain that's the woman Alan saw. Does she have a 4X4 car?"

My hand trembles as I slip the phone in my handbag. "Yes Mike. She has access to Sebastian's Land Rover. When he's in London or on the estate, Scarlett uses his car to run errands. She could very well have driven to Dorset if she was alone for the day. Even overnight." Overnight– did Alan spend nights with Scarlett? After despising sex with me for bloody *years?* The way that Mike avoids my questioning stare confirms my husband's infidelity. Suddenly I feel sick. *I need air.* Pushing my chair back abruptly, I mutter an excuse and swiftly exit the wine bar. Standing on the pavement, oblivious to people passing me by, the tears fall. A gentle hand on my arm focuses my attention back to Mike.

"Beth. Shit, I didn't mean to upset you." He runs a hand through his hair, reminding me of Sebastian. *How I miss him. How I need his strong arms around me right now, telling me everything is okay.* I feel light headed, a cloying grey fog inside my mind darkening my thoughts. "I didn't think you'd react that way after...well, you were seeing other men, love. It's not like Alan cheated first."

I deserved those words. As time passes, so my guilt becomes more profound. "If I'm honest, Mike, I need to find out what really happened to Alan and Joe, because it's something I can do for them. To right the terrible wrong that I did." He hands me a tissue from his pocket to dry my eyes. "How often did he sleep with her?"

He shifts his weight from foot to foot, apparently uncomfortable at my question. "A few times. Not overnight...well, once at my place. He told me they'd been to a hotel in Somerset a couple of times." His eyes meet mine, the pain in mine reflected in his. "I'm not trying to hurt you, love. You asked."

Ruth joins us outside, clutching my bag. "You okay Beth?" I nod. "I've paid the bill, lets get you home."

"One last thing, Mike..."

He arches an eyebrow, hands thrust deep in his trouser pockets.

"Did Alan...seem okay to you towards the end?"

"Beth, he was fucked up. To answer your question, no. He didn't seem alright."

"In what way? I saw him so little, with Christmas and all. Did he seem at all...drugged? Weird? Hallucinations?"

Mike considers my questions then, sighing deeply says, "I don't know what you mean by drugged. He was weird, yes. I remember one night, we were sat with a take-away, he'd seen her that afternoon. He looked at me and said the weirdest thing. He said the walls of my living room were running with blood. *Your* blood."

"Oh my God. So he hallucinated? Or do you

mean...he *wanted* it to be my blood?" The thought that Alan could have considered any real harm coming to me is abhorrent and unbelievable. For all his faults he was a gentle man, rarely cursing or wishing harm on others who wronged him.

"No love. He really believed he could see blood on the walls. He got weird towards the end, but then he was drinking a lot. More than usual. I put it down to the stress of your separation–it took its toll on him, you know."

"Yes I know," I whisper, ashamed.

Ruth rests a hand on my arm. "Come on, lovely. Lets get you home. Mike, you're welcome to pop in for a cuppa?" Mike shrugs and makes an excuse. It's clear that he's uncomfortable. We say goodbye, giving each other a perfunctory kiss before parting. Driving home, Ruth and I discuss the revelations of the afternoon. Ruth considers Alan to have been suffering from stress and alcoholism, but, to me, Mike's disclosure is confirmation of Scarlett's involvement in his demise.

***

A chicken is roasting in the oven. It's the first meal I've cooked for a long time and the normality of such a domestic task calms my nerves. Bella peels potatoes and Ruth pours me a second glass of red wine. My mobile phone rings just as I remove the tray of sizzling chicken from the oven to baste. Ignoring the familiar ringtone I spoon hot fat onto the crispy bird and replace the tray, slamming the oven door shut with my foot. The phone rings once more. Sebastian's photograph smiles from the phone display as I toss aside the oven glove and answer the call.

"Elizabeth?"

"Sebastian. Hi. How are you?"

"I'm fine," he says curtly. "You said you'd call when you reached Dorset. I know the roads can be bad but I'm guessing the journey didn't take over 24 hours?"

"Sorry. I meant to call you yesterday but I've had a lot to do, getting ready for Bella's birthday." I'm thankful he can't see my flushed cheeks.

"I see. I'll drive up tomorrow, I wouldn't miss my girl's birthday for the world." My Girl. His fondness towards Bella warms my heart. "I hope you're not overdoing it? The idea is that you rest, Elizabeth. It doesn't sound as if that is the case."

"Oh. I've been resting too. Anyway...how are things at Penmorrow? Are you missing me?" I try to change the subject tactfully.

"Yes of course I miss you. Are you feeling any better?" His voice is clipped and a little cool.

"You don't *sound* as if you're missing me. Is everything ok?"

"Everything is wonderful Darling. Unless of course you mean in spite of my girlfriend going nuts, running off to Dorset, my maid sulking and you not taking my calls."

"I see." Ouch. That hurts. "It's only for a short while, Sebastian. We agreed that I needed this space to get well."

"And *are* you getting well? Are you taking your medication?

"Yes, of course," I lie. "I'm feeling more clear headed. Maybe you were right about this being grief."

"Yes darling. I do think I'm right."

There is a long awkward silence. I break it. "Why is Scarlett sulking?"

"I have no idea what goes through any woman's head, Elizabeth, least of all hers."

"Has she mentioned a moving out date? Has she found somewhere to go?" *I'm skating on very thin ice now...*

"No she hasn't. She kindly offered to stay on while you are away to look after the house." *I just bet the bitch has.*

"To look after you, you mean." I can't hide the bitterness in my voice, he sighs deeply.

"Elizabeth..."

"Yes?"

"It's not forever. It makes sense that she stays until you return, it gives her more time to find another position and a place to live. I need the help too. Try and be reasonable."

"*Reasonable?*" I repeat, trying to curb the venom. "I think I've been very reasonable, given the fact that she has made it totally untenable for me to live with the man I love." He sighs deeply but I'm unable to stop myself. "Furthermore, Sebastian, it seems remarkable to me that I'm feeling better now I've left Penmorrow – now that I'm not eating her cooking, which incidentally is even more poisonous than anything that comes out of her mouth...and that's saying something."

"Have you finished?" He asks nonchalantly. "I can't do this any more, Elizabeth. I'm tired of arguing with you about Scarlett. I think, on reflection, it would be best if you stayed in Dorset, for the time being at least."

What? Oh no...this is not what I expected. I'm shocked to my core, ice coursing through my veins. "Why? Don't you love me?"

Another long silence is followed by one more sigh and my sense of panic increases. "You know I do. With all my heart," he says quietly.

*"But?"*

"But we've both been through so much and neither seems happy. Scarlett is a recurring topic for you, and I have to tell you that from my perspective, she is the one who has been my constant. I don't think you can get over your jealousy, or whatever it is you feel toward her, and I know that her help here is invaluable. So you see its stalemate." *Jealousy? Are you kidding me?*

"But the things that Scarlett does, I want to do for you, Sebastian. It's bound to be difficult with two women living in the house, one whom loves you and one who's crazy and besotted with you."

"And which are you?" he asks.

"I *love* you. For fucks sake, you know that. Don't you see what she's doing to me? To us?"

"Watch your mouth, Elizabeth."

"I won't watch my fucking mouth. You're ending our relationship because you choose a manipulative, dangerous *whore* over me."

"Then there's really nothing more to say, is there?"

"No. I guess there isn't." Tears flow down my face and I want to scream at him that I love him, not to do this to us. Instead I cut the call, my stubborn pride exceeding my desire to beg him not to leave me. *This could be the biggest mistake of my life.*

# Chapter 10

The alarm wakes me from a fitful sleep filled with erotic dreams of Sebastian. For the past six hours, since I finally drifted off, he has chained me, whipped me and declared his undying love while I lay helpless and bound in Penmorrow's inner sanctum. Now the early morning sun scatters its rays across my bed through hastily drawn curtains, as the final vestiges of sleep ebb away.

Bella is a teen who loves her sleep. She would happily languish beneath her duvet for a full twenty-four hours I'm sure, if it weren't for the distractions of mobile phones, Twitter and Facebook. This morning, as I watch her silently from the doorway to her bedroom, it is hard to imagine that once this young woman was a babe in my arms. Her tousled hair spills over her pillow, remnants of yesterday's mascara smudged beneath her closed eyelids, her chest gently rising and falling. Eighteen today, my daughter is now a woman. When did that happen? It seems not five minutes since Bella was playing with dolls and cooing over her baby brother. Closing the door quietly, I pull my dressing gown tightly around me against the morning chill and pad down to the kitchen to cook Bella's favourite breakfast of bacon, eggs and hash brown potatoes.

Ruth, still sleeping each night on the sofa is stirring. In the kitchen I fill the kettle and flick on the switch. My mobile phone is on the kitchen table, where I left it last night having consumed the best part of a bottle of red wine. A dull headache endorses the notion that red wine and I are not well suited. As the kettle noisily bubbles I wake the phone and note with dismay the absence of any missed calls or text messages from Sebastian. Just one from my mother asking that I call her to confirm what time she may call in and give Bella her presents.

"Did I hear the kettle boil?" Ruth enters the kitchen in a pair of red polka-dot oversized pyjamas, rubbing her eyes with her fists and yawning, her hair a mess of wild unruly curls.

"You did, indeed. Tea coming right up."

Taking a seat at the kitchen table, Ruth looks at my phone. "Has he called?" She nods at the mobile, I shake my head. "Men. They're so bloody moody." She tries to rake her fingers through her tangled mop but it proves an impossible task. She accepts the mug of tea gratefully, blowing on the steaming brew. "Tell me again what the plan is today for Bella's birthday."

"She has a couple of friends coming over this afternoon, they're going into town to spend the birthday money she hopes to receive. Then to a nightclub tonight." I join Ruth at the table and sip my coffee.

"Is *he* coming up?"

"By '*he*' I presume you mean Sebastian?" Even the sound of his name as it trips off my tongue is painful. My stubborn pride prevents me from picking up the phone and apologising. There is nowhere to go so it's fruitless. He won't kick Scarlett out and I won't return while she's there.

"Yes, he is coming up for Bella's birthday, as far as I'm aware."

"He adores her, Beth–don't push him out today. Let him come if he wants to." Ruth ignores my petulant sigh. "Talk to him today. Look at you, you're a mess."

"What's the point? I've given him so many ultimatums and he's chosen her so there's no way past this for us. In fact I may as well file the restraining order on her as I'm not going back while she's there. At least then the police doctor could do the blood test, although it may be too late now. It's been three days–Scarlett cooked me breakfast on Monday and since then I've been here. It's now Thursday, so the test may not show any trace of her poison."

"*Whoa,* slow down Beth." Ruth's eyes are etched with concern. "This is a blooming big step to take." She holds up a hand to stop me interrupting, I close my mouth resolutely and allow her to continue. "If you do this Beth, it will be the final nail in the coffin for you and Sebastian. He'll see it as vindictive. Is that a risk you're willing to take?"

"No, you're wrong," I stress. "Don't you see...if I file the order against her, the only way he can have me back is if she leaves as I can't be in the same house with Scarlett. He *loves* me, I know he does. He may not think that at the moment, but I'm certain that's the case. I just need to do something...dramatic, to force him to make the decision to kick her out." This makes perfect sense to me. It's a win-

win situation. The blood test may, or may not, identify drugs in my body and the restraining order sends a clear message to both Scarlett and Sebastian that I mean business. She has to go. Of course, if drugs are detected in my bloodstream, she'll be going off to prison. *Perfect. A faultless plan.*

"Kick who out Mum?" Bella drifts into the kitchen looking half asleep and slumps onto a vacant chair at the table.

"Nobody darling. Anyway, birthday girl, I'm going to cook your favourite breakfast." Leaning across, arms open, Bella flops forward into my tight embrace. "Happy birthday my darling girl. Eighteen today. I can hardly believe it."

"Happy birthday Bellaboo," Ruth, in her polka-dot finery joins the group hug and my thoughts return to my daughter's special day.

"*Whoa*...it's fab, I love it." Bella casts aside the wrapping paper and admires the small gold locket in its box.

"I hope you really do like it, love," I ask, anxiously gauging her reaction as she holds the gift in her palm. She nods enthusiastically as her thumb nail prises open the delicate clasp revealing two tiny photographs.

"It's Dad...and Joe." My daughter's eyes pool with tears as her finger traces the outline of their smiling faces.

Resting my hand on her arm, I tell her, "now you can always have them near you, Bella. Wear it and they'll be close to your heart." Ruth sniffs back her own emotion, while tears spill unbidden down Bella's cheeks and I'm a blubbering mess.

"Oh Mum. I *love* it. Thank you," she says as we all hug once more.

Ruth fetches a neon pink gift bag from the lounge and presents it to Bella with a smirk on her face. "Open it, love. Many happy returns from your mother's craziest, most generous friend...me." Bella giggles as she peers inside the bag, retrieving a miniature bottle of gin and branded glass. I scowl at Ruth who bares an admonishing frown in return. Placing the bottle and glass on the kitchen table, Bella pulls a packet of condoms from the bag. My scowl extends way past disapproval and Ruth laughs, joined by my daughter. "*Ruth!*" I rebuke. "She's my baby girl, not a drunken slut."

My friend chuckles. The next gift is far more appropriate in my opinion–a beautiful silk robe in midnight blue. Bella whoops with joy and slips the delicate robe over her purple shorty pyjamas, she looks so grown up that I start blubbing all over again.

"Thanks so much, Ruth." Bella squeezes Ruth tightly and kisses her cheek. "Love you *so* much. You're the best."

Ruth hugs her back, stroking a hand down Bella's back. "And I love you so much too," she whispers. "Not having had kids of my own, I feel like you're my daughter too."

"And you're like a second Mum to me."

At twelve o'clock, the doorbell chimes. My stomach

has been knotted all morning and, although my head is clearer, the malaise remains. The last few days seem to have sapped what meagre energy I had and I know that I'm not strong enough to face a confrontation with Sebastian. My hand hesitates on the door latch. The bell chimes once more. Ruth calls out that someone is at the door and I reply that I'm getting it. Opening the door ajar, my eyes lock with Sebastian's.

# Chapter 11

*Fuck,* he looks devastatingly gorgeous, dressed in black denim jeans, and a pale blue and cream striped shirt that enhances the vast breadth of his masculine shoulders.

"Elizabeth." He hesitates on the threshold, seemingly unsure if he is welcome. Opening the door wider, my hand sweeps in an invitation to enter my home.

"Sebastian. Come in. Good journey?"

"Indeed it was." So formal, so aloof, so very hurtful. He steps into the hallway, his gaze still locked on mine. I look away, fidgeting with the spaghetti straps on the jade green summer dress I chose to wear today, knowing how he loves me in green. He always says it suits my fair complexion and blonde hair.

"You look better," he observes coolly. "More colour in your cheeks."

"I *am* better," I confirm confidently. "The pills are helping." *Oh how the lies fall so readily upon my lips,* I reflect, telling him what I know he needs to hear.

"That is good." He thrusts his hands in the pockets of his jeans, shoulders hunched, looking uncomfortable and unsure. I wonder at what point we became so prickly in each others' company–when did the love recede?

"There's my girl. Happy birthday darling." His gaze shifts from me and settles warmly upon my daughter as she descends the stairs two at a time and leaps into his waiting arms.

"Hello you big bear," she gushes, her arms encircling

his waist, his strong bare arms locking her in a tight embrace. "Thanks *everso* for coming."

"It's my pleasure, darling. I wouldn't miss your special day, princess." Watching the two most precious people in my life together again is wonderful. *We belong together...a family, protecting and loving each other. What right have I to deny Bella the only father figure she has in her life?* As Sebastian tickles my daughter mercilessly, the knot in my stomach unwinds just a little. Leaving the giggling pair to their frivolity, I busy myself in the kitchen preparing lunch, Sebastian's favourite dish of salmon in a herb crust is on the menu. On reflection it should have been Bella's favourite 'meat feast' pizza but I know she'll understand. The way to a man's heart is through his stomach.

I sense him behind me, even before I turn to face him. He's close - his warm breath on the back of my neck so apparent with my hair clipped up while I cook. My hand trembles, the wooden spoon slipping from my grasp into the pan of dill sauce. The touch of his finger tips on the nape of my neck is so light that I wonder if it is imagined, borne of my desire to have him possess me once more. "Sebastian..." the whispered word is carried on a breath that I can no longer hold. My sex clenches as his finger weaves a path down my spine to my sacrum where it circles arbitrarily. "Sebastian..." again I say his name, though it's neither a command to stop nor an objection to his touch.

"Don't *fight* me," he rasps, his lips brushing my

earlobe, my panties drenched in my arousal. My breath catches as his body presses into mine, his erection pressing into my lower back, a muscular arm snaking around me. His hand lifts the hem of my dress with determined force, my back arching as he brushes the thin fabric of my panties. "*Fuck.* You're wet." His teeth catch my earlobe, the sharp pain melding with pleasure.

"You still want me." Oblivious to the risk of interruption, I'm lost in ecstasy as his fingers continue their assault, now slipping under the elastic, probing, seeking out my swollen bud. Clutching the counter top for support, my hips thrust forward to meet his touch. "Say you are *mine,*" he instructs, his breath hot on my neck. "Say it. I. Am. *Yours.*"

"I am yours. *Only* yours." My nipples, hard and throbbing, strain against the constraints of my bra as his thumb rubs in delicious circles over my clit, around it and over it once more. Again and again, the friction sending me into a frenzy. "Sebastian, I need you..." His touch sends tremors through my over-stimulated body, so close to climax... Fuck I need to come. I need to come for him...for us.

"*Ssh,*" he murmurs. "Come for me." His words trigger my release, the orgasm wracking my body from my core to my extremities, my sex clenching hard around his slick fingers as he thrusts them deep into my vagina. "That's right baby...oh fuck yes. You're gushing for me."

The creak of a floorboard propels me back to the kitchen, back to reality with a rush of panic. Sebastian's hand withdraws sharply as he steps away from me, tugging down my dress in a fluid motion just as Ruth appears. If she notices the red flush on my cheeks or my startled expression, she pretends not to notice. "How long until lunch? I'm famished," she asks.

"Elizabeth's just making the sauce, aren't you darling?" He is so damn cool. He arches a brow and folds his arms, resting back against the kitchen table as if he is innocence personified. "Elizabeth?"

"Ten. Ten minutes," I stammer, my legs still weak from the incredible orgasm.

"Fine," sighs Ruth. "I'll leave you lovebirds alone–it's refreshing to see you getting along. Call me when it's ready." With a toss of her unruly curls, she marches out of the kitchen as I glare at Sebastian.

"Oh Mister Innocent," I hiss. "*Elizabeth's just making the sauce, aren't you darling*. You'll get sauce, alright. On your bloody *head.*"

He chuckles softly, adding to my irritation. Seeing the tea towel conveniently close, I clutch it and twizzle it into a make-shift whip. His eyes narrow. "Don't you dare," he warns in a low growl, his lips curved in a wry smile.

"You dare me?" I goad, whipping the air with my flimsy weapon. "*Really?*"

"Really," he confirms, arms still folded, his expression dark. "Go ahead. See what happens." The temptation too great to resist, my wrist deftly whips the coiled towel landing a *'thwack!'* against Sebastian's bare arm. He doesn't flinch yet it must have stung. Unfolding his arms he looks down and regards a red mark forming on his enormous bicep. *Oh crap!* As he takes a determined step toward me, I reload my weapon–the towel coiled and ready to strike again. His teeth bite down on his lower lip as he shakes his head.

"Back off big boy," my warning is feeble, laughter catching in my throat, towel cocked ready to flick. In an instant he is upon me.

"I warned you little girl," he growls in a deep rumble as he snatches the towel from my grasp. Before I can dodge the inevitable, he whips me sharply on the hip with a stinging bite.

"You *pig!*" I gasp, shocked and rubbing my poor hip. 'Pig' was apparently an ill choice of names–he whips once more, the tightly wound towel catching my bare knee.

"Say you're sorry," he demands unreasonably.

"*Never,*" I reply but as he re-arms the towel I reconsider, my lips pushed out in a girly pout. "I'm very sorry." Dropping the towel onto the floor he gathers me into his arms and hugs me tightly. It feels so heavenly and so right, to be in his embrace once more. "I've missed you, you annoying, arrogant, sexy man."

"As I have missed you, my petulant, wilful beautiful girl. We need to talk. Right now isn't the time, though. We're neglecting Bella." He's right of course. Always so irritatingly right.

Bella's friends arrive as Ruth and I wash the lunch dishes. The house quickly degenerates to a noisy babble of colourful young women. Ruth and I exchange glances and roll our eyes as they chat animatedly in the kitchen about boys, music and makeup as Sebastian pours champagne into my pitiful selection of mismatched glasses. He's generously brought six bottles of his finest from the cellar at Penmorrow; I suspect my daughter will have a serious hang-over tomorrow. When the glasses are filled, Sebastian puts the lunch dishes away and the girls retreat to Bella's room, clutching three more champagne bottles. Silence prevails once more.

"I'm going to head back to Cornwall," he announces.

"Already?" The disappointment must be evident in my voice. "I thought we'd have that talk."

Sighing deeply, Sebastian indicates for me to follow him to the lounge. Once there, he closes the door, the atmosphere is tense between us. Sebastian sits in Alan's chair and indicates for me to sit on the sofa, such distance between us tightens the knot in my stomach. *Didn't what we just did get us past this distance?* "Okay. Talk," he says nonchalantly.

"Alright," my back ramrod straight I lock my eyes on his. His mood is difficult to read, his eyes dark and hooded. "We love each other, that's clear." He nods in agreement, the relief I feel is palpable. "The recurring issue between us...is Scarlett."

He lets out a deep sigh. "You've been diagnosed with depression, Elizabeth. How is that Scarlett's fault?"

*Damn it. We go round in a perpetual circle because of that woman.* Trying to quash the impulse to berate her, which will get us nowhere, instead I draw on my inner strength and maintain my poise. "I'm not saying everything's her fault, Sebastian. What I'm saying is that it won't work...*we* won't work if she remains at Penmorrow. It's a simple choice. She goes or you lose me."

"I won't lose you...you and Bella are all I have." He rakes a hand through his dishevelled hair, his jaw tense. "You're mine, Elizabeth, but..."

"But *what* Sebastian? But you won't give her up? Is that what you're saying? I'm yours but she's yours too?"

The lounge door opens, my questions hang in the air. Ruth peers round the door, intuitively she senses the tension and blushes at her intrusion. "Sorry to interrupt but Bella and her friends are heading into town. I thought you'd want to say goodbye."

"I thought they weren't going out until tonight," I query. The raucous gaggle of girls gather in the hall, collecting up bags and fighting for the mirror by the front door to reapply lip gloss. "You can't leave until we've done the cake." In the kitchen I hastily light the eighteen candles on Bella's chocolate frosted cake. It's her favourite and a firm family tradition since the children were small. The candles glow as I begin singing, quickly joined by everyone else, Bella squealing with delight:

*Happy birthday to you,*
*Happy birthday to you,*
*Happy eighteenth birthday, dear Bella...Happy*
*birthday to you.*

With two deep breaths, Bella puffs out the candles to a loud cheer and joyful clapping. The cake is devoured– apparently the girls aren't watching their weight–and the merry party again prepare to leave.

Sebastian hugs Bella affectionately. "Be careful, princess and have a marvellous time." He slips a fifty pound note in her hand. "Don't buy shots with this okay?" He cautions, his frown barely masking his love for her. "It's for a taxi home. I need to know you are safe. Understood?"

"Understood boss man," giggles Bella. "Thanks Seb, you're so cool."

*'Seb?' He'd never let me get away with calling him 'Seb.'* Bella hugs and kisses Ruth and I, her friends follow suit then moments later they leave, tottering down the road in their impossibly high heels, in search of a bus.

Ruth makes a lame excuse about needing milk and leaves Sebastian and I alone in the now tranquil house. Sitting in the lounge, in the same seats as previously the awkwardness returns. "Where did we get to?" My question is futile, Sebastian's aware of what we were discussing but looks reticent to pick up the topic of Scarlett, instead his eyes avoid mine, preferring to focus on an invisible piece of thread on the hem of his shirt, which he's fussing with. "I'll remind you," I sigh, hating that it's again down to me to raise the subject. "You were going to explain why you won't get rid of Scarlett, when I've made it clear it's untenable for me to return while she's at Penmorrow."

Laying his hands in his lap, he finally lifts his gaze to meet mine. He looks so weary and worn down, the sparkle in his dark chocolate eyes has fizzled out. When he speaks, his voice is low and gravelly, "you've made your position clear. I know what I have to do to get you back. You will give me time, though. I will not be dictated to by you, or manipulated, do you understand?" Tilting his rugged chin toward me and pulling back his masculine shoulders, his body language relays a commanding stance—it tells me this is not a man to push any further. He's wound as tightly as a spring and even I know when to back down. This is such a time.

"Yes," I whisper, "I understand. How much time do you think you need?" *Shit Beth, you just can't help pushing.*

"*I* will be the judge of that, Elizabeth. I will call you and let you know when she's gone. The topic is closed to any further discussion." The firm set of his jaw and steely resolve in his eyes are intimidating so it is definitely not wise to push further. My funny, complex, sexy Sebastian is not to be underestimated...he has a dark, edgy facet to his character that has shown itself before. "I'm going to head back to Cornwall now. I'll be in touch."

"You're *leaving* me?" My mouth is laced with the acrid taste of panic, my voice croaky and pathetic but he's standing and certainly looks intent on departing. "Won't you stay with me tonight? *Please?*" Damn him, he's making me beg but I need him so fiercely...need him to reclaim me as his, to take me brutally until I scream his name.

"No. I don't think it's wise. I love you...but I need some time. Lots to sort out." Does he mean that there is a lot to sort out in connection with evicting *that* woman?

"Of course, I understand. I'll wait for you to call me." A lone tear trickles down my cheek, he's noticed it but makes no attempt to wipe it tenderly away–that hurts. It's as though he doesn't care quite as much. "It was good of you to come, I know Bella really appreciates it." The champagne comes to mind. "Would you like to take some champagne home with you?" I ask him. "I'm sure Bella and the girls won't have drunk it all...at least I hope not!"

"Keep it. You and Ruth can have it tonight."

Watching Sebastian drive away kills me, it's as though a piece of my soul has gone. I have no idea when I will hear from him or be in his arms again, but I have to be thankful that he seems to finally be in agreement with getting rid of Scarlett once and for all. I've no proof as to what that evil woman did to my family, or to me...but I know just the way to find out.

# Chapter 12

The police station is a drab grey 1960's unimaginatively constructed building. Situated on a busy arterial road, it wasn't difficult to locate and thankfully there is a parking space available into which I pull, my hands trembling as the engine is cut. Without an appointment, it's possible that DI Chambers won't be available but this couldn't wait. Impetuous as ever, I'd jumped straight in the car after Sebastian left, afraid that if I delayed perhaps I may change my mind.

"Can I help you Miss?" The desk clerk is an aged man with ruddy complexion and kind face, his pale blue uniform shirt lightly crumpled, his pen well chewed.

"May I please see DI Chambers? I understand he's based in this police station."

"Is he expecting you?" he asks, smiling kindly.

"Not exactly," I tell him, " but he gave me his card and said I could get in touch with him any time." My hand pushes the creased business card across the desk, beneath the protective screen separating us. He regards it closely but shakes his head. He tells me that he thinks the senior officer is out but puts through a call to his support staff who confirm that DI Chambers is indeed away for the rest of the day. Damn. Having built up the courage to come, I'm loath to delay what I have set out to do this afternoon. As I deliberate my options, a door is unlocked to my left and a uniformed officer appears, asking if he may help me in his superior's absence. It's not ideal but I accept his invitation to follow him to a private interview room.

Officer 2973 Craig Waters, 'Drip' to his colleagues he tells me with a hint of mirth, is an amiable young man; it may be that I'm getting older but police officers look so young to me these days, as do doctors. He leaves momentarily to fetch me a cup of coffee, having gratefully accepted his offer. The room is miniscule and depressing– I can understand why people confess to crimes in here, merely to escape the confines of this little cell. The only furniture comprises the table at which I am sat, two black plastic chairs, a grey metal filing cabinet and a small corner table on which a wilted pot plant sits dejectedly. In the centre of the table is bolted a voice recording machine and a CCTV camera blinks from the ceiling to my right.

"Here you go, Mrs. Dove." He places the mug on the pre-stained pine table and places a yellow folder in front of him, resting back on his chair with a leg folded across his knee. "I've got your file here. I see DI Chambers has been dealing with you so it's probably better if he speaks to you next week. He's on leave for a few days after today. Unless it's urgent?"

"It *is* urgent. Yes." Fiddling with my watch, a present from Sebastian, my longing for him increases but my intention is clear in my mind...Scarlett is going to be exposed as the murdering manipulator she is. "I want to file a Temporary Restraining Order against someone and I want to do it today."

Sitting forward on his plastic chair now, his eyes lock

with mine–he can't fail to notice the hard determination evident in my expression. "I see. Do you believe your life to be in danger?" He takes a pen and small notebook from the breast pocket of his short-sleeved uniform shirt and opens the page, scribbling something that I can't see.

"I believe a woman has repeatedly drugged or poisoned me with the intent to *kill* me." His expression remains unreadable as he continues making notes. "Furthermore, I believe that the same woman is responsible for the deaths of my husband and son." *And breathe Beth.*

"Uh huh," he doesn't look up from his notebook. "Would you please explain why you think this is so?"

"It's in my notes," I sigh, a little exasperated at the thought of trying to explain the entire story once more and certain that DI Chambers would have recorded Ruth's telephone call in addition to his visit to my home and our conversation. PC Waters excuses himself and, tucking the folder under his arm, leaves me alone once more so that he can telephone DI Chambers and collect the necessary forms. A gentle vibration in my bag alerts me to a text message, hoping that it's Sebastian I hurriedly retrieve it.

***Hey sweet cheeks where are you? X***

Ruth. I should have left a note for her, no wonder she's worried.

***Be back soon. Think there's some champers left –***

***crack open a bottle, I need a drink! X***

I slip my phone back in my bag, resisting the temptation to text Sebastian. My thoughts turn to Bella, hoping she's having a wonderful time in town with her friends, anxious that she's safe and mostly wondering where the years have gone. Joe would have grown into such a handsome young man, he'd have turned eighteen one day, causing me the same worry as my daughter, although it's easier with boys...not the same sort of worries. He'd have gone to university, built a career and had a family of his own. The cold fury builds in me with the contemplation of what Scarlett has taken. She has snatched not only the life of my son but of *his* sons. *Their* sons. Their grandchildren. *Fuck...all the generations she has deprived this world of and for what? To satisfy her own deranged need to gain the love of a man. My man.* Glancing at the palms of my hands, the droplets of blood surprise me. I didn't realise that I had been clenching my fists with such ferocity that my nails had cut my own flesh. Taking a tissue from my bag, I dab at the small wounds relishing the pain...sometimes pain feels good. Pain is what I need to make me feel better. *Explain that to the psychiatrist, Beth, you fruit loop.*

The door opens and PC 'Drip' returns, his stride is more purposeful and he casts me a smile that tells me he no longer thinks I'm crazy. "Okay, Mrs. Dove. I've spoken with DI Chambers and he's in agreement that you proceed with the Temporary Restraining Order. He's also asked that our medic take some blood samples once you've signed the papers. Is that okay?"

Nodding my acceptance, we set to work going through the forms together.

The on-call doctor arrives at five o'clock, nearly two hours after the call is put through for him to attend and take my blood sample. After several texts to and from Ruth, I'm sure there will be little champagne left for me by the time I get home. I badly need a drink. The doctor is friendly enough, dutifully taking two vials of blood and completing his forms; he tells me the results will be phoned through to me as soon as they are available, they won't go through my own doctor. As he picks up his leather attaché case, he turns me and asks, "I just need to check, are you on any medication at the moment?" *Oh crap!* I can't lie but it will be recorded in my notes that I'm on anti-depressants...of course I haven't actually taken a single one.

"Yes. I take anti-depressants, I have them here." The doctor takes the packet from me and writes down the dose and name of the tablets. "Will they show in my bloods?" I enquire, my cheeks flushed with guilt.

"They will yes. It's a full toxicology screen," he replies before departing with a curt nod of his head.

PC 'Drip' shakes my hand firmly at the door. "We'll be in touch Mrs. Dove. As soon as we have any news. The boss is liaising with the police where Scarlett lived previously so we should have a fuller profile of the young lady shortly." He extends a hand and grasps mine firmly.

"Thank you so very much. For listening. For *believing* me."

"It's my job, Mrs. Dove. Don't mention it. You take care now okay. You need to call us if she makes any attempt to contact you or come near you. The TRO will be processed this evening so it's as good as done."

Ruth pours champagne for us both and chats light-heartedly about Bella and her friends, my daughter called during the drive home–she sounded drunk but very happy but now the maternal worry has set in. It's a cool early summer evening, almost cool enough for the central heating, English summers generally live up to expectations of being unpredictable and today is no exception. Cuddled under a fleece blanket with Ruth, sipping champagne with my best friend and knowing that the wheels have been set in motion to bring about the demise of Scarlett and restore my relationship...I feel a sense of peace which has eluded me for a very long time.

"What have you done, Beth?" Ruth could always read me like a book. She has her legs extended over my lap and is trying to steal the blanket. "You seem different. Spill the beans."

"I *did* it Ruth. I went to the police and filed the Restraining Order against Scarlett."

Ruth spits a mouthful of champagne over the blanket, her eyes wide in disbelief. "You did what? Without me?" She reaches for the near empty bottle and tops up her glass before putting the bottle to her lips and draining the last drops. "*Fucking hell,* Beth. You do realise all hell is going to break loose now, don't you?" She shakes her head in admonishment and drains her glass, as do I.

"Yes, sorry," my cheeks flush. "I would have asked you to come but it was a rather last minute decision, when Sebastian left me it just felt my only option to save us. She has to leave if he wants me back, Ruth. Under the terms of the Order, she can't be in the same place as me. I'm not sure how to tell him though ... he's going to be furious initially so it's going to require tact and timing."

"Are you sure you know what you're doing, Beth? He could view it as malicious."

"I'm sure. I'm doing this for Joe and Alan too. And for Bella. Please trust me...I know I've done some crazy things in my life but this is the right thing to do. I *have* to right the mistakes I've made and this is the first step."

Ruth leans forward and embraces me tightly. "Don't be hard on yourself, Beth. Yes you've made some mistakes–some howlers–but the accident wasn't your fault. Anyway, whatever you do, know that your best friend and partner in crime is right alongside you."

The first seeds of doubt sprout forth in my mind. If Sebastian does view this as a malevolent act, it could be the end of our relationship, but then we're screwed if I don't do something–Scarlett will never leave willingly. Sebastian said he would evict her, but then she gets away with murder. No...I have done the right thing as time will tell.

Sleep evades me in spite of the champagne. I can't switch off until I know Bella is home safely. She sent a text message at midnight to say they were having a ball and going onto a third nightclub. The clock beside me glows 02:45 and still she's not home. I tell myself not to worry, with distant memories of my own eighteenth birthday and the worry I caused my parents. Still I feel restless. The mobile phone display is blank, just the time and date blinking at me. My fingers tap out a message to Sebastian.

*Hi darling. I miss you. Can't sleep til Bella's home xxx*

Hitting the 'send' button I can visualise him in bed, his messy hair flopping slightly over an eye, dark shadowed jaw relaxed and his powerful legs on top of the white linen–he always gets so hot in bed. *Hell! He IS hot in bed!*

Letting the phone drop onto the duvet, my fingers travel to my wet folds, circling my throbbing clit in a rhythmic, quickening effort to quench my sexual need for him. The mobile phone vibrates beside me. *Sebastian.* With my available hand I answer the call, my breathing laboured, climax so deliciously close.

"Sebastian," I rasp, maintaining the steady rubbing, my pussy so wet that my fingers glide and slip over my pulsing nub.

"Elizabeth. What are you doing awake at this hour? You need your rest." The deep, sleepy growl of his voice intensifies my arousal still further. All I can do is breathe into the phone like a pervert. "What are you doing?" His words hang expectantly.

"Touching myself...thinking of you."

His breath catches, I hear the rustle of sheets and his breathing quickens. "Is that so?  Well, well my naughty girl. Describe precisely what you are doing." I suspect that he is doing the same as I. He moans into the phone and commands, "*tell* me."

My back arches as I slide one, then two fingers deep into my soaking channel. "Finger fucking myself," I purr.

"I wish it was your cock. Need you. *So* much." Orgasm is moments away, I can feel it building...just one more flick of my clit and I will be lost.

"*Fuck,*" he pants. "I'm. Stroking. My. Cock. Fuck. So hard for you. I'm oozing, baby." His words are my undoing, the orgasm wracks my body from my core the fire sweeps through me, crying out his name as the tremors persist. As I become aware of him once more, he rasps, "good girl. *Oh. Fuck.* Here it comes," and he shouts my name as he finds his own release.

"Sebastian, I miss you," my whispered words are barely audible over his laboured breathing. "I love you and want to be with you."

"Soon darling. We'll be together soon." His voice is husky, in my mind I visualise his arm around my shoulders, my head on his chest listening as his thudding heart settles. "I talked to Scarlett today."

"And? When is she leaving?"

"She's trying to find somewhere, Elizabeth. She's job

hunting. I saw her looking online. You'll be back where you belong shortly...with me at Penmorrow."

"Yes," I whisper. "Where I belong."

We talk for another few minutes, until his voice grows sleepy and he cuts the call. Soon afterwards, I hear a taxi pull up and then the bang of the front door, followed by the unsteady footsteps of my daughter and sleep claims me – Bella is home, all is well.

***

Bored at home, after too much time moping around, Ruth convinces me to go to work. I've missed my colleagues and my little office. It feels good to have a sense of purpose once more but a little disheartening that our business runs so well without me. Everyone is so warm and eager to stop by my office to say hello. Ruth has done an outstanding job of running the business in my long absence, we are exceeding our financial projections; Sebastian will no doubt be delighted that his investment is returning a handsome uplift. Ruth emails him the management accounts each month and he can't fail to be impressed though he rarely mentions it. Glossy brochures on my desk await my attention this morning. New offices have just been released in town – we have long since outgrown the current offices so a move is much needed. Sipping a mug of coffee, I flick through the brochures when my mobile phone rings. "Elizabeth Dove speaking."

"Mrs. Dove, good morning. DI Chambers here. Is it a good time to talk?"

"Yes, yes of course," I stammer, his call taking me by

surprise. "Sorry I just wasn't expecting your call, I thought you were on leave?"

"I am on leave but I wanted to speak to you. We've got some news actually...some rather disturbing news."

# Chapter 13

Chewing the end of a pen impatiently, I await the news wishing DI Chambers would spit it out, whatever it is. "Go on please," I urge.

"The blood results have come back from the lab. That is, in fact, perfectly normal. Just shows fluoxetine which of course corresponds to the anti-depressants that you are taking."

"I see." *Oh my God.* The enormity of this statement hits me squarely in the stomach and knocks the breath from my lungs. I'm aware that I'm gasping for air and can hear the officer saying my name over and over yet I can't speak. Scarlett was lacing my food–there is no other explanation for how the drug is in my blood. I haven't swallowed a single tablet knowingly. *What do I do?...think Beth. Think.*

"Mrs. Dove, whatever is the matter?" His tone is insistent. If I can't talk to him–trust him–who *can* I trust?

Taking a deep breath at last, my voice is calm, "I didn't take the medication. I have never taken a single tablet prescribed for me by the psychiatrist."

There is silence as he considers what I have just told him. When he speaks, confusion is evident in his voice. "I'm sorry, I don't understand," he says gruffly. "You told me, and the police physician, that you have been taking anti-depressants. Are you saying you *lied?*"

"Yes," I murmur shamefully, "I'm afraid I did."

"May I ask why?"

"Because everyone wanted me to take the pills. Nobody believed that I wasn't going mad. I had no choice."

"I think perhaps we should talk face-to-face. Where are you?" He asks. Having given him the address of my office, he tells me he will be here within the hour.

I am in so much trouble. *How do you get yourself in these situations?* I ask myself. *Think. I have to think. Now he knows the truth, the police will arrest Scarlett ... search her room at Penmorrow and uncover a secret stash of pills.* I wonder where she is getting them...perhaps she has a black market supplier. Maybe she has been prescribed them herself. Or is using up an old supply of Libby's. So many questions still unanswered. So much explaining to do.

Someone softly knocks on my office door. "Come in," I call.

The young, pretty secretary who was sent to us by an agency this morning to cover illness, peers around the door. "Sorry to disturb you, Beth. There's a gentleman here to see you. A policeman called DI Chambers."

"Show him in Sandra, and make some coffee please." My mouth is dry, my tongue sticking to the roof of my mouth. Nerves. *I must calm down.* "Thank you for coming," I shake DI Chamber's large abrasive hand and indicate for him to sit on the worn sofa, swivelling my executive leather chair around to face him. This puts me higher than he, giving me the advantage of power according to interview techniques. "I'm sorry to eat into your valuable time off."

"Quite alright, Mrs. Dove," he smiles, placing the familiar yellow folder beside him.

"Elizabeth. Beth. Please."

"Beth. Very good. Now then...you say you haven't been taking any of the medication prescribed for you?"

"No. That's correct. I wanted to appease my family and friends ... let them believe I was getting better by taking the pills. But, deep down, I knew that Scarlett was drugging me somehow. The hallucinations–the paranoia–they were all made worse after she had prepared food or drink for me, you see." He makes notes in a worn old blue notebook. Sandra taps lightly on the door and enters without waiting for a response, placing a tray of coffee cups and plate of chocolate biscuits on my desk. I thank her and she leaves, closing the door behind her. "Please help yourself," I indicate to the refreshments. DI Chambers takes a cup and biscuit, munching noisily as crumbs litter his lap.

"So..." I continue. "I thought that, by coming back to Dorset and away from her, that it would prove what she had done. If my head cleared and the symptoms disappeared, when I knew I wasn't taking the medication, then that would evidence her guilt."

He shoves the last morsel of biscuit in his mouth and reaches for another. "May I?" he asks, the biscuit in his mouth before I can answer.

"Please do," I smile. "The fact that the anti-depressant

has been found in my blood should be evidence enough for you to take this seriously." Leaning forward in my chair, my eyes lock on his, my look imploring and urgent.

"Believe me, Beth, we are taking this seriously or I wouldn't be sat here today. I'd be fishing right now." He spits tiny crumbs of biscuit as he talks.

"I'm sorry. I appreciate it, I really do," I ascent. "You said you had disturbing news. If it wasn't the blood results...what was it?" His initial words only now come back to me.

Brushing crumbs from his lap and crossing his legs, he regards me as only a seasoned police officer who has encountered every possible element of society can do– with professional detachment and trained composure. "What you have just told me adds a new dimension to the case, and we will be acting on the information you have shared. However, what I was more concerned about, Beth, were the findings of the local plods where she used to live, up in Rosthwaite."

"What did they find?" My breath catches, my hands nervously playing with my watch.

"It's taken a while to follow her trail. She changed her name, that's why it's been so difficult. Seems our Scarlett was in fact born Sarah Dorling. Parents, Emily and Frederick Dorling. Look at this..." From the yellow folder, he retrieves a piece of paper and hands it to me. Photocopied onto it is a newspaper cutting. "Read it please."

*'Police launched a murder investigation after a man and woman were found bludgeoned to death in Rosthwaite early this morning. The victims, in their mid 50's, were found in a house Wick Road and pronounced dead at the scene. No formal identification has yet taken place, a post mortem is due to be held later today. Detective Inspector Trevor Morefield, of the murder squad, said: "We are eager to hear from anyone who was near Wick Road, which is close to the Holiday Inn on the South Circular Road, at around 6am on Saturday 27th November. It is possible someone may have seen or heard something suspicious but is unaware of its significance. Any information will be treated in the strictest confidence."'*

The article concludes by listing the telephone numbers for the incident room and Crimestoppers. Handing the paper back to DI Chambers, I note his austere expression. He hands me another sheet of paper, a further newspaper article, this time showing the smiling faces of a middle- aged couple. "That's Frederick and Emily Dorling."

My hands tremble as I clutch the paper and read.

*'Police in Rosthwaite have today issued a statement in connection with the murder of a couple in Wick Road. The victims have been named as 52 year old Frederick Dorling and his 51 year old wife, Emily. The couple were found dead at their home on 27th November*

*having suffered blunt force trauma to their heads. Detective Inspector Trevor Morefield, of the murder squad, said: "We would like to appeal to the public for information on the whereabouts of Sarah Emily Dorling, aged 19. Miss Dorling is wanted in connection with the murders of her parents, Frederick and Emily. Anyone who knows where Sarah Dorling is, or who has seen her in the last seven days should call the incident room immediately. Miss Dorling is not to be approached by the public."'*

A black and white image of a young woman with plump face and close-cropped hair, stares coldly from the paper. Goose bumps prickle my arms, ice courses through my veins as I recognise Scarlett. *"Oh my God."* My eyes meet those of the police inspector whose countenance is dour.

He takes the paper from my shaking hands and slips it into the folder. "Oh my God indeed. It seems that Sarah Dorling has evaded capture for all this time. With a new name, place to live, sheltered life, it's no wonder she wasn't found."

"But Sebastian would have seen the news...he must have recognised her..." My hand covers my mouth, my eyes widen–the officer watches my reaction.

"Lord De Montfort will be questioned later today. He's currently helping police with their enquiries in Exeter." *Oh no! My poor darling. He couldn't have known.*

"Scarlett...?"

"Gone. Officers arrived at Penmorrow just after eight this morning but there was no sign of her. Seems she was planning to move on in any case; officers found evidence of packing in her room but it seems she fled before she had the chance to take anything with her. Very mysterious, it's almost as if she just vanished again."

*"Gone?"*

The officer nodded.

"Are the police searching for her?" *This is all too much to take in. I want to be in Sebastian's arms, to hear him whisper that all is well. Not to worry, darling. Instead my poor, dear love is at a police station. I need to go to him. Now.*

"I have to ask you, Mrs. Dove, can you think of anything that his Lordship may have said, now or in the past, that may indicate that he knew about Miss. Dorling's past?"

"Nothing...no, absolutely not," I reply without hesitation.

"Or anything he may have said to Scarlett–Miss. Dorling–that has seemed at all unusual to you?"

My mind flicks through the plethora of conversations we have had about her. So many arguments, so much said. Then it comes back to me: the distant memory of something I overheard Sebastian say to Scarlett on the phone. *"Scarlett you've done well. You'll be rewarded when I return."* It was after the accident, at the house...Dora and Brian had just left...I remember wondering what he meant at the time but everything was such a blur back then. I wasn't thinking straight. *Could this mean he planned the accident with Scarlett? He wouldn't. He loved Joe. Sebastian is not capable of such wickedness, I know him ... I love him and need him. If I tell the police, what will happen to him ... to Bella and I? I have to trust him. I will ask Sebastian about it and then decide what to do.* "No," I say resolutely. "I can't think of anything."

The officer stares at me, my face flushing a deep hot crimson. "Are you sure about that, Mrs. Dove?" *Why the formality? Why has he stopped calling me Beth? He can see through my lies.*

"I'm sure."

"Very good. If you're certain. We'll be in touch, but in the meantime, I suggest you take precautions with your safety...until she's found, we can't rule out the risk to your wellbeing. If she has already tried to harm you, which would seem the case, then there is no guarantee she doesn't present a continued risk to you."

Fear grips me, I hadn't considered that she may come after me...of course she will. I become aware of a shrill buzzing, DI Chambers retrieves a mobile phone from his trouser pocket and steps out of my office to take the call in private. He returns a few minutes later, his expression unreadable.

"There's been a development. Shoes and a black uniform dress have been found on the beach. Lord De Montfort has identified them as belonging to his maid.

Divers will be deployed there shortly but it would seem that Scarlett–Sarah Dorling–may have taken her own life.

# Chapter 14

The drive to Cornwall seems endless. Ruth was supportive as ever, insisting I leave immediately with an assurance that she will take care of Bella. The sense of urgency leads me to drive too fast, to take risks overtaking where usually I would hold back. Finally I steer the car in to the drive at Penmorrow, relieved at having arrived, nervous of how Sebastian will be with me. Scarlett is gone, for the first time we will be alone together. The police divers continue to scour the coastline but have not found a body. DI Chambers has kept me abreast of the search, he has proven to be a considerate and invaluable confidant.

The front door is unlocked. Stepping into the vast hall at Penmorrow, I set down my overnight bag and inhale the ancient aroma of wood, dust and family secrets that hang in the air. "Hello..." I call out. The only sound is the 'tick, tock, tick, tock,' of the grandfather clock. The setting sun casts shards of light through the stained glass windows, scattering rainbow coloured diamonds across the stone floor. "Sebastian?..." The silence, the aura is ethereal. Sebastian doesn't know I'm coming. Wanting to keep my arrival a surprise I didn't call him–DI Chambers informed me of Sebastian's release without charge. Just 'helping with enquiries' was all that had been required of him. Now, here I stand, alone in this great house. With Scarlett gone, the house feels markedly different...it feels as though a serenity has settled on this grand old lady. The creaks and groans that the house emits are sighs of relief now that the cancer has been cut out. She can rest at last, holding those who live here close to her loving bosom.

Setting my bag down by the grand fireplace, I tread lightly to the kitchen. The fridge is well stocked. I'm loath to admit it, but Scarlett kept a well run home. The oil heats on the hob and the chicken breasts sizzle, filling the kitchen with a delicious aroma–I realise I haven't eaten since this morning's toast, my tummy growls. The clock on the wall above the range reads seven fifty-five. *Where is Sebastian?* He hasn't answered my call nor replied to my text messages and anxiety is gnawing away at my gut. *Where the hell are you? Are you okay?*

The chicken pasta bake has been sitting on the table for almost an hour when I hear the heavy thud of the oak front door. Placing my near empty glass of red wine on the table, I pivot on the old wooden church pew and glance at the doorway. Sebastian stands, leaning against the door frame, he rakes a hand through his dishevelled hair and smiles. His eyes are encircled with dark grey rings, his stubble giving him an unkempt appearance.

"Hi," I say.

"Hi." He saunters toward me, his deportment belying his evident fatigue. A hand reaches out toward me, his fingers stroke my hair which hangs loose and tousled down my back. "You came...and you cooked," he observes, his lips forming a half smile.

"Yes. I thought you'd be hungry...and I needed to be

with you," my neck cranes as I look up at him, our eyes locking with shared misery.

His hand grasps my hair more firmly, he uses it as an anchor with which to tug my head against his firm stomach as he stands before me. I breathe in his masculine scent of sandalwood and him, the buttons of his shirt press into my face, my arms encircle his waist, my hands stroking his lower back. He shudders in my grasp. At first, I wonder if he is cold but the shudders become stronger...*dear God, he's crying.*

"My poor darling," standing abruptly, my body turning, I kneel on the pew, leaning over its back, and embrace my poor, broken man. His body heaves as he sobs and all I can do is stroke his back and whisper my love for him. His tears soak my neck and break my heart. When his emotions are spent, he pulls back and rubs his eyes with his clenched fists.

"Sorry," he croaks. "Just...fuck it, I *loved* that crazy fucking woman."

"I know you did," I whisper, his words cutting deep as a knife. "She loved you, too."

"Not in the way you think," he rakes his hand through his hair again, sniffing back the tears which threaten to spill once more. "I was always her...master...her friend...her protector. But, in the end, I didn't protect her. *Fuck, Elizabeth. Fuck. Fuck. Fuck.*" A clenched fist thuds down on the table, causing the plates and cutlery to rattle and my body to tense.

"There was nothing you could do," I soothe. "Where

have you been? You were released hours ago."

"On the beach. I've been walking...up and down the beach...again and again...calling her...looking for her. She just walked out to sea, Elizabeth. Just walked out into the dark, cold ocean and let it claim her."

"Have they found her, darling?" My hand rests on his arm, stroking, comforting.

"No. The police diver said the tide has probably washed her along the coast. They questioned me, Elizabeth. They seemed to think that she isn't...*Scarlett.* That she is someone else–Sarah someone. I'd have known. Wouldn't I have *known?*" His question hangs in the air unanswered.

"Sebastian..." I have to ask him the question which has been eating at me since my earlier conversation with DI Chambers. He looks down at me but his eyes are hooded, glazed; it's as though he doesn't see me. "I want you to listen to me and answer me truthfully. If you do that, then I am here with you one hundred percent, but only if you tell me the truth. No matter what 'the *truth*' is. Okay?"

"The truth. Yes." His voice is robotic, devoid of emotion.

"When Joe and Alan died, I overheard you on the phone to Scarlett. You said to her "you've done well, you'll be rewarded." What did you mean Sebastian? I want the truth. What did you mean?"

He sighs and wipes a hand across his face. "*Shit.* Is that what's important to you?" he asks incredulously, his eyes locked on mine. "Do you want to know what I was thanking her for? I was thanking her for arranging a fucking bouquet of flowers for *you.* Do you remember the lilies that arrived? Who the hell do you think ordered those, when I was supporting you through the hardest fucking time of your life? *Fuck!* What did you think I was thanking her for?" He backs away from me–his lip curled in a cruel sneer. *I'm losing him.*

"*No!*" The word emits as a shout that gets Sebastian's attention. "I didn't tell the police. I didn't believe that you were a party to the accident. I trusted you–I do trust you– and now you have to trust *me.*" Moving quickly, I walk around to him and gather him in my arms–his body is rigid against my embrace. "It's over, Sebastian. Don't you see? We've got each other...we *love* each other and, hell, they say love conquers all..." He relaxes into my arms, my fingers raking through his hair as he buries his face in my neck, sobbing once more. "It's okay," I soothe. "I'm here and we'll get through this together." It breaks my heart to feel my strong man cry like a baby, to feel his hot tears, his loss, his confusion. I rock him gently until his body is still.

"Take me to bed." Before he can answer, I take his hand and lead him from the kitchen–he follows, his eyes lowered, his dear face red and blotchy.

Closing the bedroom door I lead him to the bed where he sits compliantly...so unlike my dominant, confident lover. He watches by the fading light as my clothes slip to the floor forming a puddle at my feet. His eyes darken, his breathing quickens. Taking his hand once more, I pull him to standing using all my strength to raise his leaden body. Silently, I strip him...he allows me to do so, but offers no assistance. When we are both stood facing each other, naked, my hands gently caress his chest, snaking about his neck I bring his head down, his lips meeting mine in a bruising assault. He reaches a tentative hand to my hip, I step into him, his hardness pressing against my belly, grinding into him still further. His hand grips my hip so painfully that I bite down on his bottom lip as his fingers dig into my flesh, sharp and unrelenting. The taste of blood–metallic and warm–flows onto my tongue as our kiss deepens, raw and carnal. His hands grasp my buttocks, pulling me against his erection, grinding it into me in a rhythmic motion. "*Mine,*" he growls into my mouth as a hand slides up to my throat, encircling my neck, the pressure enough to make me gasp. "You. Are. Fucking. *Mine.*"

"Yes...I'm yours, darling. Always yours." He steps back a pace, his molten eyes drinking me in from head to toe. He swipes at his bleeding lip with the back of his hand, looks down at the blood and back at me, our eyes locking, mine reflecting his primal need. His mouth and hand smeared with his blood adds to our visceral desire, he shakes his head as his tongue licks at his bleeding lip. I don't see his hand lash out but feel the sting of his palm on my cheek as he slaps me. The pain feels good. I want him to do it again, feeling a warm gush between my legs as my core tightens. His hand withdraws and hovers near my face.

"*Do it,*" I goad. "Fucking *do it.*"

He hesitates, sucking on his wounded lip, his eyes hooded, his hand elevated beside my cheek. "What the fuck's happened to us?" He drops his hand by his side and stands limp and lost. "When did we start abusing each other?"

"*No!*" I cry. "Not abuse. We have to get this out. Both been through so much. It's passion...not abuse." My hand reaches out and strokes his face, he flinches at my touch. "Don't, Sebastian. Don't shut me out." He catches my hand and lifts it to his face, kissing my palm.

"I'm sorry," he chokes. "What's happened to me?" He pulls me into his strong embrace, the heat of his firm body heightening my arousal once more. "Come." He turns me so that the backs of my legs are against the bed. With a firm but tender push, he has me on the bed, his weight pressing into me. His knee parts my legs, spreading me wide, his hands pinning my arms above my head. The silky head of his cock spears me - with one hard thrust he drives it in to its root filling me so completely that I scream his name. His grip on my wrists tightens, his eyes never leaving mine as he drills me, withdrawing and thrusting into me over and over, my legs encircle his waist, heels digging into his back.

My core tightens around his hardness as the first tremors of pleasure build within. "You're so fucking *wet,*" he hisses releasing my wrist to trail his fingers to my dripping pussy. The rub of his thumb on my pulsating clitoris drives me over the edge as the first wave of orgasms crashes through my body. Screaming his name, my back arched I am lost to him, aware only of the crescendo within myself. His assault on my bud continues until the pleasure becomes unbearable.

"Stop. No more," I pant. "*Please*...no more." His hand moves from my soaked folds, trailing my juices up my stomach, over a nipple and to my throat where he pinions me. His face a mask of torment, of dark abandon he spits my name from his lips as he succumbs to his own climax. I can't breathe, panic rising–my hand tugs at his fingers about my neck, prizing them from their unyielding grip, my body twisting and bucking under his weight. He snaps back, releasing my throat. I gasp for air, panic subsiding. "Sorry. Oh God I'm *sorry*." He rolls off me, collapsing on his side and curling into a foetal ball, his arms clutching his knees.

"What the hell happened? *Sebastian?*" He's trembling uncontrollably. "Shit. It's okay. I'm okay." Tears roll down my cheeks at the sight of my broken, damaged love. Pulling the duvet up, I tuck it around him, sliding my body against his back, my arms enfolding him. Keeping him warm. Calming him. His body stills once more, his hand grips my arm and pulls me tightly to him.

"I don't know what that was," he whispers. "So sorry. Love you...*so* sorry." I soothe and stroke him until his breathing grows more shallow and his limbs relax. Sebastian is asleep. Closing my eyes, I wait for sleep to claim me too–willing it to come.

Moonlight finds its way through a chink in the curtain, casting a blue white glow across the bed. Sebastian's leg rests on my hip, we're both hot, sweaty. He's deeply asleep and I'm still awake but my eyelids are growing heavy, sleep is finally enveloping me in its comforting arms.

The shadow moves so slowly that, at first, it seems that it is not moving at all. Rubbing the onset of sleep from my tired eyes, then repeatedly blinking helps to clear my vision. The shape of the armoire, chest of draws, the mirror–all as they should be , nothing unusual–back to the armoire, a colossal wardrobe housing the dresses chosen for me by Scarlett. I wonder how she felt, forced to shop for an adversary who had stolen her true love's heart, how painful that would have been for her. The inky outline of the armoire stretches and then I realise it's another shape: the shape of a woman.

"*Sebastian!*" Shouting his name I reach to the bedside lamp, flicking on the switch with urgency–the soft yellow light banishing the shadows, my eyes blinking as they adjust to the light. He jerks and sits up, rubbing his eyes with his fists.

"What...the *fuck?*" He looks around the room then turns to me, his eyes wide and questioning. "What is it?"

"Scarlett...oh my God. *Scarlett* was here." My trembling arms grip my knees, my eyes dart about the room for a sign of her but find nothing amiss.

"Scarlett's dead, Elizabeth. She's gone." He sighs deeply, gathers me to him and holds me, stroking my hair.

"It was a nightmare, darling, just a nightmare." I know that he's right. I was falling asleep, the mind plays tricks in that half-sleep state.

"Could it be her ghost?" I whisper into his warm skin.

"No darling, no ghosts. You're exhausted and you need to sleep." His finger strokes my shoulder, his lips kiss my hair. "Did you take your medication tonight Elizabeth?"

"My pill?" *Oh my pill! When do I tell him?* "No darling, I didn't take it."

His finger stops stroking, he stiffens against me. "I'll fetch you a glass of water, you can take it now." Pulling away, he throws his legs over the side of the bed and pads over to the chaise where his black silk robe lies folded. He slips it on and loosely ties the belt. My eyes rove over his taught body, he looks so damn sexy. I'd rather he ravish me than enter into another difficult conversation but there is never going to be a good time to talk about this; it's better to get it all out now so that we can put it behind us and live our lives together in peace. *How we need some peace.*

Sebastian returns with a glass of water and my bag. "Sorry we didn't eat the dinner you cooked. It looked delicious," he mutters as he hands me the glass and places the bag on the bed beside me.

"It will keep," I reply, my tummy grumbling at the reminder of its starvation. "I need to talk to you, love."

He removes his robe and struts in all his masculine glory back to the bed, sliding under the duvet. "Can't we sleep? It's nearly 2am."

"No, Sebastian. This can't wait. I know it's probably not the right time at all to discuss this...but there likely never will be a good time." I have his attention, he sits up and plumps his pillows, resting back against them, his arms folded defensively. "I have not taken a *single* tablet prescribed by Dr. Fairfax."

He sucks in a sharp breath and spears his hair with his fingers.

"The reason that I chose not to was my utter conviction that Scarlett was drugging me." I cast a glance at his face, he's looking straight ahead avoiding eye contact, his jaw is set, his lips a poker straight line.

"Go on ... this had better be good, sweetheart," he spits.

"You all wanted me to take the medication. I know you all meant well–had my best interests at heart–but ultimately you all believed I was mad with grief, and you all wanted to believe that a little pill would cure me. Who was *I* to counter that? I wasn't in my right mind, it's true...but I was aware enough to know it didn't feel like grief or depression. I'm not denying they probably both factor in my screwed head somewhere, but this was *different*. The hallucinations, the paranoia came on so suddenly, it was like I became a different person entirely, do you *see?*" He strokes his square jaw with the palm of his hand and nods sadly for me to continue.

"So I told you all what you wanted to hear...I was taking the pills and feeling better. In fact I truly was feeling better, but not because of the medication. That confirmed to me that there really was a connection between my symptoms and here. In Dorset my head started to clear, the fog lifted and the hallucinations stopped."

He shifts and turns, his eyes finally meeting mine. "No, Elizabeth...that tells me that the moment you were away from *me* the depression lifted." His brow arches as he awaits my counter.

"Not at all. You are my soulmate, Sebastian. I'm clear on that now. Please, let me finish. After you left me, on Bella's birthday, I went to the police station and filed a Temporary Restraining Order against Scarlett..."

His eyes darken and look away from me.

"I did this so that we could be together...to force her hand, if you like, to move out of here. I also had blood taken, to test for toxins and traces of poison or drugs."

He rakes his hair again, shaking his head forlornly. "*Fuck!*"

"Fuck indeed," I sigh. "The results showed anti-depressants in my blood–fluoxetine. Do you realise what this means?"

His hand drops to his side, his eyes widen, "it means...but how could your blood show that? You weren't taking...oh Christ. *Oh God no.*"

Laying my hand gently on his arm, I nod in confirmation. "It means Scarlett was lacing my food or drink with the drug, and in large quantities apparently. I know this is painful for you but you need to know this about her–to see the full picture. You have to know that it wasn't me, Sebastian. The woman was sick in the head...very sick. Sebastian...she *murdered* her parents."

His face is contorted with pain, he lets out a low fierce growl and leaps from the bed. He begins pacing the floor like a wild tiger, his eyes narrow, his teeth bared. "Is this true?" he hisses. "All these...fucking years...I've been living with–loving, protecting–A FUCKING MURDERING, LYING, EVIL *BITCH?*"

Sliding from the bed, I tentatively approach him, scared to get too close in case he lashes out. I have never seen him this enraged–this savage–like a feral cat. "She was sick, Sebastian. I honestly believe that she didn't know what she was doing. How could she? How could a woman hold so much malice and hatred and not be extremely ill?"

He stops pacing and stands before me, puzzled and desperate. "Why? Why did she kill her parents? She told me so many lies about them..."

"DI Chambers has been liaising with the police who dealt with the case. It seems her father was abusive, used to beat the living shit out of her. Her mother, by all accounts, did nothing to stop him. Who knows why she did what she did in the end–perhaps she just snapped that day. Maybe she suffered one beating too many."

He considers what I say, his brow furrowed. "What drives a person to do that? When I think back...my own Mother...how she used to beat me, and yet I could *never* have lifted a hand or a fist to her."

"You've never really talked about her, Sebastian." I stroke the silver flecks of hair at his temples. "Would it help to talk?"

He stiffens, his mouth set in a stern line. "Nothing to tell," he mutters gruffly. "She used to drink too much and beat the crap out of me. I used to dread coming home from school for the holidays...and then dread going back to school wearing her bruises. In Mother's social circle, one didn't talk about such things. Discipline was an everyday expectation of our class. I loved her though, Elizabeth. Fuck knows why, but I did." He rubs at the back of his neck as if massaging the tension away. "I think that's why I took pity on Scarlett; she said she'd left home because of her father's cruelty. It felt like we were kindred spirits in that regard." He chuckles, "isn't it bizarre that two people who have been abused, both enter adulthood with an inherent fascination with pain."

"Not so strange, darling. It's what you both knew...what you both understood." My hand replaces his, rubbing the back of his neck. He's so tense.

"How she thrived on pain," he continues. "I've seen her. She craved the lashes, the bite of..." He lets the sentence hang unspoken but I know what he is telling me. I have always known in my heart. He sees the pain in my eyes, his face crumples and he weeps into his hands. "*Oh God!* All those times, Elizabeth. All those times she begged me to do it–and for what?"

I take his hands in mine and stoop, looking up into his sorrowful eyes. "We will never know. Listen to me.

Perhaps it was her way of taking the punishment her father would have given her...of atoning for what she did to them.   We don't know and never will." My thumb wipes a stray tear from his cheek. "It was in the past, Sebastian. I know you didn't love her as you do me."

"*Never,*" he rasps. "It was at a time when I was out of my mind.  I'd watched Libby get so sick. Oh Fuck. *Libby.* Does this mean...did Scarlett?"

# Chapter 15

Pausing to take a deep breath, my palm strokes his temple as I gently nod. "Probably, darling, yes."

"Oh fuck, *no*. My poor darling Libby ..." he sobs in my arms, the world he knows suddenly spinning wildly on its axis. "She took her. *She fucking stole Libby*...and she nearly took you too."

"Look at me, Sebastian." My hand tilts his chin so that his hooded blood-shot eyes meet my intense stare. "It's over. We have each other. We. Are. A. *Family.* You have me and you have Bella. She has *NOT* won. Do you understand?"

He wipes spittle from his chin and sniffs, shoving his broad shoulders back, he nods. "It's over. Thank God for you, Elizabeth...my wilful, disobedient, deceitful girl. Love of my life." He steps back a pace and throws me a sideways glance, his eyes narrowed, a small smile playing on his lips. "Not a single tablet, huh?"

Shrugging my shoulders, shaking my head I confirm, "nope. Not a single one." My brow forms a defiant, mischievous arch matching his.

In a heartbeat he has me on the bed. The weight of his taut body, pressing down upon me, my nails raking his back as he claims me as his. He makes love to me–possessive, powerful–taking back what is his own, stamping his ownership, marking his territory. After, as we lie recumbent in his vast bed, sleep comes to us both and I feel an inner peace so alien that it is almost unearthly. It's as though the angels have taken the badness, the evil and replaced it with all that is good–love and acceptance.

*\*\*\**

Three days have passed and police have yet to retrieve Scarlett's body from the ocean. DI Chambers advised us that there will imminently be an inquest, and it could take several years before a death certificate is issued if her body isn't found. She has left a small estate – money from the sale of her parents' house, an inheritance which she apparently never touched. Sebastian continues to wander the beach, aimlessly walking back and forth, saying he needs to see her corpse for closure. The divers have stopped looking, one told Sebastian that Scarlett may have drifted hundreds of kilometres, though more likely she will wash up along the Cornish coastline eventually. He told me that he asked the diver if Scarlett would be recognisable – the diver advised that after a few days she would decompose. I had a dream that night, that she was hooked by a fisherman and hauled aboard the trawler, her lips and eyes had been eaten by crabs and fish.

This morning is spectacular. The sun is already high in the clear blue sky, it promises to be a sublime summer day. Bella has decided to stay in Dorset, I imagine this to be a consequence of Ruth giving us time alone as she is kindly staying at the house with her. My mother is arriving on the train this afternoon. No amount of reassurance has prevented her from coming, insisting she won't believe that I am safe until she sees me. This morning, however, right this moment, is about Sebastian and I having fun–helping us to forget–if just for a moment. He has been exceedingly mysterious since waking me a little after dawn. He seemed as excited as a school boy as he led me across the yard behind Penmorrow, in our robes and wellington boots.

"Tell me," I giggled. "What have you *done?*"

He took my hand firmly and led on until we reached the stables, stopping as we reached the far box. With a dramatic sweep of his hand, he introduced me to ... the most spectacular horse I had ever seen.   "Darling, meet Brutus. Brutus, old boy, this woman is not to be messed with," he winked at the horse and I swear it winked right back as it snorted loudly through its flared nostrils.

"You bought another horse?" My hand stroked the horse's velvet nose, he was a beauty. He reminded me so much of Sebastian–wild, untamed, strong. "What about Zariya? Won't she feel abandoned?"

"No because I am entrusting her to you." He beamed with joy as he stood, hands on hips, admiring his new acquisition.

"Sebastian," I gasped, "the last time I rode her, she threw me off and I ended up in hospital," I reminded him, incredulous.

"Which is precisely why you need to get back in the saddle, Elizabeth Dove. Come. We will ride together after breakfast." He took my hand firmly in his and strutted back to the house with a firm determination and glint in his eye.

So now, here we are. He looks like a model from *Horse and Hounds*, resplendent upon his new steed, while I sit, a quivering mess, upon the beast with a death wish—my death.

"Don't let her know you're scared," he'd warned me as I mounted. "Horses are intuitive: you need to let her know who's boss." So I squeeze my heels into her flank to remind her of her lowly status and, too late, recall that this is a sign to walk on.

Sebastian's laughter can be heard behind me, damn that man. He trots alongside me, all confidence and pride, his jaw squarely jutting forward as he controls Brutus as if he and the horse are conjoined, while I cling to the reins of Zariya, as though my life depends on it.

"Race you to my tree," he quips, the challenge clear on his roguish face. "Last one there strips naked!" And off he canters, knowing very well that the most I will risk is a rising trot.

When a frustrated Zariya, carrying her sulking mount, arrives at the tree, Sebastian is lying on the long grass, his back resting against the expansive trunk of the ancient oak. He's chewing on a long blade of grass, his lips forming a perfectly satisfied smirk. "*Ah*...if it isn't Elizabeth," he grins. "I need to get that horse seen to—seems she's not running at full speed. Perhaps we're putting the wrong fuel in her...or maybe it's simply a case of bad driving."

"*Piss off*, you cheating son-of-a-bitch."

He cocks an eyebrow in response to the expletives that I fire at him. "*Really?*" he growls in return. "Take your clothes off like a good loser and come here and say that."

Stifling a giggle, I shake my head. "*Make me,*" I challenge.

He stands and languidly stretches, the blade of grass still gripped between his teeth, his eyes are dark as coal, narrowed, boring into mine. Having tethered the horses to a sapling, he slowly walks toward me, taking the blade of grass and casting it aside. His hips sway, black riding jodhpurs slung low, his hair messy where he's removed his protective skull cap. He is smouldering hot.

"Clothes. Off. *Now,*" he commands, grinning devilishly, clearly savouring my dare. "Elizabeth, either you be a good little loser, or I take you over my knee and give you a short, sharp lesson in sports etiquette–either way you get naked. Choice is yours."

"Fine," I giggle, "I take option two." My core clenches, my panties dampen.

He is close enough to grab me. I feel his hot breath panting against my face. Instinctively, my hands reach up to the chin strap, releasing the clasp and slipping the skull cap from my head, freeing my hair which tumbles over my shoulders. His breath catches.

"Fuck, you look sexy like that," his eyes roam hungrily down my body and rest on the knee-high black riding boots, before travelling up and settling on my breasts which heave beneath my tee shirt. "*Off.* All of it."

Compliant and driven by raw need for him, within a moment I have shrugged off my tee-shirt and bra, naked from the waist up. Holding a boot toward Sebastian, he clutches the heel and tugs it from my foot so sharply that I lose my balance, falling heavily on my arse. He's upon me in an instant, his mouth covering a nipple, he lathes and sucks on the sensitive bud.

My fingers fumble at the button on his jodhpurs as his more deftly undo mine, pushing them down past my hips. He sweeps my hand away from his fly and rocks back, resting on his heels. Maintaining eye contact, he slowly but purposefully frees his button and unzips his fly. Reaching inside his boxer shorts, he frees his erection – it's gloriously hard, the prominent vein throbbing along its length, the crown shining in the sunlight, a single dewy drop glinting like a tiny diamond of the tip of his cock. He towers majestic and masterful above me, my teeth bite down on my bottom lip.

"Don't bite your lip, Elizabeth," he warns, his voice a deep rumble.

My tongue licks across my top lip, my teeth clamp down on my lip once more, my eyebrow arched in defiance. With a sudden fluid motion he has me locked in a firm hold, his powerful arms heaving me supine across his lap, my face in the grass, daisies tickling my nose, my legs thrashing and arms flailing. He anchors me with a muscular forearm across my shoulder blades.

"Stay still," he barks. "You chose option two, so take it like a good girl."

"Sebastian! Get *off* me, you bully!"

He has me held firm, my buttocks feel the cool rush of air as he exposes them with a downward tug to my panties. "Don't threaten the big boys, unless you can take what's coming to you," he laughs, his hand tenderly massaging my right buttock. *Thwack!* His palm slaps against my skin–it smarts but he's holding back, capable of more. Again he rubs, extinguishing the sting. *Thwack!* Harder this time, surprise forcing a shrill laugh from my throat. "How many do we think is reasonable, darling?" he asks playfully. "Or shall I just continue until we see a rosy glow on these wonderful white peaches?" He massages and kneads my cheek, again dulling the soreness, immediately following the tenderness with a biting slap.

"Three!" I whine, "three is enough." It isn't enough– for either of us. The humiliation of being spanked in the open air is making my nipples harden and my juices flow, my thighs now wet with my arousal. The fourth slap is the hardest yet...the fifth is harder still...the sixth ceases to hurt as endorphins flood my body and by the tenth slap, I'm purring like a kitten, squirming in his lap.

"Good girl," he soothes, his hands firmly stroking the inflamed flesh. "Your arse is bright red–you're going to bruise." He flips me over and gathers me into his arms, kissing the top of my head protectively.

"I'll wear your bruises with pride," I murmur with sincerity. "I'm going to be a better submissive to you," I declare.

His rigid cock presses against my stomach, leaving a trace of his arousal in my belly button. "You are learning, darling. It just takes time, though you could start by wearing the choker I gave you, and demonstrate a little more respect." His smirking lips meet mine in a passionate kiss. His tongue spears my mouth and entwines with mine as he softly lays me on the grass. Breaking off the kiss, he removes my remaining boot and slides my jodhpurs and panties down my legs. I kick them off and wrap my legs about his waist, pulling his huge frame down onto me.

"I need you," I pant, the ache in my pussy becoming unbearable.

With his hand, he positions the crown of his solid cock at the very centre of my wetness and, with one hard thrust, slides inside me. His huge manhood fills me completely, each thrust rocking against the delicate spot deep within me, my hips rising to take all of him. So our rhythmic love-making continues–each whispering the others' name, aware of the birds chirping in the trees and the warm breeze whipping locks of hair across my face. When we climax, it is in unison–the perfect joining of two people in love, in harmony with each other–our act as fundamental as the nature that surrounds us.

Sebastian forms a mounting block with his steepled hands and hoists me into the saddle with ease. The ride home is unhurried, the horses seemingly in tune with our own relaxed pace. I shift in the saddle repeatedly - saddle sore, not because of the horse riding but by the hand of my dominant man and his twitchy palm.

Penmorrow has never looked so beautiful as it does today, from the top of the hill. The sun's rays cast a golden hue to the old stonework and shimmer on the windows; it looks like a golden treasure chest speckled with diamonds. To my right, the ocean stretches away to the horizon...white horses charging on a sea of glittering violet, the warm breeze carrying the taste of salt to my lips. Invigorated, I use the flick of my crop on Zariya's flank to quicken her pace. Sebastian looks aghast as the mare picks up a canter. Brutus, being the alpha male of the equine world, is clearly put out by Zariya's lead, carrying Sebastian home at a gallop.

Once home, we flop exhausted onto the sofa in the morning room, relaxing with the daily newspapers and steaming mugs of coffee, Sebastian still chuckling at my unexpected confidence on his mare. This is the most relaxed we have ever felt in each others' company. *It feels wonderful.*

Sebastian has collected Mother from the station, his Land Rover crunching over the gravel as they arrive home.

"Mum!" She's barely stepped from the car when I sweep her into a tight embrace. "You see–I'm in one piece. There really was nothing to worry about."

"So I see, love," she hugs me back and nothing feels as good as Mum's cuddles. I breathe in the familiar sweet smell of 'Youth Dew' perfume and hairspray, feeling safe in her loving arms. "You need to fill me in on everything,

Beth...and I mean everything."

Sebastian takes Mother's suitcase and strides on into the house while she and I saunter behind. I show her to her room, where Sebastian has already placed her case on the plush cream carpet. We have decided that Mother should stay in the farthest guest room–rarely used–so that we retain some privacy during her stay. It's small, but a delightful sunny room decorated with pretty pale pink and sage green floral wallpaper with complementing sage green silk curtains. Libby clearly had a flair for interior design, her eye for detail is exemplary, from the accent cushions on the bed, to the pastel-coloured watercolours on the walls; it has a romantic and typically 'old English' charm. Mum beams in delight as she surveys her room, I fear we will never get her to leave.

"Come on, Mum," taking her hand, I manage to prize her from the bedroom and follow me to the kitchen where Sebastian is making a start on dinner.

"Very domesticated, I approve," Mum giggles at the sight of Sebastian wearing Scarlett's apron tied around his waist. "Don't tell me he cooks too?" she sighs. "It's downright unlawful how someone with those looks is good at so much."

"*Mother!*" I admonish, smirking with hands on hips, "are you flirting with my man?"

"You flirt all you like, darling," Sebastian winks. "You have *exceptional* taste."

"Arrogant twerp," I laugh.

Mother hugs him and rocks up on tiptoes to kiss his

cheek. "God bless you for taking care of Beth for me," she whispers.

Sebastian blushes and sweeps her off the floor with one of his growling bear hugs. Sebastian hands me the apron and opens a bottle of chilled white wine, I pick up where he left off peeling prawns for a paella.

Over a delicious dinner, Sebastian and I have updated Mum on the entire events leading up to Scarlett's suicide.

At times she was distressed, she had many questions for us both, some we could answer, others we could not, but always we were open and truthful with her. By the time we have finished, it is after ten o'clock. Mother yawns and bids us goodnight. We switch off the downstairs lights and follow her up.

The house is so silent, at night this seems accentuated. The house makes its own noises and creaks but the stillness is new. Scarlett was a strong personality within the building and her absence renders it almost empty. I still refer to her as Scarlett...can't seem to think of her as 'Sarah.' Not that we talk about her all the time. I try not to raise the subject for fear of upsetting the equilibrium here. Today is the first that Sebastian has not roamed the beach for her; that is a good sign that he's coming to terms with his loss.

Snuggling with Sebastian in bed, sleep claims us both swiftly, we are both tired but more content than we have been for a very long time.

Mother is an early riser. She's cooked a full English breakfast and called us downstairs even before the grandfather clock strikes eight. Sebastian helps himself to bacon, fried eggs, sausage and black pudding–his eyes wide with greed at the feast before him. I decide upon toast and bacon, mindful of my figure. Although I have lost a great deal of weight over the past few months, I'd like to stay svelte.

"Did you sleep well, Mum?" I enquire, spreading butter thinly on the wholemeal toast.

She yawns in response. "I did dear, thank you, although you woke me when you came in. What were you looking for, Beth?"

# Chapter 16

The hairs prickle on the back of my neck. Sebastian's fork halts short of his mouth, his eyes darting to mine.

"What do you mean, Mum? I didn't come in your room last night. What time was this?"

She spears a piece of sausage and says nonchalantly, "oh I don't know, it was before sunrise, still dark. Perhaps I was dreaming–yes, that must be it, dear."

"What did you see?" The trepidation in my voice leads Sebastian to lay a hand on my knee to calm me.

"I didn't see anyone, Beth. It was dark." She chews another chunk of sausage.

"Okay. You didn't see anyone, but you thought it was me...so what made you *think* that?" I'm growing impatient with her.

"I was drifting–don't think I was fully awake, if you know what I mean–and you opened my door and came in. Or perhaps I imagined it, I'm an old lady now, we start going bonkers at my age, you know."

"No, Mum. I didn't come in your room. Sebastian, did you go in Mum's room last night?"

He shakes his head, shrugs his shoulders and mops some egg with a piece of bread. "This old pile is full of shadows, ladies. Let's not get carried away with the old 'haunted house' codswallop."

"No. Quite," agrees Mother. The subject is dropped, but I'm left with a feeling of unease that I can't shrug off.

\*\*\*

I drive Mother around the villages and hamlets scattered along the North Cornish coast. It's ironic that, as a child, my parents would bring me here for holidays. My favourite holidays were spent on a farm near Tintagel, the farmer would take me to see his lambs at sunrise. I wore a bright yellow knitted sweater that the farmer said would cheer up his sheep on a wet summer's day. Mother used to say I stank of sheep plop but I'd never let her wash that sweater. It was my 'special lambing sunshine sweater'. We'd watch the May Pole dancing in early May half term holidays, and return in August to bathe in the rock pools, Dad and I catching crabs in my plastic bucket. In later years, Alan and I had brought the children on holiday. We'd called in at the farm, but Mr Lethbridge – or Old

*Leather Breeches*–as Dad called him–had died and the new farmers weren't offering bed and breakfast any more. Such wonderful memories I still cherish though, and now here I am, a grown woman bringing Mum back to those same places. *Life goes full circle,* I reflect with a smile.

We call in at Padstow on our way home and buy Cornish Pasties, sat on the bench overlooking the harbour, devouring the warm, flaky pastries. We watch the fishermen haul their catches from their boats and inhale the fresh salty air. On the drive home to Penmorrow, we talk about Mum. I realise, with great shame, how infrequently I ask her about her life, her health or her dreams. It's been a precious day together and I make a mental note to try to be a better daughter to her.

There is a car parked on the driveway that I don't recognise. Pulling up beside it, I help Mum from the car and hurry inside to see who is visiting. Hearing voices from Sebastian's study, I tap lightly on the door and enter. Sebastian is talking to a smart gentleman of advancing years, who sips at a cup of tea.

"Ah, Elizabeth. Come in," he stands politely as I enter, ushering me to a vacant chair beside the stranger. "I'd like you to meet Jeremy Simpson."

Mr. Simpson extends a hand and shakes mine firmly. "Pleased to meet you," he says.

"Mr. Simpson is a Coroner, darling. He's going to be hearing Scarlett's inquest and wishes me to attend as a witness."

"I see," I reply, rather taken by surprise at this revelation. "What does that involve?"

"Lord De Montfort will be required to attend the inquest and give evidence relating to the death of Sarah Dorling; this is very much standard procedure in the circumstances."

"When will the inquest take place?" I play nervously with my watch, the thought of Sebastian being caught up in the inquest, and the unease at him being away, are causing a knot to form in my stomach.

Sebastian casts me a reassuring smile.

"We intend to crack on with this as a matter of some urgency," he huffs. "No point in delaying, I know the police would like to see this tied up. They are keen to close the case on this most unfortunate young lady.

Seems there has been considerable police input over the years at great expense to the public purse, you understand."

"Will you need me to attend?" The thought fills me with dread.

The Coroner shakes his head. "Not likely. If necessary we can take a statement from you, but you weren't here at the time of her suicide. That's been corroborated by a DI Chambers of Dorset Police."

Sebastian shows the Coroner out, with his promise to be in touch with an imminent date, hanging in the air.

The Coroner's clerk calls the next morning. The inquest will begin the day after tomorrow. They are already in receipt of the police documentation and don't require a witness statement from me. This is a huge relief. Sebastian will go alone and stay overnight as we have no idea how long the inquest will last. I'm disappointed, preferring that he should drive there daily, but he says he needs to be alone for this. I don't believe that it's his intention to shut me out—more that he is trying to deal with matters in his own way, and to protect me from further unpleasantness. In any case, he will be away, and I need to support him.

***

We are so fortunate with the weather. The summer is turning out to be the warmest for many years. We make the most of the time we have together, before the inquest, by picnicking on the estate. We also take Mother to the Eden Project at St. Austell, it's a wonderful day; Mum and

I enjoy the stunning gardens, exotic plants and cream tea. Sebastian is enthralled by the conservation and environmental projects, hoping to take a little of their ethos back to his estate.

The balmy evenings are spent out on the terrace, with jugs of Pimms No.1 and dishes of olives. Mum is hilarious when she's had a drink. It's a relaxed and happy time.

The two days pass and Sebastian is ready to leave. "Must you go?" My fingers play with the buttons of his shirt, my expression petulant. Although Mother is staying with me, I somehow feel unnerved by Sebastian's departure–I can't explain why, it's just a feeling I have.

"Darling, you know I must. Scarlett had no family and I feel it's my duty to go."

"She had no family, because she *butchered* them," I remind him, to which he responds with a scowl.

"That may be so but, in any case, I've been summoned as a witness. I have no choice. Hopefully, the outcome will enable a Presumption of Death Order to be granted , and then a death certificate. Only then can we truly put this behind us."

"I know, you're right. It just seems as this is going on and on. I want it *over,* Sebastian. I want us to move forward as a family. You, me and Bella."

"I know, darling. So do I. Hopefully in a couple of days this will be over." He kisses my hair and walks to his car, his broad shoulders hunched as if he carries the weight of the world upon them. After throwing his overnight bag in the trunk, he starts the engine and steers the car toward the drive. I watch from the steps of Penmorrow until his car disappears from sight, an oppressive sense of foreboding gnawing at my gut.

Bella sounds upbeat on the phone this evening. She and Ruth are having a girls night at the movies, followed by a pizza. Ruth relishes the time with Bella, never having been blessed with children herself. Ruth grabs the phone from my daughter and asks if she can 'keep' Bella for another week. I wonder if Bella will ever want to return to Penmorrow when she has so much more going for her in Dorset. She's even talked about finding a job. My girl is growing up. I wish she would go to university but she's adamant it isn't for her. Currently she wishes to explore a career in beauty therapy, she tells me. Tomorrow it will be something entirely different. *Oh to be young again.*

Mother turns in early, I've noticed that she's aged considerably over the past few months. I sometimes forget that Joe and Alan's deaths took their toll on her too. She struggles with the stairs a little more, she's forgetful and repetitious, but her eyes twinkle just as they always have. I truly am blessed to have Mum with me. Tomorrow I will spoil her again–another girls only day to rival Ruth and Bella's. Perhaps I will buy her some new clothes, she seems always to live in her old skirts and cardigans.

Our vast bed is empty without Sebastian. The crisp white linen sheets smell of his scent - pressing my nose against his pillow and inhaling deeply, I can smell him– sandalwood and him. My favourite smell in the world. My phone vibrates on the bedside table. *Sebastian.*

**Inquest adjourned until tomorrow morning. Judge sick or something! Hope it doesn't delay things too much. Miss you. Dream of me. S x**

Bless him for thinking about me. I have come such a long way thanks to this man. I tap out a reply on my phone.

If he dies, who does HIS inquest? Just a thought, LOL. Miss you too. Am snuggling your pillow – it smells of you ;) xxx

Chuckling, I wait for the reply that I know will come.

**Smart arse! Are you touching yourself?? S x**

*Dirty bugger*, I think. He always signs himself 'S', as though I don't know it's him. I love that funny man.

**Yes. Getting my rocks off thinking of you. Now go to sleep! Xxx**

Pressing 'send', I again wait for his reply which comes through in an instant.

**Glad to hear it. Sleep yourself! Nite. S x**

Joe comes to visit me tonight. He hasn't visited for a while, so it takes me by surprise when he tiptoes into my dreams.

"Hello Mummy," he says. He doesn't look any older, that confuses me. *Surely on the other side one ages still?*

"Hello darling. I've missed you terribly. What have you been up to?"

He's wearing his Manchester United Football Club shirt–the one we dressed him in–the bright red contrasting starkly against his pale skin. "I've been fine, Mummy. My footie skills are improving, Daddy says if I carry on getting even betterer, then I'll play for Man U."

"Betterer?" I chuckle, "there's no such word, you do know that darling?"

"Yes Mummy, I know. Mummy?"

"Yes darling."

"Daddy says he wants you to be careful."

"Does he, Joe? Careful of what, darling?"

"The bad lady."

"Don't be silly, Joe. Tell Daddy the bad lady is gone. She won't be in Heaven with you and Daddy–she's gone to the very hot place."

Joe thinks mulls over what I've said. His little face contorts with concentration. "Why is that big house hot, Mummy?"

"What do you mean, Joe?" I'm unsure what he means, Hell is more vast than a house. For some inexplicable reason, my mind travels back to when I was sixteen and read *'Paradise Lost'* by John Milton. *How did he describe*

*Hell? Ah, that's right.* "A dungeon horrible, on all sides round–as one great furnace flamed. Yet from those flames, no light; but rather darkness visible. Served only to discover sights of woe..." I recall the devils deciding that this was where they wanted to stay. "Joe?"

"Yes, Mummy."

"The bad lady is in Hell."

"Yes, Mummy. But Daddy says Hell is in the dungeon, like the...what was that Daddy? Like the Milton thing you just thought about.

"Hell is in the dungeon, Joe?"

"Yes, Mummy. Daddy says be careful. I love you."

"I love you too darling. Thank you for coming to see me."

"Oh...Mummy?"

"Yes, darling?"

"Tell Grandma I love her and I miss her trifle...yes Daddy?...Daddy says watch over Grandma."

"I'll tell her, darling."

"Don't forget the white feather, Mummy. Bye." His image fades, my golden child leaves me alone once more.

Pondering what Joe meant in the dream–or if indeed it was a dream–and yet my eyes are open, so how could it be a dream?...movement in my right eye snaps me back to reality. The door to our bedroom is opening. The moonlight illuminates the room with bluey hues. This dream is strange–so real. In this dream, my eyes wide open, I see the figure of a woman enter the bedroom. She stands stock still on Sebastian's side of the bed.

"Who are you?" I ask.

"It's *me*," is the whispered reply.

"Who's me?"

"Scarlett ... Sarah Dorling."

"Nonsense," I reply. "Scarlett is *dead*. She walked into the sea and drowned."

The figure laughs, a shrill sad laugh, tinged with irony and mirth. "Always so fucking *stupid,* aren't you Mrs. Dove?"

Goosebumps rise up on my arms, my scalp prickles. *Oh my God.* I'm awake. "Scarlett!"

"The penny drops."

Reaching over to the bedside lamp, my arm outstretched, I don't see the heavy weapon. I feel the breeze as it nears my head–feel the blow as it strikes me– then darkness envelopes me.

# Chapter 17

My head hurts. My eyes can't focus properly. *Where am I?* Trying to reach up to my head but my hands won't move. *Feel sick. Scared. Sebastian?*

"Well hello, Mrs. Dove. Nice of you to join me." The voice sounds as though it's at the end of a very long tunnel. It's familiar and yet foreign to me.

"What? Where am I? My head hurts."

"Does it *really?* I'm so sorry about that. Your 'headache' will be the very least of your worries soon, dear." The voice is familiar...

"Who is it?" My mouth is dry–try to swallow–no saliva.

"Did I beat your memory out of your pretty, empty little head?"

*Why won't my hands move?* "Who are you?"

"Scarlett. Remember me? Poor dear Scarlett. Do you *really* think I'd simply walk out to sea?" Her voice is shrill: cruel, sardonic. "And leave you and Sebastian to live happily ever after? *MY* Sebastian?"

"Scarlett is dead. She's gone...inquest...drowned."

"*She's gone. Inquest. Drowned.* Can you make more sense please dear?"

"What do you want with me?" My voice wavers, tears pricking my eyes. *I'm so very scared. Is this a nightmare? Am I really insane? My wrists hurt...it feels like rope cutting into them. She's tied me up? Oh fuck. Oh fuck. I want Sebastian!*

"Very good question indeed. What I want with you is for you to be gone, *E.L.I.Z.A.B.E.T.H.*"

"You're insane." My body is trembling. Shaking uncontrollably. Shock. Cold.

"You are probably correct. *Insane*...yes, most likely. *In love*...yes, most definitely."

"Let me go. Let me *go*." The tears pour down my cheeks, my chest heaving as I struggle to free myself of the restraints which only bite further into my flesh.

"Struggle if you wish. I know you enjoy pain, as do I of course. We have something in common. *Whoopseedo!* We share a common interest. Oh that and Sebastian of course. We share *Him*. My Lord. He who deserves so much more than *you*."

"Sebastian...will...be...fucking...*mad*," I hiss, my voice faltering through terror.

"Can you just please try and speak in a coherent sentence, Elizabeth. The Queen's English, if you please."

"LET ME GO...OH MY GOD...*LET ME GO!*" The fear wells up, I can't control it. *I need Sebastian. Dear God let him come home.*

"*Shh.* Please refrain from shouting, dear. Your voice echoes down here."

"Down here? Where? Cellar? Chamber?"

"Give the lady first prize. Yes, dear, you are in the outer chamber. You are in the good company of His Lordship's finest wine collection. Aren't you a lucky girl? Of course, I'd have taken you to the inner chamber–the 'chamber of pain'–but that's a private place. I won't violate that place with the likes of *you.*"

"What do you want? Whatever it is you can have it." My brain tries to rationalise the situation. Keep her calm–give her what she wants. "I'll leave, Scarlett. You can have him. I don't love him. He's *yours.*"

"Aww, thank you, Elizabeth. You really, really *mean* it?" She laughs a demonic cackle.

That's when I realise I'm naked. "My clothes...my nightdress."

"Gone, I'm afraid. I'm sorry it you're feeling rather cold, but I'll warm you up soon enough."

"*How?* How have you survived?"

"So easy," she giggles. "Smugglers' tunnel. You see I found a tiny door in the far wall of my room. Months ago, you understand. I wondered where it led. Explored one day. Takes me through the cliff, right to the beach. Been there centuries at a guess. Perfect. I stayed there for days, sneaking to the kitchen for food at night..."

"All this *time?* These days when Sebastian and I were *happy?*"

"Yes dear. When you *thought* you were happy. I'd watch you both at night. While you were fast asleep, I'd creep into your room and watch you."

"You're fucking *sick.*"

She laughs.

I feel her presence near me, if only my eyes would focus. The nausea is overwhelming. I'm so very cold, my body is trembling with fear and the biting cold. "Please,

Scarlett. Please."

"Please Scarlett...please. You're *pathetic.* Do you know that? You *disgust* me. You...you should be punished."

"No, Scarlett. Don't make things worse for yourself. I beg you," I'm sobbing uncontrollably, my body wracked with fear. "Let me go. Don't *hurt* me."

"Beg all you like, sister. You love pain. You're going to love what I have in store for you."

I can hear her. My eyes won't work properly. Damn my eyes. I can make out the shape of her; she's moving around. I think I'm on the far side of the wine cellar...*try and remember, Beth. What is on the far side of the wine cellar?*

"Saint Andrews Cross," she says as if reading my mind. "I dusted it off especially for you. Oh, I've spent many an hour tied to that. Marcus mostly. Once with Sebastian...He was the best of course." She's got something in her hand. *What is it? Damn my eyes.* "Then *you* came along. Sweet, mixed up Elizabeth."

"Please, for God's sake stop," I implore. *What is she doing?*

"As I was saying...then you showed up. It could have been the perfect family for us. Your kids were kind of cute. Perfect for Him of course. An heir and a spare."

Something tickles across my abdomen. It's soft. *Oh Christ. What is she doing? Thwack!* The flogger bites into my flesh with a painful sting.

"Alan was a lousy screw. 'Limp dick' I called him.

Had to get rid of him first of course. WHAT THE FUCK WAS THE BOY DOING IN THE CAR?" She screams, her breath hot against my cheek. I can make out the outline of her face, contorted with rage.

"Dear God. THAT WAS MY *SON,*" the strangled cry that follows isn't from me, it's from some feral animal. I realise it is from me. "*NOOOOOO!* He was a BOY. *A BOY!*" My head falls forward to my chest. *So tired. Take me Joe. Come and get your Mummy. She's ready to come to you.*

*Thwack! Thwack! Thwack! Thwack! Thwack!* The pain is bad pain. It hurts so much. It continues unrelenting until I feel a trickle of something warm running down from my breast to my groin. *Dear God please take me. I want my Mum. MOTHER.*

"Where's my Mother?" *Please, no. Don't let her hurt Mum.* I'm aware that I'm whimpering like a baby. *I need my Mum.*

"Mummy is sleeping." Her voice is ice cold. My eyes focus now. Something glints in the dim light. She has a knife. *Oh. God. No!*

The first cut burns...if someone thrust a burning hot spike into my flesh it would feel like this. The second cut hurts less, the third hardly hurts at all–then darkness comes.

"Mummy wake up." Joe's little hand tries to lift my chin. He's crying.

"Don't cry Joe. Mummy's coming."

"*Mummy. Mummy!*"

"Darling, it's fine. Mummy is nearly there."

"Sebastian is coming, Mummy. Don't go to sleep."

"Mummy's very sleepy, darling."

"Sebastian is coming. Daddy says you *have* to stay awake, Mummy."

"Mummy's tired, Joe. When I wake up, we'll be together. Won't that be lovely?"

"No, love. Wake up." The voice is deeper. A man's voice. *Alan's voice.*

"Alan? Is that you?"

"Yes, Beth. Don't go to sleep. Do you bloody well *hear* me?"

"Yes, Alan. I hear you. Are you still talking to me? After what I did to you?"

"It's done, Beth. In the past. It's too soon for you. Be strong. He's coming for you."

The voices fade, the darkness claims me. *So very tired now...*

Cold water hits my face and trickles down my chilled, aching body. My eyes snap open, my vision clear enough to see. *The cellar–I'm in the cellar. Scarlett.* She's laughing at me, standing with an empty bucket, water dripping down the red gown she's wearing. My gown. Her face is deathly pale, her lips smeared with blood red lipstick.

"Wakey, wakey, Elizabeth." She steps toward me, I recoil but have nowhere to go, my arms and feet spread wide and tightly bound. "You were dozing, dear. Did I give you permission to sleep? No I did *not*. First lesson of submission, darling...do as you're damn well told. Second rule of submission...avert your eyes. In other words, don't fucking *look* at me." She slaps my face, forcing me to look away but I can't take my eyes from the bizarre and surreal vision of her. She slaps harder, my teeth bite my lip, I wince and hot tears tumble down my cold cheek. *"Do. As. You're. Told."*

"Yes, Scarlett...I'm sorry." My teeth chatter noisily.

"Good girl, that's better. You see? When you're respectful to me, then I am lenient with you. That's the way it works."

"I...I understand." My eyes dart around the room, avoiding her sneering gaze, desperately searching for something I can use to free myself. It's hopeless. Nothing is within my grasp and my hands are bound.

She's dancing. Pirouetting around the cellar holding an imaginary man, no doubt Sebastian. "Watch me dance, Elizabeth. Don't I look the belle of the ball? Aren't all eyes upon *me?* Aren't I with the most handsome man in the room?" The sight is grotesque–my red gown hangs limp from her slight frame, the lacing undone at the back so that the dress barely stays in place. The black net underskirt trails torn behind her as she nimbly dances across the cobble stones. When the imaginary music stops, she comes to rest before me. "Don't you think the dress looks better on *me?*" She asks, holding out the skirts.

"Def...definitely. Yes." My head nods in exaggerated agreement. "May I have some water please?"

"*Me, me, me.* Do you ever think about anything except your own needs?" She hisses, wagging a finger in my face. "Sel-fish." She elongates the word to highlight my wrongdoing. "I just gave you a whole bucket of water." She roars with laughter.

*My mouth is so dry.*

"Right, my lady, we are going to play a little game." She tugs my fringe, snapping my head up so that our eyes meet. "The game goes like this. I ask you a question about His Lordship...if you get the answer correct, you win a treat. If you get the answer wrong–*uh oh*–you win a punishment. At the end of the round we shall see if you know enough about Him to be *His*...simple, yes?"

"I don't want to play...please just let me go."

She slaps my face with the back of her hand. "Don't be a bad sport, Elizabeth. Okay, question number one: What date is Sebastian's dead Mother's birthday?"

"How the fuck...do I know *that?*" The anger is boiling inside me once more. *Fuck her games. Fuck her!*

"Is the wrong answer...*whack-whack-oops!*...That's the noise from TV game-shows, incidentally." She giggles and walks away from me. Scarlett tips out items from an old wooden chest before retrieving whatever she was searching for. "Your punishment, dear contestant, is this..." she clutches a cane and approaches me, snapping it across her palm. *Thwack!* it bites the flesh across my thighs. My eyes sting with tears.

"Question number two: What aftershave does His Lordship favour? Now think about this one, I've made it easy for you to win a treat."

"Sandalwood!" I exclaim. "It's sandalwood."

"*Whoop, whoop!* And the audience go wild. Everyone loves a winner. So, your treat will be..." she walks back to the chest, returning with something hidden behind her back.

*Oh no. Oh God. Please no more pain.*

"The Hitachi wand...*Oooh!* The audience are excited!" She wields the wand around as though it is 'Darth Vader's' light sabre. It resembles a microphone a pop star would use. Pressing a small button, the wand jumps to life, buzzing noisily in her hand.

"What are you doing?" My eyes are wide, fearful, as she approaches me holding out the wand.

"Relax, bitch...you'll enjoy this." She thrusts the large round head of the wand against my crotch. The powerful vibrations clench my core against my will. My body writhes against the restrains, involuntarily. I cry out in anguish and abruptly she cuts the power.

"*Nice,* huh? I like that one too." She tosses the wand back in the chest. "Next question...it's gonna be a tough one: Give me the first name of His Lordship's Great Grandfather. Real first name, no nicknames." She laughs hard, clutching her stomach.

"Just do it! Give me...the fucking punishment, you sick, twisted, *whore!*" The words spit from my mouth, my limbs tensing as I await the inevitable pain.

She looks genuinely shocked. Her red lips form a pout. "It's no fun if you don't play properly." She looks confused, her hand scratches manically at her head. "You're not *trying*...and you're not being nice." She looks like a sulking child.

"Maybe I don't *want* to play your game." I laugh viciously at her. "Perhaps you are just such a bad game-show host that it's not any fucking *fun!*"

She cocks her head to one side, her finger playing along her bottom lip. "*Fine,*" she says, her voice shrill. "We won't play any more." She walks to the chest and slams the lid down with such force that the wood splinters. "I'm going to leave you now, Elizabeth, to think about your behaviour. When I return, I want you to apologise for spoiling the game." She pivots on her heel and leaves the cellar.

My body hangs limp, my spirit broken. I didn't plan to die like this. I was supposed to grow old and grey–die with my family at my side in some old people's home. What will they think, when they find me? What will be left for Sebastian to bury? Bella won't be able to see me, or kiss me goodbye. Too tired even to cry any more, I screw my eyes shut and welcome the sleep that comes.

# Chapter 18

Something wakes me. *Voices. Noise. Falling. Strong arms holding me. Scarlett's voice, begging. Sebastian shouting–Sebastian?* "Sebastian?"

"I'm here darling. Fuck. *Oh fuck, no!* You're going to be alright. Ambulance coming. Police. Stay with me."

"I'm cold, Sebastian. So *very* cold. Tired."

"*No!* Wake up. Stay awake. Going to find her and fucking kill her..."

My eyes open but the room is blurred again. When I blink, my vision clears. I see Sebastian's back as he runs from the room. The stone is cold under my cheek. Cold and hard. *Push myself up. Need to stand. Need to follow him. Danger.* My head swims as I sit up. I'm so very cold, my teeth chattering. His jacket is over me. I push my arms in the sleeves. *I hurt.* The pain is unbearable. My eyes dart down over my body which is criss-crossed with red lines. *How? Blood lines. Lines of blood. Scarlett has a knife...OH NO! NOT SEBASTIAN!*

The steps are steep, I hold onto the rope and pull myself, step by painful step upwards, onwards. The hallway. Sebastian's shouting. *Upstairs. Need to find him. One step at a time. Need to get upstairs. The warm stuff is running down my tummy ... mustn't stain the carpet.* I climb with a calm determination. I suddenly feel calm. I know what I must do. I must save my love. My feet travel faster, lighter. Another landing. More shouts. More stairs.

A door. Throw the door open, *the pain hurts*. The cold blast hits me. Outside. Roof.

Sebastian stands a little in front of me. The wind whips at my hair, bites at my skin. *So very cold. Scarlett...in front of Sebastian. So close to the edge.*

Sebastian is talking to her. Commanding her. "Come to me Scarlett," he says, his hand beckoning her. "Kneel before me," she remains where she is, her eyes now lowered. Her arms are stretched wide like an angel, her face pallid white like a porcelain doll. "Scarlett...move away from the edge. *Do as I say.*"

Her voice travels on the wind, "no Sebastian. For once, I'm defying you. I will always love you–belong to you–in the next life, you'll be *mine.*" and then she is gone. Just falls backwards.

*Sebastian screaming...a deep tremulous roar. He's on his knees. Sobbing...I need to comfort him but I can't move, suddenly too tired. I want my Mum. Darkness.*

\*\*\*

"Elizabeth." A voice calls to me from afar. Sebastian's voice. I must be a ghost.

"Am I dead?" My voice is feeble. Not my voice. Can one speak when one's dead?

A hearty chuckle. Sebastian's voice. "No darling, you're alive. God knows how, but you're alive. Come back to me. I need you." He's crying.

"Mum. Oh Mum. Please. I *need* you." Bella's voice.

A mobile phone ringing.

"Come on you old tart. You're stronger than this. Get

your arse in gear and get back to work." Ruth's voice. More weeping.

"Beth, love. I'm here. Pull though...*oh please*, pull through." Mum's voice.

A whispered prayer.

Sebastian's holding my hand, stroking my palm and gazing lovingly into my eyes. He looks exhausted–dark circles surround his sad eyes. "Penny for them...," he smiles.

I'm in a hospital room, attached to a machine that keeps making irritating bleeping noises. I hurt everywhere, especially my head but when I try to raise my hand to feel the bandage, *my hand won't move far enough–it seems to be attached to a line*. "I'm so thirsty," I croak.

Sebastian turns and retrieves a glass of water with a straw from the table beside the bed, then gently lifts my head so that I can take a sip.

"Thank you, that's better."

He places the glass on the table, clutching my hand in his again.

"How long have I been here?"

"A couple of days," he shifts his position on the side of the bed so that I can see his face more clearly without needing to crane my neck. "Fuck, Elizabeth...I thought I'd *lost* you." Tears mist his beautiful dark eyes. "When I saw you–what she'd done to you–I wanted to kill her with my bare hands."

My hand squeezes his. "Thank heavens you came,

darling. How did you know?"

"I didn't know. The clerk called to say the judge was still sick and that the inquest was being adjourned to a new date, so I could go home. I thought about staying in the hotel but...something told me I needed to get back to you. Thank God I did. I just...I couldn't believe what I was *seeing*. Scarlett...you, tied to the cross...the blood. My world just stopped right there, thinking she'd killed you. When she saw me, she tried to kiss me. I threw her off, cut you down with the knife she'd dropped, and then a rage took hold of me–she saw it in my eyes–she ran. I followed her to the roof, her intention was clear and suddenly, I didn't want to kill her...I felt pity for her, so sick, *so twisted*. I tried to get her to come down from the roof but she wouldn't budge. I even tried to Dom her – thought that may snap her out of it, but it didn't. Then when you appeared and she saw you...I think she knew that she'd lost me. She just fell back, darling...one minute she was there...the next she fell. The paramedics got there fast, but she was already dead...the impact." A tear escapes forming a tiny river down his unshaven jaw. "We just don't know how she got in the house, or where she'd been hiding. It's a mystery."

"She told me," I say quietly, his eyes widen. "She found a smugglers' tunnel in the cellar, in her room. She'd been hiding in there, taking food from the house at night...watching us. She never left. She *never* left Penmorrow."

"Well, I'll be damned." He rakes a hand through his

hair, shaking his head in disbelief.

"Mother...did she hurt her?" My grip tightens on his hand, he takes a deep breath and lets it out slowly, wiping his face with the back of his hand.

"She'd tied her up, Elizabeth but that was all. The police came quickly; they found her before I could. She was pretty shaken up, but she's been checked over here– had an ECG–she's fine. She's just been beside herself with worry, as we all have. Oh, and the police found a stash of pills. In the larder, would you believe? They think she'd used up Libby's supply but that wouldn't have lasted long, the rate she was feeding them to you. The police think she was buying them from a dealer, possibly locally but more likely in Exeter. They are looking at CCTV footage."

This news is welcome confirmation, if more was needed, that my recent madness was squarely down to Scarlett. I need to sit up, hug this man tightly but my body is too sore. Sebastian stops me, seeing the pain on my face, he lays a hand lightly on my shoulder.

"Am I going to be alright?" I whisper.

He smiles, his expression telling me that I'm going to be just fine. "You're an amazing woman, Elizabeth Dove. You've baffled the doctors with your resilience, you know. You had a concussion but your skull wasn't fractured–there's a wound at the back of your head which they've stitched, it's going to hurt but you're going to have strong pain killers. Also, you have superficial cuts and they're going to take a little time to heal but she didn't cut deep. You're going to have some scars, but you know what?"

"What?" I ask sorrowfully, ashamed of my disfigured body.

"I'm going to kiss and love every single one of those scars, because they will remind me every day what a strong and incredible woman I'm married to."

My breath catches, "*married?*"

"Yes, darling, married. When you're better, I'll ask you properly of course, but you *will* marry me." He arches a brow, his lips forming a crooked smile, daring me to say no.

"Yes, Sebastian...*oh, yes please.*"

He sighs, grinning, and gathers me into his arms, only releasing me when I wince with the pain of his embrace.

\*\*\*

Zariya snorts and puts her head down. I pull tightly on her reigns and urge her on. "Come on girl, don't let Brutus beat you."

Sebastian throws his head back and laughs. With a swift kick to Brutus's flank he propels him forward, taking the lead. Zariya meets his pace. We are neck and neck. Racing forth across the green meadow, the wind whipping my hair. He's ahead now.

My crop whips across the mare's flank. "Come on girl." Glancing across at Sebastian, he is hunched into the wind, racing his horse with all his strength. My crop cracks once more against the horse's flank. She whinnies and picks up her pace once more. The ancient oak stands proud on the horizon. Swaying in the breeze, it waves to us as we ride the wind.

"You lost," I pant. "Take off your clothes."

"Never," he says defiantly. "*Make* me."

"With pleasure," I reply, my brow arching.

He grabs me, pulling me down into the long grass. We roll again and again, clutching at each other, down the hill. Our mouths meet, our limbs entwine. "I love you, Sebastian. Always have. Always will."

# Chapter 19

It's a glorious day, the sun has burned off the early morning mist. Wherever I look, from my bedroom window, I see vibrant green grass, interspersed with wild flowers and ancient trees. The gravel driveway, directly below my window, is littered with cars, and people dressed in their summer finery - hats, fascinators, men in penguin suits, ladies in heels tottering on the gravel. I watch them all, my forehead pressed against the cool glass.

"Look at you...*wow!*"

Turning from the window, I beam at Mum, Ruth and Bella. "Will I do?" My hands sweep down the lace bodice and across the ivory silk skirt, loving how it rustles when I move.

"He's going to shoot his load just looking at you, love," chuckles Ruth. Mother swipes at her with her clutch bag.

Bella turns red and utters, "eww, that's just gross."

"I've never seen you looking so beautiful Beth," Mum is tearful...again. She's used up almost an entire box of Kleenex already this morning and the wedding hasn't even started yet. "Your father would be so proud." She hands me my bouquet of roses and gypsophila, which complements the gypsophila scattered through my loose curls.

My bridesmaid, Bella is dressed in a deep cerise knee-length dress with matching roses in her hair.

Ruth, my matron of honour wears a full-length gown in the same coloured silk. She looks incredible, her wild curls tamed just for today in an elegant chignon. "This colour's a bitch with my complexion," she whines.

Laughing I tell my dearest friend how beautiful she is–outwardly, if not inwardly. She punches my arm playfully with an adorable pout on her pink lips.

A knock on the door means that it is time. Bella and Ruth walk ahead, Mother and I follow behind, pausing to allow them time to walk down the stairs first. The small orchestra begins to play in the great hall–*Pachelbel's Canon in D Major*–chosen for the memories it holds for Sebastian and I. Getting the marriage license for Penmorrow had been my idea. Sebastian had taken some convincing, but finally he saw the sound business sense of hiring out the house for just ten weddings a year. Of course it also enabled us to marry here and neither of us could think of anywhere else we'd rather be on our special day, with the De Monfort ancestors smiling down–or frowning down–from the many portraits about the house.

"Come on, love." Mother taps my arm gently and I link it through hers.

"Thank you for giving me away, Mum," I whisper nervously, butterflies turning summersaults in my belly. She casts me an adoring smile and slowly we step, in time with each other and the music, toward the top of the sweeping oak staircase, which is intertwined with white roses and pink ribbon down the entire bannister. At the top step, I look down at the sea of elated faces, Theo is gazing adoringly at Bella; I'm pleased that their friendship is blossoming in spite of his father, Marcus, and Sebastian's fight.

Standing resplendent in morning suit and silver cravat, one foot on the bottom stair –as if he's going to run up the stairs and claim me if I don't hurry up–is Sebastian. Our eyes meet and lock in a private, sensual stare, at this moment we are alone, just two people who love each other and who have overcome so very much to be together. He holds out a hand, his eyes never leaving mine as each step I take brings me closer to him. When our fingers touch, my hand slips in his, tiny sparks course through us both. At this instant, I know that I am a better person for having met Sebastian. I have made so many mistakes in my life, been selfish, erratic...but the journey has changed me, and with the love we share we will continue to grow together. We'll make a life together at Penmorrow and be the best parents we can be to Bella and, in time, the best grandparents we can be.

"I now pronounce you to be husband and wife. You may kiss your bride"

As our guests clap and Ruth, it could only be Ruth, wolf-whistles, Sebastian and I embrace. The love that is reflected in his smouldering eyes melts my heart. "You are *mine*," he breathes.

"Yes, Sebastian. I am yours. Only yours ... *forever.*"

As our lips meet in a kiss that is far too passionate to be respectable, a tiny white feather floats down, swirling on a gentle breeze from the open windows...and lands at our feet.

## The End

**Facebook:**

https://www.facebook.com/JaneyRosen

**Twitter:**

https://twitter.com/JaneyRosen

**Website:**

http://www.janeyrosen.com/

**Goodreads:**

https://www.goodreads.com/author/show/6968598.J
aney_Rosen

**My blog:**

www.janeyrosen.me

**If you enjoyed this book, please write a review here:**
www.amazon.co.uk www.goodreads.com

*Also available: The Muse Keeper novella series,
available on Amazon in paperback and ebook formats.*

Printed in Great Britain
by Amazon.co.uk, Ltd.,
Marston Gate.